This book is lovingly dedicated to all the women in my family, South Dakota born and bred—past and present—who know a thing or two about resilience. . . .

NO MERCY

A MYSTERY

LORI ARMSTRONG

A TOUCHSTONE BOOK
Published by Simon & Schuster
New York London Toronto Sydney

Touchstone
A Division of Simon & Schuster, Inc.
1230 Avenue of the Americas
New York, NY 10020

First Touchstone hardcover edition January 2010

TOUCHSTONE and colophon are registered trademarks of Simon & Schuster, Inc.

For information about special discounts for bulk purchases, please contact Simon & Schuster Special Sales at 1-866-506-1949 or business@simonandschuster.com.

The Simon & Schuster Speakers Bureau can bring authors to your live event. For more information or to book an event contact the Simon & Schuster Speakers Bureau at 1-866-248-3049 or visit our website at www.simonspeakers.com.

Designed by Renata Di Biase

Manufactured in the United States of America

10   9   8   7   6   5   4   3   2   1

Library of Congress Cataloging-in-Publication Data
Armstrong, Lori
    No mercy : a mystery / Lori Armstrong.
        p. cm.
    "A Touchstone book."
1. Snipers—Fiction. I. Title.
    PS3601.R576N6   2009
    813'.6—dc22   2009015889

ISBN 978-1-4165-9095-8
ISBN 978-1-4165-9706-3 (ebook)

"Buy land. They ain't making any more of the stuff."

WILL ROGERS

NO
MERCY

PROLOGUE

In the arid summer heat on prairie rangeland, a dead body doesn't so much rot as it becomes petrified. The blazing sun and dry wind burn the most resilient flesh into dried meat.

What the sun hadn't cooked the animals had feasted on. A sunken hollow where the stomach had been. Shriveled flaps of skin resembling jerky hung from the jaw and cheekbones. The eye sockets were empty holes. The final indignity? The crotch of the athletic shorts were ripped away to reach the soft meat of the sex organs.

Poor son of a bitch had been emasculated before he'd had a chance to become a man.

A hot breeze swirled chalky dust motes and scents of decay.

Black Air Jordan athletic shoes saved the boy's toes the fate of his fingers: gnawed off clean down to the bone. Reddish-black hair floated loose around his skull, bits of leaves and insects trapped in the dulled strands. Without lips to hide behind, the crooked teeth stuck out like yellowed piano keys. The body hadn't been exposed long enough to bleach the bones white, but it'd been out here long enough to disintegrate into just another forgotten animal carcass.

Dust to dust.

Pine-tree-dotted hills and valleys of grayish gumbo made up the barren landscape. Heat mirages shimmered in the distance—a cruel illusion. There'd been no standing water in these parts for years.

The spinal column listed to the left. Like the kid's neck had been snapped.

Despite the sun beating down, a chill rippled through the air.

So how had Albert Yellow Boy ended up in the middle of no-where? What were the odds a couple of busy ranch hands would stumble over his body in this remote section of fallow grazing land?

Slim.

Had that been the intention?

More voices buzzed like angry gnats. Whispering. Arguing. Accusing.

Eerily loud caws echoed from the canyon. Bickering ceased, returning focus to tending the rituals of the dead.

ONE

One week later

Listening to bawling cows headed for the slaughterhouse is a shitty way to start a day.

I slammed the front window shut and crawled back between the cool cotton sheets. When my father's phantom voice nagged me for sleeping in, I jerked the quilt over my head.

Go away, Dad. I'm too damn old to feel guilty about not getting up at the crack of dawn to do chores.

It took me a while to get back to sleep. When I did drift off, the scorching summer afternoon from thirty years past came rushing back, dreamlike, except it hadn't been a dream:

"Momma had a baby and its head popped off." I sited my target and pulled the trigger.

Crack.

An immediate pain-filled screech morphed into prairie silence.

My heart thumped. I held the Remington tight even after the recoil pad bit into my shoulder. Heard the hollow click as the spent brass cartridge ejected out the side and chinked on the rocky ground.

Bluish smoke eddied around me. Gravel dug into my forearms. Powdery gray dirt coated my sunburned skin even as gnats buzzed around my ears and inside my nose.

I didn't care.

Exhilarated, I eyed the headless body through the scope and surveyed the bloody chunks of meat spread across the soil in the ultimate buzzard's buffet.

"Got ya dead-on, ya dirty bastard," I whispered to the decimated prairie dog, my tone reminiscent of Eastwood in The Outlaw Josey Wales.

Dad chuckled, shifting his position on the slope. "Your mom'd have a conniption fit if she heard you talkin' like that."

"Then it's a good thing she's not here."

"Yeah." He squinted at me, finding something on my face that made the laughter bleed out of his eyes. "Real good thing."

A clement breeze stirred the smell of sage, skunkweed, and hot dirt. Scents I'd forevermore associate with death.

He eased back on his haunches and stood, wincing. The lack of circulation in his legs was getting worse, though he tried to be a tough guy and hide it from me. I let him. When he held out his big hand to help me up, I let him do that, too.

"Come on, sport. Let's see what damage you done. You ain't a bad shot—"

"For a girl," I supplied.

He spit a stream of tobacco juice next to my ropers. Just like my hero, Josey. He looked me dead in the eye. "Anyone who ever says that to you, Mercy Gunderson, is a fool."

I woke with a start. At least the combat flashbacks had tapered off, but I couldn't remember the last time I'd had a decent night's sleep. Maybe I should fill that prescription for Ambien next time I was at the VA.

After I'd finished my yoga practice, I wandered outside. The thermometer read 87 degrees. In the shade. I snagged a Crystalyx feed cap off the hook by the door and detoured to the activity by the barn.

The semitruck was backed up to the loading gate. Flies buzzed everywhere. Familiar, pungent smells of dirt and manure hung in the dry air. Most people gagged at the odors, but I'd gotten used to them again, the scents of home. I hoisted myself atop the fence and watched the action unfold.

Our two hired men, TJ and Luke, were on horseback, herding the animals. The ranch foreman, Jake, culled the ones he wanted and sent the others out of the penning area with a slap on the flank.

One stubborn cow refused to move.

Jake bent down and spoke directly into the floppy ear.

The tail swished and then the cow slowly got in line.

I laughed. How cool. We had our very own cow whisperer. I would've zapped it with a cattle prod until it bellered and trotted up the ramp like a good little doggie.

Another obvious difference between Jake and me.

After the metal door to the chute banged shut, and the semi rattled down the rutted driveway, the foreman ambled toward me.

Jake Red Leaf had run my father's ranch for the last twenty-odd years. Jake wasn't a grizzled old Indian rancher, but fairly young, around forty-five. Despite spending years outside in the harsh elements, he'd aged well and was a good-looking man, so it surprised me he was still single.

What didn't surprise me, or anyone else, was that Jake knew the day-to-day operations of the Gunderson Ranch better than I did. Better than I'd ever wanted to.

I shifted my position atop the rickety fence. The wooden slats scraped my palms. I'd probably spend half the damn night digging slivers out.

"Nice to see you out in the fresh air and sunshine."

"Yeah, 'cause I so don't get enough of it being stationed in the world's biggest sandbox."

Ignoring my barb, Jake tipped back his battered Resistol and wiped the sweat from his forehead with the heel of his hand. His eyes caught mine. "How's Hope today?"

"Your grandma says she checked on her at seven and Hope was still in bed."

"Was Levi around?"

"I doubt it. Why? Was he supposed to be working today?"

"Yep. Promised to help me load cattle."

Levi was my younger sister's fifteen-year-old son. As much as I'd adored him as a baby, his wide-eyed wonder, his drooly smiles, his gurgling coos of contentment whenever I held him, these days he steered clear of me. If his recent behavior was any indication, the kid was about half a step from ending up in the juvenile court system.

Hope blamed Levi's bad behavior on Levi's daddy dying in a trucking accident when the boy was six. I blamed Levi's bad behavior on Levi. Other kids had lost a parent at a young age—Hope and myself included. Hope believed in giving Levi free reign. My mind-set? If Jake or one of the other ranch hands took a horse rein to him, he'd straighten up in a helluva hurry.

However, my opinion held no weight. I'd been an absent aunt most of Levi's life, as well as an absent sister. Add in the fact I've never given birth? Well, I'd be better off talking to a fence post.

"You act surprised he didn't show," I said.

"Not really. He's been runnin' with a rough crowd from the rez lately. Chet said he saw Levi and a buncha boys in the back of a pickup headed up toward that abandoned mine a coupla weeks back." Jake placed a worn Tony Lama on the bottom rung and propped his muscled forearms on the fence.

"Who were the boys?"

"Dunno. Some punks. Someone oughta talk to him about it. Especially in light of the fact we found his buddy Albert chewed up as coyote food in our pasture last week."

"Count me out for initiating that conversation. Hope has never listened to me, and she's completely blind where that kid is concerned."

"Funny. Your dad used to say the same thing. Of course, Wyatt wore those same rose-colored glasses when it came to his only grandson."

A black veil dropped over me as if a hail cloud covered the sun. I released a slow breath. "Don't know if I'll ever get used to hearing Dad referred to in the past tense. Maybe—"

"Stop beatin' yourself up. Nothin' you coulda done."

"I can't believe I wasn't here."

"He wouldn't have known if you had been."

"That doesn't make me feel less guilty, Jake."

He cocked his head and looked up at me. "You talked to anybody about it?"

"Like who?"

"Like one of them doctors at the VA hospital. *Unci* says you been goin' there since you got back from Iraq, eh?"

Damn Sophie Red Leaf and her big mouth. Had she ever considered maybe I didn't want everyone to know about my health problems? Especially her grandson?

I didn't respond. Instead, I tipped my face to the heavens. My eyes traced a long white vapor trail bisecting the vivid blue sky. I half wished I was on that plane, gazing wistfully at the patchwork of fields and farms from thirty thousand feet.

"Mercy? You okay?"

"Yeah. I'll see you later." I'd rather be skinned alive than talk about my feelings and failings, with Jake of all people.

I hopped off the fence. A cloud of ginger-colored dirt puffed around my bare ankles as I crossed the expanse of gravel and weeds known as the "yard" on my way to the house.

Our farmhouse was built in the 1930s, one of those "kit" houses sold by Sears Roebuck, where everything from the roof trusses to the oak trim was shipped out on railcars, transferred to flatbed trucks, and then the house was assembled onsite. Ours wasn't a typical one-level ranch bungalow, but a big two-story Victorian/craftsman–style hybrid. Five bedrooms and a bathroom upstairs, plus an enormous attic that ran the entire length of the house. The main floor boasted a good-sized kitchen, a formal dining room and living room, plus a full bathroom complete with a claw-foot bathtub, a parlor restyled as an office, and a sun porch used as a storage/laundry room.

Over the years, the Gundersons installed numerous updates. The last, when we'd added a handicapped-accessible bedroom and bathroom on the bottom floor, along with a separate entrance with a wheelchair ramp for my dad. Luckily the doorways downstairs were already wide enough to accommodate his wheelchair. For some reason that hadn't made Dad happy.

I'd always found it strange the front door faced the road, but the covered porch with the entrance to the back door was the main entrance. Very rarely did we—or any friends visiting us—use the front door.

During my teen years, the size of our home embarrassed me. Most of my friends lived in ancient trailers or tiny farm shacks.

But Dad claimed since we owned the biggest acreage in the county, it only made sense we lived in the biggest house.

Pebbles shifted beneath my sandals as I passed the abandoned chicken coop. White chunks of paint were peeling off the side panels and around the deformed round-topped door. I'd have to paint the damn thing soon or hire someone else to do it. My focus shifted to the buckled boards on the machine shed, darkened from weathered gray to moldy black. Another project requiring my attention.

Hoo-ray. Life on a ranch was never-ending, backbreaking work, which was why I'd shaken the cowshit off my boots and moved far away as soon as I was legal.

The sun seared my skin. As I gazed across the flat, open area between the hulking house and the half-dozen outbuildings—metal, wood, antique, and new—I reconnected with my eighteen-year-old self and the realization I'd been trapped in a life I hadn't chosen.

So how was it I'd traveled to all those exotic locales of my youthful daydreams only to find myself back here on the ranch? Facing responsibilities I didn't want, with a sinking feeling I'd gone no place at all?

A mourning dove cooed. Another answered. I lifted my face to the blazing sky, wishing for a draft of cool air to carry earthy scents of freshly mown hay. But with the dry conditions all I caught was another nose full of dust.

Whining was pointless. I'd made sacrifices for my country; it was time to make them for my family.

I'd reached the house when an Eagle River County sheriff's car zoomed up the drive. It parked between the Russian olive and the weeping willow, scaring a red squirrel from the bird feeder shaped like a decrepit outhouse. My sister Hope inherited our mother's quirky taste. I knew Dad hadn't chosen that kitschy piece to adorn the stalwart tree. It seemed undignified somehow.

A hat appeared out the driver's side before the body unfolded. The guy raised his head. The stoic face beneath the mirrored shades belonged to the acting sheriff, Dawson.

Despite the fact my father respected Dawson enough to get

him appointed temporary sheriff until elections were held, Dawson and I had established a guarded relationship from day one. Maybe because I had abandonment/replacement "daddy" issues on a personal and professional level with him—and wouldn't the army shrinks have a field day with that? It bugged the crap out of me that Dawson raised my hackles and my interest like no other man I'd crossed paths with in the last decade.

He skirted the front end to open the right rear passenger door. Hauled Levi out. Handcuffed. Dawson growled in Levi's ear to get him moving. Levi shuffled his big feet, untied shoelaces making curlicues in the gray dirt behind him.

"Miz Gunderson." Dawson actually tipped his hat to me before he focused on Jake. "Red Leaf."

I hadn't heard Jake sneak up behind me. So much for my powers of observation.

"Sheriff. What's going on?"

"You wanna tell her?" the sheriff prompted Levi.

Levi kept his mouth shut.

Dawson sighed. "Seems your nephew decided to break into old Mr. Pawlowski's place and help himself to some of Mr. P.'s things while Mr. P. was at Thursday lodge."

Hope wasn't around to glare at me, so I didn't bother to soften my reaction. "Levi, what the hell is wrong with you?"

Levi shrugged. And smirked. The little bastard.

"Who else was with him?"

"He claims no one."

"What did you take?"

No answer from Klepto Boy.

I directed my questions to Dawson. "What did he take?"

"A couple bottles of booze, a couple bottles of pills."

"What kind of pills?"

"Viagra."

Imagining my ninetysomething neighbor with a hard-on was almost enough to make me shut my mouth.

Almost.

"What other kind of pills?"

"Vicodin."

B&E with a narcotics charge? Levi was screwed. The cynical

side of me thought maybe he'd finally done something serious enough to get him to straighten up. "Why did you bring him here?"

Jake sighed.

Guess I'd blown my chance for Aunt of the Year.

"Normally we'd send him off to the Juvenile Corrections Center in Rapid City, but Mr. Pawlowski isn't pressing charges."

My mouth dropped open. "Then why did he even call you?"

Sheriff Dawson crossed his arms over his chest and braced his feet wide. "Said he wanted us to 'be aware of the problem' but claims no harm was done since he got back his meds and his Lord Calvert."

"That's it?"

"No. He rambled about how he'd known the boy's grandfather for more'n fifty years and remembered how tough it was when he'd lost his own pappy back in '31."

It amazed me how the old-timers talked like 1931 was last week, not last century.

Dawson added, "Mr. P. also swore your dad would've wanted this sort of thing handled by family."

Levi glared at me from behind his fall of greasy brown hair. "Yeah? Well, she ain't my mom."

"Son, I got no problem taking you back to jail if you'd rather. Count yourself lucky I brought you here since nobody answered the door at your mom's place."

Super. In addition to dealing with my delinquent nephew, I had to worry about my delinquent sister.

"Can you keep an eye on him?" the sheriff asked.

Jake stepped up. "No problem, Sheriff. I've got lots of bales to unload."

"Appreciate that." Sheriff Dawson spun Levi around and unlocked the cuffs.

Levi rubbed his wrists, aiming his sullen face at the ground and trudging behind Jake toward the barn.

"You okay?" Dawson murmured.

My cap didn't quite shield the sun from my eyes but I glanced up at Dawson anyway. Like my dad, Dawson was a big guy—six feet three inches, built like a Vikings linebacker. He even looked

Nordic, with short-cropped blond hair and a broad forehead, razor-sharp cheekbones and a square chin. If the deep laugh and frown lines on his tanned face were any indication, he had a couple of years on me, which put him in his early forties.

I didn't know much about him since he wasn't a local, a transplant from "back east." Most people think that phrase means the East Coast, but in South Dakota, "back east" means any midwestern location east of the Missouri River—in Dawson's case, Minnesota.

"Just so we're clear, Sheriff, Mr. Pawlowski had it wrong. My dad would've tossed Levi's dumb butt in jail, family or not."

"I figured as much. Didn't seem productive to argue. Besides, I'm still feeling my way around being sheriff. Wyatt Gunderson left some mighty big shoes to fill."

Sadness descended on me again. "Yeah, I'm sure he did." I sucked at offering platitudes, so I didn't bother.

I awaited a response that was a long time coming. Dawson tried to stare me down behind those dark glasses. An exercise in futility for him, because I always won. Always.

Finally he said, "Can I ask you something personal, Miz Gunderson?"

"Sure, if you call me Mercy. 'Miz Gunderson' makes me feel like an old maid."

"Only a fool could set eyes on you and see an old maid."

Whoo-boy. I'd be lying if I said his flattery rolled off me like water off a duck's back. I wasn't an ugly duckling, but I'd never been rodeo-queen material either. Mostly I'd gone out of my way to blend in. Still, it'd been years since I'd fallen for that "aw-shucks, I'm-just-a-good-old-boy" routine.

"Ask away, Sheriff."

"Seems odd, with a spread this size, that Wyatt didn't stick to ranching."

If Dad had handpicked Dawson as his successor, why didn't Dawson know the story? I hated rehashing personal family history. I leaned my backside against the dirty patrol car.

He followed suit.

"After my mom died, his heart wasn't in ranching. Wasn't in anything, really. He didn't take care of himself. His diabetes got worse. Then he couldn't do half the chores after they took his leg."

"With Wyatt being handicapped, it surprised me he wasn't behind a desk all the time at the sheriff's office."

"It was hard enough for him to be in a wheelchair. Strictly desk duty would've killed him."

The diabetes eventually did. The image of my strong father lying weak in a hospital bed made me shudder, not that I'd seen his indignity firsthand.

"So, strapping on a gun and helping the community gave him a purpose?" Dawson asked.

"Yeah. But he couldn't bear to sell his birthright outright, so he turned over day-to-day ranch operations to Jake. Jake's cousins, Luke and TJ, work as hired hands."

"Sounds like Red Leaf has been in charge a long time."

I nodded.

"He must've been pretty young to take on such a big responsibility."

"He was. But he knows what he's doing. Makes sense when you consider members of the Red Leaf family have worked for us, in some capacity, for over a hundred years. It's what Jake and Dad both wanted."

"What about what you and your sister wanted?"

I shrugged. "She was young and I was uninterested."

The thud of the wooden barn door echoed like a sonic boom. Jake, TJ, and Luke shouted to one another.

"You still ambivalent about running this ranch?"

I shrugged again.

"Are you gonna sell it?"

"Why?" My gaze snapped to his. "You interested in buying?"

"On my salary? You kidding?"

I wasn't gullible enough to believe his rapid-fire denial.

He said, "I'm just as curious as the rest of the folks around here to know if you've lined up potential buyers."

I scowled. "Don't these people have anything better to do than gossip about me?"

"Nope. Long as we're talking about it, lots of folks are plenty interested on what you'd been up to in the army."

"It's not that interesting, actually."

"I hear ya. I was in the marines during Desert Storm." He paused. "You've been in Iraq?"

I nodded.

"Wyatt didn't talk much about your military duties."

Because he couldn't. How I'd earned my keep in service to Uncle Sam was on a need-to-know basis, so Dawson's interest won him an abrupt subject change. "Why aren't the locals talking about the Yellow Boy case?"

"They are."

"Discovered any new info?"

"No." His demeanor changed from amiable to brusque. "I don't expect anyone will come forward with any either."

"Why not?"

Dawson faced me. "Truth is, no one's surprised that Indian kid ended up dead. He'd run away a half-dozen times before he was reported missing. Spent more time in trouble than he had at home recently."

I remembered Albert's parents, Estelle Apple and Paul Yellow Boy, from high school. Evidently neither of them had fallen into that brutal cycle of alcoholism and abuse that affects so many Indians living on the rez, and Albert's disappearance and death sent shockwaves through the family. Since Levi and Albert were pals, and Levi was a pallbearer, Sophie had dragged me to the funeral. I'd gotten the impression Albert hadn't been a troubled teen for very long. Then again, eulogies extolled virtues, not faults.

"So his death wasn't from foul play?" I asked.

" 'Foul play.' You sound like Wyatt. You really are a chip off the old block aren't you?"

"That surprises you?"

"No." He sighed. "I don't know if it was an accident or something else."

"That mean you're done investigating?"

"Not a lot I can do at this point when no one will talk to me."

He sounded a little whiny. Didn't he know it'd take years for him to build up the trust my father had been granted?

Then again, maybe Dawson didn't want that trust. Appeared he'd already written off the death as an accident. Wouldn't be hard to believe he was another redneck who believed the only good Indian was a dead Indian.

I'd known more than my fair share of people sporting that attitude. I was temped to shoot them and eliminate their racism from further tainting the gene pool. Most days I refrained.

Most, but not all.

The screen door squeaked. My housekeeper/surrogate mother/ babysitter/cook/chief meddler and Jake's beloved grandmother, Sophie Red Leaf, limped down the porch steps. She shielded her eyes with a frayed kitchen towel. "Sheriff? Everything all right, hey?"

"Everything's fine, Miz Red Leaf."

"Not exactly fine," I corrected. "Levi's in trouble. The sheriff brought him here since Hope wasn't home."

"Where's Levi now?"

"He and Jake are unloading hay bales."

Sophie's hard black stare nearly pinned my ears to my head. "Alone?"

Guilt kicked me in the ass; I could've been helping. But ranch duties were Jake's job, not mine. I was JR to his Dusty. "No, TJ and Luke are here. Besides, the sheriff and I were discussing some other things."

"Out here in this heat? Lord, Mercy, where are your manners?" She flapped the towel at me. "Sheriff, why doan you come on inside where it's cool? I jus' made a pitcher of iced tea. Think I can round up some of them gingersnaps you like so much, eh?"

Sophie knew Dawson's cookie preferences?

"Hate to say no to those tasty sweets, Miz Red Leaf, but I have to get back to the station."

"Lucky for you I'm bringin' a fresh batch to the community center tomorrow night. But I'll only share if a handsome young man such as yourself promises to save a dance for a gimped-up old *wigopa* like me."

My head whipped to Sophie. Did she just bat her eyelashes? God help me, was my seventy-nine-year-old housekeeper . . . flirting with him?

"Gimped up? You? Hah. You'll be dancin' circles around me, for sure." Dawson angled his head at me. "You goin'?"

Before I could scream *no way* Sophie clucked her tongue.

"Course Mercy will be there. Mebbe you'd better save her a dance, too, eh?"

"Be my pleasure." The sheriff pushed away from the patrol car, brushing the dirt off his butt as he rounded the front end. He paused before climbing in. "When Hope turns up, tell her to call me at the sheriff's department as soon as possible. Remind her she doesn't want me to come lookin' for her again."

Again?

Puzzled, I watched dust devils engulf his car. When I turned around to ask Sophie what he'd meant, I found myself staring at her gingham apron strings as the screen door slammed behind her.

TWO

Hope waltzed into the house half an hour after the sheriff left. Perfect timing—avoiding confrontation, as usual.

Ignoring me, as usual.

Hard to believe we were full-blooded sisters; we were exact opposites in so many ways. She was small and round—softly feminine with an ample chest, hips, and ass—whereas I was tall, long limbed and leanly muscled. Not a soft thing about me, inside or out. Hope's fairer skin, blue eyes, and curly light brown hair were courtesy of our father and his Germanic forbearers.

My straight hair was the color of mahogany, as my mother's had been. My skin wasn't the reddish gold of our grandmother's tribe, but as a quarter Minneconjou Sioux, my pigmentation held enough of the darker undertones that allowed me to easily pass as an ethnic woman in Afghanistan, Iran, Iraq, Bosnia, and the other war-torn countries I'd been lurking in for the better part of two decades.

Hope and I did share the sharp Aryan facial features of Dad's European ancestors. I had mom's eye color: an odd shade of hazel that changed from green to brown with my mood.

What was Hope's mood today?

Dressed in a floral-patterned gauzy tunic and frayed 501 cutoffs, she looked like a teenage hippie. A hippie who'd either scored some premium grass, or who'd just gotten laid, if her rosy cheeks and glassy eyes were any indication.

Either scenario made me shudder. But I'd inherited Hope and all her problems along with the ranch.

She plopped in Dad's Barcalounger and lifted the damp ringlets from the back of her neck. Then she snatched the remote from the TV tray and flicked on the TV like she lived here.

An ad for Depends blared. Apparently Sophie had caught up on her soaps over lunch. Hope left the volume at 200 decibels and scrolled through channels.

"We need to talk about Levi," I said loudly.

"In a sec." She flipped to *Oprah* and popped out the footrest.

I snagged the remote and vanquished the Queen of Daytime TV.

"Hey! I was watching that."

"Tough. Did you hear me say we needed to talk?"

"Can't it wait until my show's over?"

"No."

Flower-child appearance aside, the petulant act wasn't becoming on a thirty-three-year old woman. I inhaled a deep *uji* breath. Dealing with my sister required patience, and mine was in short supply today.

Hope had suffered more emotional trauma before age five than most people did their whole lives; consequently, when we were kids, I'd always let her have her way. Our father had fallen into the same trap. As an adult I refused to get sucked in.

"Where'd you go today? Sophie said she saw you at seven and you were sleeping."

"Out."

"Out where?"

"Just out, okay?"

I sipped my tea, the picture of nonchalance. "Out where?"

"I don't report to you."

"You do when your kid's been in trouble and no one knew where you were, including the sheriff."

"What happened?" She scrambled out of the chair. "Is Levi okay?"

"He's fine."

Hope sagged next to me on the loveseat. "Where is he?"

"Unloading hay with Jake." During my brief rundown of Levi's transgressions, her anxious expression changed to defeat.

She reached for my hand. Hers was so soft and frail. In

comparison, mine felt hard and tough as an old baseball glove.

"I'm sorry. You got enough to worry about without adding Levi to the mix." Tears spilled down her cheeks, leaving black mascara tracks on her ashen face.

I softened my tone and passed her a Kleenex. "The last month has been rough. On all of us."

She delicately blotted the corners of her eyes. "Know where I was today?"

"Where?"

"At the cemetery."

"Doing what?"

"Talking to Daddy."

"Really?" To keep a conversation going with her, I had to respond to every question. Luckily one word answers were sufficient.

"Yeah. I go there sometimes. Do you?"

"No."

"I feel like I have to go, because I don't want to forget him like I did her."

Her. My pulse quickened. "It's not the same, Hope. You were only three when she died."

The window air conditioner kicked on and packed the void with cold white noise.

"What do you remember?" she asked softly.

My breath froze in my lungs.

"I mean, what do you remember about her? Mama."

An unwanted image of my mother appeared—sprawled face-first in the horse stall, blood matting her hair, pink splotches soaking through her white eyelet blouse. Tan leather riding glove clutched in her right hand; the pulpy red mass that'd been her left forearm stretched out in the filthy hay. The rank smell of nervous horse sweat. Horseshit. My own urine-soaked jeans. The horse's continual, loud, moist grunts of distress.

Mostly I remembered my helplessness, peeking through the slats at her motionless body.

Three decades later, the scene still haunts me. I'd neglected to take the saddle off the Thoroughbred we'd been boarding before I'd corralled her. The saddle had slipped beneath the horse's belly, and the temperamental mare spooked. When my mother entered the stall to correct my oversight, the horse's powerful hind legs connected with her head. Several times.

"Sometimes when I'm out there I try to talk to her," Hope continued, oblivious to my guilt and grief, "but I can't remember the sound of her voice."

I'd never forget my mother's high-pitched shrieks of pain. Her last words, garbled from a broken jaw. How she screamed at me to stay out. Screaming at me to run and get my father.

In her confused state, she'd forgotten Dad and Hope were in town, spooning down ice-cream sundaes so she and I could go riding alone. My mother had understood my obsession with horses. She'd shared it. Encouraged it.

That day cured my equine fascination. I haven't been on a horse since.

Hope giggled, a tinny sound that startled me back to the present. "I'm sure folks who were driving by the Gunderson Cemetery thought, 'There's that crazy Hope Arpel, talking to herself in the family graveyard again.'"

"No one thinks you're crazy," I lied.

Before I braced myself for the million reassurances Hope always needed, the kitchen screen door banged.

Levi stormed in and slumped in the doorway, sweaty, covered in muck and fine pieces of hay, disaffected scowl distorting his face. "About time, Ma. Can we go home before Jake finds another shitty job for me to do?"

"Watch your mouth."

"Why should I? Aunt Mercy swears all the time." His brown eyes challenged me. "She even swore at me today. In front of the sheriff."

Traitor. Next time we were alone I'd do worse than swear at him.

"Don't blame her because you were caught breaking the law. I would've cussed you out too if I'd seen the sheriff hauling you from a cop car in handcuffs. You're just lucky your grandpa ain't around to see how you've been behaving."

"Ma—"

"Don't you 'Ma' me. You aren't stupid. Why would you break

into Mr. Pawlowski's house? He's such a sweet old man. Never been anything but nice to us."

"Like you care."

"That's not fair. I care and you know it."

"No, you don't. You told Aunt Mercy where you've been?"

I lifted a brow.

Hope's cheeks flushed, but she didn't acknowledge his taunt. "That's why you stole? To make me worry about you? To punish me for not being at your beck and call?"

His scraggly hair curtained his face as he dropped his chin to his chest.

"Why'd you steal, Levi? For the money?"

"Jeez, Ma, I didn't do it for the money."

"Then why? I'm serious, Levi. You better come clean about every sneaky thing you've been doing lately."

My focus shifted to Hope. Raking Levi over the coals? Almost a responsible parental reaction from her for a change.

Levi kicked the doorjamb.

"Stop acting like a two-year-old and answer me."

"I did it for an initiation thing, for a . . . club."

"A club? Or a gang?" She leaped to her feet and got right in his pimply face. "Don't even think about it. Those gangs on the rez are bad news. You know that."

"It ain't a gang."

"Then what is it?"

"I told you. A club."

What type of "club," besides a gang, made potential pledges commit illegal acts?

None.

"Besides, it don't matter now," Levi added. "I got caught. They ain't gonna let me in. Can we go? Shoonga's been cooped up all day. Probably ripping the place apart."

Shoonga was Levi's corgi, a gift from Dad on Levi's seventh birthday. While Levi had debated on what to name his new pet, Sophie and Jake had taken to calling the unruly pup the Lakota word for dog, which stuck.

That was the only year I'd been home for Levi's birthday. Now, as I watched my nephew and the surly teenager he'd become, I wondered what'd happened to the boy with the ready grin and sweet disposition.

I half listened while Hope harangued Levi for another minute, which seemed to last an hour. When Levi began kicking the oak molding again, I said, "Enough. Take him home. Make sure you call the sheriff."

Levi shot me a grateful look. It shocked me. Maybe getting arrested had been a good thing for him. For us all.

Hope twirled her keys and brushed past me. "We're leaving. Right now."

No good-bye. No thanks. No surprise.

Sophie didn't stick around after she'd made me supper. I could've terminated her employment after Dad's funeral—as a single woman I didn't need full-time help in the form of a maid and a cook. I insisted on washing my own clothes and cleaning my space upstairs. But Sophie had taken care of our family since my mother's death, and she'd struggle without the salary we paid her. In some ways, it'd be like throwing her out of her own house.

I wandered through the main floor, at loose ends. I hadn't revived my TV habits since I'd been home from the war because I couldn't stand watching the news. Protestors and pundits and pansy-asses blathering on about what we were doing wrong over there—without having stepped a goddamn foot on foreign sand. They had no idea what it was like spending a night waiting for the patrols to return, not knowing which one of your fellow soldiers was headed home in a flag-draped coffin.

I had no interest in reading the thriller Sophie had bought at Besler's grocery. I had lived that edge-of-your-seat thrill ride every damn day, and it wasn't nearly as fun as depicted in fiction.

Sadly, no lover waited in the wings for my call. Too early for bed. Too late to head into Rapid City to catch a movie. When in doubt, I exercised. I laced on my running shoes and took off.

The gravel road in front of our place has little traffic in the early evening. I hated to run. But there's nothing like it for keeping in aerobic shape. At times my life depended on being able to make a quick getaway.

But I almost stopped when I realized it was the worst time of day for me to see. Hazy purple twilight: not quite day, not quite night. I've always taken my perfect eyesight for granted. I never believed my body could fail me. Or medical science couldn't cure what ailed me.

Retinal detachment. The words were like shrapnel in my soul.

It'd come as a total shock when black shadows obscured the vision in my right eye. I'd been alone in Hilah, two days away from medical help. By the time I made it back to camp, a shrapnel wound and severe dehydration accompanied the eye injury.

Luckily, a Mobil Ophthalmic Surgical Team (MOST) performed the surgery on my eye immediately. Chances were good I wouldn't completely lose my eyesight, a better prognosis than initially expected. I should feel thankful.

Instead, I felt restless. There was no gray area in my field of expertise. Either I was 100 percent or I'd be reassigned to a military desk/teaching job.

Or I could take my twenty and retire. Put my skills to use in the real world. Problem was, there isn't a big market for female snipers.

With my assorted injuries, the loss of my career, the grief and stress of losing my father, and my having to make a decision on the ranch, I doubted my life could get more complicated or out of my control.

Famous last words.

THREE

The next morning my edgy feeling continued. For years my life had been scheduled down to the nanosecond. During rare downtime I reconnected with my family. Revived my sex life. Hit the firing range.

Spending the day between the sheets with a naked man wasn't an option. I'd endured as much family time as I could stand. That left one thing. I pulled my guns out from beneath the bed.

Although I'd already cleaned them, I double-checked anyway. I shoved the ammo in the duffel bag alongside the gun cases and zipped it shut.

Sophie turned from the sink when I hit the last creaky stair tread. Her eyes zeroed in on the bag. "How many times do I have to tell you? I can do your laundry."

"It's not laundry. I'm going out for a little while to shoot."

"Good thing Hope isn't here to see you hauling around a bag of guns, eh?"

"Probably."

"She still has nightmares," Sophie said.

My hand momentarily stilled on the shoulder strap of my little black bag of death. I turned away and grabbed a bottle of water from the fridge. As I uncapped it and drank, my neck burned from Sophie's hawklike eyes boring into me. I couldn't blame her for her overprotective instinct when it came to my little sister. We all felt sickened and guilty for what'd happened years ago, and yes, I knew Hope still had nightmares. We all did.

Sophie made a harrumphing noise. "You're exactly like your

father when it comes to dealing with stuff, Mercy. Anyway, I wanna ask you about something else."

I faced Sophie and couldn't keep the grumpiness at bay. "What?"

"You thought any more about talking to Estelle? She called me at home last night."

"About what?"

"About you helping find out what happened to Albert."

I forced myself to count to ten. "No, I haven't thought about it. I don't know why she's pestering you anyway. Why does it matter that Albert was found on our land?"

"Mebbe she sees it as your land, your responsibility."

"Have her take her concerns to Dawson. That's his job—his responsibility—not mine. Besides, it's not like I don't have enough to do around here."

"You?" Sophie's eyebrows lifted. "And here I thought you was passing everything off to my poor, overworked grandson, eh?"

"You really want to get into Jake's job description with me, Sophie?"

She sighed. "I don't know what happened to you, Mercy. Now you and Jake don't talk about nothing."

"So?"

"So, you never used to be like this."

"Like what?"

"Cold. Hard. Mean. Unforgiving."

Sophie and Hope knew how to push my buttons. Rather than take the high road, I loomed over her. "I'm exactly who I always was, so don't go coloring the past rosy and painting me as some Pollyanna who turned evil when I left the stabilizing influences of home and hearth. I've had darkness and secrets inside me since the day my mother died. The only difference is now I don't try to hide them."

A bleak expression flitted through her black eyes.

I didn't feel like appeasing her. And I sure as hell wasn't about to explain myself any more than I already had. "Forget it. I'll be back later."

Sophie gave me one last wounded look before she returned to the dirty breakfast dishes.

The ATVs were missing, which meant Jake and the ranch

hands weren't around. He'd left my dad's old Ford 250 diesel backed up to the barn door. Too much trouble to unload the posthole digger, roll of barbed wire, and assorted tools cluttered in the truck bed. I shinnied up the thick nylon rope dangling from the rafters in the barn. From the open hayloft door, I heaved a hay bale on top of everything and rappelled down.

In the pasture, I maneuvered the truck around rock piles and holes, swerving hard to avoid a rusted car door from a '57 Buick propped up like the start of Carhenge, the quirky tourist spot in Nebraska, where a few enterprising farmers had replicated Stone-henge—not with stones, but with vintage, American-made cars.

Tacky? Maybe. But not nearly as bad as the tourist trap that is Graceland.

Out here the vegetation was fairly high, indicating this section hadn't been grazed recently. From a distance, pockets of orangish-red and brown soil were laced with drought-resistant tallgrass; blue grama, fescue, prairie dropseed, and the slender green stems of quack grass. Up close, the shorter buffalo grass spread out as a spotty carpet of gray-green sod. Velvety-soft lamb's ear plants ringed large and small clumps of silver sagebrush. Yucca spikes poked up intermittently. When the fat, dried yucca seedpods shook in the wind, it sounded like dozens of rattlesnakes coiled in wait.

In the grove of half-dead elm trees, I parked beneath the larg-est one, not for shade, but to stand on the cab roof to reach the branches. Climbing trees wasn't a hobby left over from my tom-boy years; it kept me agile, kept my senses sharp. In my line of work, a clear shot was a rarity. Preparation for every contingency was a necessity.

I unwrapped a package of neon orange targets, small dots the size of a dime. When I'd scattered twenty targets, I cracked the case for my H-S Precision takedown rifle. I swapped out the modified barrel and was good to go.

No sunglasses, no cap to shade my eyes from the morning sun. Just me, my gun, and my scope. If I missed a shot, I couldn't blame it on anything besides my shitty marksmanship.

That familiar tickle started low in my belly. Fear. Anticipation. Confidence.

It'd taken longer to set up the course than to empty the

magazine. My self-assurance deflated when I studied the targets. Berating myself, I disassembled the rifle and packed it away. As I readied my handgun, a 9 mm Browning High Power, I knew my ego needed better than 50 percent accuracy, especially when I was used to 95 percent.

Tires crunching on bone-dry vegetation signaled unwanted visitors. A burgundy Dodge Silverado dually crept toward me. No clue who these people were. With a body discovered a week ago, I wasn't taking chances. I slammed a full clip in the gun, letting it dangle by my side.

My face remained neutral. My body appeared loose-limbed and relaxed. Inside I was wound tight as a new ball of baling twine.

The door opened. Bluish-white ostrich-skin cowboy boots thumped on the chrome running board. I gave a mental whistle. Those babies were high-end Lucchese boots, if I wasn't mistaken. I tamped down my envy as my mystery guest hopped down. He kept his back and the brim of his silver Stetson to me as he slammed the door.

When he faced me I groaned. Kit McIntyre. Real estate tycoon wannabe. My gaze flicked over the shiny truck. More than a wannabe if he could afford to drop $65K on a rig and $3K on boots. Still, he was a pain in my ass. He claimed a friendship with my father that Dad hadn't appreciated or reciprocated.

Old Kit had cotton white hair and a matching goatee. Add in his rotund carriage and he was the bastard child of Boss Hogg and Colonel Sanders—a description Kit wouldn't find the least bit distasteful. He even wore an off-white western suit with a bolo tie, and a silver-studded white leather belt with a buckle the size of my great-grandma's prized silver serving tray.

The passenger door opened. Hiram "Hi" Blacktower scrambled around the front end. Hi, a Lakota Sioux man, was tall as a spruce, broad as a barn, and dumb as a turkey. Dad always said Hi would be dangerous if he had any ambition. It appeared his ambition was to be a carbon copy of Kit. Hell, they'd even dressed the same.

Kit grinned at me. "We was wondering if we'd ever find ya, Mercy. Whatcha doing all the way out here by yourself?"

"Target shooting." I lifted the gun. Neither of them had noticed it. Kit's name fit: he had the survival instincts of a kitten.

"Is that military issue?" Hi asked.

"Nope. Personal. Why?"

"My brother Josiah was in the Gulf War, and he had a gun like that before . . ."

Before coming home a broken man in a wheelchair, courtesy of a land mine. My father had been freaked out about Josiah's injury when I accidentally let it slip I'd been in that exact area right before that particular bloody offensive.

"Anyway, it's good to see you, Mercy," Hi said.

"How'd you know where to look?"

"Sophie was kind enough to point us your direction."

Sophie earned herself a free ass chewing. "So, why are you guys trespassing? No one would blame me if I shot first, given all that's happened round here in the last month."

Kit softened his good-ol'-boy grin until his jowls sagged. Blinked at me with puppy-dog eyes. "I sure am sorry about your daddy, Mercy. I know it's got to've been hard, coming back here after Wyatt's death and handling all this stuff, the ranch, your sister—bless her soul—and the estate legalities. Lot of responsibility for a single woman."

I didn't have to guess what Kit was getting at. Surprised me it'd taken him a month to get around to it.

"I saw Hope at Besler's grocery. She told me she's anxious for you to make a decision on what you're gonna do with the ranch."

"Did Hope talk to you about it?"

"Yep. Sounds to me like you might be convinced to sell." His eyes searched mine. "That true?"

"What's it matter to you if I sell it or not?"

"Well, now, I'm glad you asked. 'Cause I've put together a sweet opportunity. It's real exciting."

"Real exciting," Hi chimed in.

They paused, letting the silence build drama.

I made the on-with-it gesture. With my gun.

"First off, let me tell you I know better than anyone what this ranch means to the community. It's a piece of living history.

We'd all like to see that history preserved, Mercy. In a beneficial manner to the Gunderson family, for all they've done over the years."

I muttered, "What a bunch of bullshit," but old Kit heard something else because he beamed an indulgent smile.

"Saddens me to see young folks being forced away from the country way they was raised in because they can't afford to ranch. Either because their older brothers and sisters are carrying on the family traditions, or because the price of the land is too damn high for a young couple just starting out. I'd like to keep some of them around here and offer them the same chance that was given to their daddies and granddaddies. Keep the community young and thriving."

"I imagine you've got something in mind?"

Dollar signs lit his eyes. "As a matter of fact, I do. I've rounded up a group of investors that would like to buy the Gunderson Ranch from you. In its entirely."

"Yeah? What are their plans for it?"

"We'd keep a large chunk of it intact. The rest we'd parcel out, about five hundred acres each. It'd give some of these young ranch couples a place to start."

Five hundred acres might mean a lot of land in fertile prairie-farming communities, but as far as ranching in western South Dakota? Forget it. Not enough room to run a decent herd of cattle. Not enough cattle meant not enough money to live on. Which meant the people buying the land wouldn't be ranching.

In essence, he was proposing to turn the "historic" seventy-thousand-acre Gunderson Ranch into a bunch of hobby ranches. Where white-collar professionals could play cowboy. Dress up in new Wranglers, fancy cowboy boots, and custom-made hats. Talk about low cattle prices, the lack of moisture, the high price of feed. Build a half-million-dollar house next to the quarter-million-dollar barn where they could stable their expensive hobbyhorses and fleet of top-of-the-line ATVs.

They'd throw branding parties in the spring. Sit in air-conditioned three-season porches in the summer and watch satellite TV while chatting on their cell phones about "real" country livin' with their stockbrokers. Then in the fall, they'd invite their buddies with purebred Labrador retrievers for a week of roughing it out West to do some *real* hunting.

God. Maybe I was channeling my friend John-John's abilities to see visions. A shudder ran through me. I actually felt my dad spinning in his grave.

What bothered me more than Kit's offer was Hope discussing our private family business with this big mouth. No wonder everyone in the county gossiped about my intentions. No wonder Dad left the final decision about the fate of the ranch to me and not my flaky sister.

"Whatcha think? Would you be willing to sit down and talk to the investors?"

"Sure."

Kit looked so happy I was afraid he'd lay a big honking kiss on me. Eww. I'd pop him one first, and not necessarily with my fist.

"When?"

"That's the thing, Kit. A group from Florida has asked to come and check the place out."

His white eyebrows rose clear to his hairline. "Florida? How'd they hear about it? Why would you even be talking to them kinda folk?"

I shrugged. "Don't know how they heard, but they offered to buy the whole property, sight unseen, as an investment." I grinned nastily and lied, "In cash."

Now old Kit looked like I *had* plugged him in the heart with my trusty gun. "B-but. You ain't seriously thinking about it, are ya?"

"Yes. Seems these other folks really do have the Gunderson family's best interests at heart."

Kit's sagging shoulders snapped straight with indignation. "You saying I don't?"

"I'm saying none of the people who have contacted me are pretending they want this chunk of land for any altruistic reasons."

"But—"

"You think I'm stupid, Kit? You think I don't know what this land is worth? You think because you paid me a personal visit I'll be inclined to sell it to you? Or will you bring up my *daddy* and your great friendship with him and lie about what *he* would've wanted?"

His brown eyes turned as cold and hard as frozen cow chips. "For years your daddy hoped you'd come back here and take over. Except we all know he was delusional when it comes to you and your crazy sister."

It was on the tip of my tongue to defend Hope. No one had the right to call her crazy but me.

But Kit wasn't finished. "You always thought you was too good to stick around these parts. You couldn't even be bothered to show up before your daddy passed on. No big surprise you're finally back here, now that you don't have to look him in the eye as he was wasting away to nothing. I'm glad he ain't around to see the heartless creature you've become, God rest his soul."

Wind rustled through the elm leaves. A drawn-out, high-pitched hawk's screech made me twitchy.

Hiram moved in. "He don't mean it, Mercy."

I stared at Kit. Revulsion stared back at me. "Yes, he does. So now that I know how you really feel, Kit, don't hold back."

"Fine. Here it is: you don't know all the problems you'd be causing if you sell out to someone who ain't local. Who's it gonna hurt? Your neighbors. Remember them? The ones who helped out your family when your mama died? When your daddy's diabetes got so bad they chopped off his leg and he couldn't take care of this place? When your granddad nearly lost everything in the dirty '30s? Oh, and let's not forget way back when your great-grandma Grace nearly lost her mind."

Seemed old Kit knew my family history better than I did.

When he spit a wad of tobacco out the side of his mouth, I expected to see a forked tongue.

"Think those fellers from Florida give a rip that your daddy's been letting the Marshall family hunt here off-season so they don't starve in the winter? Them rich snobs will close the land off to all hunting except for their bigwig buddies.

"Sure, they're willing to pay you top dollar. They don't have to worry about some damn conglomerate moving in next to *them*, sending ag-land values through the roof and forcing them out of *their* heritage. By then they'll probably already have bought up half the damn county and sent the people who've lived in this area for generations into town so's they can work for Wal-Mart."

His venomous declaration wasn't a revelation to me. So far he'd been the first person to voice his concerns to my face. For that alone I ought to have given him props. I might have, if it weren't for the sneaky-ass way he'd gone about it.

Oh, and his shitty opinion of me and my family.

"You done?" I asked coolly.

"No. Some powerful people are backing me on this. Life on the ranch is mighty rough, especially for a city girl like you."

Whoa. That was a name I hadn't been called. Ever. "City girl?" I repeated.

"Yeah, you ain't cut out for this life. Never were. Wyatt kept you in the dark about what it really takes to run a ranch this size. Neither you nor your sister has the guts to do it. 'Sides, you never know what can happen around these parts. Accidents and the like." Kit lifted his hand and casually studied his fingernails.

Oh. My. God. I could hardly keep a straight face. Talk about him acting like a caped villain in a bad melodrama. He should've been cackling evilly while he twirled his mustache. Was he secretly imagining tying me to a railroad track as I cried for help?

Screw that. Screw him.

"Don't got nothing to say?"

"You threatening me?"

"Consider it a fair warning. You may act tough, but when it comes down to it, the years away made you soft. With the right kinda pressure, I suspect you'll give way like a marshmallow in the sun."

Soft. With that suggestion my humor vanished. My gun arm lifted of its own accord. I fired at the right headlight on his truck. Metal chinked. Glass exploded. Gun smoke hung in the air. I didn't flinch, although Hiram hit the ground pretty damn fast.

Kit screeched, "What in the *hell* are you doing?"

"My way of warning you that I don't deal well with any kind of threats, Kit."

"You're just as crazy as your sister and the rest of the women in your family."

"Maybe."

"You just made a big mistake." He shook his finger at me. "You're gonna pay for that."

"Yeah? Then go ahead and put this one on my bill, too." I shot out the other headlight just for fun.

Hiram crawled away.

Chicken.

Kit's face matched the color of his rig. "You just bought yourself a whole passel of trouble, Missy."

I swung the barrel away from his front tire and aimed at his sweat-covered brow. "Wrong. You breathe one word of my little misfire to anyone and I'll come for you." I inched closer, and he backed up. "When you're all alone, Kit. I'll have you pissing yourself in the dark before I shoot off your worthless dick. Then we'll see who's tough and who's soft." I pointed at the driver's-side door. "Now get the hell off my land."

Hiram scrambled to his feet. "Come on, Kit. Let's go."

"Next time I see you trespassing I'll shoot you—or anyone else—on sight. Feel free to pass that around."

I fully expected Kit to crank down the window to shout out something lame and ominous like, "This ain't over." But he hauled ass away as fast as his ten-cylinder allowed.

After they'd gone, I slumped against a hay bale. This was the first confrontation, but I knew it wouldn't be the last. And I couldn't get rid of all my problems by shooting them.

Pity.

FOUR

Sophie gave up trying to get me to wear a dress to the community dance. If boots and jeans were good enough for the guys, they were good enough for me. Instead of showing up in my beloved Viper, I drove my dad's truck down County Road 11, country music on KICK 104 my companion.

Despite the dust and bugs, I rolled the windows down. I slowed for a baler taking up half the gravel road. I waved at Tim Lohstroh as I passed, inhaling the deliciously sweet scent of yellow clover.

The breath-stealing heat had abated, leaving a perfect summer evening, where the air is velvety soft. I glanced across the horizon at the myriad of colors: a swirl of sapphire, salmon, and scarlet, indicating the sky's magical transformation from day to night. I'd seen sunsets all over the world. Nothing beats a summer sunset on the high prairie. Nothing.

I parked in the dusty field at the Viewfield Community Center. The knee-high bromegrasses were dead in places from lack of moisture and flattened from Buicks, pickups, and ATVs leaving skid marks on the concretelike ground.

I slid the beer cooler across the truck bed. Alcohol wasn't allowed inside these family events, so we all snuck out for a nip between songs. Or we tucked a flask in our boots. The Wild Turkey in my ropers sloshed with every step.

It was hard to believe that barn dances were still the summer highlight in Eagle River County. Was it because country and ranch people clung to traditions, rejecting anything new or different on principle?

Nah. These gatherings were actually fun. As a kid I'd loved dances, even when Dad—as sheriff—kept an eye on every cowboy who asked me to two-step.

Tonight's festivities weren't taking place in a barn, but in a steel building a few enterprising souls had remodeled from an abandoned wool-shearing shack into a much-needed community center. As it was the biggest building in the county, we'd held the finger sandwiches and sympathy assembly here after my father's funeral. At the time I hadn't paid much attention to the surroundings.

The interior owed more to function than decor. A big, open kitchen, lined with assorted old stoves and refrigerators and a huge concrete dance floor with a wooden platform serving as a stage. Flags hung from the metal rafters: Old Glory, the pale blue South Dakota state flag, local chapters of FFA, 4-H, Stockgrowers Association, SD Beef Council, SD Pork Producers, VFW—banners that meant something and were hung with pride.

In the far back corner chipped white Formica folding tables were piled high with sweets. Crisp, sugary cookies covered in sprinkles, drenched with powdered sugar, and bursting with nuts and chunks of chocolate. Pans of bars coated with frosting in every color of the rainbow. Thick, gooey brownies and rows of fruit pies with perfectly browned crusts—all homemade goodies, not a Keebler bag in sight.

Four watercoolers abutted the wall between the men and women's bathrooms. Six industrial-sized coffee urns were set up beside the dessert station. Each pot would be emptied and refilled at least three times before the evening's festivities concluded. My mother used to say, "Those Lutherans sure love their coffee." Not all the attendees were Lutheran. Methodists, Catholics, Presbyterians, and Episcopalians were welcome, too. We do have *some* religious diversity in South Dakota.

Coffee was one thing we all agreed on: black. The rage for lattes, espresso, cappuccino, and confections topped with whipped cream and flavored syrups hadn't caught on. A few people preferred cream and sugar, but mention a half-caf, sugar-free, caramel macchaito with light foam, and you'd get a blank-eyed stare like you were speaking Farsi.

I'd barely stepped foot inside when people descended on me like a pack of locusts. Most everyone in the county felt entitled to grill me on my plans for the ranch. When I hedged, they gave me a suspicious look usually reserved for outsiders. Then they left me standing alone like I'd developed mad cow disease. In that moment I missed my father with an ache so painful I almost turned and ran out.

A Gunderson never runs.

As I debated ignoring Dad's phantom words of wisdom, Hope materialized by my side.

She looked worse than dog crap. Makeup didn't mask her waxy complexion, and the thick black mascara accentuated the hollowness in her eyes. Why couldn't Doc Canaday figure out what was wrong with her? "You sure you should be here, sis?"

"I'm sick of being at home. I want to have some fun and dance."

A hairy head the size of a moose popped between us. "Did someone say dance?" Tubby Tidwell wrapped a flabby arm around each of our shoulders. "You're in luck tonight, ladies, because 'Tubby the Texas Two-Step Master' is here. Who's first?"

Hope giggled and leaned into him.

I resisted pulling out my flask right then.

Without warning the lights dimmed and the band launched into "Whiskey River."

"Mind if I steal this gorgeous young thing for a while, Mercy?" Tubby yelled over the music.

I glanced at Hope. Her eyes pleaded with me. I smiled tightly. "She's all yours, Tubby."

He whooped and dragged her to the crowded dance floor.

Hope's defection spurred mine. No such luck I'd get away easy.

Our neighbor Iris Newsome cornered me. "Mercy. I'm surprised to see you here, although I am glad I ran into you. I've been meaning to come by. How are you holding up?"

I'm drinking more than usual and my career is toast, but besides that, I'm peachy keen.

Nah. Not a good response. "I'm taking it day by day."

"I know how that goes." She smiled sadly and turned to focus on Hope and Tubby twirling around on the dance floor.

Dealing with Iris always set my teeth on edge, mostly because I didn't know how to deal with her.

When Hope was five, she was playing cowboys and Indians in the shelterbelt behind our oldest barn with her best friend, Jenny, Iris's daughter. Somehow Jenny had managed to sneak her father's eight-inch Bowie knife into her Barbie backpack.

Hope's jealousy that Jenny had the real thing, while she had to make do with a plastic toy gun, spurred Hope to sneak inside and grab Dad's snub-nosed Ruger revolver from his nightstand drawer.

After Hope captured Jenny, she'd tied her up and interrogated her. Just like on TV. When Jenny's answers weren't to her liking, Hope placed the gun barrel to Jenny's forehead. Just like on TV. But unlike on TV, when Hope pulled the trigger and fired, she blew Jenny's brains all over the barn and all over herself.

When Jenny didn't hop up and laugh, just like on TV, Hope started to scream. She screamed until her voice gave out and she went into a catatonic state.

Dad literally picked up the pieces.

Even through their grief, Jenny's parents hadn't blamed Hope. They knew everyone in our part of the world kept their guns loaded; the circumstances could've easily gone the other way and we'd have been buying a pine box and planning a funeral.

The incident became another turning point in our lives. Dad burned the barn to the ground and purchased a gun safe. Within two months he quit wallowing in the grief and whiskey that'd followed my mother's death and signed on with the sheriff's department as a deputy. Hope still suffers from random periods of depression. Rather than medicating her, we all tread lightly during these episodes and use our family strength to shield her from others and herself.

The catastrophe hadn't dimmed my love of firearms; it merely increased my respect for the deadly consequences of misuse. Killing, even accidentally, will make some people delicate, like my sister. But killing is the one thing I'm good at, even if the payoff is some sleepless nights.

Iris faced me. "I'm calling a meeting next week with Bob Peterson about some of the changes those LifeLite people who bought the old Jackson place have made." Her eyes narrowed. "Have you been by there yet?"

"Ah. No." It was hard to imagine the kind of changes that could require the attention of our county commissioner.

"It's an abomination. Eight-foot-high electric fences and manned gates twenty-four hours a day? They've got to be doing something illegal, especially with so many new outbuildings popping up practically overnight . . . heaven only knows what for."

"What can Bob do?"

"First of all, he can check to see if their permits are up to snuff."

"And if they aren't? What then?"

"He can bring it to the county commission and stop any additional building. Hopefully all of the landowners with adjoining property, who are affected by the blight on the landscape, can make our voices heard. Or at least encourage the county to enforce legal actions and heavy fines for building violations. If enough of us sign the petition to enact some sort of covenants to keep it from happening again, we can bring it to a countywide vote."

I snorted at her casual use of the word *covenants*. No rancher I knew would ever consider voting for that type of restriction. Sure, they may hate what those outsiders were doing to the property, but they'd never allow their own personal freedoms to be dictated by local government. Or the local busybody.

"I got you thinking, didn't I?" Iris asked smugly.

"No. I don't see what this has to do with me."

"But as a landowner—"

"Which is in question right now, isn't it?"

Her mouth tightened. "You aren't seriously considering selling?"

I offered her a greasy politician's smile. "I'm seriously considering peeing my pants if I don't get to the bathroom pretty damn quick."

Iris retreated, taken aback by my rudeness.

She was probably thinking if my mother hadn't died, I would have better manners. Or if her daughter Jenny had lived, she certainly wouldn't have uttered such a crude comment.

Mumbling "Excuse me," I made a break for the bathroom,

locked myself in the stall, and dug the whiskey flask out of my boot. After sucking down three gulps of liquid fire, I closed my eyes and enjoyed the burn.

Mature, Gunderson. How often in the last month had I looked to Jack Daniel's or Jim Beam for strength? Too many.

Reluctantly I exited the stall. At the crowded sink, I glanced in the mirror as I dried my hands. Molly, the oldest daughter of my oldest friend, Geneva, winked at me and grinned. "You hiding in here?"

"Yep. Are you?"

"We both are." She nudged the lanky Indian girl standing next to her. "Sue Anne, this is my mom's friend, Mercy." Molly added slyly, "She's also Levi Arpel's aunt."

Sue Anne's brown eyes widened. "Really? Is Levi here?"

I'd forgotten to ask Hope if Levi had tagged along. "I don't know. I could ask his mom if you want."

"No, no, don't, it's okay. Maybe we'll see him around."

"Sue Anne thinks he's a total hottie," Molly said. "They're actually sneaking—"

"Shut up!" Sue Anne blushed and pushed her.

My nephew a hottie? Whoa. Hanging out with these girls for even two seconds made me feel every one of my thirty-eight years. "If I see Levi, I'll tell him you're looking for him."

I ducked out of the bathroom and considered leaving. As I debated, I saw Hope slow dancing with some guy I didn't know. Weird. I scanned the group of kids lined up against the far wall like they were facing a firing squad, but didn't see Levi.

"Hey-o, you *are* here."

"I told you I would be, Sophie."

"You're not smiling. No wonder you're standing here alone while everyone else is out dancing, eh?"

"Don't you have grandchildren to harass or something?"

Sophie shuffled into my line of vision. "*Shee*. They don't fight back. They say 'yes *Unci*' or 'no *Unci*,' where you snarl like Devlin's pit bull. You're more fun."

I gave her a droll stare. "Comparing me to a dog to see if I bite? You must be bored."

"Curse of the elders. Got nothing to do but stir up trouble."

Her wrinkled face brightened, and she waved to someone across the way.

"Well, have fun mixing things up. I'm going home."

"Wait." Sophie grabbed my sleeve. "There is someone here who wants to talk to you."

Visions of Sophie's (bad) matchmaking attempts twisted my guts into a knot. "Who?"

The song ended. A round of applause broke out.

Jake sidled up behind Sophie and squeezed her hunched shoulders. "Ready for that dance, *Unci*?"

"Afraid you're too late, *takoja*. I'm off to sit with some friends. But Mercy told me she would like to dance."

Talk about stirring up trouble.

I opened my mouth to protest, but Jake led me to the dance floor. Tempting to glare at Sophie, but her genuinely happy smile doused my burning look. Plus, if I stuck around, she'd probably fix me up with someone worse than Jake.

One dance. What could it hurt? It'd probably be something fast like the "Cotton-Eyed Joe" anyway. But the singer belted out the mournful, slow ballad, "A Thousand Miles from Nowhere" by Dwight Yoakam, and I ground my teeth.

Jake put his hand in the small of my back, pulling me close. I set my free hand on his shoulder and pretended this was no big deal. Like we danced together every weekend, not once every two decades.

We started to move, a slow, *one* two three, *one* two three. I shut my eyes for a moment as we fell into the familiar rhythm. But when I couldn't see him, my other senses kicked in. The feel of his rough palm on mine. The heat from his hand on my spine. Clean cotton, tangy lime aftershave, male musk, and the underlying hint of horseflesh. Scents that were uniquely Jake and hadn't changed in twenty years. Scents I'd spent a lot of time trying to forget.

His smoothly shaven cheek grazed mine. "Sorry. I'm probably the last man you wanted to dance with tonight, eh?"

"It's fine."

"Then relax. I remember when you used to think this was fun." He twirled us into the middle of the dance floor.

I'd relaxed when he blew it all to hell by softly whispering in my ear, "Are we ever gonna talk about it?"

"I haven't made my decision on the ranch yet."

"You know that ain't what I meant."

His disappointed tone grated on me but proved I wasn't any more anxious to spill my guts now than I'd been years ago. "Drop it."

He did.

During the slide steel guitar solo, we'd glided to the outskirts of the dance floor again. Soon as the song ended, I pushed away from him and made tracks for the exit.

The balmy evening cooled the sweat on the back of my neck. In the darkness, I stopped to get my bearings, angry about the resurgence of memories. Of me as a hopeful teen. Of Jake. Of what we'd had and what we'd lost.

When footsteps shuffled behind me, I snapped, "Go away. I already told you I didn't want to talk to you."

"Sorry. I thought Sophie said . . ."

I whirled around. Not Jake forcing me to face my demons and our past. It was Estelle Yellow Boy.

"I'm sorry, Estelle. I thought you were someone else."

Sophie sidled up beside her. "Estelle wants to talk to you about something."

Sophie's meddling knew no bounds.

Estelle sidestepped the bluish circle of light next to the doors and hid in the darkness. "Bet you think it's weird, me wanting to talk to you, hey?"

"Maybe a little."

"It's about Albert."

I figured as much.

Estelle spoke to the ground. "I ain't gonna lie to you. Albert was going through a rough patch. Running off all the time. Growing up on the rez is hard. We thought it was a phase and he'd straighten out. He won't get the chance now. So, I wanna know if you'll help me find out who killed him."

"Run that by me again?"

"That's why I come here. To see if you'd help me."

Happy people milled past, laughing, joking, living, as we lurked in the shadows. Sobering, that Estelle wasn't at the dance to kick up her heels, to forget about her sorrow for a while, but for the express purpose of talking to me. "What do you think I can do?"

"Anything you'd be willing to do would be something. As it sets, the acting sheriff, Dawson, ain't done nothing. He ain't talked to none of Albert's friends. He ain't even really talked to us. If I ask him questions, he looks at me like if I'da been a better mother, Albert wouldn't be dead. Looks at me like I'm wasting his time. Acting like my boy is just another dead Indian."

My feeling of disquiet grew.

"Your father was a good man and a good sheriff. Fair. If he was still alive, he'da done everything to find who done it."

"Though I appreciate that you thought so much of my dad, I honestly don't know how I can help."

"I can give you the names of them kids he'd been hanging with. They started some club. Albert didn't talk much about it, which makes me think them boys might of had something to do with him getting killed."

"Estelle, I don't know the first thing about—"

"I don't expect you to do it for free. I ain't got no money, but I can give you this." She withdrew a piece of white flannel from her jacket pocket and carefully unfolded it.

Nestled in her palm was an elaborately beaded necklace. Beautiful primary-colored beads surrounded a simple circular design. Pieces of polished bone attached the medallion to the chain, which looked to be a thick black braid fashioned from the hair of a horse's tail. Red, black, yellow, and white beads—colors attributed to the Earth's four directions—dangled from curly buffalo leather strips below the pendant.

I touched it. I couldn't help it. It was magical.

"This belonged to my great-great-great *unci*," Estelle said. "Been in my family longer than the Gunderson Ranch has been in yours."

"I can't possibly—"

"You have to. I need somebody's help, and only someone who's lived through a buncha horrible things knows what I'm going through."

I bristled, expecting her to mention specifics about the woes that'd plagued the Gunderson family for generations: death, death, and more violent death with a dash of crazy stirred in just to spice things up.

Instead, her voice broke. "His neck was snapped like a twig. Whoever done this left his body like it weren't no more'n a deer carcass. I can't forget about it and move on like everybody wants me to."

Shiny tears skimmed the pockmarks before dripping down her brown face. "Paul don't know I'm here talking to you. He thinks we oughta stay out of it." She sniffled. "I tried, but I just can't."

Maybe it was the crack in her stoicism. Maybe it was because I'd seen broken and forgotten bodies scattered all over the world—more than most people could imagine. Maybe it was a need to connect with another woman to band together against men's indifference. Whatever it was, something inside me shifted. The theme song from *Underdog* began to get louder and louder inside my head.

"Okay. I'll see what I can find out. No promises though."

Estelle's chin dropped to her chest. "Thank you."

"Do you have a list of his friends? A place for me to start?"

"Estelle? Where are you?"

She looked up. Panic flitted through her eyes. She hastily swiped her tears and pressed the flannel into my hand. "I'll call you. Or get the list to you somehow. Please don't say nothing to nobody about this." She hustled away to deflect Paul's suspicion.

Before I could give the necklace back to her, she vanished. So I hid the package in my boot. Desperate for a cold beer, I wove through the cars and trucks. Tripped over my own damn feet when I didn't see a pothole because of my altered vision. I probably looked like just another drunk. Or maybe the guilt of taking that family heirloom even temporarily added extra weight to my imbalance.

After I wiped the dirt from my knees, I locked the necklace in the glove box. As I reached for my cooler, a couple of shouts caught my attention, followed by the unmistakable sound of a body hitting metal.

A fight.

No kidding. Nothing cowboys liked better than to get drunk and brawl. Mostly the young cocky ones, but I'd seen my share of forty- and fifty-year-old guys duking it out over a slight, real or imagined.

I zeroed in on six or seven kids circling two punks mixing it up in the dirt. Couldn't tell if any of the gawkers were adults who should've stopped the asinsine show of testosterone. I peered over the edge of the crowd to see if I had to be the voice of reason.

And I noticed his shoes right off. Good thing. His face was so damn bloody I doubt his mother would've recognized him.

Levi.

He'd pinned the other guy on the ground. He was so tired the wild punches he swung didn't land.

The situation left me in a dilemma. If I broke up the fight, Levi's friends wouldn't let him live it down. If I didn't break it up and Levi ended up hurt . . . I couldn't live with that option either. As I debated, I heard a sharp male voice bark, "What's going on back there?"

Both boys jumped up. Wiped blood from their faces, glaring at each other from bruised eyes. "Keep your fucking mouth shut about this, Arpel."

"You don't tell me what to do, fuckface."

A short-lived respite. More words were exchanged, and they were back at it again. Pushing. Shoving. Swinging. Missing.

I attempted to diffuse the situation by trying to insert myself between them. Yeah, I probably should've waited the full thirty seconds until the Samaritan showed up, but I'd broken up my fair share of fights. Mostly between drunken adult male military personnel, so I didn't consider the danger of coming between a couple of pissed-off hormonal high school boys.

I should have.

"Stay out of it. It don't concern you." This free advice was snarled from a bystander the size of an oak tree.

"Shut your big mouth, Moser," Levi panted, keeping his eye on his opponent. "*You* stay out of it."

"Make me, Arpel."

Levi growled.

"Ooh. Tough guy."

"Don't hafta be tough to take a pussy like you."

Then Levi charged Moser. I ended up in the middle and fell into a tangle of punching arms and kicking legs. Took a shot to my shin. An elbow to the gut. A glancing blow off my jaw. That one hurt. I braced myself for an opportunity to (a) escape or (b) inflict some damage.

Before I'd implemented either plan, both guys were pulled off me and I stared at the angry face of Sheriff Dawson.

Crap. I huddled on the ground, trying to make myself inconspicuous.

"What's going on here?" Dawson had one meaty fist twisted in Levi's tank top and the other in Moser's baggy Denver Nuggets basketball shirt.

When neither answered, he shook Moser. "You. Tell me."

Moser flashed Levi a nasty, bloody grin. "Nothing's going on, Sheriff."

Dawson scowled and focused his attention on Levi. "What about you? Gonna tell me why a couple of you guys are covered in dirt and blood and the rest are standing around watching?"

"Nothing going on. Sir."

He released them. "Either go inside or get on home. I see any of you guys out here again, doing *nothing*, and I'll throw you in the back of my patrol car and you can do *nothing* from a cell, understand?"

A bunch of murmured "yes sirs" then boys scattered like aspen leaves in a windstorm.

Dawson finally noticed me. "What the hell are you doing down there in the dirt, Mercy?"

"Nothing."

He scowled and extended a hand to help me up, but Levi beat him to it.

I hid my shock that my nephew actually acknowledged my presence, and grunted as Levi jerked me to my feet.

"You all right?" Dawson asked me.

"I'm fine. Nothing ice and Excedrin won't cure."

Dawson's gaze pinned Levi like a bug. "Want to say anything now that your buddies abandoned you?"

Levi dropped his chin. His tangled hair fell in his face.

"Didn't think so." He sighed. "Levi, I need to talk to your aunt alone."

From beneath his fall of hair, Levi glared a you're-gonna-rat-me-out look.

I couldn't do that to him. "Sorry, Sheriff, it'll have to wait. Levi's face is hamburger. If I don't get ice on it, his jaw will swell up like a toad's."

"You headed home?"

I didn't answer. Let him think we were leaving. "See you around, Sheriff."

He cupped my elbow before I'd made it two steps. "I haven't forgotten you promised me a dance." His husky whisper vibrated in my ear, sending a pleasant shiver through me. "Don't think I won't collect. Drive safe."

Huh. His declaration was as curious as my reaction to it. I tried not to think about either as I led Levi to my truck.

FIVE

I unearthed a roll of gauze out of the first-aid kit stashed under the seat and ripped off the paper packaging.

"Thanks for umm . . . covering for me with the sheriff."

"I didn't cover for you. I didn't know what you and that kid were fighting about. Why'd that guy Moser jump in?"

"Because he could. Fucking jerk-off. Thinks everybody oughta bow down to him, like he's some alpha leader."

I let his foul language slide because—hello? Pot? Calling the kettle black? I unwound a healthy chunk of gauze, snipped off a strip with my pocketknife, and dipped it in the melted ice from the cooler. "Normally I don't offer advice, but if I were you, I'd clean off some of that blood before your mom sees you."

"That bad?"

"Take a look."

Levi ducked down and peered at himself in the passenger's-side mirror. "That asshole Donald Little Bear really marked up my face, eh?"

He'd said it with pride. Boys. Men. Some things never changed. "You won't be winning any beauty contests."

After he'd become mildly presentable, he hopped up on the tailgate next to me.

I dug out two icy cold cans of Bud Light. Put the first one against my jaw, and popped the top on the other. I sucked down a mouthful of ambrosia and sighed.

Levi asked, "Can I have one?"

"For your eye?"

"No. To drink."

"Hell no." I sipped. "Does your mom let you drink beer?"

"Hell no." His lips formed a smarmy grin. "But I do anyway."

"You been drinking tonight?"

"Nah. Probably why being at this dance sucks."

I slid him a sideways glance. "Were you having fun until you and Mr. Little Bear decided to make each other bleed?"

"Are you serious? These things are so lame."

"Yeah? I always thought they were kinda fun."

"Not when everyone is watching you all the time."

Who was watching him? Not his mother. "Think you've got it bad? My dad was sheriff. When I was your age? Every time some guy he didn't like asked me to dance, he'd cut in. In his wheelchair."

Levi laughed. It was a pure, sweet sound. Not yet man, not quite boy. I didn't know if I'd heard him laugh at all in the last month.

"I s'pose that's worse."

I waited a beat. "Worse than what?"

"My mom. Treating me like a little kid. Making me come to this thing in the first place, so we could spend some time together, then sneaking off with Theo the first chance she gets."

"Who's Theo?"

"Her boyfriend."

The next swallow of beer hit my stomach like liquid nitrogen. "Since when does she have a boyfriend?"

Levi looked torn. Obviously he needed someone to talk to, but his loyalty was to his mom, even when he wasn't happy with her. "For a couple months."

"*Months?* Since before Dad died?"

"Yeah. Right after Doc told us about Grandpa." He paused. "With all the people dying in her life . . . Ma can't handle stuff like that. No one but me really knew that Gramps took care of her more than she took care of him. And when he couldn't anymore, she . . . had to find someone else who could."

"Why couldn't you be the one she leaned on when Grandpa got sick?"

His soft brown eyes were a mixture of bitterness and sorrow. "Because she still sees me as a little kid."

Oh damn. My heart crumbled, my stomach lurched, my eyes

stung. Damn my sister. Did Hope have any idea how badly she'd hurt her son by turning away from him? To a strange man? When Levi needed her?

I chugged the beer. Angrily chucked the spent can behind me in the truck bed and opened the second one. "I understand why she might've been hesitant to tell me at first. But I've been home for well over a month. Seen her every damn day. Why hasn't she mentioned it?"

"You ain't missing much, believe me. Grandpa would've hated him."

"Is that why hasn't she brought this Theo guy around to meet me?"

"Yeah. She's afraid of what you'll think of him."

"What's he do?"

"He teaches summer classes at the rec center on Lakota culture."

"Is he Indian?"

"Some kind. I have to go to them classes because I failed social studies this year. He's teaching that old shit that nobody cares about. He totally creeps me out."

"Why?"

"Besides the fact that he's doing it with my mom? After he spends the night, Mom acts all giggly and shit. It's sick."

That'd creep me out, too. "So, Theo was the guy she was dancing with a little while ago?" Levi nodded. No wonder she'd been plastered to him. I couldn't believe she hadn't told me. I couldn't believe my powers of observation were so piss-poor I hadn't noticed she was mooning around in love.

"It kinda surprised me they were dancing in public. They ain't exactly been telling anyone they're together."

At least I wasn't the only one in the dark.

"Can I ask you something, Aunt Mercy?"

"Shoot."

"Do you like being in the army? I mean, I know you gotta like it some because you been in it for so long."

"You asking if I had it to do over again if I'd join up?"

"Yeah, I guess."

Talk about a loaded question. Hope hated my military service.

The guns. The potential for killing. But this wasn't about Hope. I wouldn't blow the first real connection with my nephew and lie to him because his mother would want me to.

"Yes, I would. Even though we're at war and the chances of getting stationed in Iraq or Afghanistan after enlistment are pretty much guaranteed, I can't imagine what my life would've been like without the army."

"So's it true what Mom said? You selling the ranch? Going back to being a soldier?"

"I'll never be the soldier I was." I drained my beer. My grimace had little to do with the tart taste of the barley and hops.

His head whipped toward me. "Whaddya mean?"

"Look. If I tell you this, swear you won't tell your mom. Or anyone else. This is top-secret stuff."

"I swear."

With the complete absence of street- and yard lights, the sky was a swath of pure black punctuated with silver dots. It never ceased to amaze me it was the same sky I'd seen on the other side of the world. "The reason I didn't come back until after Dad died was because I was in the hospital."

"Why? What happened?"

"Shrapnel injury."

"Holy shit! Where?"

"Iraq."

"No. I meant where on your body did you get hit?"

"Oh. In the leg." I wasn't ready to talk about my eye to anyone.

"Cool! Can I see it?" Guilt distorted his face. "I mean, not cool that you were hurt—"

"It's okay. I know what you meant."

The wavering tent walls of the military hospital in Balad flashed in my mind. I'd waited damn near a day for treatment since my injuries weren't life threatening. As I writhed in pain, I wondered if the injured Iraqi on the cot next to me had spent the day executing American soldiers. In those hours I basted in heat and hatred, I realized the antiseptic scents never masked the odors of blood, urine, death, and despair. And my utter sense of hopelessness expanded to near hysteria when they'd finally

tracked me down amid the hundreds of injured soldiers to give
me the message my father was dead.

The band belted out a countrified version of "Satisfaction."
Car doors slammed and people shouted, yet silence hummed
between us. I spied a young mother pacing in the shadows of the
building, trying to soothe a screaming baby wearing nothing but
a diaper and tears.

"So how come you don't want no one to know? *Shee.* You're
like . . . a hero! They would've had a parade for you and stuff."

I didn't answer. I wondered if he'd come to the right conclu-
sion without my having to explain.

"You didn't want none of that, did you? Not because Grandpa
had just died either."

Surprisingly astute kid. "No."

Cricket chirps rose and fell.

"Can I ask you something else?"

"Sure."

"Have you ever killed anyone?"

My natural inclination was to lie. Yet, if he was serious about
the military, he deserved to know killing was part of the job.
"Yeah." I yanked the flask from my boot and emptied it in my
mouth. "Why?"

"Just curious."

"Come on, Levi, that's crap. Tell me why."

He didn't look at me. Instead, he picked at a gummy chunk of
unknown origin imbedded in the tailgate. "Mom tells me you've
liked to shoot stuff since you were little."

"Lots of people hunt," I said cautiously.

"She wasn't talking about hunting. She was talking about killing. In cold blood."

I didn't point out that Hope had no room to be judgmental
when talking about killing.

He blurted, "Did you really shoot your dog when you were
kids?"

Whoo-yeah. Hope had a high opinion of me.

It'd been a long time since I'd thought of Rufus, our Austra-
lian blue heeler.

That brutally hot afternoon became so clear in my mind I

could almost smell the cherry Kool-Aid. Dad was working second shift. Sophie had gone home. None of the ranch hands were around. Just Hope and me and a lazy summer day.

We were swinging on the porch when we heard the most god-awful howling. We followed the yelps to the end of the driveway and found Rufus cowering in the ditch.

He'd been hit by a car, back legs broken, hips crushed. He couldn't even drag himself out of the gully.

Hope raced to pick him up. Happy as Rufus seemed to see her, in his paralyzed state he couldn't even wag his fluffy tail.

I'd stopped her. "Don't touch him."

She wailed, "But we have to help!"

The insistent cawing of black crows brought my attention to the cloudless blue sky and the bluish-black wings of the birds circling above us. Nature knew. I knew. Nothing would help poor Rufus.

"Call Daddy," Hope begged me over Rufus's howls. "He'll tell you what to do. He'll send Doc Kroger. Hurry!"

The vet was too busy to waste time on a lost cause. My stomach churned the Kool-Aid into battery acid. I knew what Dad would've done. No one liked putting down an animal, but it was a harsh reality of ranch life.

My heart pounded. My palms dripped sweat. I'd made myself look at Rufus, the cattle dog my mom loved. Blood poured out his muzzle. Diarrhea matted the black-and-white fur on his rear haunches, proving he'd lost control of his bowels.

I had no choice. "Stay here with him for a minute, okay?"

Relief crossed Hope's face. She'd nodded and dropped to her knees to stroke his head.

At the house I'd unlocked the gun safe, removed the Remington, grabbed some ammo, and shoved them in my shorts pocket. I'd dragged a shovel, letting the distortion of metal grinding on rocks and gravel fill my ears as I trudged to the end of the driveway.

Hope was bawling. When she saw the rifle, she began to scream.

"Unless you want to watch, go on and get in the house."

"No! You can't do this! I won't let you!"

I was on the prowl. I tugged on my skintight Rocky jeans with the leather lacing down the outside seams and slipped on my beat-up red Justin ropers. Snapped the pearl buttons on my favorite shirt, a short, sleeveless red-and-white-gingham number from Cruel Girl.

I pawed through my extensive collection of rhinestone belts: b.b. Simon, Kippys, 20X, Montana Silversmiths, Old Man River. You could take the girl out of the country, but a gaudy bit of rodeo queen always remained. The Swarovski crystals on the skinny red Nocona belt glimmered as I threaded it through the belt loops, adjusting the silver studded buckle below my belly button on the low-riding jeans.

Damn. No place to put my gun.

As a civilian I didn't need to carry everywhere I went. Still, it was hard to remember a time in my life when I wasn't loaded for bear.

I clomped down the stairs and paused on the landing leading into the kitchen. The warm smells of home cooking hung in the humid air. Mashed potatoes and peppery gravy. Roasted meat, sugar-glazed baby carrots, and onions. Chocolate cake with white buttercream frosting. When I saw Sophie and Jake seated at the big table, plates set for Hope and Levi, and the empty melmac plate in my usual spot, I ignored my growling stomach.

"Why you all spiffed up for dinner, hey?"

Guilt, go away. "I'm not staying for dinner."

"Where you going?"

"Out."

Sophie's eyes were curious as a crow's. "Out where?"

As I snagged my straw hat off the coat rack and shouldered my purse, I swallowed the retort reminding Sophie I didn't answer to her. I pocketed the truck keys and debated on racing back upstairs for my Walther, just in case.

"Mercy? You gonna tell me where you going?"

"No, Sophie, I'm not. I'll see you tomorrow." I left before she could change my mind.

The heat inside the truck blasted me like a woodstove. With the windows rolled down, the interior cooled as I zipped along the series of gravel switchbacks, a shortcut to my bar, my darling Clementine's.

I belted out "Redneck Woman" along with the radio. The neon Coors Light winked at me across the barren field, the shadowy purpled Badlands a backdrop for the shadowy bar.

Clementine's is a total dive. A cobbled-together shack where only the toughest locals dared to tread. A mix of cowboys, Indians, ranchers, bikers—anyone who wasn't in the mood to exchange pleasant conversation. A place to knock back a shot, knock in a few pool balls, or knock heads together. Clementine's was the roughest bar in five counties, and I considered it my own personal Island of Misfit Toys.

Oddly enough, Jake's cousin, another one of Sophie's grand-sons, John-John Pretty Horses, owned the joint with his partner, Muskrat. I didn't know Muskrat's real name; everyone just called him Muskrat. Since he was about ten feet two inches and re-sembled Sasquatch, no one questioned him.

John-John and Muskrat were partners in the truest sense of the word. Woe to the idiots dumb enough to utter the phrase *Brokeback Mountain*.

The dusty parking lot was clogged with beat-to-crap Harleys, pickups with gun racks—loaded, of course—rusted-out midsized American-made sedans, and an SUV or two.

The steel door flew open as I walked up.

Muskrat had a scrawny biker in each ham-sized hand; two pairs of boots barely touched the weeds. He threw the guys to my left. They landed on hands and knees in a patch of creeping Jenny. "When I tell you to take it outside, I mean it." Muskrat whirled on me.

Instinct had me bracing for a fight.

But his pale brown eyes lit up. "Mercy! Where you been keep-ing yourself? You'll make John-John's night." He scanned the parking lot behind me. "You bring Jake along?"

My back stiffened. "No. Not my day to entertain him."

"No need to snap at me."

"Sorry. Habit. I'm just sick of everyone around here assuming Jake and I are still some star-crossed lovers. That time apart has mended our broken hearts and we'll ride off into the sunset to-gether on white horses and live happily ever after."

"Ain't a romantic, are ya?"

"Not a single bone."

"Good. You can find someone better'n him anyway."

My brows lifted with surprise. "You think?"

"Yeah. Jake might be John-John's cousin, but I ain't got much use for him. Takes that wooden cigar Injun bit too far." He held the door open for me.

I ducked under his beefy arm without commenting.

Creedence Clearwater Revival blasted from the jukebox, which separated the central core of the bar from the back room. Both pool tables were in use. Ditto for the dartboards.

In the far corner, several guys straddled chrome bar stools, sipping mugs of beer, vacant eyes glued to some sports event on a big-screen TV suspended from the metal rafters.

I'd barely stumbled in when I heard my name shouted as a benediction. I was wrapped in a bear hug so tight my eyeballs threatened to pop out. A feather tickled my nose.

The burly bear in question, John-John, resplendent in black jeans, a black silk shirt, purple velvet vest, and a matching beret (complete with a red feather) gave me a slow once-over.

"Don't you have the wholesome Mary Ann from *Gilligan's Island* meets slutty Daisy Duke look? Love the belt."

"Thanks. You can borrow it anytime."

"Honey, if I had a waistline like yours, I'd take you up on that."

"Aw. Turn a girl's head, you talk so sweet, John-John."

Muskrat snorted.

"Trey, you're in Mercy's spot," John-John said, and shooed a very good-looking, whipcord-lean young cowboy off my favorite bar stool.

"I'll move. No problem."

I smiled at him. "Thanks, Trey."

He gifted me with one of those playful, cocky male grins, and my stomach actually fluttered. "I'll be over there if you need anything. Anything at all."

My flirting skills were rusty, not corroded. I winked. "I'll keep it in mind, cowboy."

I set my forearms on the shellacked bar top, elbowing aside the ashtray Trey used as a spittoon.

"Whatcha drinking?" Muskrat asked.

"Double shot of Wild Turkey and a Bud Light chaser."

John-John grinned. "Bad day?"

"Might say that."

He slid the first shot in front of me. The bitter taste hit the back of my throat and ate a path through my stomach lining. I could afford expensive whiskey, but old habits die hard.

It made me laugh, those pretentious people who looked down at the Scots and the Irish and their homemade hooch. Now those same snobs consider themselves whiskey aficionados and search high and low for the "real thing." Spare me. Only two types of whiskey in my book: free and not free.

I chased the shot with an icy cold glug of beer. "Ah. I'm feeling better already."

"That's why we're here." He murmured something to Muskrat and Muskrat lumbered to the other end of the bar.

John-John's soulful black eyes connected with mine, mirth gone. "We need to talk. I had a vision about you."

I sucked down another mouthful of beer, fortifying myself.

John-John and I had been best pals since we were kids. He is what the Lakota Sioux people call *winkte*, or two-spirited, a person born with both a male and female spirit.

In the days before Indians were relegated to reservations, it was a sign of good luck from the Great Spirit if a *winkte* was born into a family. The *winkte* was allowed to hunt with the men. Cook and sew with the women. It didn't matter which sexual organs the *winkte* was born with, he/she had always been an honored and welcomed member of the tribe.

Part of being two-spirited also meant a closer tie with *Wakan Tanka*—the Great Spirit—and what I considered the woo-woo factor in Lakota religion, so it'd always freaked me out that John-John experienced visions. Mostly because they were dead-on.

I shivered.

He saw it. "If you hadn't come in here tonight, I would've stopped by the house tomorrow."

"That bad, huh?"

"Subject to interpretation, as always, but yeah, it is disturbing."

"Well? Let's have it."

John-John squeezed my hand. "Somebody wants to hurt you, Mercy. Real bad."

"Physical or emotional kind of hurt?"

"Physical."

"I don't suppose in this vision you've seen who?"

"No."

"You have any idea when this will happen so I can try and stop it?"

"No." He winced. His eyes filled with pain and guilt as he remembered. We both remembered.

When we were kids, John-John had had a vision about my mother's death. Nothing that could've prevented it, just an impression of blood and horses.

It wasn't until a year after we'd buried my mother that he'd mustered the guts to tell me of how, on the day of her funeral, he'd confessed to his *unci* Sophie what he'd seen.

Sophie realized the onset of puberty had started John-John on the sacred path. She'd taken him to the tribal elders for advice and guidance. John-John was lucky his grandmother hadn't abandoned the traditional Lakota ways, or he could have floundered for years to understand who and what he was. Unlike kids who struggled with a conflicting sexual identity, he'd always been comfortable in his own skin.

"Mercy? Hon?" John-John prompted.

"Sorry. Lost focus for a sec. What did you see?" I asked, even when I really didn't want to know.

"Red ground, red sky, red water. Though the impressions were blurry." He frowned. "Don't you believe me?"

"Of course I believe you. I just wondered if I should avoid blow-drying my hair in the bathtub or shoving a knife in the toaster."

"Don't be flip."

"I'm not. I hope nothing happens tonight because I left my guns at home."

"Don't you think you've killed enough, *kola*?"

What else had his vision revealed about me? God forbid anyone found out what I'd seen. Or what I'd done. I pushed the empty shot glasses at him. "Another round, barkeep."

He pressed his lips together and turned away.

I used the lull between us to drain my beer. The jukebox was silent. I twirled around on my stool to rectify the situation when I noticed someone was already making selections.

Whoo-yeah. A tall male someone with an ass to die for, a perfect butt gift-wrapped in a pair of tight-fitting, faded Wranglers. A black-and-gray-plaid shirt stretched over wide shoulders and a broad back. I couldn't see the color of his hair beneath his black Stetson, but I knew I was looking at a gen-u-wine cowboy.

God save me. I've had it bad for cowboys my whole life. Since the first time I'd seen Clint Eastwood. Since my first rodeo, watching bareback and saddle bronc riders getting tossed on their asses in the dirt and then climbing right back up into the saddle and doing it again. Around age thirteen I fell in love with bull riders. I mourned the death of Lane Frost like some mourned the loss of John Lennon.

Something about cowboys speaks to me on a visceral level. Rugged-looking men making a living from the land. Wearing dirty, mangled cowboy hats. Hearing the jingle of spurs. Seeing work-stained ropes draped over tired shoulders. Tight jeans. The faded circle on the back pocket of those jeans from the ever-present can of chew. Scuffed boots covered in manure. The tougher-than-shit attitude. The gentlemanly way a cowboy held a woman as they two-stepped. The brawling in the name of honor, dishonor, or just because a good fight seemed like a good idea.

Oh, and don't get me started on their big . . . belt buckles and pickup trucks.

Being born on a ranch, I'd never stood a chance at wanting any other kind of man besides a cowboy. I'd tried to expand my horizons after I'd left South Dakota. Law enforcement guys and a few sweet-talkin' soldiers from Dixie had come close, but ultimately they'd fallen shy of the mark. My dad—a throwback to the old cowboy ways and an honest and decent man—had set the bar high.

I silently willed my object of lust to turn around.

From the speakers, Toby Keith demanded, "Who's Your Daddy?" and my cowboy sidled into the back room without letting me see if his front matched his back.

Damn. Win some. Lose some. Maybe if I planted the seed

with John-John, he could conjure up a vision of the next time I'd get laid. It'd been a while.

John-John slid the Wild Turkey in front of me. He lit a Salem and blew the smoke out the side of his mouth. "*Unci* said you're helping Estelle Yellow Boy."

"Sophie told you that?"

He nodded. "Did she railroad you into it, Mercy?"

"Doesn't she always?"

"Yep. That doesn't mean you have to do it." John-John set his elbows on the bar. "In fact, I wish you'd blow her off."

My gaze zeroed in on him. "Why? Is there something in your vision you're not telling me?"

"No. I never know what events can be changed by a single decision. I think poking around on the rez and asking the bad kids Albert hung around with questions is a bad idea."

"How do you know they're bad kids?"

"Didja forget I grew up there? I know firsthand what cruelty teens can inflict on one another, especially angry Indian kids. It'd be best if you stayed out of it."

"I don't know how deep I'll look, but I can't blow off Estelle completely. She's hurting. We both know there'd be no living with Sophie if I don't do something." I scowled. Shot number four joined shot number three gurgling in my stomach.

I saw John-John debate on mentioning the amount of booze I'd sucked down, but he thought better of it and shoved a bowl of pretzels toward me.

The music streaming from the jukebox became sappy and sentimental. I love a good he-done-me-wrong-so-why-don't-I-just-get-drunk-and-screw-someone country song as much as the next woman, but I wanted a more upbeat tune.

You want to see if Mr. Tight Ass is still hanging around in the back room.

Yeah, maybe that, too. I hopped off the bar stool and headed for the jukebox.

The rainbow strobe lights flashed as I punched in the number for the Trick Pony song "Pour Me." I snickered at Big & Rich's "Save a Horse, Ride a Cowboy." An image I didn't need in my present hormonal state, but I played it anyway. Followed by

"Unwound" by George Strait. When I spun away from the juke-box, there was my cowboy. Before I mentally begged him to turn my direction, he did.

Holy shit. My Sexy Tight Ass Cowboy was Mr. Tight Ass himself, Sheriff Dawson, looking decidedly unsherifflike without the uniform, the shades, and the perpetual stick rammed up his butt.

I groaned. It figured.

He did a double take when he saw me.

Too late to pretend I hadn't seen him. Wasn't life just a big bowl of rotten chokecherries?

He ambled over. "Mercy Gunderson. I didn't expect to see you in a place like this."

"Yeah? I could say the same, Sheriff."

"I'm off duty."

"If I remember correctly, my dad was never really 'off duty.'"

"Maybe, but as I'm in here enjoying myself, I'd rather you called me by name, not my job title."

I drew a mental blank. "What's your first name again?"

"Mason."

My eyes widened. "Like the jar?"

Dawson scowled. "Nothing gets by you, does it?"

Typical marine. What a jarhead. I'd had enough whiskey to want to slug him. Fuzzy logic, but if he wasn't here in official capacity . . . maybe I could get away with it. As I contemplated the repercussions, a baritone voice yelled, "Hey, Mad Dog," from the back room.

The sheriff's head whipped around. "What?"

"You're up."

"Okay. Be right there," he yelled back.

"Mad Dog?" I repeated.

He shrugged. "An old nickname."

"From your football glory days?" I snickered.

"Nah. From my bulldoggin' and bull-riding days."

Ah hell. Maybe John-John's violent vision was nothing more than my beating my head into the bar top from my questionable taste in men. "Well, *Mad Dog*, see you around."

Back at the bar, I drained my beer. Chatted with Muskrat until two guys caused a ruckus in front of the TV. I'd signaled to John-John to tally up my bill, when the hair on the back of my neck prickled and someone crowded in behind me. I didn't grab the guy and toss him on his ass, which was a huge step toward civilian normalcy for me.

Or it could've been a sign I'd had too much to drink.

I rotated my bar stool.

Dawson grinned at me—pure cowboy charm.

Shit.

"Can I buy you a drink?"

"I was just leaving."

"Come on, Mercy. One drink."

"I thought you were playing pocket pool, Sheriff?"

He didn't bat an eye at my dig. "Game is over."

I sighed like I was doing him a favor. "One drink. But I refuse to call you Mason. Or Mad Dog."

"Fine. Call me whatever you like." I opened my mouth, and he amended, "Within reason."

The jam-packed area around the bar pressed us together like saltine crackers. "You here alone?" I nodded. "Doesn't seem like your kind of place. A little rough."

"Not as rough as the club I mistakenly stumbled into in Bosnia. Makes this joint look like a church." My finger unconsciously sought the souvenir, a three-inch scar above my ear, now hidden by my hair.

Dawson didn't push. He didn't look away either. "You ever want to talk, I did my stint in the marines during Desert Storm. I imagine we've seen some of the same things."

Maybe it was the booze. Maybe it was his condescending offer. But for once I let the horrors I'd witnessed and perpetrated flit through my eyes. "You can't begin to imagine what I've seen."

Most people would've missed his tiny flare of alarm. Then again, I'm not most people. I'd scared him. Good. But I knew he wouldn't let it slide.

"Who are you? Maybe a better question is: *What* are you?"

"Just a simple enlisted girl keeping the country safe from the evils of terrorism."

He tipped up the brim of his hat so he could bend down and

whisper in my ear. "I don't buy it. You can fool other people, Mercy, not me."

"Then I'll be careful to watch my step around you."

Dawson angled his head back. Still too close for my liking. "Speaking of . . . I didn't get my chance to two-step with you the other night."

I made out the strains of "Boot Scootin' Boogie" above the usual bar noises and the strange pounding in my heart.

A dark brown hand with ruby nails appeared on his chest. Teased and frosted hair brushed my jawline as a woman crammed herself between us.

"I'd love to dance with you, Mason. You wandered off and left me all alone in the back room."

Dawson's face stayed neutral at her little-girl pout. "Just getting a fresh round. Laronda, this is Mercy. Mercy, Laronda."

"Nice to meetcha," she said, leaving her hand on his shirt, practically digging her claws in as a sign of ownership.

This was the type of woman Mad Dog went for? Beauty queen meets Elvira? I could understand his liking her huge boobs. But having to put up with a bad dye job, fake nails, a fake tan, clown makeup, and a quart of perfume just to get his hands on those enormous jugs? Not worth it.

Plus, she couldn't have been more than twenty-two. That made him roughly twice her age and me . . . in desperate need of another shot. I caught John-John's eye. He poured the Wild Turkey and slid it in front of me. It went down the hatch smooth as honey.

"You from around here?" Laronda asked.

"Used to be. How about you?"

"From Belle Fourche, originally. What do you do?"

Kill people. Nah. Not a good midwestern response. "I'm a rancher. You?"

Her witch's beak wrinkled as if I smelled of cowshit. "I'm a secretary. For now. I'm studying for my real estate license."

"Sounds interesting."

Awkward silence.

Laronda looked from Dawson to me. "How do you two know each other?"

"We don't." I swallowed a big drink of beer. "Actually, I was trying to pick him up and drag him back to my place to have my wicked, nasty way with him. You've got incredibly bad timing, Laronda."

She glared at me.

Some people have no sense of humor.

"She's pulling your leg. Mercy's dad used to be sheriff. That's how we know each other."

"Oh."

When Laronda made no move to skedaddle, Dawson said, "I ordered a round. Let me settle up and I'll be right there."

"Don't be too long." She smiled at me—a feral flash of crooked teeth—and raked her talons down his arm.

After she stomped off I said, "She seems nice."

Dawson stared at me like I'd grown horns.

John-John swept up the empty shot glasses. "Need anything else?"

"Four pitchers for the back room." Dawson tossed thirty bucks on the counter.

"Mercy?" John-John paused in front of me. "How you doing?"

"I'm good."

"You're never good, Miz Mercy."

I half chided, "Not the best information for you to share with the sheriff, John-John."

"True. But I'm hoping he's talking some sense into you."

"About?" Dawson asked casually.

"Keeping her from getting involved with the Yellow Boy family's troubles."

The beer mug stopped halfway to Dawson's mouth. "Come again?"

But John-John was oblivious to the tension. "*Unci* had no right guilting Mercy into helping Estelle, no matter how close she was to Estelle's grandmother."

As if Sophie could guilt me into anything. I had this perverse habit of finding trouble on my own, and I had just stepped into a heaping pile of it. I sent John-John a cold look, but he'd fled the scene.

Dawson's eyes burned with fury. "You messing in my investigation, Miz Gunderson?"

I fiddled with my empty shot glass.

He crowded in. "Answer me."

"Since my dad was sheriff I know I'm not legally obligated to answer a damn thing."

Dawson got his mean on. "I don't give a damn how long your daddy was sheriff. If I find out you've uncovered information on an active case that you're not sharing with me, I'll throw you in jail so fast it'll make your head spin."

"You threatening me?"

"Bet your sweet ass I'm threatening you."

"Nice try. On what grounds are you going to lock me up?"

"The dead kid found on *your* land, who just so happens to have a tie to *your* family via *your* nephew. That's enough right there."

He was bluffing. Had to be. "Try it."

"Don't tempt me."

"My lawyer will eat you for lunch. Let me tell you something else, Sheriff. If you were doing your job, this wouldn't be an issue."

His gaze turned razor sharp. "What in the hell is that supposed to mean?"

"Why is it that a grieving parent is hounding *me* for answers?" I paused. "Because she isn't getting the answers she needs from you. You think I enjoy having my friend begging *me* to figure out why her child was killed?"

His mouth tightened.

"Just because my father was sheriff she thinks I have some magic fucking insight into the criminal mind and how to catch them. I don't. But I sure as hell won't brush off her concerns."

"And I am?"

"Goddamn right you are. It's been over a week since they buried Albert. According to Estelle, you haven't talked to his friends or his other family members. You haven't done a thing besides piss and moan that people aren't flocking into your office to unburden themselves. You want people to talk to you and stop treating you like an outsider? Then start acting like you give a shit about what happens inside this county."

I didn't wait for his response. I grabbed my purse, ducked under his arm, and made a dash for the bathroom before I did something I'd regret. Good thing I hadn't brought my gun.

In the stall, the strength of the Wild Turkey shots hit me full force. My vision doubled. I felt sick to my stomach. I'd pay for this in the morning. Guaranteed.

Dawson wasn't hanging around when I'd slunk back to the bar. With any luck, he'd left and was brushing up on his riding skills with Laronda.

The loud people and the thick smoke made my head throb and my lungs seize up. Although I wasn't in any shape to drive home, the thought of being cooped up another second made me nauseous. I slipped two twenties in John-John's hand and bolted.

Outside, I sucked in several breaths of fresh air. I could sleep this off in the truck. Wasn't like I hadn't done it before; wasn't like I wouldn't do it again. Hell, wasn't like I had anywhere to go tomorrow.

On my way to the back of the parking lot, I stumbled over empty beer cans. Bottles. My own damn feet. Muskrat really ought to install lights out here. I couldn't see a thing.

Your vision is limited out of your right eye at night anyway, even when you're sober.

Nice timing for that cheery reminder.

I tipped my head back and studied the stars. Ooh. Bad move. Made me dizzy. I closed my eyes for a minute, and the keys tumbled from my hand.

As I bent over to pick them up, footfalls echoed, something struck me in the back of the neck. I fell forward and everything went black.

SEVEN

Callused fingertips caressed my cheek. Mmm. Nice. I angled my face into the insistent touch. And a piece of grass poked up my left nostril like a railroad spike.

I froze. Where the hell was I?

I wiggled my arms and legs. Not tied up. Definitely on the ground. Not in the desert. No sand shifting beneath me, but sharp rocks and dirt with the faint odor of skunkweed.

No skunkweed in Iraq.

"Shit." I couldn't remember where I was.

"Hey. Take it easy."

The male voice didn't ring any bells. "Where am I?"

"In Clementine's parking lot."

Clementine's. Things started to come back to me. Sort of. "What happened?"

"I don't know. I came out here to take a leak and I tripped over you." Heavy pause. "You okay?"

"I'll be fine as long as you didn't actually pee on me."

He chuckled. "I didn't."

"Good." I tried to sit up but didn't quite manage it.

"Easy." Then, "How much've you been drinking?"

"Not enough to make me pass out." I made it into a sitting position and opened my eyes. My rescuer squatted down. The young hottie with the great grin who'd gallantly given up his bar stool. "Cowboy Troy?"

His white teeth lit up the night like a beacon. "*Trey*. Not Troy."

"Well, Cowboy Trey, thanks for not leaving me out here to get run over. Although I feel like I've been a speed bump for a cattle truck." I scooted back until my spine hit solid metal. I lifted my arm and touched the back of my neck. Even that little motion made me wince. Nice goose egg. No blood, though.

"Maybe I should get John-John or Muskrat. See if they can help you. I ain't real good with first-aid stuff."

"No." I gripped his forearm. "John-John will freak out and blame himself."

"Maybe he should. It ain't right, letting a pretty woman wander out here alone at night. He don't have the most trustworthy customers."

"Except you, apparently."

Trey grinned. "He should've asked me to escort you to your truck. It would've been the high point of my night."

I blinked. "You flirting with me, Cowboy Trey?"

"Yeah. Is it getting me anywhere with you?"

I didn't answer. I felt too crappy to flirt back.

Encouraged, he scooted closer. He plucked a piece of dried grass out of one of my braids. "You're in no shape to drive home, Mercy." Trey stood, stuck his hands out, and jerked me to my feet.

The second I was vertical . . . *hello, vertigo.* I fell right into him.

"Come on. My rig is over here. I'll take you home."

"You know where I live?"

"Everyone knows where you live."

I frowned at his odd comment. He helped me into the passenger's side of his truck.

Next thing I knew, Trey shook me awake. I sat up, as stiff as if I'd suddenly developed arthritis. Even after a short nap my head felt like a cannonball teetering on my shoulders. I squinted at the darkened windows of the kitchen. Would it have killed Sophie to leave a light on?

On the porch, Trey said, "Key for the door?"

I snorted. "Please. Like everybody else in this county, we don't lock the door."

"Makes it easy. Whoa. Steady. Where is your room?"

"Upstairs. The one in the far left corner."

"I'd offer to carry you—"

"Not necessary."

We trudged up the stairs, Trey following behind me in case I fell backward. I insisted on stopping in the bathroom first, where I downed two codeine-laced Tylenol I'd hoarded for emergencies. With the way my head screamed, this qualified.

I stretched out on the bed. The last thing I remembered was giggling as Trey pulled off my boots.

The mattress jiggled. I cracked one eye open at a time. Bright sunlight burned through the blinds, creating a cockeyed pattern across the patchwork pillow. I raised my gaze.

And saw a naked man roll out of my bed.

Holy cow. A muscled back and an excellent backside were inches from my face. The second I saw those lean hips swivel, my eyes snapped shut. As much as I wanted to see the front side of his body, I was too embarrassed to look.

"Mercy? You awake?"

I groaned. What had I done last night? I rolled over. Looked down at what I was almost wearing: a white lace camisole that doubled as a bra and my bikini panties with big red lips and the words *kiss my ass* printed everywhere. "What time is it?"

"Almost eight."

Clothes rustled. I peeked over to see Trey sliding wrinkled jeans over his smoothly muscled naked ass. "At the risk of sounding like an idiot, what happened last night after we came up here?"

"My ego is crushed you don't remember."

I think I stopped breathing.

"Just kidding." He gave me the million-dollar smile that'd so thoroughly charmed me last night before I'd knocked back a hundred shots. "Nothing happened. You undressed yourself to what you're wearing now. I bunked down with you because you were really out of it."

Passed out next to a strange man. In my own bed. Yeah, I'd taken stupidity to a whole new level. I kept it light; wasn't his fault I was an idiot. "Sorry you had to babysit me."

"It's all right. Wish it'd turned out different. Maybe next time it will."

Flattering, that he wasn't scared off by my haggard morning

appearance. So why in the light of day did his megawatt smile seem forced?

"You want me to run you back to Clementine's so you can get your truck?"

"If it's not too much trouble. Let me hop in the shower first. I'll meet you downstairs." I snagged my robe and made a beeline for the bathroom.

Clean, dressed, and in need of caffeine, I was in fairly decent spirits considering the knot throbbing on the back of my neck and a hangover . . . until I realized I'd sent Trey downstairs without warning him about Sophie.

Crap. I wouldn't have put it past Sophie to whack him over the head with the cast-iron frying pan and tie him up with the clothesline cord before asking questions.

But the kitchen was empty. The aroma of freshly brewed coffee lingered in the air. I'd sort of expected Trey to be sitting at the table, patiently waiting for me. I peeked into the living room.

The toilet flushed, the old pipes rattled, and the bathroom door creaked open. Sophie stepped out in a cloud of rose-scented air freshener and frowned at me. "What?"

"Ah. Have you seen—"

"If you're looking for that young feller, I think he's out by the barn."

I refused to blush. Dammit. I was a thirty-eight-year-old woman. This was *my* house. I would not feel guilty for having an overnight male guest in my own house. I blurted, "Nothing happened."

She rolled her eyes, clucked her tongue, and shuffled to the sun porch.

Back in the kitchen, the screen door slammed as I filled my coffee cup. I turned around as Trey trooped into the kitchen with Sheriff Dawson trailing behind him.

I managed not to choke on the hot liquid. What was Dawson doing here at eight thirty in the morning?

"Good. The coffee's done." Trey sauntered over, snagged a cup from the rack, and poured, acting like he'd been in my kitchen dozens of times. He glanced over at Dawson. "Sheriff?"

"No," Dawson said curtly. "I didn't come here to drink coffee."

"So why *did* you darken my doorstep this morning?"

His hard gaze zoomed from me, to Trey, and back to me. "Because when I drove past Clementine's this morning, I noticed your truck was still in the parking lot. I wanted to make sure everything was all right and you made it home okay."

Trey and I exchanged a quick look. I didn't give a crap if Dawson misread it. "Thanks for your concern, but as you can see I'm fine."

When Dawson continued to stare, I bristled. "Is there something else you need, Sheriff?"

"The other reason I stopped by was to ask you some questions about what we talked about last night."

"Refresh my memory. Some things from last night are a little fuzzy." I smiled coyly at Trey. I didn't care if Dawson misread that look either. "And some things not so much."

"Fuzzy from too much to drink?"

"No, fuzzy from someone smacking me in the back of the head with a tire iron."

Dawson was by my side in two steps. "Where were you hit?"

"Forget it."

"Like hell. Where?"

"On the left side of my neck."

"Let me see."

The words *fuck off* danced on the end of my tongue. I bit them back and angled my neck so he could look.

Dawson's dry fingers lightly traced the swollen spot. I withheld a shiver at his touch. "Did someone look at this?"

"No."

"When did it happen?"

"About half an hour after you went into the back room."

"Why didn't you report this?" Dawson's gaze lasered into me. "I was right there in the bar."

"After you made a big point of telling me you were off duty?"

His mouth tightened. "I'm on duty now."

"I'll go get the truck ready," Trey said, and vanished.

What a little chickenshit.

Dawson pointed to a chair. "Park it. I want to talk to you."

I sat.

"Last night you talked about digging for answers in the Yellow Boy case. I'm here to ask you to stay out of it."

"Why?"

"A number of reasons."

"Give me two."

"First off, I'm not convinced this is a homicide. The county coroner's report was inconclusive as to the nature of death. But she's tagging it as accidental."

"That's one."

"Two, if I do suspect foul play, as you so eloquently phrased it last week, I can't have you running around spooking people before I get a chance to talk to them."

"You've had time. My understanding is you haven't contacted any of the people who might know anything about why Albert ran away."

"Who told you that? Estelle?"

I nodded.

"Mercy. Think about it." Dawson angled forward, the picture of sincerity. "Nothing I do is enough. Albert was her child. She wants this case solved yesterday. She doesn't realize things don't happen overnight or like it does on TV."

"So you *are* working on Albert's case?"

"Yes. Just because I have other daily duties occupying my time doesn't mean I've blown the case off." He frowned. "There's some funky things happening around here. Things that don't fit. But it's nothing I can share with Estelle at this point."

"Why not? God, Dawson, give her something. Some hope that whatever secret thing you're working on might eventually lead you to why Albert is dead."

He didn't say a word. Which in my mind meant everything he'd just said was a bunch of hogwash. I stood. "Fine. I'll tell her you're doing your best and she shouldn't worry."

"And you'll stay out of it?"

I smiled at Trey through the screen door. "Come on, cowboy. We got places to be."

A chair scraped. Dawson loomed over me. "I mean it. There are plenty of other things to keep you busy without messing in my business."

"Like what?" If he suggested joining a quilting club, I'd club him.

"Like have you made a decision on whether you're selling this ranch?"

I crossed my arms over my chest. "Gee, Sheriff, the way you keep bringing it up makes me think you might have designs on it yourself."

"I don't. But some folks around here do." He dropped his guarded expression for a second. "That knot on your neck wasn't an accident."

His words sent goose bumps across my flesh. I looked at Trey. He had the oddest expression on his face. Probably he was as confused by this cryptic conversation as I was.

We left, and I didn't look to see if Dawson followed.

Hope's Honda was parked out front when I returned home. She and Sophie looked up when I dragged ass into the kitchen.

My sister smirked. "Hear you got yourself a new beau. Or was he hanging around because you were babysitting him?"

I should've let it slide. Instead, I spun the chair around and straddled it. "Tell you what. If you dish the dirt on the guy Theo, who's been warming *your* bed, I'll return the favor."

Her face went as milky white as the tea in her cup.

"Didn't think I knew, did you? How long before you planned to tell me?"

"Mercy, be nice," Sophie warned.

I ignored her. "When you bringing him by so I can meet this great new love of your life?"

"See? That's why I didn't tell you. Because you'd get all sarcastic and mean."

Sophie patted Hope's hand and murmured to her, her shiny black eyes shot deadly daggers at me.

My focus shifted to a bottle of pills in the middle of the table. Thank God. A jumbo container of aspirin. Just what I needed to stop the throbbing pain in my head.

"Hey! Gimme that! It's mine!" Hope said, trying to snatch the bottle from me.

"Relax. I'm just gonna borrow a couple."

"You can't. It's private!"

Private aspirin? I turned the bottle in my hands to the read the contents. A prescription. In the name Hope Arpel. For pre-natal vitamins. Prescribed by Doc Canaday.

Two months ago.

My mouth dropped open. "You're pregnant?"

She wouldn't look at me. Sophie suddenly seemed mighty interested in the cow and chicken wallpaper border above the refrigerator.

Stay calm. "That is why you've been so sick? And you didn't think I deserved to know? Instead, you let me worry because no one could figure out what was wrong with you?"

"It's not your job to worry about me. I've been doing just fine without you." Her self-righteousness vanished, and her chin wobbled. "I knew you'd come back and take over everything."

"Someone had to."

"This baby's got nothing to do with you and is none of your business."

"Wrong. As Dad made me executor of his estate, *everything* that happens within this family or on this ranch is my business."

No smart answer from Hope.

"How far along are you?"

She and Sophie exchanged another look.

"Tell me, goddammit."

"Stop swearing at her," Sophie said sharply.

"I will when she answers the question."

"Three months or so."

My mind whirled. "Did Dad know?"

Hope shook her head.

"This Theo guy is the father?"

She glared at me.

"Am I the only person who doesn't know?"

"No. She didn't bother to tell me neither." Levi was sagged against the doorjamb separating the kitchen from the living room.

My anger escalated at the hurt look on his face. Damn my selfish sister.

"Levi, honey, I can explain—"

"Save it, Ma. Aunt Mercy is right. She ain't the only one who's been worried about you. But like usual, you don't care about nobody but yourself."

"That's not fair!"

"You know what ain't fair? If you think I'm gonna be your built-in babysitter once that brat is born. I won't stick around. You can't make me. You probably wouldn't notice if I was gone anyway. But I can guarantee you Theo ain't gonna be changing diapers. He'll expect you to do it since he follows the 'traditional' ways of the Indian, the separation of men's and women's duties within the tribe and home."

"You don't know that."

"Yeah, I do. I take his culture class; you don't. And he's a different person around me than he is around you."

Sophie tried mediating. "Why don't we all just calm down and talk about this, eh?"

"Screw that. I'm outta here." Levi stormed out before anyone could stop him.

Hope jumped to her feet. I blocked the door. "Let him go."

"No. I have to explain."

"You should've explained long before now."

She blinked back tears.

I hated it when she cried, but I steeled my resolve not to let her off the hook this time. "Give him some time to sort through this. He's hurt, and he has a right to be upset."

"But I need to talk to him!"

"No, you need time to figure out why you kept something this important from him. *He* is your family. *I* am your family. What were you thinking, shutting us out?"

Her eyes thinned to malicious slits. "You don't have kids and you haven't been around him, so what makes you think you know anything about how he's feeling, huh?"

"It's obvious he's pissed off at you. And how do I know that? Because you've pissed me off more times than I can count, *sis*. So leave him alone. You'd better figure out a way to make this right with him, because he sure as hell deserves better than you've given him lately. And so do I."

I slammed the door with enough force the screen popped out

and bounced off the porch slats. I didn't care. It would still be there when I returned, just another damn thing in my life I'd have to fix.

Levi peeled out across the pasture on an ATV, Shoonga racing alongside him, and he headed south toward Old Woman Creek. I could've let him go. But I suspected he's spent more time alone than he'd let on. I hopped on an older four-wheeler, trailing behind him. If he noticed me following and it made him mad, so be it. He could take his anger and frustration out on me.

He killed the engine beneath a cluster of cottonwood trees. Thin puffs of dust kicked up as he shuffled to the ledge of the steep bluff.

I doubted he'd do anything stupid, like pitch himself over, but I wondered how many teenagers' last thoughts before suicide were ones of remorse.

Levi backed away and dropped to the ground. He huddled into a ball and shouldered Shoonga aside until the dog flopped beside him. It reminded me that Levi might act tough and grown-up, but he was still young and vulnerable.

Shoonga panted heavily, too tired to bark at me as I climbed off the machine and ambled across the hard-packed soil.

"I ain't gonna kill myself, if that's what you're worried about," Levi said.

"I'm not."

"Then why'd you follow me?"

To see if you needed me. "To see your secret brooding place."

Levi straightened up. "How'd you know I had one?"

"All teenagers have them."

"Even you?"

"Especially me."

"Where was yours?"

"Which one?" I plopped beside him and narrowly missed jabbing my ass on a tiny barrel cactus.

"You had more than one?"

"Don't you?"

His cheeky smile was there and gone. "Yeah."

"I liked to keep people guessing. I thought they'd gnash their teeth and weep and wail, distraught with guilt if they couldn't find me in my usual spot."

We watched a red-tailed hawk perform a loop-de-loop and soar higher on a thermal.

"Didja ever tell anyone where you was going?"

"Nah. But I think they knew. How about you?"

"Not usually. Ma don't care. This is my favorite, but there is another spot with one old gnarled tree. It's like I can see for a thousand miles."

I knew that place, but was surprised he did, as it was fairly isolated. "How'd you stumble across it?"

"The person who showed it to me meets me there sometimes." He tossed a flat piece of toffee-colored sandstone over the edge. It made a hollow chink. "She's cool. She listens to me whenever I'm mad at my mom. Which has been a lot lately."

"My brooding spots were directly related to who I was mad at. If it was Sophie, I usually stomped around the kitchen. Drove her crazier than if I'd taken off and left her in peace."

The corner of his mouth twitched.

"If I was mad at my dad, I hid in that grove of old elm trees. I'd climb to the highest branch so I could see far away, since that's where I planned to go."

"Is that the grove where you practice target shooting now?"

"Yeah." I fiddled with a knobby cottonwood twig and peeled the bark away, revealing the whitish-green meaty wood. "If your mom pissed me off, which was pretty regularly, I holed up down by the creek. I'd stand on that big boulder, shaped like a chef's hat, and whip rocks in the water."

Neither of us spoke. The hair on the back of my arms prickled from the heat. The occasional insect buzzed past my ear. No wind meant the leaves in the trees were as quiet as the air between us.

"Why didn't she tell me?" He absentmindedly scratched behind Shoonga's ears.

"No clue. What she did was wrong, Levi. I've explained the reasons for her actions most of her life. I guess maybe it's easy for her to avoid taking responsibility for anything."

"See? You're still doing it. Making excuses for her."

Smart kid. "You're right."

"Well, I ain't gonna do it anymore."

"Do what?"

"Make excuses. And I'm sick of hers. She's gonna be pissed, and Theo will give me a lecture on respecting my mother if I say anything, and I cannot deal with either of them."

"Does Theo do that a lot?"

"What?"

"Try to act like your father?"

"*Shee.* If he ain't yelling at me, then he's ignoring me. Whenever Ma starts crying, which is all the time lately, he starts acting like it's my fault . . . like if I were a better kid, she wouldn't be sad. I hate it. Makes me wanna run away like Albert had been doing." Levi nudged me with his shoulder. "Hey, maybe I could stay with you at Grandpa's house for a while. I used to stay there a lot. That'd be fun, doncha think? You and me hanging out? Like we did that summer you were here? When you showed me how to make those cool native friendship bracelets?"

Like I needed more friction in my life, especially between my sister and me, but Levi needed someone on his side. Truthfully, it touched me he'd remembered those funky, wildly popular friendship bracelets we'd made the year he'd turned seven. I'd been determined to reconnect with my nephew during the four short weeks I'd been on furlough. And because the "craft" gene skipped me, I'd secretly burned the midnight oil, learning to braid, just so Levi and I could do an activity together that interested him. Some people are scared of guns; I have the same reaction when faced with embroidery floss.

"So what do you say?" Levi prompted.

"Sure. But I want you to do one thing first. Go home. Talk to her. Tell her how you feel."

"About what?"

"About how she treats you. About your issues with Theo."

"In other words, make sure Ma knows it wasn't your idea."

"Pretty much."

"All right. I'll do it tomorrow. I won't be around tonight."

"Where you going?"

"Out." He sighed. "Trying to make new friends sucks, eh?"

Thorny silence again. No easy way to lead up to what'd happened to his friend, so I dove right in. "Speaking of friends . . . Do you think someone killed Albert?"

Levi looked at me strangely. "I dunno. Why?"

"His mom doesn't think his death was an accident."

He didn't seem surprised by that observation.

"She thinks someone killed him and dumped his body here," I added.

"Is she blaming *me* because he was found on our land?"

Our land. I liked how that sounded coming from him. "No. Why?"

"Because me and Albert were fighting for a while before he disappeared. He was drinking and shit all the time, not just on weekends. Every bad thing he was doing revolved around that Warrior Society. It pissed me off. That's really the only reason I wanted to join, so I could see for myself why everyone thought that club was so fucking great, because it sure wasn't great for Albert. But I'd never do nothing, to like, *hurt* him. Man. He was my friend."

"Relax. She asked me to poke around, see if I could find out anything new from you or his other friends."

"Good luck with that. None of them Warrior Society guys will talk to you because you're white."

My automatic rebuttal—*I'm not entirely white*—stayed stuck in my mouth.

His head fell to his chest, his hair blocking his face. "They ain't talking to me for the same reason. Seems everyone I know is ignoring me or is dead."

Poor kid. "I'm not dead."

"Yeah, but you were ignoring me up until a couple of days ago."

Oof. Guilt kicked me in the gut.

"Gramps is gone. And I miss having Albert—the old Albert—to hang out with. Me and him could talk for hours." He toed the ground, unearthing stones, sending a mini-rock slide over the edge. Shoonga barked at the sudden noise, and Levi petted his head. "I could still talk to him, I s'pose, but he ain't gonna answer back so it won't be the same."

Sometimes I thought if I talked to my dad out loud I could pretend he was there. But the Gunderson women already had the reputation for crazy behavior, no need for me to add fuel to the fire. "You have anyone else you can talk to?"

"One other person. She's been through some nasty shit in her life, so it's like she knows what I'm talking about."

I didn't ask if "she" was Sue Anne. I stood and brushed the dust from my butt. "Don't stay out here too long, okay? Call me and let me know what's going on."

"Thanks, Aunt Mercy."

"No problem." I resisted the urge to ruffle Levi's hair. Instead, I reached down and rubbed Shoonga's sun-warmed fur. When my hand brushed Levi's, I squeezed it once before I backed off.

He didn't watch me drive away. He stared straight ahead, lost in his own misery.

I knew exactly how he felt.

EIGHT

The next morning the demand "Where is he?" bounced off the living room walls.

I glanced over the screen of my laptop at the grandfather clock, reading nine a.m., and then at my sister. "Who?"

"Levi. He's staying here, right?"

"Why would he be here?"

"Don't patronize me. I know you told him he could move in with you after all the junk that happened yesterday." She angled her head so her crown nearly touched the door frame. It made her neck look broken. I thought of Albert Yellow Boy and fought a shiver.

"We talked about it, but nothing was set in stone. He was supposed to discuss it with you first."

"He didn't talk, he yelled. And he wasn't in his bed when I checked on him this morning. But he left that damn dog locked in his room, barking like a fiend. I swear . . ."

I tuned her out for a second. Levi wouldn't have gone far without Shoonga.

" . . . besides, he's never up this early."

"Maybe he's turning over a new leaf."

She gaped at me as if I'd lost my mind.

"Did you ask Jake if he's seen him?" A couple of times since Dawson brought him here in cuffs, I'd seen Levi hanging out and helping Jake early in the morning.

"He's not with Jake. Whenever Levi gets his mad on like this, he runs off. I don't know where."

You should. "Give him some time."

"Time? I've hardly seen him since Daddy died. Acting all secretive. I think he's sneaking off to meet a girl."

Sue Anne's pretty face swam into my mind's eye. "Would that be so bad?"

"No. But why wouldn't he tell me?"

"Why didn't you tell him you were pregnant?"

Temper put color back in her cheeks. "You trying to turn my boy against me?"

I powered down my computer, using it as an excuse to gather my thoughts and smack a lid on my anger. When the screen blanked, I looked at her. "That's what you think? I'm trying to turn Levi against you?"

Her lip wobbled. She nodded.

Instead of responding with a nicety, the devil on my shoulder jabbed the pitchfork in my tongue. What came out was, "Why would I have to turn him against you when you've been doing such a good job of it yourself?"

"That was mean," she whispered through her tears.

A man metastasized beside her. "I agree."

"Who the hell are you?"

"Theo Murphy."

Great. Mr. Wonderful. Mr. Fertile.

"Hope thought we should meet."

I heaved myself off the couch and thrust out my hand. "Mercy Gunderson." I studied him. Didn't care if it made him uncomfortable. He epitomized the soft, intellectual type, who tried too hard to be hip. Square glasses centered on a pudgy face that would've been handsome a decade ago. Limp, dulled brown hair, thinning on top. He'd secured his shoulder-length hair in a leather tie at the base of his neck. A tan, V-necked tunic, probably made of hemp, hung off his slight frame like an antique flour sack. Stick-thin, hairy calves stuck out from the bottom of faded khaki cargo shorts. On his feet were ratty-fringed moccasins the color of bleached deerskin.

Wow. *So* not impressed.

I gestured to the kitchen. "We can talk in there."

After he pulled out two kitchen chairs, he set his elbows on the table and smiled earnestly. "I imagine you have all sorts of questions."

Yeah, like why the hell have you been lurking in the background?

Probably not the best way to phrase it. "I do. First off, why the secrecy about your relationship?"

Theo gave Hope an indulgent look. "Your father was dying. I didn't want to intrude on the time he had left with his family. And Hope didn't want to cause him any more worry. Especially when you didn't come home before he passed on."

Bringing up my daughterly failing first thing? Zero brownie points for him.

"I can see where Dad would've been stressed about some stranger knocking up his daughter and then that guy not having the balls to face him." Dammit. It just slipped out.

"Mercy!"

"It's okay, Hope, your sister has a right to her concerns." His shit-brown eyes never wavered from mine.

Maybe I was being too hard on him. "Let's start over. Why don't you tell me about yourself, Theo? Where you're from, what you do for a living, all that jazz."

"I'm from Oklahoma."

"Are you Indian?"

He preened. "My great-grandfather was part Cherokee."

I barely resisted rolling my eyes. A big joke on the rez was if everybody who claimed to have some Cherokee blood stood in a line, it'd stretch from reservation to reservation across the country, without a single red face in the crowd. "What did you do before you moved here?"

"For the past few years I worked in North Dakota doing research and studying the effects on the land and the culture of introducing buffalo back to their native habitat."

"Research like returning a big chunk of the Midwest to a gigantic buffalo commons?"

"You've heard about it!"

Crap. The gleam in his eye meant one thing: I was in for a lecture if I showed my ignorance. Or interest. I was so screwed. When in doubt, pull a standard South Dakota trick and change the subject to the weather. "It must've been a big change, from humidity to the desert-dry conditions here."

"Yes, but I missed teaching."

"So that's all you do? Teach summer school part-time at the community center?"

"Mercy!"

"I can provide for Hope and the baby, if that's what you're insinuating."

Whoa. Testy. "And Levi?" I prompted. "You willing to provide for him?"

"Until he's of age."

A pall fell over the room.

"So tell me about you." Theo smiled benignly. "What do you do in the army?"

"Heavy-equipment transportation."

"A truck driver? Seen any combat situations?"

"A couple of close calls. We were out of range in the field outside of Beiji and majorly affected by a massive communication breakdown, which is a big reason I didn't know about Dad." That lie never got easier.

He nodded sympathetically and reached for Hope's hand. "Well, you're here now, if only temporarily. Hope has talked about the decision you two have to make and how much she's going to miss this place."

Hope's mouth opened, ready to dispute him, but Sophie bustled in. Hope compressed her lips and looked at her hands.

Sophie's gaze encompassed the empty table. "You didn't get them coffee, Mercy?"

As far as I was concerned, company manners didn't apply to my sister and her freeloading boyfriend.

"That's okay, Sophie. We were just leaving. I'm dropping Hope off before I head out of town for a seminar in Rosebud." Theo pushed to his feet. "I'm sure we'll be seeing each other again."

For one scary second I was afraid he'd try to hug me. Instead, he helped Hope up. Whew. I probably would've punched him. Overgrown pothead. He was the pseudo-intellectual type who'd call marijuana *peyote* and pretend smoking it was a cultural thing when in actuality he just liked getting stoned.

Yeah, doubtful he and I were going to be best friends.

"—called again. You really should call them back, Mercy," Sophie chided.

Everyone was looking at me. "What?"

"That pushy nurse from the VA. Second time this week. Said you never called her back."

Was nothing around here private? How many people had Sophie told about my visits to the VA?

"VA? Is everything okay?" Theo asked.

My answering smile was pure plaster. "Fine. Just some routine tests while I'm stateside."

He patted Hope's stomach. "Plenty of doctor appointments coming up for us, aren't there, blossom?"

Blossom? Oh, you've got to be fucking kidding me.

They'd nearly reached the door when I remembered the real reason Hope barged in here. "Let me know when you hear from Levi, okay?"

If the hangdog expression on her face was any indication, she'd completely forgotten about him.

That's when I started to worry.

By two I'd gone from edgy to freaked out. So acute was my bad gut feeling I considered contacting John-John to see if he'd had any more visions. I called Dawson and demanded he organize a search party—for a teenager who probably wasn't missing, just brooding. Talk about paranoid. Dawson blew me off and assured me Levi would show up eventually.

To ease my mind, I decided to look for him. Yesterday Jake had chewed me out for using ranch vehicles whenever I pleased without letting him or anyone else know where I'd gone. With spotty cell-phone service out in the middle of nowhere, having equipment breakdown was a real concern. So it was standard procedure for everyone who worked on the ranch to leave instructions on where they'd gone, what vehicle they'd taken, what they were doing, and when they planned to return. I left Jake a detailed note before I hopped on an ATV.

Gnats filled my mouth and nose as the sun beat down, reminding me of my impulsive action. No water, no hat, no protection from the heat. Not to mention the fact that I hadn't even bothered to grab a gun. I'd be dead if I headed into the desert so unprepared. Civilian life was making me soft.

I hit the gas, standing so the motor wouldn't bog down.

Once I cleared the rim and spied the copse of trees, I knew Levi wasn't there. The kid was probably holed up at a friend's house drinking beer, playing video games, and ripping on parental authority.

Still, it wouldn't hurt to double-check. Levi had mentioned another spot. Had he told me where? Or had he just alluded to it? Man. The sun was frying my egg. I took a break in the shade. What had we talked about? The need for wide-open spaces. A lone gnarled tree.

Whenever I pondered life's big questions, I liked to be where I could see for miles. Where I didn't feel cooped up. Only one place like that within walking distance of both his house and ours.

I sped across the field. In greener years this sweeping vista had shown off the simplistic, yet spectacular prairie splendor. In spring, delicate lavender crocuses, purple rockets, scarlet globe-mallow, and wild yellow snapdragons were sprinkled throughout the low-lying meadow. But in the middle of drought, pretty flowers and green grass were scarce. Succulents like yucca and the cactus held their own even as the wind blew red dust, covering them so they were nearly unrecognizable bumps.

Land is one thing that doesn't change. It'd been nearly ten years since I'd been on this section. The flat top of the bluff was within view. I floored it, aiming the ATV to the right, climbing the gentle slope instead of trying to spin my way to the top between two colossal boulders.

As I closed the distance, I decided if the shape my eyes locked on was indeed my nephew, I would chew him out. If he planned on living with me even temporarily, I'd have to know where he was at all times. Even times he thought he needed to be alone.

I parked the ATV and squinted at the lump in the middle of the bluff. Yep. It was Levi, all right. I shouted, "Hey, lazybones. You better have a good reason for dragging me out of the air-conditioned house."

No answer.

Maybe he was sulking. "Levi? I was kidding. Come on. Get up and let's head back to the ranch and we'll talk."

Shadows flickered across the ground. I looked up and saw the misshapen circle of birds flying above my head, heard the caw-ing of gleeful crows.

I ran.

But I was too late.

Levi was already dead.

He had been shot once in the head. Once in the heart.

I fell to my knees and touched his cheek. His skin felt warm. Supple. He hadn't been out here long. A gust of wind swirled his hair, and the strands slowly floated down to conceal his face. I frantically brushed them away. I never liked it when he hid behind his hair.

I sat down hard as the finality hit me.

Oh-God-oh-God-oh-God-oh-God.

How could this have happened? How could Levi be dead? How could I possibly tell my sister her son was dead? *Dead dead dead* repeated in my head until I screamed to stop it.

I clasped my hands around my knees and rocked, staring in absolute disbelief at puddles of blood beneath his lifeless body. I couldn't look away. I couldn't do anything but rock, cry, and gape at my nephew's rapidly cooling remains.

Time had no meaning. I probably would've stayed locked in my grief and shock until sunset. Shooing away bugs and preda-tors. Hoping like hell I'd wake up and realize this was just an-other fucked-up combat nightmare. But the ground rumbled. Some part of my brain recognized hoofbeats. In a normal frame of mind, I would've panicked at the sound.

The rider brought the galloping horse under control. I didn't look up. Instead, I slammed my eyes shut. *Go away. If you're not here, this isn't real.*

Leather creaked, sounding abnormally loud in the afternoon lull. Spurs jangled. The stirrups smacked against horseflesh after the dismount. Dust and the rank smell of horse sweat eddied around me. A shadow fell across Levi.

I heard Jake's garbled, "No."

My tears fell harder.

I didn't speak. I silently begged Jake to let me fall apart out here alone. To let me temporarily get my grief out of my system so when I had to face my fragile sister, I could be strong for her. I'd always been the rock. I didn't know any other way to be.

Tears poured down my face, blurring my vision. I wasn't sure who I felt the sorriest for: Levi, because the last minutes of his life had been hell, or Hope, because her life would become a living hell.

Hot wind whirled over the bluff, rattling the leaves of the bushes clustered at the bottom of the ravine. Delivering the scent of sage. The scent I associated with death. I squinted at the heavens, allowing the breeze to dry my cheeks as I studied the wispy white clouds.

In that moment I realized I did know who to feel the most sorry for. The person who'd killed Levi.

I'd find them. And when I did? The "one shot; one kill" motto of the U.S. Army Snipers wouldn't apply.

No cell service meant Jake had to ride back to the ranch to call the sheriff. I stayed with Levi. Offering explanations and excuses on why I hadn't been a bigger part of his life in recent years. I whispered my deep regret that I'd lost the chance to get to know him better, the offbeat, tough young man Hope and Dad had loved so much.

Hope. Another wave of bitter tears choked me. Jesus. Jake better have his wits about him and not bring my sister out here. She didn't need to see her son's final desecration.

I stood to block the blazing sun as I scanned the horizon. The only access to this remote area was by horse or four-wheeler. Or by walking in, as I suspected Levi had.

Who had he trusted enough to bring to his brooding place?

Without moving, I glanced at the hard-packed ground surrounding Levi's body and a few feet beyond. I didn't see footprints, or horseshoe marks. Animal or ATV tracks. Sheriff Dawson had his investigative work cut out for him.

No way could he chalk this up to another accident like he'd done with Albert Yellow Boy.

I didn't waste energy worrying about Dawson. Strangely enough, I didn't plan out the best way to tell Hope about Levi. Of all the millions of words in the world, I doubted I could come up with the right ones even if I had a lifetime to prepare.

• • •

An eternity passed before the sheriff showed up. Jake led him to the location on horseback, then spurred away. Two ATVs zipped along behind Dawson, who sat astride a horse. A stretcher was hooked to the side of one machine. The other was piled high with duffel bags. Probably a body bag.

The motley group parked a hundred feet from Levi's body. Out of respect? Or to preserve the crime scene? When Dawson motioned me over like he expected me to hold the reins of his horse, I turned away. Didn't give a damn if it pissed him off. I hadn't stuck around watching over Levi all this time only to be treated as Dawson's stable hand.

Mad Dog and I were going to butt heads on this, guaranteed.

Heavy footsteps stopped behind me. Followed by the thud and scuffle of bags being dropped in the dirt. No conversation, just the *flap flap flap* of the nylon straps on the ATVs, the dry wind constantly beating in my ears, and the sorrow screaming in my soul.

Sheriff Dawson didn't offer condolences. He sidestepped me, inching closer to look at my nephew's body.

He didn't move for the longest time. "How long have you been here?" he asked, without facing me.

"I don't know. Couple of hours."

"He was like this when you found him?"

No, you stupid cowboy, I shot him in the chest so he wouldn't blow away.

A lifetime later, he asked, "You gonna answer that?"

"Yes, he was like this when I found him."

"Did you walk around? Check things out?"

"Are you asking me if, in my rage and grief of finding my nephew *murdered*, I fucked up your crime scene?"

Dawson wheeled around. "Take a deep breath, Mercy. I know this is hard as hell, but we're on the same side here."

Where was the cold, detached part of myself I'd honed to a sharp edge? I inhaled. Exhaled slowly. Started over. "I didn't mess with anything. I saw him and knew it was too late. I didn't walk around, didn't do anything . . ." *But cry.*

"Did you see anyone? Maybe off in the distance?"

I shook my head. The motion made me dizzy.

No. Not the same. Not at all.

Wasn't it?

Sophie sent me outside to dump the garbage. I thought I'd been holding it together fairly well . . . until Jake pulled up with Shoonga. The dog bounded from the pickup bed, sniffed me, smelling Levi on my hands. He barked and whined, rubbing his body on my lower legs, trying to herd me to where I'd hidden his master. When he looked up at me with those expectant brown eyes, tongue lolling out of his mouth, I fell to the dirt and sobbed quietly in his fur until he'd had enough and darted away.

Beyond heartsick, I pushed to my feet and returned inside to pace and hover over my sister.

During a rare quiet spell, I left Hope lying on the couch. In Dad's office I made a list of people to call, but ultimately, I couldn't even pick up the phone. As I rooted around for a pen, I found Dad's last prescription for Valium. I'd never consider offering it to a pregnant woman, but I looked at it longingly, wishing I could down a pill or ten. After accomplishing nothing, I tiptoed into the living room in case Hope had fallen asleep.

Not only wasn't Hope asleep, she wasn't alone. Jake sat beside her on the sofa. They didn't notice me. I lurked in the shadows. Hiding. Listening. Waiting. Doing what I do best.

Hope clutched Jake's hand. "I'm sorry—"

"Ssh. It's okay."

"It's not okay! I've been stupid and selfish."

"I never blamed you."

She cried harder. "See? You should blame me. I'm so sorry. I planned to tell him." Her breath hitched and she was having difficulty speaking. "Now it's too late and he never knew." Sobs burst forth and her whole body shook.

The knots in my stomach tightened. I shifted slightly, intending to show myself, and berate Jake for whatever stupid thing he'd said to upset her, but Jake's words froze me to the spot.

"Even when *he* didn't know, I knew. I always treated him like my son." He gently smoothed the damp curls from her brow, as if he'd done it a thousand times before.

My mother always cautioned me nothing good ever came

from eavesdropping. For most of my life I thought it was bad advice. Now I wished I'd taken that advice and slunk away when I'd had the chance. Maybe I should've swallowed that whole bottle of Valium.

Levi was Jake's son. Jake was Levi's father. Not Hope's late husband, Mario Arpel. The phrase repeated in my head like a bad song lyric: *Jake was Levi's father. Jake was Levi's father.*

My spirit shriveled; I felt my muscles and bones threaten to liquefy. A burst of white light rushed past me as the years disappeared to a spring morning my senior year in high school. I sang along with Tanya Tucker on the radio. When I climbed out of the shower, I noticed blood between my thighs. A trickle rapidly became a torrent. Blood discolored the sunny yellow bath mat. Cramps seized me, and I had to bend over the bathtub from the intense pain.

I could barely crawl across the hallway to use the phone. Sophie had gone into Rapid City and I hadn't wanted my father to worry, so I called my best friend Geneva. By the time she arrived, I was floating in and out of consciousness and lying in a pool of blood.

Geneva called 911. All dispatch calls went through the sheriff's office first, so my father pulled up the same time as the ambulance.

The rest of the images from that day were blurry. One memory is crystal clear; the ghostly paleness of my father's face as they loaded me in the back of the ambulance.

Spontaneous abortion at age eighteen isn't uncommon. But nearly hemorrhaging to death and having a hysterectomy at age eighteen is.

I hadn't even known I was pregnant. Once the pregnancy ended it was pointless to talk about it. To Dad. To Sophie. To Geneva. Especially to Jake.

Within a month, my body hadn't shown signs of menopause. Within two months, I left the ranch, my childhood, and the memories of Jake and me far behind.

Or so I'd thought.

A floorboard creaked in the kitchen. Jake lifted his head and saw me by the china cabinet. Our eyes met. No reason for me to hide the murderous rage in mine. I felt triumphant at the fear in his.

He leaned down to whisper in Hope's ear, then slipped out the front door.

Coward.

I dug deep until I found the tranquil mind-set that helped me to survive combat situations. I inserted myself into the warm spot Jake had vacated and fussed over my sister, tucking the afghan under her elfin chin.

Her face resembled one of those wax carvings at the tourist traps in Keystone outside of Mount Rushmore. When her bloodless lips moved, I nearly leaped to the ceiling.

"You heard, didn't you?" she whispered.

"Yeah."

More tears fell. "Do you hate me now?"

"I couldn't ever hate you, Hope."

"Really?"

"Really. I know we haven't always been close . . . I don't know if it was because I was gone, or because of stuff from when we were kids, but I am here for you now. I'll always be here for you."

"Thanks." Her throat muscles worked, but her voice was still scarcely a whisper. "For the first time I really feel like you mean that, Mercy."

"I do." I changed the subject lest I start crying again. "Sure you don't want me to have Doc Canady give you something to help you sleep?"

"I won't take anything, so stop badgering me about it." She wiped beneath her eyes. "And stop asking me if I can keep quiet about how he"—her breath hitched in an effort to finish—"how Levi died. I'm good at holding a secret."

Boy, was she ever. "All right." Needing something to do with my hands, I fiddled with the fat gold yarn tassels on the afghan.

"Where's Shoonga?"

"On the porch. You want me to get him?"

She nodded.

I cut through the kitchen and opened the screen door. The dog looked up from his usual spot by the stairs. "Shoonga. Come."

Shoonga cocked his head like it was a trick. We never let animals in the house. He'd been on the receiving end of Sophie's broom a time or two, so I didn't blame him.

I patted my thigh. "It's okay, Shoonga, you can come in."

The dog stood and slunk past me, tail tucked between his short legs. He waited in the kitchen, whining, until I led him to Hope's side. Shoonga licked her hand and dropped on the carpet next to the couch.

"You need anything else?"

"Will you stay with me until I fall asleep?"

"You don't even have to ask." I sat beside her and rubbed my knuckles over the baby-fine hair on her forearm, like my mother used to do when I was sick as a child. Hope had known so little of our mother; I wanted to give her something that'd always calmed me. The repetitive motion helped her relax until her breathing slowed. When I was certain she was out, I briefly snuck upstairs, then came back down and grabbed a bottle of Wild Turkey and a glass on my way outside.

The night air retained the day's dry heat. I poured three fingers of whiskey and knocked it back. Don't know why I bothered with a glass. According to my best guess, I'd drained half a bottle throughout this nightmare day. I wasn't drunk; I was absolutely numb.

As much as I didn't want answers about Hope and Jake, I knew I'd have to ask questions. Since waking Hope wasn't an option, that left me one other choice.

I drained the bottle, loaded my Sig .357, and melted into the shadows.

NINE

The tiny foreman's cabin was far enough away from our house that I had time to consider how many times I'd done this in my life as a sniper, slithering through the darkness in silence as elusive as smoke.

I owed a good part of my skill to the shooting basics my father had instilled in me from the time I'd been old enough to curl my small fingers around a trigger. Shooting was what I'd loved best and where I'd excelled. In basic training I'd finished at the top of my class in marksmanship.

The army noticed and optioned me to join their elite team, The U.S. Army Marksmanship Unit (USAMU). But I didn't want to be a competitive shooter; I wanted to be a soldier. Actually, my dream was to be an Army Ranger. When I'd told my sergeant, he'd laughed in my face. A woman an Army Ranger? Never happen.

A month later his female CO, Major Martinson, yanked me out of the duty roster. She offered me an opportunity of a lifetime. For several years she'd petitioned for a chance to prove women could excel in stealth combat. With cases all over the country decrying the military's sexual discrimination policies, General John Ehrlich relented and gave Major Martinson the go-ahead. She selected an elite group of six women, all army, all with specialized skills, all with a medical anomaly that wouldn't differentiate us from the boys, so "female issues" when in the field wouldn't be an issue.

The army grudgingly, stealthily trained the six of us, figuring we'd ring out.

We didn't.

No one in our group received the official Army Ranger designation, but we completed every required training course, and that'd been enough for us.

Our troop was officially attached to the 82nd Airborne Division out of Fort Bragg, North Carolina, specifically, the 525th Battlefield Surveillance Brigade. Unofficially? We were in the murky designation of the Division of Special Troops, part of the 519th Military Intelligence Battalion, Tactical Exploration.

The bottom line was our covert group didn't exist on paper anywhere. We still were promoted, we still bitched about the stupidity of the brass, we still spent time in the crappy barracks in the armpits of the world. We were afforded all the privileges of regular enlisted army grunts, save one tiny thing: we weren't allowed to tell anyone—including our families—our military objective.

When military personnel of any branch, past or present, enlisted or officer, are asked about women participating in "black-ops" programs, they laugh. Or argue the ridiculousness of the suggestion, which is fine by us. Who'd believe American women soldiers were running around in the Mideast dressed like the oppressed local chattel, picking off terrorists with specialized weapons designed to stay hidden beneath *niqabs* and *burkas*? Because of religious and social traditions frowning on physical contact between men and women, we easily slipped past checkpoints.

The global conflicts—the Gulf War, Bosnia, Croatia, Afghanistan, and Iraq—kept us busy and behind enemy lines. Most of our assignments involved close-range work with smaller-caliber firearms than the standard large-caliber, long-range, heavy sniper rifles.

We were a tight-knit group, though we mostly worked in pairs. The major told us there was less competition between us than in male squads similar to ours. Extensively defined leadership roles weren't as important to us as teamwork and finishing the job. Men had egos. That's why there were wars.

There is a common misconception about snipers, that we are cold-blooded killers in love with the act of snuffing lives. That's not true for me. Wasn't true with any of the other snipers I've worked with. The reason we're so good at our jobs is because we can separate ourselves emotionally from the situation.

In all the years I lived behind a scope and prowled behind enemy lines, I never rationalized that my assigned target was inherently evil, therefore death by my hand was justified. My commanding officers and the military brass had to wrestle with the ethical and moral dilemmas of who had to die, why, and what would follow in the aftermath. I just had to pull the trigger.

Once it was done, I didn't dwell on it any more than a contractor would after successfully constructing a building according to the architect's blueprints. Cross it off the list as a completed project and move on to the next one.

I didn't have a montage of all the faces in my crosshairs over the years, swirling around inside my subconscious when my head finally hit the pillow. I'd be hard-pressed to describe any specific facial features of my targets—save one or two. Those instances were memorable only because I'd missed my shot the first time.

The hardest part for me is the continual sense of detachment. Hard to be part of a raucous crowd when silence in body and mind is a constant necessity in my work, not only to perform at an optimum level, but in winding down from the execution. I don't get a killer's high, per se, but a certain amount of adrenaline is produced and needs to be released in a productive manner. Male snipers let off steam by getting blow jobs. I let off steam by blowing *uji* breath in and out of my body. Different strokes for different folks.

And being a sniper was just a job for me. Granted, a job where I signed someone's death warrant with a .50-caliber bullet made me a paid killer. Uncle Sam's rigorous and expensive sniper training wasn't a job skill I could put on a résumé. My contract was with the United States Army. Once that contract ended, so would that part of my life.

So why was I loitering in the darkness, holding a gun, contemplating going against everything I believed in, considering killing a man in cold blood?

• • •

In the moonless void of his bedroom, I was ready when Jake Red Leaf awoke and realized he wasn't alone.

Before his hand inched from beneath the covers to reach for the light on his nightstand, a click echoed at the foot of the bed. A click signaling my gun was cocked.

"No quick movements. Sit up. Put your hands where I can see them."

"Mercy?" His bare feet dug for purchase as he scrambled backward.

"Do as I say. Don't make me shoot you, Jake."

He shrank away from my clipped, icy tone. Or maybe it was from the gun.

"What are you doing here? At"—the whites of his eyes were huge in the dark as he glanced at the clock—"one in the morning?"

I let deadly, ugly silence linger.

Jake reclined against the headboard, his hands white-knuckling the star quilt. "What's going on?"

I sensed it spooked him that he couldn't see me or hear me breathing. It was almost like I wasn't there.

But I was. My anger poisoned the air. "Why, Jake?"

Even if I hadn't aimed my gun at his head, he knew better than to play dumb with me. "Why what? Why Hope?"

"Yes. Was it because she was here?"

"No."

"Did my father know?"

"Know what, Mercy? That Levi was actually my son?"

"No. Did he know you were fucking my sister?"

Jake flinched. "Don't be so crude. There was more to it than that."

"More than betrayal by the man my father trusted above any other? Did he know you screwed him over by knocking up *another* one of his daughters?"

"Yes. He knew."

I wondered what other secrets this family had kept from one another.

"I don't expect you to understand."

"Oh, I understand, all right. You blew your chance with me, so you set your sights on Hope. The poor, confused girl didn't stand a chance against your strong, silent Indian charm, did she? How long after I left before she crawled into your bed? Did you pop her cherry, too?"

"I'm telling you, you weren't here. You don't know nothing about it. And I don't owe you any explanation."

Before he blinked, I pressed the barrel against his forehead. "Wrong. Tell me. Give me a reason not to blow your fucking brains all over the wall, Jake. We both know Dawson won't do a goddamn thing to investigate. You've got three seconds."

Perspiration snaked down his temple.

"One."

It was as if he were paralyzed by fear and his mouth was wired shut.

"Two."

The *snick* of me thumbing the safety untied the knot in his vocal cords.

"I was with her because I loved her."

The gun stayed in place; I ground the muzzle deeper into his skin. "You loved her? Is that what you told her, or what she believed?"

"It's what I told her because it is the truth."

"You are a liar. The only thing you've ever loved was the idea that someday you might own this ranch."

"Not everything revolves around this piece of earth."

"Were you with her to get back at me?"

"Not everything revolves around you either."

My neck flashed red-hot. "I never pretended it did, but that's not a good enough answer." I shifted, so did the gun. "Why did you love her?"

Jake wasn't stupid; he read between the lines. He knew I'd never stoop to ask the real question: why he'd loved Hope and not me.

"Because Hope needed me in a way you never did."

"She couldn't have needed you that much because she bailed on you, too, didn't she?"

He winced.

It didn't faze me. "If she needed you so much, why'd she marry someone else, Jake?"

"I wanted to marry her. She told me she was getting an abortion. Instead, she came back five months later married to Mario Arpel. Still pregnant, and I knew it was mine."

I taunted him into giving me an emotional reaction, just to see if he would. "Weren't you pissed off? She left you and wouldn't admit Levi was your child, then she returned to rub it in your face."

"After she left me and came back, she was happier than I'd ever seen her. She deserved a chance at happiness, so I didn't interfere."

"How noble." I removed the gun and tried to stay disconnected.

"Noble? At least I'm not pretending to be superior. You're not any better off now than you were when you left twenty years ago. What is it you're searching for that you can't seem to find here or anywhere else?"

"This isn't about me. This is about you and my little sister. And the secret love child you fathered," I added with a sneer.

"Is that why you're here? To tell me I don't get to mourn my son?"

I felt his fury. But it was too little, too late. "You didn't see fit to acknowledge him during his short life, so you sure as hell don't get to act the part of anguished father now that he's dead."

Even as the words left my mouth, I knew I'd struck a blow equal to gut-stabbing him. Was this what I really wanted? To be at odds with everyone in my life?

Yes. If only for tonight. If I could keep the rage boiling on the surface, I could keep the grief at bay.

"What'd they do to you in the army, hey?" he asked softly.

Jake knew how to get to me. I almost broke down.

"Mercy?"

Almost.

"They taught me to hold my emotions in. To be cold. Kind of like you, huh, Jake?"

Evidently he'd had enough. He snapped, "Either kill me or get the hell out."

My answering laugh was decidedly mean. "Maybe you have grown a backbone after all, *kola*."

Pause. "We've been many things, Mercy, but never friends."

I'd made my point; it was time to make my escape. From the doorway, I said, "Night, Jake."

I wasn't sure, but as I passed by his open window, I thought I heard him retching.

And I didn't feel a bit of regret.

TEN

The next two days passed in a blur. There were so many people in and out of the house I couldn't keep track. Sophie and our neighbors Iris Newsome, Kathy Lohstroh, Jackie Quinn, and Bernice, from the sheriff's office, all took turns organizing the food dropped off by various church groups and friends. I'd forgotten how a community pulls together at the loss of one of our own. I guess I hadn't paid much attention after my dad died.

Then again, Wyatt Gunderson hadn't been murdered. My cynical side wondered if the support was borne out of voyeurism.

Being around a crowd without a clear purpose drove a loner like me crazy. I'd escaped from the living room, where a half-dozen women were tending to Hope. Some were parents of our friends, who knew our sad family history. I could almost hear them, wondering what other tragedies could befall the unlucky Gunderson family. Speculating on why I was hiding outside with the menfolk rather than sipping tea with them.

Levi's funeral was set for two o'clock. I would've preferred earlier in the day, to avoid the heat and just to get the damn thing over with, but it wasn't my call. I glanced at my watch. Barely ten. Too soon to break out the Wild Turkey? Everyone grieves in their own way. Whiskey works best for me.

Tires on the gravel driveway caught my attention. Great. More company. A quick feeling of relief bloomed when John-John's El Dorado parked.

John-John was dressed sedately in dark slacks, a light gray

polo shirt, and black loafers. Even the row of silver hoop earrings was small and understated.

"Hey, *kola*," John-John said. "Whatcha doin'?"

"Taking a breather."

"Can I join you for a minute?"

"Sure. Shoonga. Down." The dog jumped off the swing and rearranged himself by the door.

John-John flopped next to me on the porch swing. The cushions slid around and the chains jangled as he settled his bulk.

"You here to see Hope?"

"No, buttercup. I'm actually here to see you."

My stomach revolted. "Another vision?"

He shook his head.

We let the momentum of the swing carry us because the conversation was at a standstill.

"I wondered how you were holding up."

I shrugged. Ignored the hollow feeling in my chest. "I'm doing okay." I wasn't. But I didn't want to share my misery. Levi's murder had returned my father's passing to the forefront, just when I'd seemed to get a handle on the idea Dad was really gone. Now I had another loss to compound it and the guilt.

The porch swing creaked with each pass. The constant *squeak shuffle clank* of the chains soothed me. The silence between us stretched, not awkward, just . . . there.

"You don't want to talk about it?"

"Nope."

John-John sighed. "I remember when you used to tell me everything."

"That was a long time ago."

"Some things might've changed, doll, but my ears still work the same as they did twenty years ago."

"I'll keep that in mind."

Another long pause. I heard the water valve kick on in the kitchen. Someone was doing dishes. Seemed like those church ladies were always washing dishes.

"We're worried about you."

I faced him. "Who's we? You and Muskrat?"

"No. Sophie and me."

"Sophie needs to mind her own damn business and stop talking about me behind my back. She keeps it up and I'll fire her."

"You don't mean that."

"Yes. I do." I couldn't look him in the eye when I said it; he'd see the lie. "Anyway, I hate that everyone is watching me, judging how I grieve. Just because I'm not bawling and cutting off all my hair or slicing my skin in a Lakota mourning ritual doesn't mean I'm not affected." Doesn't mean I'm coldhearted. I told myself looking for solace in the bottom of a whiskey bottle didn't mean a damn thing either.

"No one believes you're unaffected by Levi's murder. It's just our nature to reach out to you."

And it was my nature to retreat inside myself. None of these well-meaning souls would leave me alone unless they felt they were "helping" me. Damn. I had no choice but to let them think they were helping me while I followed my own agenda.

"I appreciate it, really, I do. It's just . . . driving me crazy to sit around. I want answers *now*. Kids don't get murdered here. And we've had two murders in two weeks."

John-John stopped nervously pinching the crease in his pants. "You think there's a connection between Albert's and Levi's deaths?"

"Don't you? Doesn't everyone? Everyone except for Dawson." I slapped a mosquito on my forearm, leaving a smear of blood. "I don't know why Dad hired him. Dawson wouldn't know investigative work if it bit him on the ass. Now I understand why Estelle was so upset. Why she wanted me to do something. Somebody has to." I'd called Estelle, and she'd agreed to meet me later, after the funeral, when she got off work. Getting that list had become urgent.

The swing stalled. "I don't like the sound of that."

I said nothing.

"Come on, girl. Whatcha got up your sleeve?"

"Just my arm."

He frowned.

"What makes you think I'm planning anything?"

"Let's just say my spidey sense is tingling."

"I have some of that 'spidey sense' myself."

"I know. About damn time you owned up to it; you ain't all white, you know." He playfully slapped my thigh. "Nice try, changing the subject. You ain't gonna tell me what you're up to, are you?"

"Probably not."

"These visions are disturbing, Mercy. Trust me when I tell you it'd be best if you don't get involved."

"Best for who? Not best for Levi. Maybe if I'd acted a little quicker helping Estelle, Levi might still be alive."

John-John reached for my hands. He peered into my eyes, and I swear he saw all the secrets I'd buried. "You're wrong. Don't do this to yourself. You have enough guilt burning holes in your soul. Levi wouldn't—"

The screen door banged. I jumped. John-John swore and Shoonga barked once before rolling over on his back into a patch of sunshine.

Iris Newsome stopped, readjusting the avocado green Tupperware bowl sliding off the Pyrex casserole dish. She looked up at us. "Oh. Sorry. I didn't mean to interrupt."

"You didn't. Here, let me help you." I shot off the swing, thankful for the interruption, and caught the plastic bowl before it crashed to the porch.

"Thank you. I have a case of butterfingers today."

I followed her to her car. She stacked the dishes in the passenger seat and straightened. She didn't smile; instead, she stared at me, waiting for me to say something.

I almost wished she'd broach the subject of the countywide petition drive and break the thorny silence between us. "Thanks for bringing food, Iris, and helping out. We appreciate it."

"It's the least I could do. I just wish I could do more." Her gaze flicked to the house. "Poor Hope. First losing her dad. And now this?" She looked back at me with watery eyes. "I know what it's like to bury a child."

I stood there like an idiot. Not knowing what the hell to do. Words of comfort escaped me. I wasn't much of a hugger. I couldn't even offer her a stupid Kleenex.

Iris wiped the tears with the tips of her fingers and gave me a wan smile. "Sorry. It's just hard, seeing her like this. It's not fair."

Nothing seemed to kick my vocal cords into use.

"I'd better get going. I'll see you at the service."

As she drove off I glanced at the empty porch swing. John-John had gone inside. Good. He couldn't ream me for sneaking a nip or two.

Then again, given his spidey sense, he probably already knew.

After the short service and the burial in the Gunderson Cemetery, we headed to the ranch. The women congregated in the house; the men milled outside. I alternated between hovering over Hope and waiting for Estelle to show up.

I watched Kathy Lohstroh rip off a chunk of plastic wrap and cover a pan of pumpkin bars. She gave me a sympathetic half smile and set about tidying the kitchen.

After she joined the throng of women in the living room, I grabbed the flask I'd stashed in the junk drawer. I'd just poured a generous splash of self-medicating goodness into my coffee when I felt a tap on my shoulder. I turned around guiltily.

Hope's loser boyfriend, Theo, said, "There are some guys outside who want to talk to you."

"I'll be right there." I assumed more offers of condolences. I drained the coffee and stepped into the late-afternoon heat.

Never assume. Two shiny matching Chevy pickups parked in the middle of the yard blocked in a half-dozen cars. Several men dressed in black pseudo-fatigues leaned up against the pickup's side panels, talking in low voices and pointing to the area past the barns.

Not locals. Hunters? We had a great number of guys—local and out-of-staters—who stopped at the house for permission to hunt on our land. Dad usually said yes if they asked. But if we caught people hunting on Gunderson land without permission? I'd learned the "shoot first" philosophy straight from the horse's mouth—good old Dad.

The men straightened up as I approached. "Is there something I can do for you guys?"

The bulky guy with a buzz cut—no doubt a former soldier—stepped forward. "Hi, Miz Gunderson. I'm Richard Amiotte."

I frowned. His name sounded familiar.

"We've been playing phone tag. I'm with the Swamp Rats Investment Group in Florida? We've been trying to set up a time to check out this property. We were on our way through from a fishing trip in Canada, and were in the area looking at other properties and thought we'd stop by."

"Sorry, Richard, we've been dealing with some family issues in the last few days—"

"Sorry to hear that. Unfortunately, we are pressed for time, so we understand if you'll just want to do a quick overview."

"Excuse me? An overview of what?"

His gaze narrowed on the cars and trucks, the men dressed in western suits. Finally back on me in my little black dress. "Is this an auction? You already sell this place?"

"That's hard to do when it isn't even listed."

His face relaxed. "Then what's the problem with letting us take a look around?"

A crowd had gathered behind me. Before I could answer, Theo said, "What would it hurt, Mercy? Whoever he is, he might make a better offer than Kit McIntyre's group."

How did the pompous asshole know about Kit's offer? I whirled on him. "What would it *hurt*? We buried my nephew today, you moron."

Theo turned beet red. Then he glared at me as he brushed past and headed back into the house.

"We don't need a guided tour," Richard said quickly. "We can get all the information we need just by a drive-through."

"Not possible. I'd appreciate it if you'd leave."

Another man, around sixty, tanned, his hair bleached from the sun, and dressed for an afternoon on a sailboat, sidled up beside Richard. "What's the problem? We contacted you weeks ago about purchasing this tract of land here in the Dakotas."

Several ranchers behind me snickered. *The Dakotas*. Didn't this southern-fried idiot realize North and South Dakota had been recognized as separate states since 1889? Probably pointless to mention that the Gunderson Ranch had been in my family since the 1890s.

I paused, giving him a moment to rethink his stupid, smarmy statement. He didn't. He merely stared at me. Dared me. Creeped me out to the max.

Too bad these guys hadn't listened to their damn voice mail. I'd left them a message renouncing my intention to sell, or to consider their offer. "There's been some misunderstanding. The Gunderson Ranch is not for sale. I'd appreciate it if you'd leave immediately."

"But—"

"I'm not asking again."

Murmured conversation began behind me. The rumor mill would run rampant in Eagle River County in another hour. My neighbors figured the conversation was over. They dispersed, leaving me alone with these gate-crashers.

The other men with Richard climbed in their trucks. I watched until their pickups were a red blight on the landscape and then gone.

After the Swamp Rats scurried away, I snuck into the house. My black satin heels were scuffed from the rocks, caked with dust, and completely ruined. No wonder I never wore girly shoes.

In my bedroom I changed into worn boots and jeans, carefully placing the flannel-wrapped bundle inside my right boot. Downstairs I made nice with our neighbors for the next couple of hours. Hope seemed to appreciate me sticking around.

When I'd endured my limit of politely restrained conversation, I wandered outside. Leaning against the weathered fence, I wrapped my hands around the rail and propped my foot on the bottom rung.

Some of the cattle wandered in from the pasture and circled the stock tanks. The calves were getting big. A few brave babies even ventured away from their mothers. We weren't running a full herd. It didn't make sense to lay out that kind of money for stock upkeep when the ranch's future was up in the air.

I closed my eyes. Even the blistering rays from the sun didn't burn away the cold reality of saying good-bye to Levi. Tears dripped down my face as I listened to swishing tails, buzzing flies, the sucking sound of hooves caught in the muck, and the occasional disgruntled moo.

Lost in sorrow and misery, I jumped when "Mercy?" sounded behind me.

I whirled around and saw Estelle Yellow Boy.

"Didn't mean to scare ya." Estelle crossed her arms and set them on top of the fence. "Sophie said I'd find you out here."

"A lot more peaceful than in the house."

"I've always liked this time of day. Too hot for most folks."

Two calves frolicked by the fence connected to the barn.

"Sorry about Levi. He was a good friend to Albert."

I didn't know how to respond, so I didn't.

"I can't stay long. Paul thinks I'm working late because I took time off to go to Levi's funeral earlier." She turned and looked at me. "It was a nice service. Considering."

It saddened me that more of Levi's friends hadn't shown up.

"Here's the list you asked for." Estelle slid a piece of rose-colored stationery from the pocket of her skirt. "This should be enough to get ya started."

"Good." I rolled up my jeans and removed the package containing the necklace and handed it back to her. "Thank you, but I can't take this."

"Why not?"

"Because I don't need a financial incentive to do what's right, Estelle."

Her eyes darkened with skepticism. She held her tongue for a minute. "And what *are* you gonna do if you figure out who done this to Levi and my boy?"

"I'm not sure." What a lie. I'd do what I do best: kill. I doubted the predator instinct that defined my life resided in Estelle. I wouldn't lose sleep over vengeance. She would. Whether or not she understood, carrying out revenge was my burden to bear, not hers.

"Will you keep in touch with me?" she asked.

"You really want Paul to know what I'm—we're—doing?"

Estelle shook her head. Without another word she left.

I remained in the great outdoors as the sun expanded to a fat orange ball and the clouds puffed out to pastel waves on the never-ending blue horizon.

Jake meandered over from the barn, Shoonga on his boot heels. He didn't make eye contact with me. Not surprisingly, he stayed a good distance from me, too.

We both stared across the field like it held the secrets to the universe.

Finally, his silent routine got to me. "You come here looking for an apology?"

He snorted. "Be waiting a long damn time since I know you ain't sorry. And you're just like your dad in that respect; he said false remorse is as bad as an outright lie."

Dad. What would he think of my murderous intentions? Would he do the same thing if he were in my shoes? No. But he wouldn't be sitting on his hands like Dawson was either.

"You plan on quitting and telling me to go to hell, Jake?"

"No. But I'd like a chance to say my piece, without you interrupting me like you always do."

"Fine."

"We're opposites, Mercy. Always have been, I suspect we always will be. I know you think a man who doesn't fight back—even when provoked—ain't a real man." He rubbed the heel of his hand on the exact spot where I'd shoved the gun barrel into his forehead. "I'm not gonna defend the way I was raised, and I don't wanna argue with you about the hard-assed way Wyatt brung you up."

I kept quiet.

"I'm tired of fighting you. No matter what happened in the past, or hell, even the other night when you showed up at my place armed and angry, we need to figure out a way to work together, not against each other, since it appears neither of us is going anyplace anytime soon."

"True." Jake had been forthright; he deserved the same from me. "But to be honest, the idea I can't pick up and leave here whenever I want is suffocating me. It always has."

"I know," he said softly.

"So what do I do?"

"Come take a ride with me."

"How's that gonna help?"

"Maybe you won't feel like you're choking on your responsibilities when you have a clearer view of them."

I squinted at him. "Do I need to get my gun?"

He rolled his eyes. "I'm checking that old stock tank in the south section. Thought I reminded TJ to fill it, but with all that's been going on . . . I ain't sure if I did."

A hot wind blew my hair across my face as I looked over my

shoulder at the house. Sophie and a few other women were still there. Hope should be all right, but I didn't feel comfortable passing her on to someone else.

Jake moved and laid his hand on my arm. "We won't be gone long. I promise."

"Okay, but I'm driving."

"How'd I know you were gonna say that?" He tossed me the keys.

We settled in the ancient truck, Shoonga panting between us, water sloshing in the tank in the truck bed. After we were through the first gate, which Jake opened and closed, he harrumphed. "You're driving just so you don't gotta be on gate duty."

"Yep. Pays to be the big boss."

"So, you know where you're going, boss?"

"I'm sure if I get it wrong you'll be more than happy to correct me."

A smile ghosted around his mouth.

Bumping along in the stifling heat had a cathartic effect. Somehow Jake knew I needed a reconnection to solitude and a reason to focus on the external problems rather than the internal ones, if only for a short while.

We drove in silence for fifteen minutes. I'd automatically followed the tire tracks without really paying attention to where we were headed. When I veered left to crest a small rise, I hit the brakes. I hadn't been out in this section for years.

Memories arose of the hours and years Jake and I had spent just like this, driving around in the cab of a dirty truck, bound by circumstances and our love for the Gunderson Ranch. Testing the boundaries of friendship. The spring I'd turned seventeen we'd stopped circling each other and crossed the line from friends to lovers. Right here. On this very spot.

For the next year we weren't "out" as a couple, although everyone suspected. The secrecy was partially because I was underage, partially because Jake worked for my father, but mostly because sneaking around heightened the relationship's appeal. Accidental touches, stolen kisses, lingering looks seemed more meaningful when given and taken covertly. Even our couplings were quick—a frenzy we mistook as passion.

Dad disapproved of his oldest daughter and ranch foreman

Escort, and old VW Bug in the driveway. A Chevy Blazer on blocks under the drooping carport roof. No clue which vehicle was his. Didn't know if he was even home.

I drove to the end of the road, four trailers from Rollie's place, parked in the driveway of a 10x13 with a FOR RENT sign tacked in the front window. I jammed the gun in my back pocket, untucked my shirt, and hopped out of the truck.

On the set of wooden steps, I peered inside the porthole-shaped window, acting like a potential renter. Knocked for good measure. When no one answered the door, I reversed course. Avoiding a huge pile of dog crap by the propane tank, I made my way the length of the trailer.

Individual metal clothesline poles ran parallel to the barbed-wire fence separating the trailer court from Rollie's horse pasture directly behind it. I hid in the shadows until I reached the house next to Rollie's. The windows were covered, two with tinfoil, the rest with cheap plastic blinds. I didn't hear a window air conditioner, a TV, or a boom box.

Suddenly I felt ridiculous. What was I doing, slinking around a trailer court? What had I hoped to accomplish by stealth? This wasn't Iraq, where an ambush lurked around every corner.

I marched up to Rollie's front door and banged on it.

The door cracked only wide enough for a girl to squeak, "Go away. We don't want none."

"I'm not selling anyth—"

She slammed the door in my face.

I rapped again. Harder.

The door flew all the way open and a very pregnant Indian girl, no more than seventeen, demanded, "Jesus. You deaf? I said go away."

"Not until I talk to Rollie."

"Don't know who you're talking about, lady."

"Tell him if he doesn't get his ugly ass out here in about a minute, I'm coming in after him."

I heard the footsteps behind me.

"You ain't in no position to be making demands." The soft click of a hammer cocking next to my right ear was followed by, "You got a minute to get *your* ugly ass outta here."

Rookie mistake.

I pivoted, grasped his gun arm with one hand, and threw him down. His revolver—a S&W .38—crashed to the ground and discharged a shot. The girl shrieked. I placed my boot on the back of the kid's neck, twisted his arm, and aimed my Walther P22 at his head. "Tell Rollie I want to talk to him right now."

Rollie's raspy voice drifted to me before I saw him. "Still feisty as ever, I see."

I briefly glanced over at his form stuffing the door frame. Besides wrinkles and gray hair, he hadn't changed much in the three decades I'd known him. He was six feet two inches, 250 pounds, with long gray hair plaited into two braids. Despite his last name, Rollie looked Sioux.

One hundred and fifty years ago his horny French ancestors had traveled down the Missouri River as fur trappers, mixing DNA with the various Plains tribes. Although Rollie claimed he was 100 percent Indian, it'd never stopped him from betraying his own kind for a buck. Which was exactly why I was here.

He eased down the steps. "Let him go and I'll talk to ya." He crouched and spoke to the kid on the ground. "I'm cutting you some slack on your poor protection skills this time, Junior, because no way could you've gotten the drop on her."

"Junior?" I said. "This is your son?"

"Yeah, one of."

I angled my head toward the girl in the doorway. "So is that one your daughter?"

"No, I ain't his daughter, I'm his girlfriend!"

Rollie sighed. "That's enough, Verline."

Girlfriend? Yowza. She could've been Rollie's granddaughter. Not touching that one. Maybe Rollie and Mr. Pawlowski were setting an example for the local senior citizens on the benefits of Viagra.

"I almost had her," Junior complained.

"Almost ain't good enough." Rollie spit a stream of tobacco at an anthill. It exploded into dust the color of powdered milk. "They still calling ya No Mercy?"

"Only once." I released Junior's arm. He scrambled away and scowled over his shoulder.

Rollie's gaze met mine, but he wasn't smiling. "You look just like her."

Her. Meaning my mother, Sunny Fairchild Gunderson. Rollie dated her before my father barged into the picture and "stole her away"—or so Rollie claimed. My mother swore it'd been love at first sight between her and Wyatt Gunderson. Consequently, there'd been no love lost between Rollie and my dad. The fact my mother had been killed by Rollie's Thoroughbred—and Dad shot the horse upon discovering my mother's body—only increased their animosity. Rollie had a soft spot for me. Probably because we both felt a measure of guilt over her death.

"Although you're still acting like him," he added slyly.

"Rollie. Never insult a woman with a gun." I flipped the safety and returned it to my pocket.

He grinned. "So what brings you here, Mercy girl?"

"I need some information."

"You know it don't come for free." He spun the cylinder on the revolver, dumped the bullets, and put them inside his beaded suede vest.

I traipsed behind him through the garage, dodging ratchet sets, wrenches, and crushed beer cans. We passed a disembodied welding torch and ended up at a resin table with a dilapidated umbrella. He settled himself in the chair in the corner between the garage and the crooked fence. I sat beside him. No way was I leaving my back exposed.

"How long you sticking around?"

"That a subtle way of asking if I'm selling the ranch?"

Rollie grunted. "You ain't gonna sell the ranch."

"You sure?"

"Yep. I know your dad. Bet he demanded some kinda 'deathbed' promise from ya, didn't he?"

"I wasn't here, remember?" I said tightly. "He died before I could promise him anything." He'd died before I could say goodbye. That raw, grating sensation I knew would never go away coiled in my gut like a pile of old, rusty barbed wire.

"*Shee*, don't matter. Wyatt guilted you into keeping your heritage long before he died." He gave me a crafty smile. "John-John ain't had no visions, telling what you oughta do?"

"No. Maybe I should talk to your brother Leon. John-John told me his *yuwipi* skills were in demand. Tell me. Did Leon reconnect with his Indian roots in prison?"

Rollie scowled. "Old fool. Between him and Verline, I can't get a moment's peace with all that claptrap. It's driving me to drink."

"You don't believe in that woo-woo Lakota stuff?"

Absentmindedly he fingered the stone hanging from his necklace. "Be easier if I didn't." His eyes narrowed. "Don't matter. Ask your questions. I ain't got all day."

"Fine. What do you know about Judd Moser and Donald Little Bear?"

"Why you interested in them?"

Rollie had the uncanny ability to smell a lie, so I didn't bother concocting one. "Initially, Estelle Yellow Boy asked me to poke around to see if Albert's friends would talk to me about why someone might've killed him."

"But now?"

"Now? It's personal. Those two names I gave you keep popping up. Those boys started some kind of an Indian Warrior club. Albert was a member; Levi wasn't."

Rollie measured me. "Seems strange that Estelle would ask you to help her. You hiding investigating experience I don't know about?"

"No. And don't get pissy. I'm not looking to hang out my PI shingle. This is strictly a one-shot deal." South Dakota was one of the few states where private investigators didn't have to be formally licensed by the state. I could call myself a PI if I wanted, and Rollie or Dawson couldn't do a damn thing about it. Which, near as I could tell, allowed me lots of leeway.

Ironically, Rollie considered himself a PI above all else, touting his "modern-day Indian tracking" skills. He'd work for anyone who could pay his hefty fees. As a council member of the tribe, he had access to people and information white people didn't.

No matter how many times Rollie turned in his brethren, those Indians still confided in him. Some folks claimed he maintained files on every tribal member and their families, dating back decades. Others claimed he had spies everywhere on the rez and knew everything about everyone. So though he was generally reviled, no one dared cross him. Even my father had had to play ball with Rollie a couple of times.

"So you know anything about this group calling themselves the Warrior Society?"

He looked at me consideringly. "Not much. An elder heard a rumor some young punks were doing their own version of the Seven Sacred Rites. According to one of the kids who was there, they did 'em wrong, not in harmony with traditional at all."

Even among Lakota people discrepancies abounded about which ceremonies were "traditional" to Native religion, and which ones were transformed after Christianity gained a foothold on the reservation. I knew a few, simply because Jake and John-John participated in the common ceremonies: the sweat lodge, vision quest, making of relatives, and the Sun Dance. The other rites, preparing a girl for womanhood, spirit keeping, and the throwing of the ball, weren't as prevalent. And contrary to popular belief, the Ghost Dance, which played a part in the Wounded Knee Massacre in 1890, wasn't part of Lakota ritual at all.

"Who's leading them?"

"I don't know. I just know them rituals weren't about dancing for healing or a prayer offered to the Great Spirit for guidance, it was more like a . . . sacrifice."

"What kind of sacrifice?"

"Blood. Flesh. Tears." His troubled gaze connected with mine.

I played devil's advocate. "But isn't that what the Sun Dance is all about? Men piercing their flesh? Crying to the Great Spirit as they dance in the sun? Then blood flows from the wounds after they've ripped away the sticks attaching them to the sacred pole?"

"That's the simplified version, yes. But what I'm talking about is blood, flesh, and tears from *unwilling* participants."

Chills tracked down my spine. "Like Levi?"

"I ain't sure." Again, Rollie touched the teeth and stones on his choker like it was a talisman. "You been to the rez and talked to them boys?"

"Not yet."

An engine revved down the street. A woman's screech was lost in spewing gravel and the thump of rap music.

"Lemme offer you a piece of advice before you go charging in. The only thing those punks understand is fear. Don't think of them as kids; think of them as animals. Get the upper hand right away." He chuckled. "But you don't have no problem invoking fear in people, do you?"

I shrugged.

"I recognize the hardness in your eyes, Mercy."

"Yeah?"

"Uh-huh. I saw it in the mirror when I came back from Vietnam. That look will fade in time."

"And if I don't want it to fade?"

"Then your past deeds will eat you from the inside out until there's nothing left but a bitter black hole where your soul used to be."

Rollie summed it up better than the army shrink. But he was just as wrong. The hardness in me *was* the truest part of me. I'd accepted it long ago. Why couldn't everyone else? I didn't answer, merely stared at him.

"What're you gonna do when you find whoever killed your *tunska?*"

"If you have to ask, Rollie, I haven't made myself clear."

He nodded. No judgment.

I released a pent-up sigh. "Is there anything else you know about the Warrior Society?"

"For whatever reason, there's at least one adult tribal member helping them with these so-called rituals. Which is why it's so disturbing that he's teaching them wrong."

"Any whispers on who the elder might be?"

"A couple. Paul Yellow Boy, for one, which was why I was surprised when you said Estelle asked for your help."

No wonder Estelle wanted Paul kept out of it. But surely she didn't suspect he had something to do with Albert's death?

"You'll let me know what you find out, Mercy girl?"

"Is that the price of the information you gave me? I share mine?"

Rollie harrumphed. "You ain't getting off that easy."

"I figured as much."

"Tell you what. Feel free to use my name whenever you're in Eagle River. It'll probably open a few more doors for you. Anyone gets nasty, tell 'em you're working for me."

"Do I need an official business card, boss man?"

"Smarty-pants. No. If anyone calls me to double-check your credentials"—he smiled broadly—"I'll set 'em straight. Of course, that means as my *employee* all information you uncover pertaining to this case or any other belongs to me. Along with any monetary compensation you might be receiving. You getting paid?"

"No. Doing it out of the unkindness of my black heart, Rollie."

"Then I rescind my offer of employment."

"Indian giver."

He laughed. "My advice is never do no work for free. People don't appreciate it. Charge the heck outta them and they think it's worth something."

An interesting philosophy I'd have to remember.

"Long as you're here, did your dad ever find out who was causing all them problems for the Lohstrohs?"

I frowned. "What problems?"

"Some outfit from out of state offered them big money for their ranch. They said no, and some weird things started happening."

"Was their ranch for sale?"

"No, that's why it struck Wyatt as odd."

The Lohstrohs were one of our neighbors to the north. Because our ranch was so big and an oddly jagged shape, it was bordered by three other ranches on the north side: Lohstrohs', Mattsons', and TJ and Luke Red Leaf's small family operation. On the east side, our neighbors were the Newsomes and the Quinns. I wasn't sure about our west-side neighbors because the land that'd been known as the old Jackson place had been sold twice in the last twenty years. Our border to the south was the Eagle River National Grasslands. "When was this?"

He scratched his chin. "Wyatt called me from the ranch a coupla days before he took sick the last time. He didn't sound too good. Asked me to dig around and see what I could find. I said I would but . . ."

"But you didn't." Because Dad was dead. "What kind of stuff happened?"

"Small, random fires. Kathy Lohstroh was run off the road twice. Fences ripped down. More'n just usual kids' pranks. Let me ask you something else."

I nodded.

"After Frank Jackson died, why didn't Wyatt snatch up his place when everyone knew he'd had his eye on that chunk of land forever?"

Easy: no money. We might be land rich, but when it came to cash, we were dirt poor. "You think we need another fifteen thousand acres to worry about?"

"Never know what kinda land baron you'll end up being; it's in your blood, that's for damn sure. You might could get another chance to add to the Gunderson legacy. I heard the Quinns was looking to get out."

Why were all our neighbors bailing? A weird feeling rippled through me. Had the Swamp Rats approached them? Or another group?

I'd bet a year's worth of hay that Kit was circling the Quinns and the Lohstrohs like a vulture. So if Kit got his hands on my land and the Quinns, he'd have most of Eagle River County turned into hobby ranches.

Why was that a bigger betrayal than the corporate hunting groups? "Why didn't anyone tell me this before now, Rollie?"

"Don't know. I'm just as curious as you are as to why all this land is going up for sale, besides the drought. This part of flyover country is considered the armpit of the nation. Makes you wonder why it's becoming so popular, eh?"

"Good clean air, good clean living, low taxes, and a low crime rate." My stomach clenched and I scowled. "Guess with two unsolved murders in two weeks, the crime rate claim isn't necessarily true anymore."

"From what I've heard, Dawson is a real stickler on patrolling. He picked up Junior for speeding over by the Newsome place last week."

A perfect opening. "So, what do you think of Dawson?"

"Sneaky."

"That's it?"

Rollie blinked at me. "Ain't that enough?"

He had a point. "Yeah. Thanks for the help, boss. I gotta run."

"*Boss*. Heh." He smiled, even as he said gruffly, "G'on, Mercy girl. Get outta here."

It was still early enough to tackle a few names on the list. Estelle mentioned Albert's friends didn't show up at the rec center until evening. She hadn't mentioned whether they held jobs, but since the unemployment rate on the Eagle River Reservation runs 80 percent it was unlikely they'd be pulling fries at Burger King.

Jake's remark about Chet Baker seeing Levi and a bunch of boys a few weeks back prompted me to stop there first.

Chet delivered propane for the local co-op. When I rolled up to his place on the other side of the Viewfield city limits, I wished Rollie had given me an official PI badge.

As I waited for Chet to get off the phone, I studied his cramped office. The place stank of cigarettes, motor oil, and body odor. Catalogues were piled on top of dingy filing cabinets. Grungy windows lined one side of the building. The linoleum was stained black from never seeing a can of Mop & Glo. The coffee machine hadn't been near a scrub brush in months. Several years worth of "girlie" calendars—circa 1970—decorated the paneled walls. The joint harkened back to the days when ladies avoided men's domains—garages, filling stations, and hardware stores.

Chet hung up the receiver, plucked a yellowed hankie from the front pocket of his denim coveralls, and blew his nose. "So what can I do for you, Mercy?"

I asked him what he remembered about Levi and his friends riding around in the back of a pickup.

"Was the damndest thing. I figured they was up to no good, so I followed them."

"Where'd they end up?"

"By that abandoned silver mine offa County Road Nineteen. I seen beer cans around there, so I knew it was a place them fellas partied."

"Were they drinking?"

He shrugged. "Probably. But that's not the main reason they was up there."

Because he didn't get many visitors, Chet dragged out the drama. "What were they doing?"

"They were loading rocks in the back of that truck."

"Rocks?"

"Yeah. Know those big flat ones? Kinda yellowish-orange shale? Well, some of the Indian guys on the rez use 'em for different kinds of ceremonies. Couldn't imagine what those punks wanted with 'em."

That stumped me. Entertainment was a scarce commodity on the rez. "Did you see them doing anything else?"

"Nah. When I saw they were ready to take off, I did, too. Didn't want them to see me taking notice of what they were doing. Don't need trouble from them." He fiddled with the stapler in the center of his desk. "Mind if I ask why you're asking all these questions, Mercy?"

It was tempting to play the I'm-a-PI-and-I-work-for-Rollie card since it was brand-spanking new, but I refrained. "I'm trying to track down some things Levi loaned out. Now that he's gone . . ." My gaze fell to my boots, then I looked at him with sorrow that wasn't faked. "Hope would like to have those things back. We don't want Levi's friends to think we suspect they ripped him off, so we'd appreciate it if you didn't mention it to anyone."

"No problem. I sure hope you find what you're looking for."

Oh, I will.

I hopped back in my truck and hit the road. My next stop was my best friend Geneva's house, to talk to her daughter, Molly, about the names on the list. Although I knew Geneva was busy with a houseful of kids and a ranch to run, it bothered me a little that she'd come around only a few times in the aftermath of my father's and my nephew's deaths.

Still, Geneva was my oldest friend. She'd married her high school sweetheart, Brent Illingsworth, right out of high school, and they took over Geneva's family ranching operation. I wasn't the only one who'd bailed from Viewfield; Geneva's parents had flown the coop with the rest of the snowbirds and hightailed it to Arizona.

A hot, hay-scented breeze stirred my hair as I motored down
Geneva and Brent's driveway. I parked in front of the small two-
story farmhouse. Chaos ruled here. A Big Wheel was overturned
in the sandbox next to an orange plastic slide. Vacant tree swings
swayed in the wind. Boards were hammered in a haphazard line
up a gigantic elm tree, a tree house in progress, or one that'd
been abandoned. Clothes in graduated sizes flapped on the line.
The doors flew open on the huge metal barn and kids raced
from every direction.

Six-year-old Krissa grinned at me. "Mercy! Wanna see the new
kitties?"

"Sure. In a minute. Let me—"

"She don't wanna look at no dumb cats. Leave her alone." This
from twelve-year-old Doug.

Two tugs on my pant leg. I peered into Nikki's angelic face.
Wispy blond ringlets, enormous blue eyes, pink cheeks, and a shy
smile. At age three, she was still small enough for me to scoop
up. "Hiya, Nikki."

She set her head on my shoulder. I melted.

"We're s'posed to bring you inside. Right away. No goofing
off." Doug rolled his eyes. "Mom and Molly are so bossy."

The old ranch house had seemed bigger when Geneva and
her brothers Rome and London lived here. The kitchen still
smelled like molasses, sugar, fresh coffee, and laundry soap.

Geneva saw me holding Nikki and smiled. "You're a sucker.
Next she'll be rifling through your purse for candy."

"I don't mind." It surprised me how easy it was to indulge in
my softer side with Geneva's kids and how easily they accepted
it. And me.

"There's cookies and Kool-Aid in the sun porch. Then I wanna
see some kids outside picking up the toys in the yard. And keep
an eye on Tiffany."

At the mention of cookies they vanished.

"Sit," she said. "Coffee?"

"Sure."

She poured two cups and joined me at the table. Molasses
cookies were piled on a china plate.

I studied her over the rim of my cup. Geneva had been
the prettiest girl in our graduating class. Natural honey blond

hair, dark blue eyes, razor sharp cheekbones, and a thin, regal nose. Early on she'd grown into a woman's body, full hipped and curvy, with big breasts the envy of every girl in school. I would've hated her if we hadn't been best friends since kindergarten.

She was still gorgeous even though she'd plumped out considerably. Now, deep fatigue lines were etched around her eyes, and she didn't smile as often as I'd remembered.

"Molly will be right down." Geneva sipped coffee, leaned back in the chair, and sighed. Probably the first time she'd sat down all morning. "How is Hope doing?"

"She sleeps a lot. She cries a lot. She doesn't talk much."

"I can't imagine losing one of my children." She shuddered. "I don't even know what to say. God. Molly and her friends are just numb. We all are. Stuff like this doesn't happen around here."

"I know." I bit down on a cookie and sighed softly because it was so crisp and sweet and tasty. I hoarded two more and glanced up guiltily when Geneva didn't keep the conversation going. As longtime friends we rarely had awkward pauses. It didn't matter if we hadn't seen each other in two days or two years, we always picked up where we'd left off. Her silence left me unsettled. "What?"

"I don't know how to say this."

"Then just say it straight out."

"Why are you talking to Molly?"

I snapped a cookie in half. "Has the sheriff been here to talk to her?"

"No."

"Then there's your answer. Dawson is doing nothing to find who killed Levi, and it isn't because he's busy working on the Yellow Boy case."

"No offense, but what can *you* do?"

"Figure it out on my own."

"Good Lord, the rumors are true. You are turning into your dad."

I blushed, but I wasn't surprised she'd made the connection. "Kids can't keep secrets. Somebody knows something. Even if I have to talk to every teenager on the rez and in the county to find out who might've wanted Levi dead, I'll keep at it until I get some answers."

"What happens if you run out of time? Don't you have to go back to active duty?"

I paused a beat too long because Geneva demanded, "Well?"

"I'm on medical leave."

The blood drained from her face. "What happened?"

"Had a freak eye injury that won't allow me to return to my former position." The army liked their snipers to take out targets on the first try. If I couldn't, there were plenty of younger shooters who could.

Geneva slapped her hands on the table. "I cannot believe you didn't tell me this before now. Jesus. I oughta smack you."

"You'd hit an injured soldier?"

"No. But I'm still pissed off."

"You'll get over it. You always do."

Geneva made a face that read *maybe I won't*. "So is that why you've been dragging your feet? Because if you can't go back to duty, you might have to live here?"

"*Have* to live here? Nice dig."

"You know what I mean. You couldn't wait to get out and see the world. You never wanted to be a ranch wife with a half-dozen kids. . . ." She clapped her hand over her mouth.

Wow. That was another good dig. I didn't react this time.

"Damn, Mercy. Sometimes I don't think before I open my mouth. I don't get out much."

"Forget it."

Geneva babbled to cover the awkward silence. "Sometimes I wish we could sell this place. Move into a split-level in Rapid City with three bathrooms. The kids could walk to school. Brent could get a normal job, and there'd be enough money for Dan to go to college. I wouldn't have to worry about making ends meet." Color spread across her cheekbones. "Sorry. Then I think about what Hope's going through and Estelle's going through . . . I got nothing to complain about."

"You will complain once you see what Krissa and Nikki did to the bathroom," Molly said from the doorway.

I faced her. "Don't you look bright and fresh."

"Only until I clean stalls later this afternoon."

Geneva scrambled out of her chair like she couldn't wait to get away from me. "The weeds in the garden are calling my name." She squeezed Molly's shoulders and left us alone.

Molly and I sat in silence. I could be polite or I could get to it. "Tell me about Levi and these kids he'd been hanging out with lately."

"I don't really know Moser and Little Bear, but I've heard they are bad news."

"How so?"

"Drinking and driving. Stealing stuff. Starting fights, especially with the cowboys." Her eyes met mine. "The white cowboys. Until recently Levi hung around Albert and Axel. Then Albert and Axel were both in Moser's group and they left Levi out. From what I've heard from Sue Anne, Moser and them guys didn't want Levi because he wasn't Indian enough."

How little they knew. But it fit with what Levi told me.

"To show you how mean those guys are, Moser and Little Bear teased Levi, letting him hang out with them sometimes, making him do stuff, acting like they might let him in, all the while knowing their elder wouldn't accept Levi into the club."

"Do you know who this elder was?"

"No."

"Did Albert want to leave the group after this leader wouldn't let Levi in?"

Molly nibbled her cookie like a mouse. Crumbs fell on the plastic tablecloth. She stayed quiet as a mouse, too.

I forced myself to be patient. "Molly?"

"No one can leave once they're in. I guess Moser and Little Bear told Albert he couldn't be friends with Levi anymore."

"Or what? What could they do to him?"

"Punish him."

Damn. This just got more and more bizarre. "What kind of punishment?"

"I'm not sure." She rearranged the cookies on the plate in a flower pattern.

I placed my hand over hers. When she looked at me with in-nocent eyes, I hated what I had to do. "My nephew is dead. His

mother is home bawling her eyes out because she can't understand why someone killed her son. I need to know what these
so-called friends are doing before they hurt anyone else."

"I can't tell you because I don't know. I'm white. I'm not in
the group."

I needed a different tact. "Who *would* know about the punish-
ments?"

A long pause. Then she softly said, "Sue Anne White Plume."

The Indian girl from the dance. Why wasn't her name on the
list? "Was she dating Levi?"

"They liked each other a lot, but they were both quiet about
it. I think they were sneaking around behind Moser's and Little
Bear's backs."

"What's the best way for me to contact her?"

"You can't go to her house. Her parents are like total drunks.
They'd freak out and use it as another excuse to beat her."

I forced myself to ignore the *beat her* portion of Molly's warning. "Does she have a cell phone?"

Molly shook her head. "She doesn't have enough money for
food half the time, which is why she works at Taco John's."

Few kids in this country had it as bad as the kids on Eagle
River Reservation. "When's her next shift?"

"She said she's working tomorrow from ten to two." Molly
chewed her lip and pulverized the cookie in her fingers. "You
won't tell her you talked to me? Because I don't want her to be
mad."

"I'll try to keep you out of it. One other thing. If Sheriff
Dawson stops by and asks you questions, I'd appreciate it if you
didn't mention my name."

"Why not?"

"Let's just say the sheriff and I don't see eye to eye on a lot of
things." I scooted back from the table and tried to lighten the situation. "Krissa said something about showing me some kitties?"

Molly smiled softly. "Poor things. She loves those little babies
so much we tease her that she's gonna love them to death."

As if that were possible.

TWELVE

Late the next morning I made the trek to the Eagle River Reservation. The scenery was spectacularly diverse. Flat land, which wasn't quite prairie and therefore not conducive to farming, gave way to the scalloped edges of hills outlined with scrub oak and misshapen cedar trees. A few flat-topped buttes, colors ranging from butterscotch to vanilla, were interspersed among the desertlike stretches. Sagebrush, sweetgrass, and yucca were prevalent. Cattle grazed. The occasional deciduous tree peeked out from a ravine, a shimmer of green in an otherwise monochromatic landscape.

In the two hours before Sue Anne's shift ended, I figured I'd scope out the rec center, the ice-cream joint, and other places where Levi's friends hung out.

As I closed in on the town of Eagle River, clusters of houses appeared. Abandoned cars stood next to piles of garbage and bald tires. Old mattresses, busted refrigerators and stoves. Most homes looked worse than junkyards. Surprising that diseases like the bubonic plague weren't running rampant, since dead dogs and cats were discarded and left to rot on the side of the road.

Geneva's four-bedroom house crammed with six kids and two adults was nothing compared to the housing situation in Eagle River. Not uncommon for a dozen or more family members to live in a two-bedroom, one-bathroom house. Indians had lived together like that for thousands of years.

Although I had some Indian blood, that lifestyle was a foreign concept to me. My mother hadn't been raised that way.

After my Minneconjou Sioux grandmother, Caroline Longbow,

married my white grandfather, William Fairchild, he'd removed her from the reservation. Their only child, my mother, Sunny, cared little about her Indian heritage. She hadn't enrolled in the Minneconjou tribe and hadn't seen the point of enrolling her daughters. She'd taught us the Gunderson lineage was the only one that mattered.

Why hadn't that ever bothered me?

Several sprawling buildings housed the multitude of tribal offices. Most people employed on the reservation worked for the tribe, for the state, or for the Bureau of Indian Affairs. Others worked at the Indian Health Services Hospital. In addition to early childhood development programs, there were two colleges.

Yet few young kids who'd graduated with marketable skills ever found jobs on the reservation, since there was zero economic development. A small number of businesses survived, a couple of convenience marts, the fast-food joints, a grocery store. The funeral home. Luckily the tribe funded the community center and rec center, or neither would've lasted.

As I drove through town, it saddened me to see little had changed in twenty years. Same decrepit buildings. More cheap housing.

I passed several groups of kids, some as young as four and five, running around unattended. Many didn't wear shoes. Their clothes were tattered, their faces dirty, their hair matted and uncombed. I had to look away.

I'd seen some of the worst areas on the planet. Ghettos in big cities. Barrios in third-world countries. War-torn cities where death and destruction is a part of everyday life. This was somehow worse. Since we were the most prosperous nation on Earth, there was no excuse for such poverty and hopelessness. Shoving aside my morose thoughts, I pulled into Taco John's parking lot.

The lunch crowd had dwindled. Sue Anne worked the register. She didn't look at me as she asked, "Can I help you?"

I glanced at the menu. "I'd like a Taco Bravo, a large order of Potato Olés, a large Diet Coke, and an Apple Grande."

Sue Anne poked the buttons. "Would you like sour cream on the Taco Bravo?"

"Please. And on the Apple Grande."

"Is this order for here or to go?"

"To go."

"Your total comes to seven twenty-nine." The register spit out my ticket, and she grabbed a pen.

I handed her a twenty.

"Your name?" Sue Anne asked as she passed back my change.

Taco John's still asked for a first name on every order? I remembered in high school my friends spent way too much time thinking up kooky names. Mine was odd enough. I said, "Mercy," and waited for her reaction.

She finally looked at me. "Omigod. I'm sorry. I can't believe—"

"Sue Anne. Order!" the line cook shouted.

She turned away, dropping a napkin and a plastic cup of hot sauce in the paper bag on the counter. She slid my order under the metal tab and called out, "Virgil?"

An Indian man around sixty snatched the bag. He didn't look me in the eye as he shuffled out. Not a snub. Typical behavior for a Lakota man when faced with an unknown white woman.

But you aren't white.

Ignoring my racial identity crisis, I rested my shoulders against the back wall and waited for my order.

A large red wax cup appeared. Sue Anne bagged my food. "Mercy? Your order is ready."

The moment of truth.

"Can I get you anything else?"

I said softly, "Yes. I need to talk to you."

"I can't. I'm working."

"Please. This is important. It's about Levi. You name the place and I'll be there."

She squinted at the clock. "I'm off in thirty minutes. I'll meet you out back at the picnic table."

"Thank you."

Half an hour later Sue Anne slid across from me. I noticed she'd removed the ugly polyester hat and changed her clothes, yet she smelled of taco meat, fryer grease, and powdered sugar. She dumped out five tacos from a carryout bag. "I'm starving."

I purposely shifted my focus to the cars on the main drag.

Seemed like only a minute passed and she was crumpling spent wrappers.

Sue Anne sipped from a supersized cup. "I'm really sorry about Levi. He was . . . great."

"Thanks. I didn't see you at the funeral."

"I had to work."

Uncomfortable silence descended, broken by the hum of the air-conditioner compressors kicking on at the rear of the restaurant.

"Why do you wanna talk to me?"

"Because I'm trying to find out who killed my nephew."

"I don't know nothing."

"That's where I think you're wrong."

She finally looked at me.

"When was the last time you saw Levi?"

"The night before he . . . at the Custard Cupboard."

"Who was Levi with that night?"

"Me. Then Bucky showed up, and he and Levi got into a shouting match."

"About what?"

"Some stuff about Albert." Sue Anne slid the elastic band from her hair. "Levi was pissed when Moser stepped in and wouldn't let Bucky talk to him anymore. After them guys left, Levi quit talking to me and called for a ride home."

"Who'd he call?"

"Pretty sure it was his mom. Looked like her car anyway. That was the last time I seen him."

I knew Hope hadn't picked him up. So who had?

"Is that it?" she asked tightly.

"No. Tell me about the group."

"What group?"

"The Warrior Society. Albert was in it. But Levi wasn't. He wanted to be a part of it so bad." I watched her closely. "Were you in it?"

"Yeah."

"So what is this group, Sue Anne?"

She twisted the hair band around her index finger. "Nothing big. Started as a way to celebrate our heritage. We're all like fifth- and sixth-generation rez kids. Ain't none of us jocks. Or druggies. Or none of them crusading no-sex, no-alcohol religious freaks. We'd get together and talk about learning Lakota. We even built this sweat lodge in the grasslands and had an *inipi*, which was way cool. We did a couple of ceremonies."

"Who's 'we'?"

"Moser. Little Bear. Albert. Bucky Two Feathers. Randall Meeks. Lanae Mesteth. Me."

Lanae was a new name. "Axel Rouillard?"

"At first. Then Axel didn't want any part of it."

"Why not?"

"Moser and Little Bear decided we'd train to do the Seven Sacred Rites. Axel was a total dickhead and said we needed a Lakota holy man to teach us. When Moser and Little Bear found someone, Axel said a bunch of nasty shit about them being stupid puppets because it was being done wrong."

"Who was the leader helping with the rituals?"

She shook her head.

I almost snapped, "Tell me." Instead, I switched tactics. "If I paid you, would it convince you to help me?"

"It ain't about money."

"Then what is it about? Honor? Levi told me how much he wanted to be in this group, and the next thing I know, he's dead. Please, Sue Anne, I need some answers."

She gnawed on her straw, avoiding my gaze as she debated. Finally, she sighed. "I'll tell you this much. It started out one leader, then another guy started coming around. The leader told us we had to pass a bunch of tests to prove our worthiness before we could do the actual rituals."

"What kind of tests?"

"Mental. Spiritual. Physical. Endurance."

"Endurance for what?"

"For pain."

It was pointless to berate her or judge her. I'd blindly followed military orders my whole life, even to the point of excruciating pain. "And did these tests hurt?"

"The first couple weren't so bad. Then we started the harder ones, like the Warrior's Challenge." She squirmed. "The leaders passed around fire water to help us with the pain so I was sorta drunk when it was my turn."

"What do you remember?"

Her eyes lost focus. "Facing a pole in the center of a sacred circle with my hands tied above my head. Then my back was whipped with a willow branch while the other warrior candidates watched."

I must've made a noise; her answering look was defiant.

"Everyone participated. It was a spiritual cleansing. My Indian blood mixed with my tears on sacred ground as I cried a lament to the Great Spirit. Then the leader cut me from the pole and gave me the willow branch as a symbol of my bravery. Afterward we sat in a circle, chanting, drumming, and finishing the ritual by smoking the peace pipe."

My stomach roiled. Bet there was wacky tobaccy in that peace pipe. Bet they passed the bottle around again.

"And before you ask, I used the whip on my friends. The whipping may sound cruel, but we thought it was a celebrated part of our heritage. Toughening us up to honor our warrior ancestors."

"How else were they toughening you up?"

"By cutting us."

Holy shit.

Sue Anne fell silent. When she finally spoke, I strained to hear her muted voice. "We believed the cutting prepared us for the piercing rituals of the Sun Dance."

A pickup load of young kids drove by. Sue Anne ducked her head from view. "Look. I said enough. I gotta go."

"No. Please stay. Please finish. I'm not judging you. I'm just trying to understand."

Angrily, she said, "I don't know how any of this will help you. Levi didn't even know what we were doing. Moser and Little Eagle were using him, making him do things, then laughing behind his back, knowing they'd *never* let him in. After the sick shit that happened with the last so-called ritual, I don't know why he or anyone would want to join such a fucked-up group anyway. I realized they was even using me. I was so stupid—" She made a move to leave.

My hand circled her wrist before she could run. "What happened?"

Sue Anne twisted out of my grip. "Of the Seven Sacred Rites, the *Ishna Ta Awi Cha Lowan* is supposed to be about purifying a girl after she gets her first period. It's meant to be a time where her mother and sisters and aunts prepare her for womanhood. But these advisers, and the guys, they fucking *twisted* it. . . ."

Dread expanded in my chest. "Into what?"

"Into a gang rape. They called it a 'mating ritual.' During the spring equinox they tied Lanae up and took turns raping her. I wasn't there, but Lanae came to me and told me afterward." She swallowed. "That's when I knew Axel was right and the stuff these 'leaders' were making us do was bullshit. There ain't nothing like that in our Lakota traditions."

"But you stuck it out up until that point?"

"Yeah. We were so . . . *crazy* for a group to call our own, to belong to something that was *ours*, that we did anything they told us to. Stupid, huh? Lanae went to live with her sister in North Dakota. Most of them guys think she's just spending the summer there, but I know the truth. She's never coming back here."

"Couldn't you tell an adult or a tribal elder what happened?"

"Yeah, right."

"Someone has to know about it. Especially since these leaders are adults. Not only is it morally wrong, it is against the law."

Sue Anne laughed. "Everyone looks the other way. Or they're part of the ceremony stuff. Or they're making up their own ceremonies to rip off stupid white tourists for money. Or they like screwing young girls. Plenty of that shit around here."

Briefly, I thought of Rollie and his young paramour, Verline. I pressed her for more answers. "Were you the only girl after Lanae left?"

"Yes. That's when I knew I wanted out because I'd be next. I knew that's the only reason they ever invited me was to rape me." She shook her head violently. "I stopped going to the meetings and started hanging out with Molly. But I didn't tell her all of it. I just wanted to be normal. I just wanted out."

"Who else wanted out? Albert?"

No response.

"Could a member of the group have killed Albert because he tried to get out? And Levi was helping him?"

She fixed her gaze on the mangled straw in her cup.

"Mercy?" A male voice called out behind me.

I turned around.

Theo was behind the wheel of an old white Honda Accord in the drive-through lane. He poked his head out the window. "I thought that was you. What're you doing here?"

"Having lunch. Why are you here?" Why wasn't he taking care of Hope, like she'd told me? Damn him. Was she sitting in the trailer alone?

"Just finished a staff meeting and needed a bite to eat." He focused his dumb-ass smile on Sue Anne. "I haven't seen you in a while. You coming to class tonight?"

"Umm. No. Sorry. I'm working a split shift."

He was teaching class tonight? Then who was staying with my sister?

"You know this is a graded class, Sue Anne. So if you want the credit to count toward graduation, you have to pass—"

"Yeah, yeah, I get it. I know, all right?"

"Good."

The pickup ahead of him inched up. "Catch you both later." His engine made a clicking rattle as he shot forward and yelled his order into the speaker.

When I looked back, Sue Anne had made it halfway across the parking lot. I raced to catch up with her. "You need a ride so we can finish what we were talking about?"

"No. Forget it. Forget everything. I said too much."

"Sue Anne—"

"Go away. Levi is dead. I'm sorry. But I didn't have nothing to do with it. I-I just . . . just leave me alone." She shouldered her backpack and walked along, head down.

As a last-ditch effort I yelled, "At least think about what I said. Tell someone what happened. Someone will believe you."

She didn't respond.

I felt pushy and mean as I watched her disappear into the distance like a heat mirage.

On a whim I decided to stop at the grocery store for a cup of *wojopi*—a starchy pudding made from roots, nuts, and berries.

Something sweet might counteract the bitterness left by my conversation with Sue Anne.

A flash of sunlight on metal drew my attention to the Tribal Police Department across the street. Weird. An Eagle River County patrol car was parked out front next to a beige Taurus. Before I theorized it couldn't possibly be Sheriff Dawson's vehicle, he strode out the door.

Dammit. Ours was a small community, but this was ridiculous. Too bad my window wasn't rolled down; I would've dived through it *Dukes of Hazzard*–style to avoid Dawson. But as the only luck I had was bad, Dawson spotted me right away.

If I sped off now, I'd look guilty as hell.

Well, aren't you?

No.

He moseyed over in a way that shouldn't have been sexy and commanding but was. I had no choice but to wait for him. And watch him. And grind my teeth.

"Mercy."

"Hey, Sheriff. How's it hanging?"

"What are you doing here?"

My inner vamp wanted to growl, *"None of your goddamn business, Copper."* Instead, I said sweetly, "Running errands for Sophie."

He frowned at the grocery bag clutched to my chest. "Seems out of your way."

"What are *you* doing in Eagle River?"

"County business."

"Seems out of your jurisdiction."

Dawson floated a deliberate *you're-a-smart-ass* pause.

Perfect time to take my leave before I said something I'd regret. It was downright mortifying that I acted like a hormonal thirteen-year-old girl around Dawson: nice one second, nasty the next. The hell of it was, he reacted just about the same way to me. "I'll let you get back to it. See ya."

His hand curled on my shoulder to keep me from climbing in my truck. I stared into his mirrored shades. "What are you really doing here?"

"I already told you."

"Are you messing in my investigation?"

I blinked innocently. "What investigation?"

Dawson laughed. "Right. Don't play dumb."

"I'm not. As far as I know, you've done no investigating, which means you've got no investigation. If you'll excuse me."

He blocked me in. "If I find out you were nosing around, asking questions, or harassing people I have interviewed, or want to interview for any of these active cases, especially your nephew's, I will take action."

"Last time I checked, this was still a free country and I can go wherever the hell I want or talk to anyone I please." I paused. "Especially now that I'm working for Rollie Rondeaux."

"You're joking."

Ooh. That look of surprise was totally worth any favor I owed Rollie. "Nope. Call and ask him."

"Why in the hell would you . . ." Dawson thrust his hand through his hair. "Because he's a PI."

"Yep. And because of confidentiality laws, I'm not allowed to share details about why I'm nosing around. Sorry."

"Jesus. Added to what I'm already dealing with . . . talk about a fucking nightmare."

"Welcome to my world."

He retreated and allowed me to scramble into my truck. I'd barely started it when he tapped on the window.

I rolled it down. "What now?"

"How is Hope?"

His genuine concern surprised me. But the snarly girl inside me deemed it too little, too late. I punched the clutch and rammed the stick into reverse. "She'd be doing a helluva lot better if you caught the person who killed her son." I hit the gas and peeled out without looking back.

I expected to see red and blue lights flashing in my rearview at some point on the drive home. But the only thing I saw in my rearview mirror were miles and miles of deserted blacktop.

Darkness had fallen by the time I'd donned my workout clothes. Didn't matter. I needed to sweat and push my physical endurance to the absolute limit.

I needed to run.

Away?

Maybe.

That's what John-John had accused me of when he'd called. As I'd stretched my muscles, I listened to him list my recent risky behavior. When he couldn't convince me not to go for a run, by being his nice and reasonable self, he yelled until I tired of it and hung up on him.

Jake had finished the last of the chores and waved good-bye from his truck, Shoonga riding shotgun, as I laced up my running shoes.

Hope had finally gone home. She'd hung around with Sophie all day. I didn't blame her for not wanting to face her house without Levi in it. I'd even asked if she'd rather spend the night here. She hedged, knowing Theo wouldn't be welcomed at the family homestead as easily as he was at her place.

I didn't mention seeing Theo in Eagle River. Be interesting to see if he'd mention it himself. Another disconcerting thing I noticed: Hope hadn't brought up Levi's name all day. Maybe she was sick of his murder being the sole topic of conversation. I'd let it slide, but I recognized the behavior pattern. It was a trait Hope and I shared: denial.

My cardio workout had suffered the last few days. Consequently, my lungs burned. My hamstrings were tight as rubber bands. My quads screamed. My knees ached. My Achilles tendons were ready to snap. I kept plugging along. I knew it would pass.

And it did. I hit my stride, and I could think about things other than how badly my body hurt.

As my shoes pounded the gravel, I replayed my conversation with Sue Anne. Talking to her hadn't answered my basic question: Were any of the group members capable of killing Levi? The whippings, the mutilation, and the gang rape would lead me to believe, yes, any one of those kids was qualified.

But Sue Anne's comment about someone picking Levi up the night before his murder bugged me. He wouldn't climb into a car with Moser or Little Bear. Maybe at gunpoint. I couldn't see Levi inviting any of them out to his trailer either. But Levi had walked to the bluff with someone.

Who?

Right after I'd returned home from the rez, I had unearthed a small spiral notebook from the kitchen junk drawer and jotted down what Sue Anne told me. For the first time since I'd spoken to Estelle, I had felt I might have a knack for investigating. It had filled me with a strange sense of kinship with my father.

I wiped the sweat from my face with the bottom of my shirt. Despite the temperate air, I was roasting. My legs were noodles. I glanced at my watch. Forty-five minutes. Almost done.

Headlights swept behind me, highlighting the purple clover. I jogged to the side of the road. The row of pine trees marking the turnoff to the ranch was finally within view. I couldn't wait to stand under a cool shower. And treat myself to a couple of shots of whiskey.

The vehicle's lights blinded me after I'd been out in the dark. The truck whooshed past, spitting gravel, leaving dust thick as fog. I coughed and flapped my hand to clear it.

At twenty feet the truck's brakes locked up. The white reverse lights flashed. The vehicle backed up.

Maybe it was someone I knew.

The truck whipped a U-turn, gunned the engine, and headed straight for me.

Then again maybe it wasn't.

I turned and ran.

The truck followed, gaining speed.

I cut to the left for the ditch.

Bump bump bump reverberated as the truck skidded off the gravel into the grass.

Shit. When I could practically feel the heat from the engine burning the back of my calves, I launched myself sideways and sailed over the barbed-wire fence like a high jumper on amphetamines.

I landed hard on my left side. I scrambled to my feet and sprinted. When I didn't see the headlights behind me, I chanced a look over my shoulder.

The truck plowed over a fence post.

Adrenaline crashed through me as I dropped behind a decent-sized rock.

The vehicle swerved out of the ditch, the back end fishtailing. The motor revved, and it disappeared in a dusty haze.

I waited for that flash of reverse lights to appear again. I was half afraid the driver was screwing with me. How long before the truck stopped, turned around, and came back?

When sufficient time passed and I didn't see headlights, or hear a motor running, I stood. And promptly fell on my ass. I'd twisted my ankle. I felt searing pain, but luckily it was sprained, not broken.

I considered my options. Not good to loll in the field where we housed the bulls. I'd rather take my chances with one three-quarter-ton truck than four one-ton pissed-off bulls. Since I'd landed only about fifteen feet away from the road, my best bet was to follow it back to the house.

I hobbled to the break in the fence line and did a three-limbed crawl through the ditch. The short walk was excruciating. I winced whenever I put pressure on my left foot.

Who had tried to run me over? A couple of punks screwing with me because I was dumb enough to be out on the road alone at night?

I made it to the mailbox. While I took a breather, a vehicle turned onto the gravel road, coming the opposite direction from the death squad. I froze. Listened. Even from a distance the engine didn't sound the same. Then again, fear distorts things. I squinted. Couldn't tell if the headlight pattern was familiar. One thing was for sure: this truck wasn't going nearly as fast as the one that'd chased me.

In fact, it slowed about twenty feet from the turnoff to the house. When I tried to hide behind the post holding the mailbox, I lost my balance and fell right into the middle of the road.

My life flashed before my eyes. Just my luck. I'd survived combat situations in hell only to be run down by a redneck in a pickup a hundred yards from my front porch.

I felt the absurd urge to giggle.

Brakes locked up and gravel sprayed everywhere.

A door slammed. Footsteps pounded until they were right next to my head. I heard, "Jesus Christ, Mercy. What the hell are you doing laying in the middle of the road?"

I looked up.

Dawson.

That bitch fate has a cruel sense of humor.

He knelt down. His gaze swept over me. "What happened?"

"Hit-and-run."

"Where's your truck?"

"Wasn't hit-and-run with the truck. Someone tried to hit *me* with their truck when I was running, and then they took off."

"Where are you hurt?"

Everywhere. "Mostly my left ankle."

"Can you walk?"

"Barely."

"Hang on. I'll help you up."

He wrapped his hands around my biceps and lifted me. Once I was upright, I collapsed into him.

I hissed from the pain and humiliation. "Shit. Sorry. Give me a minute." I tried to squirm away, but he wouldn't let me.

"Stay still. Might be best if I carried you."

"No."

"It's not that far to my truck."

"No."

"Dammit, Mercy, quit being so stubborn."

I inhaled a deep breath. Let it out. He was being helpful for a change and I . . . wasn't. "Fine," I said through clenched teeth.

"Hold tight." He muttered something else, then slid one arm behind my knees and the other across my back. One second I was airborne against a warm, hard body; the next I was nestled in a squishy leather seat.

We putted down the driveway. Without a word, he came around to the passenger's side, picked me up, and carried me inside the house. In the living room he deposited me on the couch.

"Do I need to call an ambulance?"

"No."

"Then I want to see how bad you're hurt. Where's the light switch?"

"Over by the doorway, halfway down the wall on the left side." The fixture buzzed and fluorescent light glowed from the ceiling.

Dawson crouched beside me and propped my left foot on an embroidered pillow. "Can you move it?"

"Yeah." I gritted my teeth and tried to twirl my ankle. Sharp pain shot up my shin. "Shit!"

"We need to get this shoe off."

I struggled to sit up. My normally pliant body was strung so tight I couldn't even reach my shoelaces.

"Here. Let me do it."

I held my breath as he loosened the laces, figuring he'd rip the shoe off like an old Band-Aid. But Dawson gently eased the shoe off and peeled away my sock.

He prodded the swollen skin around my anklebone. "You think it's broken?"

"No. I broke the right one a couple of years back, and it doesn't feel like that. Just a sprain."

"A bad one." He slowly pressed his fingers in a straight line up my shin, watching my face. "Does any of this hurt?"

"A little."

He stopped at my knee. Frowned at the scratches and scrapes on my left leg from my tumble in the pasture. Good thing the right side of my body was against the couch so he couldn't see the shrapnel wounds on my right thigh. "Where else are you hurt?"

"Nowhere. That's the worst of it."

Dawson looked like he didn't believe me.

I slumped back into the cushions. "Okay. My left shoulder took the brunt of my fall, and I smacked my head into a rock. Happy now?"

"No. Why would seeing you beat to crap make me happy?"

You tell me. For once I kept a smart comment to myself.

A heavy sigh. His. Not mine.

"You gonna let me look at it or not?"

"Look at what?"

He grinned.

Why did my stomach do a little flip at the sight of his devilish smile? Hell, maybe I *had* cracked my skull harder than I realized.

"Come on, Mercy. Let me look at the spot where your head hurt that poor defenseless rock."

"Asshole."

His grin widened.

I closed my eyes and dropped my chin to my chest so he could reach my neck.

Warm, dry fingers prodded the bump behind my ear. I sucked in a harsh breath when he pushed too hard.

"Sorry. Better get some ice on that."

He rattled around in the kitchen. My head began to pound in time with the throbbing in my ankle.

"Here you go."

I opened my eyes. He held out a Ziploc bag filled with ice and a kitchen towel. I put it behind my head. "Thanks."

"Another one for your ankle." He positioned the plastic on top of my foot, tucking it around the swollen area like a pro. Then he perched next to me on the couch. Close to me.

"Thanks, Dawson."

"You're welcome. I just wish I'd gotten here sooner."

Why hadn't I thought to ask why he'd been driving past my house? At nine o'clock at night? It seemed . . . coincidental. "There a reason you were coming out here?"

"Two reasons actually." He thrust a hand through his hair. "First, to apologize for being a jerk this afternoon. I was having a bad day and shouldn't have taken it out on you. But, God, I hate dealing with the tribal cops."

My dad complained about the same thing. Ditto for the FBI and U.S. Marshals.

"They called me about a report I'd filed a month ago. They couldn't fax me the information because their fax machine was broken. I get there and the officer who contacted me had a family emergency and wasn't around. The other cops didn't know what was going on and didn't care. So, I sat there for two hours, twiddling my thumbs, while the receptionist sifted through file folders, only to hand me the same paperwork they'd sent me after the incident occurred. A month ago. Nothing new. Story of my life." Dawson readjusted my ice pack. "Sorry."

"Apology accepted. I wasn't exactly Mary-fucking-sunshine today either."

"We're a pair, huh?" He relaxed a bit. "And before you turn

back into that pit bull, my trip to Eagle River had nothing to do with Levi's or Albert's case."

"Fair enough. What's the second reason you stopped by?"

Dawson sighed. "It'll sound lame."

"Try me."

"I had a bad feeling. A real bad feeling. With all that's happened around here, I thought I'd drive by to see if everything was okay."

He didn't appear to be lying. In fact, Dawson looked embarrassed. For once, I cut him some slack. "You aren't the only one who had a bad feeling. John-John called me right before I left the house and yelled about me taking unnecessary chances."

I heard the ice cubes melting in the sudden silence.

"And yet you still went for a run in the dark by yourself?" Dawson asked.

"I run most every night by myself."

His gaze turned shrewd. "Who knows you do this?"

"Anyone who hangs around the ranch on a regular basis."

"And anybody in the bar listening to John-John's very loud phone conversation with you tonight."

"Which leaves half the criminals in the county," I said irritably. "What are you getting at, Dawson?"

"Somebody knew you were on that road tonight and came after you."

"Why?"

"You tell me."

"So you don't believe this was an accident?"

Dawson scowled. "No. Maybe once your head is clear and we fill out the incident report, something will click."

My eyes went big as pie plates. "You're filing a report?"

"Standard procedure. Don't act so surprised."

I was. Didn't make sense. He'd drag his feet on tracking down a murderer, but he'd waste time trying to find out who'd played a game of chicken with me? A smart retort danced on my tongue, and I bit it back.

"I'll swing by tomorrow morning with the paperwork. You look exhausted." He casually swept a hank of hair that'd escaped from my ponytail. Rather than flinch at his touch, I had the strangest urge to purr and demand more.

"Anything you need before I go?"

"Would you grab the prescription bottle of Percocet from my bathroom upstairs?"

"Be right back."

I'd about dozed off when I felt the warm weight of his hand on my shoulder. "Mercy?"

My eyes opened.

"Here are your pills and a bottle of water."

I popped two and swallowed. Nestling my head back in the pillow, I said, "Thanks, Dawson. Would you shut the light off on your way out?"

"Even I can take a hint that broad." He laughed softly. "Night. Sweet dreams."

THIRTEEN

The constant *brrrr-rat-a-tat-tat* of machine-gun fire echoed in the distance. A series of angry shouts dragged my attention from the window across the street. I peered around the corner, careful not to give away my position. A man climbed out of a baby blue Cadillac and started up the steps of the mosque just as happy kids streamed out the front door.

My heart thumped a warning too late. The car and the man exploded simultaneously. I couldn't even scream when hunks of metal, small chunks of flesh, and blood rained down on me.

I jumped and was instantly awake. Disoriented by the darkness and the nightmare, my eyes frantically searched for something familiar. When my gaze caught the whir of the ceiling fan blades, I realized I was on the couch in the living room. My ankle throbbed, reminding me of the incident from the previous night.

I looked at my foot propped on the pillow. The ice pack on my ankle had melted. The one beneath my head felt like a water balloon. A leaky balloon.

I yelled, "Sophie?"

No answer.

Why hadn't I heard her clattering around in the kitchen? I squinted at the grandfather clock. Six. That explained it. Sophie didn't get here until after eight . . . unless she decided to come early. Or later. I didn't make her punch a time clock.

I sat up and bent forward to check my ankle. The swelling was down. No bruising. I flexed and pointed. Still sore. It'd probably be all right if I didn't put too much pressure on it. I swung both feet to the floor and put my weight on the arm of the couch so I could stand. I half limped/half hopped to the kitchen.

I glanced out the window over the sink. Didn't see Jake's truck. He was always here at the crack of dawn. I didn't make him punch a time clock either. I hobbled to the door. Twisted the handle and the lock popped. I never locked the door. Dawson? Concerned for my safety last night? How . . . sweet.

I pushed on the screen door. It wouldn't open all the way. What the hell? Did nothing in this place stay in one piece? Just another damn thing I'd have to fix. I pushed again. The bottom corner kept hitting something. I stuck my head out the top of the door, looked down, and froze.

Couldn't be.

I blinked. My vision swam. I slammed my eyes shut and chanted: *please be a dream, please be a dream, please be a dream.* Slowly I peeled my lids open.

Still there.

I couldn't breathe. I couldn't make my mouth move. I couldn't work up enough spit to even swallow. My eyes kept straying to the horrific scene on my porch.

Black goo ran in a river down the steps. A large puddle had crusted over, looking stark against the white boards on the porch.

Not a nameless black substance. Blood.

Blood from the dead person blocking the door.

I curled my hands around the screen door until metal cut into my palms. The pain meant it was real. This wasn't another bad dream.

Heartsick, I choked back the acid crawling up my throat and scrambled for the kitchen phone. Dialed 911. After I explained the situation to dispatch, I added, "Make sure you call Dawson and tell him I've got another body at my place."

Only after I hung up did I allow myself to fall apart.

I loaded the cordless in my purse, along with my cell phone. In my dad's office I found my grandfather Deke's old oak cane. Leaning on it kept the pressure off my bum ankle. I shuffled down the handicapped ramp.

Outside, I dropped my backside onto the bumper of the truck. Unfortunately, I had an unobstructed view of Sue Anne.

I could've closed my eyes. Or gazed at the pearly morning sky. Or focused on the red geraniums and pink petunias in the flower boxes. But I forced myself to look. To see what had been done to her.

She'd been placed on her left side with her knees drawn up, facing the steps. Her slender arms were bound behind her back with nylon rope. Blood coated her neck. Her teeth, clamped over a blue bandana serving as a gag, stuck out from beneath her swollen lips, giving her a feral look. Her long hair had been pulled away from her face and tied with a white bow, which matched the white gown she wore. The front of the dress, at least the part I could see, was discolored reddish brown.

Somehow I'd managed to keep myself somewhat together until my purposefully detached gaze landed on her bare feet. Her toenails were unpainted and unadorned except for a silver toe ring on the second toe of her right foot. A rainbow-colored braided friendship anklet was tied around her left ankle. Just like the bracelets Levi and I had made years ago.

I lost it again. What a waste. What an absolute fucking waste. I dropped my head to my knees and cried.

Even as I sobbed for Sue Anne, a cold fear invaded my soul. Had I played a part in getting her killed by forcing her to talk to me? How did I live with that? How could I possibly justify snooping around when it led to more deaths?

I kill for a living. There's no PC way to say it. I've never tried to pretend I was an assassin with a heart of gold. I can't afford to think of anything but the job when I'm on the job. Study intel, get in position, pull the trigger, get out. Repeat as necessary. Simple.

Do I have sleepless nights? Yes. Do I have regrets? Some. Not as many as I should. I'd ended more lives than what's listed in my kill book. I hate having to document my assignments. Yes, it's important to keep track of all the technical stuff, wind velocity, range ratios, and humidity. Build a better soldier by being better prepared. But to list names? Dates? Times? And methodology? That requirement bordered on psychotic bragging.

Terrorists deserved to die. Sue Anne didn't. Some things really are black-and-white in my world.

The sirens snapped me out of the black hole I'd sunk into.

Baby-faced Deputy Jazinski crossed the yard and stood beside me. Nervous. Fidgety. Could've been his usual behavior since I didn't know him. I'd heard Dawson hired Jazinski right before my father's death with Dad's blessing. Still, the kid gave me a weird vibe.

"Has anybody been through that door besides you, Miz Gunderson?"

"No. And I didn't come out that door; I came out through the front."

He asked me a bunch of questions. My response was nonsensical at best, curt at worst. By the time he'd finished, the second patrol car and ambulance arrived. As had Jake. At least he'd retained a clear head. Not only had he immediately tied up Shoonga behind the barn, he called Sophie to delay her coming to work. My brain was scrambled.

Photos were snapped. Distances measured. I would've stayed frozen in shock in that same spot until they loaded her body, but Jake forced me to the picnic table by the gazebo. He stayed with me, lending me his unspoken support until Dawson loped over.

Dawson crouched down and poked my ankle. "Looks better. How's your head?"

"Fine."

"Did you sleep?"

"Yeah. Apparently I slept through someone dropping a dead girl on my doorstep." I flinched. Dammit. I hadn't meant to sound so callous.

He straightened and rubbed the back of his neck.

I recognized it as a sign of his agitation. "What?"

"I don't know how to tell you this."

"Tell me what?"

No answer.

It hit me. "Jesus. Am I a *suspect*?"

"No."

"Then what?" When he peered at me, I realized he wasn't wearing his mirrored shades.

"Sue Anne wasn't dead when she was dropped there. I would guess she was unconscious. But whoever killed her slit her throat right on your porch."

I gaped at him. No wonder there'd been so much blood. "You're serious? She bled to death here?"

"Unfortunately, yes."

I could scarcely find my voice. "How long had she been there?"

Dawson's steely eyes seemed to soften. "You couldn't have saved her, Mercy. The damage was too severe."

"But, maybe—"

"No maybes. She was nearly decapitated. There was nothing you could've done."

This had to be another nightmare. Please. Let this be another bad goddamn dream. I squeezed my eyes shut. Maybe when I opened them, I'd see the lace doilies decorating my dresser. At this point I'd take olive green canvas tent walls.

"Look, I feel guilty as hell, too. If I had stayed to keep an eye on you last night, maybe I would've heard something. . . ."

My eyes flew open. "Did you see anything on your way home?"

"No."

"Did you tell Jazinski you were here?"

"Yeah."

"Great. So he thinks you and I are knocking boots." Which meant within the hour everyone else in the county would hear the story. Dawson and me screwing like rabbits, while some psycho murderer took a hacksaw to an innocent teenage girl on my front porch.

"Wrong. If you and I were knocking boots, Mercy, I would've been here all night, not just until ten o'clock."

The shout from the front of the house didn't make a dent in the unwieldy silence between us.

He sighed. "Besides, Jazinski needed to know someone tried to make you a hood ornament last night. The paperwork is in my car. You feel up to answering some more questions?"

"No. Not now."

"I understand."

I wish he would've been a jerk and demanded I take the time now. It'd be easier to handle my anger than my sorrow. "Look,

I don't want to seem . . . cold and self-centered, but is there a chance I can get back into my house?"

"Sure. Soon as they're done cataloguing the scene."

I felt the need to explain. "I have to take a shower. Everything happened so fast this morning. I feel . . ." *Guilty. Grimy. Worn out*. I cleared my throat. "I still have dirt and grass stains all over from last night. I need to clean up."

Even if I remained under the hot spray for hours, and scrubbed with lye soap until my skin bled, my soul would still feel dirty. How would I ever get clean?

Clean. I thought of Sue Anne's bloodstains on the porch. Had those ugly black spots seeped into the wood? I couldn't expect Sophie to scrub them off, and I sure as hell couldn't do it.

"Hey." Dawson hunkered down until he was right in my face. "After we've released the scene, why don't you let Kiki's sister Vivi take care of cleaning up? She does this sort of thing. I can call her."

Spooky, how he'd known what I was thinking. "Okay."

He tucked a strand of hair behind my ear. For a moment his sweet touch lingered on my cheek and I let myself be comforted by the fact he wanted to offer me solace.

"Sheriff?" Jazinski shouted. "Can I see you for a sec?"

"Be right there." His hand dropped. He stood and slipped on his sunglasses before he jogged around the corner.

A few minutes later Kiki came by. "Sheriff said you can go inside now. I called Vivi. She's on her way."

"Thanks, Kiki. I don't mind telling you I'm pretty sick of seeing you."

She smiled sadly. "I hear that a lot. You need help getting upstairs?"

"I'll manage." Once I was inside, rather than use the cane, I crawled upstairs on my hands and knees straight into the bathroom and dry heaved. Repeatedly. No wonder. I couldn't remember the last time I'd eaten anything.

The shower helped my aches and pains, but not the images in my brain. Naked, I studied my limited wardrobe choices. Since I hadn't done laundry for a week, I pulled on a denim skirt and buttoned a white sleeveless blouse over a navy blue camisole.

Sophie was sitting at the table snapping green beans when I hobbled downstairs. She looked as surprised to see me as I was to see her. Her wrinkled face looked troubled and sad. "You okay, *takoja?*"

Her calling me grandchild almost made me lose my hard-won emotional control again. "No. Not really."

She nodded. "Didn't think so. Maybe this is the last of it. Bad things always come in threes."

"But counting my father's death, finding Sue Anne would make this number four, not three."

Her gnarled hands stilled.

"You think there's more to come, don't you?"

"I know you don't believe in the woo-woo stuff, but—"

"You're wrong. I've seen and heard too much to chalk it up to coincidence." I paused. "John-John had a vision about me."

"I know."

"You do? Did he tell you about it?"

"No. The important thing is he told you."

Rarely did Sophie act like the wise old Lakota woman, so when she did, I paid attention.

Snap snap snap. The beans were tossed in the ceramic bowl.

She also had a flair for the dramatic.

Finally she asked, "How many of what he seen has come to pass?"

I thought back to John-John's words. Red sky, red ground, red water. My mind flashed to the day I'd found Levi and how his blood stained the ground. "As far as I can decipher? Just one."

She shook her head. Evidently she didn't have any additional wise words to add.

I snatched a can of Coke from the fridge and drained it in three long swallows. I held back a burp and realized Sophie had been staring at me. "What?"

"You look nice. I like to see you dressing like a girl, hey."

I scowled. "Don't get used to it. I'm out of clean clothes."

Snap snap snap. "You know, you are paying me to do stuff like that. No shame in needing help now and again, Mercy. You want me to run a coupla loads today when you're at the doctor's office?"

"Sure, thanks. What time is Hope's appointment?"

"Hope ain't going to the doctor. You are."

My eyes narrowed. "Did Dawson put you up to this? I'm fine. It's just a mild sprain."

"Don't have nothing to do with your ankle. Your appointment is at the VA at two o'clock."

"What?"

"That nurse kept calling, so I just had her make an appointment." She frowned. "I know I told you about it last week."

She probably had. With all that'd happened I'd blocked it out. "Well, I can't go. Someone needs to stay with Hope."

"I am here."

"Dawson has paperwork for me to fill out. I don't know how long it'll take."

"He's gone. Said he'll be in touch with you."

I opened my mouth, but Sophie shook her finger at my pitiful attempt at another excuse.

"I ain't gonna pry. I don't know why you're so scared to hear what them docs are gonna say. It'd be better to know what you're facing instead of trying to hide from it, eh?"

Even I couldn't argue with that.

I hate hospitals. No one but the army knew how much time I'd spent in various hospitals around the world.

The VA hospital was typical for a government facility. About thirty years past its prime. One half of the main building housed long-term patients; the other half short-timers. Checkups and nonemergency appointments were held in the various outbuildings.

The single-lane road curved through the compound. Clusters of oak trees and lilac bushes blocked the employee's quarters from view. Beds of flowers were a beautiful flare of color among the drab buildings.

I parked in the lot of Building C. Alongside the wide stone steps was a handicapped ramp. A well-used ramp. Seeing it snapped me out of feeling sorry for myself about my injuries. I'd been damn lucky. I knew several soldiers who hadn't been.

The round-faced girl at the check-in desk—she looked all of fifteen—smiled at me. "Can I help you?"

"Yes. I have an appointment at fourteen hundred."

"Name?"

"Gunderson."

She stared at the computer screen as her fingers flew over the keyboard. "I don't need any additional paperwork filled out today, Sergeant Major. You can have a seat."

"Thanks."

The waiting room wasn't as full as I'd feared. The VA was notorious for overscheduling appointments. Puke-yellow plastic chairs were aligned between end tables strewn with magazines. A TV (no big flatscreen to entertain the vets) was bolted in the darkest corner. CNN blared. Several guys in wheelchairs watched the coverage detailing yet another suicide car bomber in Mosul. I shuddered, thinking of my early-morning flashback.

Once again I was the only woman in the room. I was used to the stares and the hostility from older vets who believed a woman had no place in the service, which was worse than getting hit on by new recruits who weren't intimidated by a woman in uniform.

Names were called. None of them mine. I'd cracked another copy of *Reader's Digest* and skimmed Humor in Uniform when a wheelchair rolled up.

A bearded guy pointed to the magazines on the chair beside me. "Done with those?"

"Yeah. Have at them."

"So can you tell me why everyone on the planet is interested in Brad Pitt and Angelina Jolie? Because I sure don't understand the fascination."

He smiled and I realized he was an attractive guy, in a Kurt Cobain/'90s grunge metal kind of way.

"Probably because sex sells," he said, answering his own question. "Plus, it's easier to stomach trivial stuff than the truth of what's going on over there."

"True."

"This is the first time I've seen you here." He groaned and hung his head. "Jeez. That probably sounded like some lame pickup line. Moving on. Which branch owns your soul?"

"Army. You?"

"Marines. I assume you're retired?"

"No. I'm active."

"And you're here?"

"My dad died recently, so I'm home on leave."

"Oh, man, that bites. I'm sorry. My folks are both gone."

Neither of us said anything.

He smiled sheepishly. "Well, that was another conversation killer."

"You do have a knack."

"Let's start over." He held out his hand. "Maxwell."

I clasped it and we shook. "Gunny." My military nickname popped out automatically.

"Name or designation?"

"Both."

He whistled. "A hot chick that can shoot. Be still my heart."

At any other time his flirtatious comment would've made me grin, but today I couldn't shake off the impact of my ghastly morning discovery. The other men were scowling at us, not because we were being too loud, but because we had the audacity to strike up a normal conversation. No one was normal here. For some it was a point of pride, for others a mark of shame.

War redefines normalcy for those of us in the service. Even the most gregarious soldiers can pull back into themselves after recurring combat situations and long-term deployments. Some never recover. Sadly, all these guys giving us the stink eye appeared to be alone. Had they isolated themselves on purpose? Was it easier to deal with horrific memories and life-altering injuries when you didn't have to explain yourself and your unpredictable moods to people who could never understand it unless they'd lived it?

One guy kept glaring at me. Rather than offer him a friendly smile, I returned his glare until he spun around and gave me his hump back.

Hah. Take that. The guy was too damn young to be acting like a bitter old coot.

That could be you if you keep pushing away everyone who cares about you.

Care isn't the same as need, my inner loner argued. Hope needs me now, but does she care about me for the long run?

Sophie's care felt . . . forced at times and based on Hope's needs, not mine. Jake needed me because of the ranch.

Sobering to think the only person who really needed me was Levi and he was dead.

The nurse called a name—Maxwell's apparently—and he rolled away with a jaunty salute.

I took the opportunity to look around at the other vets, hoping a dose of self–tough love would wake my hermit ass up, when I noticed an Indian man in a wheelchair at the back of the room.

Sunglasses covered his eyes beneath the brim of a battered ball cap, the front emblazoned with the SCREAMING EAGLES emblem of Eagle River High School. I squinted at him. He'd been a big man at one time, wide shoulders, long, thick neck, large head, but with both his legs gone above his knees it was hard to gauge how tall he used to stand. My eyes kept flicking toward him, not because of his disability. Something about him looked familiar, yet I couldn't put my finger on it. Despite my mother's voice reminding me it wasn't polite to stare, I did it anyway.

The door swung open. A nurse approached him and spoke loudly. "Blacktower?"

"I'm blind, not deaf, so you don't gotta shout."

The nurse blushed. "Sorry. The doctor sent me out to tell you he's running behind."

He didn't bother to look up when he grunted.

Blacktower. Now I knew why he looked familiar. He was Hiram Blacktower's brother, Josiah, the disabled and partially blind Gulf War veteran.

A woo-woo feeling rippled through me again. What were the odds I'd run into him here?

My pragmatic side assured me those odds were above average in our sparsely populated state. Since I was seeing the VA eye doctor, who rotated into this facility only once a month, logic dictated Josiah would be here at the same time. Health-care choices for veterans were limited, and Indian veterans even more so. The Indian Health Service had a worse reputation than the Veterans Administration, so no surprise he'd chosen the lesser of two evils.

I tossed the magazine on a side table and headed toward him. "Mind if I sit here?"

Josiah grunted.

I flopped down. "Nice ball cap. Does that mean you are a Screaming Eagle alumni?"

No answer.

"I'm from Eagle River. Or I was. I've been gone the last twenty years in Uncle Sam's army. You a marine?"

A slight nod.

"Look. We haven't met, but when I heard your name and saw your ball cap, I realized I know your family. Hiram Blacktower is your brother, right?"

He mumbled.

"Excuse me?"

"I said yes. I'm sorry you know him."

Whoa. That was unexpected. "You two aren't close?"

"No. I keep my distance from him and have asked him to do the same."

"Why's that?"

Another pause.

"Come on. You wouldn't have said something if you didn't want to talk about him."

Another affirmative chin bob. "How well do you know Hiram?"

"I've crossed paths with him, mostly on a professional basis."

"Professional. Right." He snorted. "Even half blind and crippled I ain't the embarrassment to our family name and our heritage that he is as a 'professional.'"

"You the only one in your family who's feels that way?"

"There is only us these days. The rest of our line has died out."

"I hear ya there. No more males are left in our family to carry on our name either."

Hightower cocked his head. "I can't tell by the way you speak . . . are you Lakota?"

I nodded, realized he couldn't see it and said, "Some. My mother was part Minneconjou."

"Ah."

I couldn't tell if his response was meant to be insightful or condescending. "What?"

"Then do you know the old stories? Of Iktomi, the trickster?"

"A little."

"Then think of Hiram . . . like Iktomi."

Sweet baby Jesus in a manger. Parables were my least favorite part of Indian mythology. Why couldn't he just say what he meant? Rather than comparing a person to a rock or to a turtle or to smoke and expecting me to draw my own conclusions? I pretended to contemplate his wisdom for thirty seconds before I asked, "How so?"

"No matter how many times Hiram sheds his skin and tries to become someone else, the flesh beneath that skin remains red, not white."

Just another barbed reminder that race was always an issue in our culture, even within the same family.

"Being Indian isn't a hobby. Neither is being honorable."

Okay. I'd missed something. "What's being honorable have to do with anything?"

"It has to do with everything," Josiah chided me. "You ask him if what he's been doing is honoring our ancestors."

"Is this about him working for Kit McIntyre?"

Another no-answer, stoic-Indian moment.

Which pissed me off. If Josiah wasn't tight with his brother, how the hell did he know what Hiram was up to? I said as much.

Josiah faced me. I swear a jolt of power shot through me.

"When you see Hiram next, you ask him if he's proud. Tell him I told you to ask."

Before I could demand clarification, the nurse called his name and chattered loudly as she rolled him out of sight, leaving me with more questions than answers.

My appointment was a waste of time. Nothing'd changed with my eye or my vision. I'd say it was a relief, but it just added another layer of frustration of being stuck in limbo in all aspects of my life.

I called Jake to check in, but mostly to get directions to Hiram Blacktower's place. I don't know what I hoped to accomplish. Josiah's remarks unsettled me, and since I'd already gotten into a pissing match with Hi's boss, I didn't have anything to lose by paying Hiram a friendly visit.

Hiram's place was more run-down than I'd anticipated—not a good indication of his success in real estate or that Kit was paying him better than slave wages. I unhooked the lopsided gate at the entrance, pulled through the opening, got out again, relatched it behind me, and then putted up the driveway.

The house looked to be a one-room shack. The siding was a morass of colors plastered at odd angles in a poor man's attempt at a mosaic. The lone front window was covered in tinfoil. Probably switched out with plastic wrap in the winter months.

Four vehicles were parked in the yard. A Ford F-150, a Pontiac LeMans with the front end accordioned, a Dodge truck, and some type of foreign economy car. For a second I had an urge to check around the front end to see if chunks of grass hung off the grilles of either truck. Or if the sides were scratched from barbed wire. Or if it'd make that grinding noise if I started it up.

Did I suspect Hi had played the make-Mercy-a-hood-ornament game last night? Hell yes. I suspected everyone with a pickup, which left roughly 99.9 percent of the entire population of South Dakota.

My gaze tracked the high line wire that swooped from the pole by the road to the house. At least Hi had electricity out here; some folks didn't. I doubted he'd dug a well, so he'd have to haul water. I saw the faded blue plastic tank centered in the back end of the Dodge and knew he hadn't been the one who'd chased me—at least, not with that truck.

A horse stared at me from behind a rickety fence. I shivered and looked away. Horse one; Mercy zero. As I looked beyond the broken-down corral, I noticed a thatch-covered hut that resembled a dirt igloo. A sweat lodge. A heap of good-sized rocks stood off to the left. Wood was piled around the perimeter. Smoke snaked out of the top of the hut. I glanced at the clock in the truck. Hiram was performing a sweat? At this time of day? When it was already a million degrees? Just another reminder Hi wasn't the brightest crayon in the box.

Hiram stretched out of the tiny door of the sweat lodge and squinted at me. I couldn't see his lower half, and I knew most guys did the sweat naked. I so didn't want a glimpse of Hiram's dangly parts.

He waved vigorously.

I especially didn't want to see swaying dangly parts. I almost threw my truck in reverse.

Hiram strode toward me, not buck-ass nekkid, but wearing a robe and a gigantic grin.

I climbed out of the cab. My ankle was still sore and I didn't feel like walking to meet him halfway, so I leaned against the driver's-side door and nonchalantly looked around at where he hung his moccasins. Stacks of stripped, long pine poles, probably for tipis, were evenly stacked on the other side of the fence. That bit of neatness surprised me, given all the rest of the broken, worthless crap piled everywhere else.

"Mercy Gunderson. What're you doing here?"

If the gleam in his eye was any indication, he believed I'd shown up to talk to him about Kit's offer. I'd keep that as an option to keep him talking. I used the old standby: "I was in the neighborhood."

"Really? So you here on official business?"

"Might say that. I was just at the VA. I ran into your brother."

Hiram stopped. "You saw Josiah? Umm. How is he?"

"As good as a partially blind, crippled veteran can be, I suppose. He said you don't come to see him much." The little white lie was a test to see if Hiram regarded his relationship with his brother in the same light that Josiah did.

"Nope, I don't. I ain't got a lot of free time," said the man standing in his bathrobe, late in the afternoon.

I nodded. "I imagine working as Kit's gopher keeps you scrambling."

"I am not his gopher. I am his assistant." His hands came out of his pockets, and he crossed his arms over his chest in a defiant posture. "He's taking me to a real estate seminar in Spearfish next week."

"Sounds promising."

"Josiah put you up to this? Making me feel guilty for having a job?"

"No, I just wondered why Josiah's so unhappy about you

working for Kit. When it seems you're apparently having some success. Is it jealousy?"

Hi relaxed slightly. "No. Josiah just don't understand how the world works; he never has. He went from Ma taking care of him to the marines taking care of him to the VA taking care of him. He ain't ever had to punch a clock. Never had to worry about being hungry. Never had to worry how he was gonna come up with money for living expenses. And he thinks being a wounded Indian soldier makes him a warrior like our ancestors, and gives him the right to . . . forget it."

I understood what Hi left unsaid. Some guys in the service were total jerks before getting injured, and a permanent disability made them only jerkier, more demanding and, in most cases, more impossible to be around. "Well, he talked about honor and pride, saying something along the lines about you doing stuff he didn't approve of."

"Which would be almost everything, in his opinion."

I pointed to the sweat lodge. "Does Josiah know you take part in the sweat?"

"It ain't something I advertise."

Neither did Jake or John-John. "Too bad I've got another stop to make or I'd ask you to show me how to do a cleansing ritual."

"Why? Seeing my brother make you feel dirty or something?"

"No, I need one after finding another dead body at my place this morning."

Hiram's twitchy body went still. "What?"

"You haven't heard? I figured it'd be all over the county by now."

"I haven't been to town. I've been out here all day getting ready. Who'd they find?"

"Not 'they'—I found her. Sue Anne White Plume."

Her name didn't bring any reaction. Hiram was just as stone-faced as his brother.

"Did you know her?"

"Just because I'm Indian don't mean I know every Indian around these parts," he snapped.

"I didn't mean—"

"Forget it." Hi looked over his shoulder, then back at me. "So now that you're done nagging me about my brother and spreading bad news, didja wanna talk about Kit's offer on your place?"

I must've gotten that deer-in-the-headlights look because Hiram offered me the sly, mean smile he'd learned from Kit.

"Didn't think so. I got stuff to do. See ya."

Don't let the gate hit you on the way out went unsaid. He trudged to the sweat lodge and disappeared inside.

Despite my desire to go home, I had to stop by the sheriff's department to fill out the paperwork from last night.

Jolene, the second-shift secretary, gave me a sympathetic look as I approached her desk. "Mercy, hon, how you holdin' up?"

"I admit all this crap is getting to me."

"I imagine so. Anything I can do?"

"No. But thanks." I peeked around the corner. "Is Dawson here?"

"I'm sorry the sheriff isn't in." She smiled wistfully. "Seems strange, saying that to you. When your daddy ran the county, we knew better than to make either of you girls wait. Didn't matter what he was doing, whenever you called from overseas, he gave me explicit instructions to patch you right through."

Jolene had worked for my dad forever. I wondered how she fared working for Dawson. "Bet *you* didn't love those interruptions."

"I didn't mind." Jolene straightened a stack of folders on the corner of her desk. "What can I do for you?"

"There's some paperwork floating around I'm supposed to fill out. Thought I'd try to catch Dawson before he went home."

"Too late. He's gone."

My raised eyebrows weren't entirely faked. "Dad never took off before six. Dawson keeping banker's hours?"

"Not usually. Seems he's always here. Think he's afraid if he isn't he'll get lost in your dad's shadow."

"That would be easy." I hesitated, hoping she'd buy my unease. "Can I ask you something about my dad and the department?"

"Sure."

"Why'd he pick Dawson as his successor when there were other deputies who'd worked for him longer?"

Jolene lived to gossip. She tossed a quick glance over her shoulder to make sure the coast was clear before she mock-whispered, "Caused a big stir. Bill O'Neil was the only one interested in the position. And he's close to retirement. Wyatt wanted new blood in here; that's why he hired Dawson."

New blood or bad blood? nearly tripped off my tongue. Instead, I manufactured a puzzled look. "Remind me again where Dawson came from?"

"Bennett County Sheriff's Department in Minnesota. He called here about a year ago and asked if we were hiring."

"Convenient."

My sarcasm was lost on Jolene. "Very. Dawson moved here right after his interview. He's renting that old trailer on the Lohstroh place."

"You'd think if he planned on sticking around he'd want to buy, not rent."

"Oh, he's talked plenty about it. He even keeps regular contact with McIntyre's realty office. But I suspect he's holding off on buying anything permanent until he knows how the election goes."

"Sounds to me like he's got it sewn up."

"Not necessarily." She looked at me expectantly.

"What?"

"Some folks are hoping maybe you'll stick around and give him a run for his money."

That absolutely floored me.

Jolene laughed. "Hadn't considered running for sheriff? Ain't that the way it goes in this county? If it involves you, you're always the last to know."

I practically ran out of the building, visions of Suzanne Somers's bad '80s sitcom *She's the Sheriff*, replaying in my head.

As I reached the door Jolene said, "Don't write it off as craziness, Mercy. There's a lot of your dad in you. He always did the right thing. You will, too."

As I drove, I thought about Dawson and his place in the sheriff's department. My dad had always been an exceptional judge of character. He definitely would've double-checked Dawson's background before he'd hired him. So Dawson's apathy bugged the crap out of me.

But was it truly indifference?

Dawson wasn't doing his job solving murder cases. But . . . if I gave him the benefit of the doubt, his lack of progress could be blamed on inexperience. Homicides were rare in Eagle River County. With three suspected cases of murder, Dawson might be in over his head and trying to hide it.

Naturally he'd bristle if the former sheriff's daughter started questioning his experience, his commitment to the community, and his methodology. Especially in light of the rumors circulating I might have my eye on his job.

Jesus. No wonder he always seemed to be following me, showing up when I least expected it, and asking me a million questions.

The more scenarios I ran, the more guilt I felt. Yet my main focus hadn't changed: finding out who'd killed Levi. As soon as possible. By any means necessary. With or without Dawson's help.

However, the next time Dawson and I crossed paths, I'd be . . . nice to him. Pleasant even.

Yeah, that oughta throw him off balance.

I pulled up to the house. A bag of trash was piled alongside the outer wall on the porch, and for the briefest second, it morphed into the shape of a body. Sue Anne's body. My stomach lurched. I closed my eyes. When I reopened them, it was just garbage. I didn't have the mental fortitude to walk across the porch. My ankle hurt as I limped around the corner of the house and entered through the front door.

Despite the ghastly vision of Sue Anne's bloody body propped on my porch, the time had come to track down Moser and Little Bear. Chances were slim they'd talk to me. Chances were high I'd try to change their minds.

Tomorrow. I'd had enough of today. Exhausted and in pain, I wolfed down a protein bar and crawled into my bed.

Some time later, loud voices in the kitchen woke me. I ventured downstairs. Theo's arm was draped across Hope's shoulders. She rested against him, her posture the picture of dejection. My chest cavity ached, as if she'd jammed her hand inside and squeezed my heart in her fist.

Theo looked at me and frowned. "I didn't think you'd be here."

I live here, asshole. "Yeah? Well, I didn't think you'd be here. After what's happened, maybe this isn't the best place for Hope to be."

Hope raised her tear-filled eyes. "Is it true? Was that girl found here today Levi's girlfriend?"

"'Fraid so."

"First Albert, then Levi, and now her? What is going on?"

"Dawson can't believe those kids were some kind of random victims," Theo said angrily. "Isn't it obvious there's a common tie? Especially when Levi and Sue Anne were seeing each other. This certainly is a—"

"Clusterfuck?"

Poor Theo seemed pissed I'd cut off his impromptu lecture.

"Funny. If you were in my class . . ."

He rambled. I tuned him out until something clicked. "Hey, wasn't Sue Anne in your class?"

"Yes. I hardly see what that has to do with anything."

"Did she come to class last night?"

"No. Lately she's been missing more than she's been there, which makes it difficult to talk to her about her excessive absences, doesn't it?"

"It's kind of a moot point now." I took a mental step back. Hope would probably appreciate it if we dropped it. "What are you guys doing tonight?"

"Theo is making supper at his place." Her eyes glistened again and she said softly, "I have to get out of that house."

"And I have to make sure she eats properly."

I was afraid they'd invite me over. Okay, when a decent interval passed and they didn't issue even a half-assed invitation, I felt slighted. Hypocritical, I know. Just to be ornery, I asked Hope if she needed a ride.

"No. I'll drive myself."

"You sure you're feeling up to it?"

"She'll be fine," Theo assured me. "I live about four miles out of town. Small place, but it does have a barn. Nothing slick like

your setup here. You should come out and ride with me sometime. I've got an old paint horse that won't spook you."

I went rigid.

Panic flared in Hope's eyes. She stepped away from Theo.
"Mercy doesn't ride horses. Ever."

"Why not?"

Hope waited for me to answer.

I didn't. Instead, I said, "See you," and scrambled up the stairs.
By the time I'd reached the top, my ankle hurt and my heart
hammered. I flattened myself against the wall to regain control.
Normally I didn't have such a visceral reaction at the mere mention of horseback riding. The blood and the death and the bad
memories were getting to me.

I heard Hope say, "I can't believe you said that to her."

And Theo's smarmy, "Not my fault she freaked out. It's
been . . . what? Thirty years since your mom died? I say your
sister needs to get over it. Climb back on the horse that threw
her, so to speak."

"Know what? Mercy doesn't deserve you being an asshole to
her in her own house, Theo. Sometimes you just plain piss me
off."

The door slammed behind her.

I don't know which surprised me more, that Hope had stood
up to Theo or that she'd stuck up for me.

FOURTEEN

The following night I sketched out a rough plan.

The rec center on the Eagle River Reservation was the hot spot for teens. With Sue Anne's murder, I assumed kids would band together, if not to grieve, to gossip. I'd hang out and see what was what.

No reason to disguise myself. None of them had attended Levi's funeral, but Little Bear, Moser, and that group had seen me once in the dark parking lot at the barn dance. I'd spent the majority of my life blending in. If I couldn't stay off the radar of self-absorbed teens, it was time to hang up my spy gear.

I grabbed my Walther P22 and hid it in an ugly crocheted purse Sophie had crafted that I've always hated—be a good reason to get rid of it. Yeah, carrying a firearm to an Indian reservation where I'd be around minors probably wasn't smart. But I'd had enough of being on the receiving end of violent acts. Time to go on the offensive.

Not having streetlights was a double-edged sword for Eagle River. It masked the poverty but provided the ideal situation for criminal activity.

Vehicles cruised the main drag. People of all ages staggered beside the road. Alcohol wasn't permitted on the reservation. Didn't seem to stop it from flowing. Two liquor stores were set up on either end of the highway running through the center of town. Deaths from drunk driving were commonplace.

I hated that the tribal police didn't try harder to control the amount of booze brought in. But the cops spent so much time dealing with the aftereffects of alcohol—drunks, accidents, and domestic violence—that preventative measures were impossible to sustain.

I parked in front of the rec center. Hide in plain sight, that's my motto. I jammed a ball cap on my head and slid into the corner booth by the snack bar.

Quick recon revealed the building consisted of two main rooms and hallways running opposite directions from those rooms. Levi had mentioned to Jake that his group hung out by the pool tables. I ordered a pitcher of Coke and a cheese pizza while I waited.

Nobody paid attention to me. An hour passed. My bladder was full. Time to check out the bathrooms and exits.

No cameras and the men's room was at the end of the corridor, next to a utility closet. And score—an emergency exit. Despite the placard exclaiming ALARM WILL SOUND, I figured it'd been years since the alarm had functioned.

By the time I'd returned from the restroom, Moser, Little Bear, and the entourage held court in the two booths across from the pool tables. Thank God no music thumped from the speakers to hamper my eavesdropping.

I studied the dynamics of the group and decided it'd be nearly impossible to get Moser or Little Bear alone. I'd have to try for one of the other kids.

Two stood out as potentials. The reed-thin boy with long stringy black hair, a goiter, and a nervous habit of checking his wristwatch. Randall Meeks? Or Bucky One Feather? The other good-sized kid with the group could be a threat, so I set my sights on the geeky one.

As I sat in the booth and watched these thugs, my anger grew. It wasn't fair Levi was dead. It wasn't fair these kids were laughing and joking while Sue Anne was lying on a steel table with her throat cut.

I wanted to bang their stupid heads together until I got the answers I needed, or until their blood spilled. I caught myself making a fist on the table. For a second I closed my eyes and sought the internal black void where emotions didn't exist.

Calmer, I pretended to flip through a community newspaper, keeping an eye on the trash talking and the movements of the players.

Randall Meeks weaved through the crowd of preteens to the bathrooms.

Showtime.

I allowed him about thirty seconds before I followed. In the shadowed hallway, I pulled out my gun, tossing the purse in the corner behind the mop bucket. I stuck the compact pistol in my back pocket.

The door to the women's restroom squeaked. Giggling female voices faded behind me.

I positioned myself by the utility closet.

Randall exited the bathroom and tried to blow past me. I blocked him.

"Hey. Whatcha doing? Get outta my way."

"No. Turn around and walk to the emergency exit."

"What the fuck? Did Moser put you upta this?"

"Start walking."

"Fuck off. I ain't goin' no place with you."

He turned sideways. He made it two steps before I wrapped my arm around his throat and jerked him to a stop. I hissed in his ear, "You had a choice. Now you don't."

A strangled sound emerged. "You're choking me."

"No shit. Not another word." I propelled him out the door.

The emergency exit opened into the back parking lot next to the Dumpster. Immediately the gag-inducing odor of old grease and the sour stench of moldy cheese assaulted my senses. Once we hit the pavement, I switched my hold, twisting one arm behind his back in addition to keeping the choke hold.

He yipped with pain.

"Your name."

"Randall M-meeks."

"Tell me about the Warrior Society, Randall."

"I don't know nothing about it."

I increased the pressure on his arm.

He moaned.

"Try again. The Warrior Society."

"Okay, okay. I'm in it."

"Why are two members, Albert Yellow Boy and Sue Anne White Plume, dead?"

"I don't know."

"Who killed them? Was it you?"

"No!"

"Maybe it was one of your buddies? Did Moser snap Albert's neck like this?" I amplified the force by jerking my arm harder around his throat.

"Stop. Jesus, that hurts."

"Who tried to cut off Sue Anne's head?"

"I don't know! Sue Anne ain't been around, and the rest of us been laying low for a while."

"During this time you decided to 'lay low,' did you come up with a plan to keep Levi Arpel out of your club by killing him?" As I said Levi's name, I rammed Randall's hand further up his spine.

He whimpered. "You're hurting me."

"Not as bad as you're gonna hurt if you don't answer the fucking question." I bent his thumb until it reached his wrist. "Tell me everything or I break it."

"We didn't have nothing to do with Levi. And after what happened with Sue Anne, some of us want out. We're having a meeting with the leaders."

"When?"

"In the next couple days."

"Where?"

"I ain't sure. Lemme go."

"Yeah," a deep voice said behind me. "Let him go."

Keeping my grip on Randall, I wheeled around, using him as a human shield in case these idiots were armed. Satisfied they weren't, I threw him at Moser's feet. Everyone jumped back. Randall stayed on the ground.

"I don't like nobody fucking with my friends," Moser said.

"Yeah? We have something in common then, 'cause I don't like nobody fucking with my family."

"So who's your family?"

"Levi Arpel was my nephew."

Moser, Little Bear, and Bucky exchanged a look.

"What do we care? He's dead."

"That's why I'm here, Moser. For answers on *why* he's dead."

Little Bear grabbed his crotch. "I got answers for you right here, bitch."

The guys behind him laughed.

"But I'm looking for big answers, Little Bear, not small ones."

That got real laughs until Moser sent them a dirty look. "What makes you think we know anything about it?"

"It's too goddamned coincidental that Albert and Sue Anne were both in the Warrior Society, but trying to get out, and Levi wanted to be in, but you kept him out, and now all three of them are dead."

Moser shrugged. "Shit happens."

"I don't buy that." My gaze swept the other pimple-faced beanpole. "Bucky and Levi had a fight the night before Levi was murdered. Maybe I oughta drag Bucky to Sheriff Dawson and let Dawson question him."

"You can't force him off the rez because of the sovereign nation laws," Moser said smugly. "Besides. He's a minor. That's kidnapping."

The little bastard thought he was so smart. Time to smack his pride and point out his stupidity. "Wow. Almost sounds like you're still calling the shots, Moser. But I heard your so-called spiritual leaders horned in and took over."

"Shut up, bitch," Little Bear snapped.

"Bet that burns your ass. You're nothing but a whipping boy. Literally. I heard about the 'toughening' rituals. Do these advisers let you do anything without their permission? Or do you obey like good little conquered Indians and do what they tell you?"

Randall leaped to his feet. "How'd you know? That big-mouthed bitch Sue Anne—"

Moser punched Randall in the jaw and Randall hit the dirt like a hailstone. Then Moser focused on me. Little Bear flanked his left side.

"You don't know shit."

"Yeah? Sue Anne told me a bunch of stuff. So did Levi."

Moser's nasty, snaggle-toothed grin appeared. "Whatever Sue Anne said was a lie. And Levi didn't know nothing. Besides, ain't like you can ask him."

Little Bear laughed.

"Gang-raping Lanae Mesteth wasn't a lie, and I know that's why Sue Anne stopped going to meetings." When none of the guys disputed my statement, I had that sinking sensation in my gut.

I grasped for something solid. A threat they hadn't considered. "If I call Lanae and tell her Sue Anne was murdered, she'll come back here and testify against all of you and your leaders."

No response.

Someone a lot more intimidating than me kept these boys on a short leash. "Why is their identity such a secret? Why are you guys protecting them? You know they wouldn't do the same for any of you."

That got Moser's attention. He muttered in Lakota to Little Bear and they each took a step sideways.

Ooh, I didn't like the looks of divide and conquer.

As I reached for my gun, a banshee wailed behind Little Bear. My fingers froze on the grip. Next thing I knew, a broom handle thwacked Little Bear across his upper back with enough force he crashed to the ground.

Swish swish crack. Another grunt of pain. This time from Moser. I saw he'd curled his left hand over his right bicep.

Before Moser recovered, another loud *crack* sounded as the stick connected with his shins. Moaning, he fell to his knees.

I looked up to see who'd come to my rescue.

Hope.

I blinked. *Hope?* What was she doing here?

Before I could warn her to get the hell back, she brandished the long stick above her head like a Valkyrie poised for battle. "Which one of you bastards did it?"

No one uttered a peep.

"Somebody better start talking." Hope pointed the end of the stick at Bucky, jabbing him hard in the sternum. "You. Now. Talk. Why is my son dead?"

"I-I d-don't know."

"Liar!" She swung the stick so fast if Bucky hadn't ducked, his fat head would've been pulp. "Try again."

I'd never seen this side of my sister. It was as beautiful as it was scary.

"We didn't have nothing to do with Levi getting killed," Bucky said.

"Then why all the intimidation and shit, huh? Why'd you act like you were gonna beat the crap outta my sister if you haven't done nothing wrong?"

Randall blurted, "Because we're scared! And now she comes around asking the same questions we been asking each other—"

"Shut the fuck up, Meeks," Little Bear snarled.

Hope's shrill laugh could've shattered glass. "You should be scared. Of me. So help me God, if I find out one of you punks killed my son, I will track you down and beat you to death."

I moved to stand by Hope, poised to make an escape. Someone would notice us before too much longer, and, like Dawson, I'd rather avoid dealing with tribal cops.

"If you guys are telling the truth, and you didn't have anything to do with your friends ending up dead, I guess I'd worry if the secrets I was keeping are worth dying for. I'd be freaking out that I'd be the next one."

They had nothing to say to that either.

Hope warned, "Don't follow us. Stay right there until we're gone." She wielded the stick as we backed away.

We rode in silence to the Indian Health Services Hospital and parked in the visitors' lot.

An SUV towing a fishing boat screamed up to the emergency room entrance. I couldn't see what injury constituted an emergency, so out of habit my mind supplied all sorts of gruesome images involving fishhooks, fillet knives, and propellers.

I rolled my window down. The night air smelled stagnant: old sweat socks mixed with sewer gas and dead animals. "Thanks for coming to my rescue tonight."

Hope smiled slightly.

"How did you happen to stumble across me in Eagle River? When we're both miles from home."

"Does kinda smack of coincidence." She sighed. "I don't know. Maybe I'm channeling John-John's psychic abilities. I just knew I needed to get away from Theo after supper."

Get away from lover boy? That was new.

"Whenever I'm on the rez, I'd swing by the rec center because Levi usually needed a ride home. Old habits die hard, I guess, and I noticed Daddy's truck. Then I heard you talking and saw those guys surrounding you. I ran back for a weapon."

Good thing she hadn't seen my gun. "Whether a fluke or divine karma, thanks."

"You're welcome." Hope settled her neck against the headrest.

"Is everything okay?"

"Not really."

"What's wrong?"

"I've been thinking about what Levi said, about the baby, before he . . . Maybe Theo is expecting me to take care of the baby on my own. I already did that once. Not something I want to go through again."

I knew little about her husband. During the few years she'd been married, before Mario died, I'd come home less than usual. "Mario wasn't around much?"

"Hardly ever. Sounds mean, but I was so damn mad at him when he got killed in that accident. He didn't leave us money. Don't know what I would've done if Daddy hadn't given me the trailer. I had no other place to go. I couldn't tell Jake about Levi and take his charity."

I shivered, unnerved by the feeling I didn't know my sister at all.

"Know what's kind of funny, though?"

"What?"

"I always wanted to be like you. Leave here, leave Daddy. Start my life over away from the damn ranch and the folks in town who always look at me with pity. 'Oh, that's Hope Gunderson. A horse killed the girl's mother when she was only three. And then, the poor little thing blew her best friend's head clean off when she was barely five. Such a tragedy.'"

Why had I thought Hope had it easier? A strange thought niggled. Maybe *she* wasn't the selfish one in our family.

"Now maybe I finally have the chance to leave."

"Do you want to?"

"I want to run as far as I can whenever I hear the people talking about me being a bad mother."

"Who? I'll give those self-righteous biddies a piece of my mind."

"It's okay, Mercy. Some of what they're saying is true. I know I didn't always do right by Levi."

"Hope—"

"I'm not making excuses. I loved him. He knew I loved him." Her voice was a raw whisper. "Lord, I loved that kid so much.

My life isn't ever gonna be the same without my boy. My guts are tied up in knots every morning when I wake up and realize I'll never see his sweet face again."

My deep sigh resounded in the anguished quiet.

She reached for my hand and squeezed, but she didn't look at me. "You were starting to love him, too. That means a lot to me."

"I'll find out who did this to him. I swear."

"I know you will."

We held hands, but I couldn't tell if it was for her benefit or for mine.

Finally, Hope gathered herself and started the car. "I'll take you back to your truck and follow you home in case one of them boys gets a fool idea about doing the same thing. We crazy Gunderson women gotta stick together, don't we?"

"Yeah."

When had the tables turned and she'd become my ally? My protector?

It didn't matter. I was just glad I wasn't alone.

My morning yoga practice didn't offer me the usual sense of calm, which disturbed me on several levels. The last fifteen years I'd come to rely on yoga, not only to keep my muscles pliable, but also as a mental refuge where I existed only as deep breath and flowing poses.

Firing a gun gave me the same sense of otherworldliness. The repetition of loading clips. Reconfiguring. Firing. Replacing targets. Loading more clips. More firing. Then the smell of clean cotton and gun oil as I performed my cleaning ritual.

I could drag out my guns and complete my mental health regiment. Ooh. I could call it *Yoga Zen and the Art of Assassination*. Maybe that's what I should do—make a DVD.

On the other hand, I hadn't done any shooting since before Levi's murder. Seemed a waste of time, trying to keep myself on top of my game, when the truth was I'd pretty much fallen to the bottom of the heap.

I'd put in my twenty. My choices were re-up for another four or get the hell out. Contrary to popular myth, the U.S. government did not bar soldiers from retiring during wartime. Still, I dreaded making the phone call. I left a message for my CO with a personal update on my health condition, and requested she start the paperwork.

Paperwork. Ugh. I hated paperwork, and it was a reminder of another chore I'd put off: cleaning Dad's office.

I'd mostly avoided his sacred space since his death. First, because it was an ungodly mess. Second, it'd feel too much like snooping. I'd heard horror stories about the bizarre things adult children uncovered about their aged parents. I doubted Dad horded a stash of porn. Or hid letters from a secret admirer.

Once, when I still believed in happily-ever-after, I asked Dad if he ever considered remarrying. His reply? Any woman would be a step down from my mother. He'd been a man of few words, so the potent ones always stuck with me.

The coffee was fairly fresh, so I reheated a mug and ventured into the mouth of the beast.

When I opened the door, grief hit me like a Bradley assault vehicle. The room smelled like Dad: the spicy scent of Red Man chewing tobacco, Old English aftershave, and newspapers. A trace of cow shit. He'd never quite mastered wiping off his boots. After they'd taken his leg Sophie quit pestering him about it.

I braced my shoulders against the door and fought a prickle of tears.

Dammit, Mercy, get ahold of yourself.

I forced myself across the room. Another wave of sadness tightened my gut when I saw the month on his desk blotter hadn't changed since March—the last time he'd been in here. I moved his monstrous office chair out of the corner and over to the desk. It'd nearly killed him to give it up after he'd become wheelchair bound.

My fingers traced the cracks in the seat. White stuffing stuck out like milkweed puffs. Grease stains darkened the tan leather headrest where Dad leaned back to "think" but most likely to sneak in a nap. Damn chair hadn't seen a can of WD-40 in years. The lever to adjust the height was busted, leaving it in the lowest position. When I squeaked up to the mahogany desk, I really felt I was playing grown-up.

I sighed. Where to start? Piles teetered on every horizontal surface. I grabbed a random file folder and opened it. Invoices from Nelson's for hay. Holy shit. *That's* how much hay cost? I squinted and double-checked the date. That was the price of hay last fall.

Jake handled the day-to-day expenses and writing checks from the ranch account. Our accountant, Carol, managed the rest: payroll, filing taxes, and all the legal junk I knew nothing about. Saint Carol also paid my bills while I was overseas, not that I incurred many. Because of the war, I hadn't traveled much in recent years even if I was granted a rare leave, so I had one indulgence: my Viper.

Maintaining the ranch books was a tradition passed down to the females who'd married into the Gunderson family. My mother, Sunny; my grandmother, Faith, before her; and my great-grandmother, Patience, before she took over the reins from my crazy great-great-grandmother, Grace. Bet she'd produced some creative numbers.

I made three piles. Keep. Throw away. And no clue. Most of the paperwork hit the trash bin. Receipts for cowboy boots from 1993? Newspaper clippings about rodeo results? A bull sale catalog from Montana?

One box of files dealt with cattle bought and sold. The lineage, both bull and heifer. Milk weight-gain ratios for the calves up to weaning. Grain weight-gain ratios for the calves after weaning. Feedlot weight gain and the sale prices.

It made my head spin. All this information needed to be logged in a computer program and the Gunderson Ranch brought into the twenty-first century.

You'd think I'd know this stuff, growing up on a big working cattle ranch. Not so. Kit McIntyre had been right about one thing: Dad had kept Hope and me sheltered from everything but the surface stuff. Now I wondered if my lack of interest in something so dear to his heart had hurt him.

I tackled the files on the left-hand side of his desk, which held the most recent bills and bank statements. Ten years ago I'd set up an emergency-cash fund for the ranch after Dad let it slip things were tight. Despite his pride, he agreed to borrow money from me rather than the county bank. Dad grew up hearing

stories about the dirty '30s and he didn't really trust banks, so
he also squirrel-holed a chunk of cash in the safe, just in case the
banks went bust again.

No one knew about the financial arrangement but us. I'd
never demanded an accounting of how he'd spent the funds. Yet
seeing that account $85,000 less than the last time I'd checked
made my eyes bug out of my head.

No doubt we were cash poor. Thank God the county provided his health insurance and he'd purchased a modest life
insurance policy before his diabetes diagnosis or we'd be in big
financial trouble. He'd spent two months in a nursing home. I
feared he'd been sentient enough to know he hadn't been dying
on his beloved ranch.

As I stacked the last file, I noticed a manila envelope sticking
out from under the desk blotter. An oversight on Dad's part? Or
had he hidden it for a specific reason? My heart pounded a little
as I opened it.

Nothing incriminating, just loose paper, handwritten notes
and business letters. The first note scrawled in his precise pen-
manship read:

    The Swamp Rats—investment company based in
    Florida

Had the Swamp Rats contacted Dad? Or had he contacted
them?

No. He'd never sell. Wouldn't even consider it.

Would he?

I flipped to the next page. For several seconds I blinked in disbelief. My eyes had to be playing tricks on me. I tracked the legal
gibberish on a contract with a Montana real estate assessment
firm to assess the value of the Gunderson Ranch.

Dated six months before he'd died.

Goddammit. Why hadn't Dad told me? And if he'd paid for
the assessment, where was it? I knew it hadn't been in the stack
of legal documents dealing with the estate. What was this place
worth? My best guess—somewhere around $30 million—was
probably way short of the mark.

I carefully picked through the rest of the paperwork. Nothing more.

My coffee had gone cold. In just a couple of hours I'd basically cleared the desk. I stood, stretched, and looked around the cluttered room. It wouldn't take long to get this space spic and span. Dad wasn't big on sentimentality.

Six pictures decorated his desk. A wedding photo. Not a stiff pose of the couple poised on the altar—rather, a close-up of young Sunny and Wyatt, gazing into each other's eyes, smiling like crazy-in-love fools. Another one of him and me, posing next to the eight-point buck I'd shot the year I'd turned twelve. Hope's senior photo. A pic of me in my uniform after graduation from basic training. A snapshot of him and Hope; she cradled a red-faced baby Levi, and he grinned with grandfatherly pride. Levi's most recent school picture.

Anger supplanted my melancholy. Levi had his whole life ahead of him and someone snuffed it out. Why was I sitting in this stuffy office when I should've been out finding answers?

While I stewed, the front doorbell rang. Weird. No one used the front door.

I opened it to see Kit McIntyre soiling my welcome mat. He didn't bother trying to charm me. "Can I come in and talk to you?"

"About?"

"A couple things. Please. I won't stay long."

Stupid inbred midwestern hospitality: I let him in. He headed for the kitchen. By the size of his belly he was probably trolling for Sophie's famous gingersnap cookies.

"So, why are you here?"

"Lots of people are talking about what happened the day of Levi's funeral. When you run off them out-of-state guys."

"They didn't show any respect for my family. Someone needed to let them know we don't put up with that."

Kit nodded vigorously. "I know what you're saying. I had the same problem with those folks who bought the old Jackson place. Not a friendly one in the lot. I stopped there. Even though they bought the place from me last year, they ain't got the time of day for me."

I frowned. I couldn't imagine they'd be reselling so soon. "Why were you there?" Iris had kept hounding me about heading over and seeing the damage they'd done in hopes I'd sign her petition, but I'd put social visits on the back burner.

He paused.

And then I knew. I waited for the lie.

"Just being neighborly."

The west side was the most accessible section of our land that showcased the river flowing through the canyon. Of all the places on the ranch, that gorgeous vista would bring top dollar. So I figured Kit tried to schmooze the owners of the old Jackson place into letting him onto the Gunderson Ranch. Why? Because I'd denied him access and he wanted to prove my threats were idle?

I didn't know whether to be pissed off or pissed off. And . . . pissed off won.

"Kit, I told you what I'd do if I caught you trespassing."

Out came the good-ol'-boy grin. "Now see, Mercy, that's where you and I don't see eye to eye. I don't think of it as trespassing. I think of it more as a sneak peek at the potential uses for such a unique piece of property."

"It is a shame and a waste of your time. No one needs a peek because the Gunderson Ranch is not for sale."

His face fell. "But . . . I thought you told them guys no because we had an agreement that you'd at least consider the offer from my investment group first. And Hi said you'd stopped by his place. How can you say no when you haven't even heard it?"

"Because it doesn't matter. You could offer me $100 million and I wouldn't sell a single inch to you."

He sneered, "It ain't worth that kinda money."

I didn't respond. Just waited for him to pull the noose a little tighter.

"So that's it?"

"Yep. I'll show you out." I stood and walked to the kitchen door.

His big belt buckled scraped the table edge as he pushed away. "Trey was right. You are stone cold."

He'd succeeded in jarring me. "You know Trey?"

"Could say that. The boy's been working for me for the last year."

Kit's nasty smile curled my innards.

A thought occurred to me: had Trey knocked me out that night at Clementine's on Kit's orders? Then "found" me and offered to take me home? He'd actually slept in my room, in my bed, right next to me. The opportunistic little fucker could've slit my throat in my sleep.

Just like Sue Anne's.

A worse thought arose: had Kit or someone else killed my nephew in the ultimate ploy to cause us additional grief? Thinking neither Hope nor I would want to stick around after such tragedies befell us? He'd threatened me. Had he executed his threat by executing my nephew?

My violent streak surfaced. I pushed him hard. The sudden move knocked Kit's hat off his head, as well as the John Wayne collectible plate off the wall. Using a wristlock, I whipped him around and rammed his face against the wall. "Did you kill Levi? Or did you use that rhinestone cowboy Trey?"

He squirmed. "What is wrong with you?"

I shoved harder, trying to catch his bulbous nose on the nail that had held the plate. "I'm pissed off, Kit. So if I were you, I'd start talking before you see what I'm like when I'm"—another push from me—"*extremely* pissed off."

"W-wh-what do you want to know?"

"To know if you had anything, and I mean even a fucking whisper, to do with Levi being murdered."

"No! What kind of a man do you think I am?"

"Slimy, but I assumed you weren't stupid enough to mess with me."

"Let me go."

The vicious part of me longed to inflict more damage. I had to force that part to let go of his hands. Immediately I backed up, in case he decided to come out swinging.

Kit grunted as he bent down and plucked up his hat. He fingered the bent brim and wouldn't meet my eyes. Embarrassed to have been shown up by a woman. Too bad.

"I don't know why you're acting like this. I'm chalking it up to grief. But I will tell you that if you ever come at me like that again, you'll be sorry."

He stomped past me and out the door.

I let the adrenaline fade, picked up the broken plate, and poured myself a glass of water.

Christ. It'd already been a long-ass day. But it'd be an even longer wait until nightfall.

After a lunch of peanut-butter crackers and grapes, I called Geneva. No answer. I called Rollie. No answer. I called John-John. No answer. Why didn't people answer their damn phones? I hated talking to machines, but I left messages anyway.

I hated to admit I was lonely and wished Sophie and Hope were around.

Sick of silence and my own crappy company, I flopped on the couch and indulged in an entire afternoon of TV. All classics: *Petticoat Junction*, *Green Acres*, and *Hogan's Heroes*. Reminded me I'd always wanted a pet pig named Arnold. Maybe it was time to seriously look into it. Wouldn't Sophie have a fit? Cheered by that thought I roused myself and ventured outside.

It neared Jake's usual quitting time, and I needed to talk to him before he left. I assumed he'd be in the place he loved and I hated: the old wooden barn. As far as barns went, it was considered antique. Constructed of wide oak planks, painted red, with a hayloft; a Norman Rockwell portrait come to life. Charming, right? Wrong. For me it was a mausoleum.

I inhaled a calming breath and scooted inside. With the hayloft door closed, it stayed dark. The narrow walkway to the stalls was littered with loose pieces of hay. The smell never changed, even after everything had been scrubbed down. Horse sweat, horseshit, wet leather, wet wool, hay dust, dirt, and feed. Mud. Plus the chemical odor of the pesticide needed to keep the flies down.

Three of the four stalls housed horses. I didn't linger, just made a straight line to the tack room.

Jake looked up at me with surprise. "Hey. What's up?"

"Nothing. Just needed fresh air."

"Then you're in the wrong place. The air's mighty stuffy in

here." He glanced down at the ropes in his hands instead of at me when he remarked, "Didn't think you came out here."

"Not if I can help it."

"I seen Kit McIntyre's fancy-ass rig pull up. What'd he want?"

"To buy the ranch. I said no. He didn't listen. I said no with a little more force. Don't think he'll be back."

"*Shee*. Watch out for him. He's a sneaky one."

"He doesn't scare me." I forced my foot onto the plastic milk crate by the wall so I wouldn't run out. "Anyway, think you could get some specific information about the next meeting time and place for the Warrior Society from Bernie?"

Jake's work-roughened hands stopped twisting the rope. Slowly his gaze met mine. "Why?"

"Randall let it slip they're meeting with the leaders in the next couple of days. I want to know where and when."

"I don't know how much Bernie can help. Bernie said a couple of months after Axel was initiated into the group, Axel quit."

"From what I've heard, no one can quit."

"Huh. He did. Anyway, Axel refused to tell Bernie who the leaders are because of some secret oath."

"Would Bernie talk to me?"

Jake frowned. "I don't know. He's kinda closemouthed. What'd you learn from Rollie?"

"About the same thing you just told me. But he gave his blessing for me to poke around on the rez."

"Think you mean curse."

I smiled. "What're your plans for tonight?"

"Hang out. Watch TV." His eyes narrowed. "What're you doing?"

"Taking the Viper out for a spin. The girl gets antsy. Might see what's up at Clementine's."

"I don't like the look on your face, Mercy."

I smiled again. Wider. "Just be damn glad that look isn't aimed at you tonight."

FIFTEEN

So I went looking for trouble.

I called John-John. Trey was at the bar, knocking back a couple of beers. Maybe my luck was about to change.

Gravel roads are hell on metallic paint. By the time I'd bumped into the parking lot at Clementine's, an amethyst glow cast the Badlands in shadow.

The metal door banged open. An angry ranch woman stamped out. I paused to see if her significant other would chase after her. But she climbed in her Chevy truck alone and roared off in a powdery puff of dirt.

I sauntered inside and John-John came out from behind the counter to give me a big hug. He whispered, "I don't like the gleam in your eye, Mercy."

I almost said, "Which eye? The good one or the bad one?" but I offered him a toothy grin. "Trick of the light, *kola*."

"Uh-huh. What can I get you?"

"A Coke. Straight up. But make it look like you dumped whiskey in it, okay?"

"You're scaring me."

I playfully slapped his cheeks. "That's the nicest thing anyone has said to me all day."

Trey returned from the back room the same time John-John slid my drink in front of me. He'd even added a maraschino cherry. I lifted the lowball glass in a mock toast. Trey loped over with a big cowboy smile.

"Hey, Mercy. Ain't seen you around much."

"Haven't really been in the party mood."

His grin died. "Yeah. I heard. Sorry about your nephew."

"Thanks. I needed to escape from the house for a while, so I took my car out for a spin. Thought I'd stop in and get a little something to wet my whistle."

"Car? You ain't driving your truck?"

I shook my head. "Wanted to drive fast so I rolled out the Viper."

Trey's mouth hung open like a broken cellar door. "You have a Viper?"

"Yep."

"No way."

"Way."

"A Dodge Viper?"

"Is there any other kind?"

"You pulling my leg?"

"Nope."

"It's out there right now? In the parking lot?"

"No. I parked it on the roof."

He blushed. "Shit. Sorry. Can I see it?"

"Sure. Let's go." I downed my Coke and waved good-bye to John-John.

Even without light the black metallic paint on the car gave off its own radiance.

Trey was mesmerized.

"Pretty, isn't she?"

"Yep." Trey's hand caressed the front quarter panel like the curve of a woman's backside. He whistled. "This is one sweet machine, Mercy. How fast will it go?"

"It'll blow the doors off anything around here."

"Bull."

I looked at him. Tried to keep from glaring at him. "Name one."

"Boxy Jennings's 1969 Barracuda."

"Still won't beat what's under this hood."

"You've raced her? On the track or on the road?"

"Both. Don't argue with me on this point, Trey, because you cannot win. Some pissant forty-year-old muscle car can't hold a candle to the performance of this baby."

"What's the fastest you've ever gotten it up to?"

I angled across the hood and flashed him a bit of cleavage. Smiled seductively as I twirled my keys. Yeah, I was feeling wild. Cocky. Cruel. "Wanna hop in and see what she'll do?" *Come on, I'm danglin' the rope, cowboy. Grab for it with both hands.*

His blue eyes lit up bright as the neon Bud Light sign. "Hell yeah."

"A couple of conditions first."

"Name 'em."

"No telling me how to drive. No grabbing the steering wheel at any point. And we stop only when I say we stop."

"That it?"

"No. If you mess your pants, you're cleaning it up."

"You're serious? Like I'll be so scared I'll . . ." He drawled, "I ain't skeered a' nuthin'."

At any other time that might've charmed me. "Remember you said that."

"Anything else?"

"Before you ask, no, you don't get to drive it. Ever."

"Shoot. That ain't no fun."

"You drop ninety grand on a car, Trey, and come talk to me about who you'll let drive it. I guarantee the list will be short. Very short." I stumbled in a sinkhole and caught myself on the driver's-side door.

"Ah. Maybe this ain't such a good idea. How much you been drinking?"

"Why?"

"'Cause you seem a little . . . I don't know. On edge. You all right?"

No. I'm not all right. Half my family is dead. My military career is over. My sister is pregnant with some bozo's spawn. My friends and neighbors wish I never would've returned home. To top it off, I'm lonely as hell even though I'm hardly ever alone.

My life had been going to shit for months, and it didn't look to end anytime soon.

"Mercy?"

"What?"

"If you wanna go back in and have a beer or something, I'd understand. We could—"

"You gonna talk all goddamn night, or are you gonna get in the goddamn car, Cowboy Trey?"

"Getting in the car." After he'd buckled up, he said, "Never seen orange leather before. Sweet. You have it customized?"

"No. The interior is original and part of the reason I bought it." I let my fingers drift over the dashboard. "I love this color. Like being Cinderella inside a pumpkin."

"How'd you afford something like this?"

"What else do I have to spend my money on? I'm overseas living in barracks most of the year and my wages are tax free."

"Do you keep it at the ranch when you're gone?"

"Nah, I store it in Denver. When I hit the wide-open spaces of Wyoming I open her up and blow the cobwebs out."

The engine made a throaty growl as I started her up. I switched off the radio. Drove slowly out of the Clementine's weed patch and putted to the end of the gravel road.

"Thought you were gonna show me how fast this can go."

"I will. Soon as we get on the pavement."

Trey's lips curled into a sneer. "What? It's picky on driving conditions?"

"No. I'm picky. I hate rock chips."

"That's why a car like this ain't practical."

I turned onto the blacktop and said, "Fuck practical," as I hit the gas.

The speedometer went from 0 to 60 in 4.2 seconds.

Trey whooped. "All right! Do it again."

I slowed down. Stopped. Punched the pedal again. 0 to 60 in 4.2 seconds. Dodge engineering was nothing if not precise.

I kept the speedometer at a steady 65 mph. Be nice to have the windows rolled down, but at high speeds the velocity of the wind made conversation impossible. Not that Trey and I were yukking it up.

My lone set of headlights swept the black pavement. No other cars. No streetlights. No yard lights. Shimmering silver clouds covered the stars and moon.

When I was surrounded by pure black, the compromised vision in my right eye was less noticeable. Luckily enough, tonight everything seemed to be in perfect focus.

A long, flat stretch loomed ahead. Time to give the girl her legs.

I shot Trey a sideways glance. He was relaxed, gazing straight ahead, drumming his fingers on his knee. I increased the pressure on the gas pedal.

When we'd reached 85 mph, Trey took notice. "How fast we going now?"

"Ninety."

"Huh. Don't feel that fast."

Just wait.

The needle crept up to 100.

The dotted white lines bisecting the road started to blur into one long ribbon.

One hundred and ten.

"You're right. This thing hauls."

Ol' Trey didn't seem so relaxed now.

I pressed the pedal to the floor. I actually felt the tires dig into the pavement. The engine hummed approval and we hit 120.

"Okay. Okay. I get it."

"Get what?"

"This is one bad-ass car."

"I know."

"Can you just slow down now?"

"No."

"But—"

"Did I warn you about not telling me how to drive?"

The dial on the speedometer jiggled toward 130.

I can't describe the sensation of driving 130 mph. Most people don't have cars that can reach that level of performance. And about two-thirds of the idiots who do purchase high-performance cars don't have the balls to rod the piss out of them.

I'd never had that problem.

At this speed everything outside the windows blurred like a Mondrian painting. The rush of power was incredible. One false move, one tiny twitch, one little lapse in concentration, and we'd become airborne and spin end over end like a baton.

Usually I pushed the girl to her limits when I was alone. But Trey had pissed me off, not only because I'd discovered who wrote his paychecks, but because I realized he'd masked his sneering attitude toward me behind a helpful demeanor. That was not the cowboy way; he was an insult to men (and women) who lived their lives by that simple code of ethics.

He was undoubtedly on edge. Might be juvenile, but I wanted to see what it would take to push him over.

My hands clutched the orange wheel. I saw his white-knuckled grip on the dashboard. I imagined his heart pounding. Sweat popping up all over his body. I smiled. Knew it looked mean and didn't care.

By the time you see the red lights on a semi at a cruising speed of 135, it's time to pass. Since the road was straight, I wasn't worried about coming up on another car.

"Watch this." I cut the headlights.

"What the hell are you doing?"

"Playing chicken."

I eased over into the passing lane. *Whoosh*. We were around the truck and back on our side of the road before Trey choked out a curse word.

I turned the lights back on and slowed down. To 100. I said, "Bet that trucker thinks he had an UFO experience."

Trey didn't respond.

"You lay an egg over there?"

"You're fucking crazy."

"Oh, you ain't seen crazy yet."

"You trying to kill me?"

"Maybe."

"Let me out."

"Uh. Let me think about that." Pause. *"No."*

I think he whimpered.

"I'm not kidding, Mercy. Stop the car."

"Fine." I lifted my foot off the gas. Took a while for the car to slow. When we hit 30 mph I slammed on the brakes.

Even with his seat belt on Trey smacked into the dash. Hard.

I whipped around 180 degrees so we were in the other lane and floored it.

"Jesus Christ! I said stop the fucking car!"

"And I did." The needle on the speedometer ripped past 70.

"You're gonna kill us!"

"Only if I lose control. So quit whining. It's distracting. Let's see what this bitch feels like when you push her. You like to push, don't you, Trey?" My eyes left the pavement for a second. "Guess what? I push back."

At that point Trey started praying. For a second I thought I smelled urine. It required every ounce of concentration to let her run at 120 and then let her fly.

We reached 130 mph five miles from the turnoff to Clementine's. Once I hit that magical number, I whooped, "Yee-haw!" and gradually dropped back to the legal speed limit. "Feels like we're crawling now, doesn't it?"

Trey didn't say a word. Poor baby appeared to be pouting.

Didn't mean I had to put up with his sullen attitude. We were in my car. "Swallow your tongue, sugar?"

"Just shut up. Jesus, Joseph, and Mary, you need professional help, Mercy. I swear to God, if you were a man, I'd—"

I slammed on the brakes again and skidded to a stop on the shoulder. "Get out."

"What?"

"Get the fuck out of my car."

"But . . . We're a mile from the bar."

"I don't give a shit. Get out."

He opened his mouth. Shut it when he noticed my expression.

"You ever threaten me again, I will cut you open and yank your tongue out through your nose, got it?"

His hand froze on the door handle.

"I said, *got it?*"

He nodded.

"I know you're working for that son of a bitch Kit McIntyre. I don't know what you've done for him in the past, or whether it involved me and my family, but I'm warning you now: if I see you put one toe on my property, I will shoot you. And I will make it hurt before I let you die."

Trey ran away from me so fast his boots were smoking.

I smiled and headed home.

The TV was blaring in the living room when I walked into the house. It was surprising to see Hope's Honda parked out front. Normally she'd say her good-byes after Sophie left.

But tonight she looked more fragile than usual. Pale and wan and I just wanted to . . . feed her. To take care of her. To mother her, which was a new sensation for me. "Can I get you anything?"

She said, "No," but she followed me into the kitchen.

"You sure?" I rummaged in the fridge until I found the foil-wrapped baking pan. "Sophie made peach cobbler. That wouldn't upset your stomach."

Hope shook her head.

"Where's Shoonga?" I asked, just to make conversation.

"Jake took him."

I dished up a healthy portion for myself and saw her watching the digital clock on the stove. "You don't have to sit here with me, Hope."

"I don't mind."

"You want to talk about what's bothering you?"

She didn't answer for so long I was afraid she wouldn't.

"I miss him. Everywhere I go in that trailer I see him. Yesterday I tripped over a pair of his stinky old running shoes. Know the ones with grass stains? The shoelaces are completely frayed, they're too small, and I hated those shoes. Couldn't make myself touch them, but I can't make myself toss them in the burning barrel neither."

Tears poured down her ashen face.

My hands clenched into fists on the table.

"And last night, I woke up about midnight and laid in my bed, listening for him to come home. Waiting for that cheap tin door to slam. Waiting for thumping rap music to turn on. I lay there and lay there and I worried. I worried something happened to him. Then I drifted off again, and when I woke up, I realized something *has* happened, the worst thing I could ever imagine has happened to my boy."

"Hope—"

"Oh God, why would someone do that to him?" Blindly, she reached for my hands. "Shoot him like a dog? Why? I don't understand . . ."

Hope cried so hard I was afraid she'd forget to breathe. She squeezed my balled fists like they were lemons. But my bitter tears stayed inside me, acidic as vinegar.

"I can't go back there. Not tonight. Maybe not ever."

"You can stay here as long as you want. This is your home, too."

She pulled away and dabbed her eyes with a soggy tissue. "Yeah? But for how much longer?"

A warning screamed in my brain. Her mood could change at the drop of a hat. Rarely was the change for the better. "If you've got an opinion on what you think we should do with the ranch, I'd like to hear it." I emphasized *we*.

"No, you don't."

"Yes, I do."

Hope paused and studied me. "I guess when you came back I thought you'd keep things the same, letting Jake or whoever run the ranch until Levi was old enough to take over. Not that it matters now."

Tick tick. The pressure valve on my patience was about to blow. "Your opinion matters to me. I don't know why you don't understand that."

"Yeah? Know what I don't understand?"

Off on another tangent. Big surprise. "What?"

"Why Daddy made you the executor. Why he left you in charge when I've always been here. When everybody knows you don't want nothing to do with this place."

"You think you could handle all the details?"

Eyes completely dry, she gave me a dull stare. "We'll never know, will we? Unless something tragic happens to you and the responsibility would fall to me by default."

At least she had full grasp of the situation. "Dad made that decision, not me. What do you want me to say? I can't change it."

She harrumphed.

"You know, I'm tired of pissing around with this. People second-guessing me. Trying to sway me on what I should do." I angled closer and locked my gaze to hers. "If *you* had to make a decision right now, what would it be?"

Hope didn't even blink. "Sell it."

My jaw nearly hit the table.

"Not what you were expecting?"

I shook my head.

"If you'd asked me two weeks ago, I would've said keep it. Now I agree with Theo. I need to put all this behind me and move on."

Move on? Levi's funeral had been a few days ago. Yeah, Theo was the father of Hope's baby, but his advice seemed a bit harsh and more than a little selfish. "Has Theo been staying with you?"

"Sometimes. Might sound mean, but since Levi died I don't care whether he's around. Most days I wish he wasn't. That's part of the reason I'd like to stay here."

"I'm sure Sophie made up the guest room."

"But I always sleep in the front bedroom," she said softly, pleadingly.

It figured she'd want my room; it was the nicest, and she always wanted what I had.

Truthfully, it didn't really matter where I tossed my pillow since I wasn't sleeping much these days anyway. However, it'd be a complete bitch to move my guns. But I'd do it. I slapped on a happy face. "No problem. I'll grab my stuff right after I finish eating."

While Hope indulged in a bath, I indulged in Wild Turkey. I sat on the porch swing, soaking in the beauty of the night.

When my vision doubled and the harsh edges of the day blurred, I stumbled into the house. I shut off the lights. Checked on Hope. She'd fallen asleep sprawled in the middle of my bed with a pink towel wrapped around her head turban-style. I covered her with our mother's wedding-ring quilt.

The mattress in the guest room sucked. I can take hard beds. I'd rather sleep on the ground than spend the night tossing and turning on softball-sized lumps, so I curled up on the braided wool rug, next to my guns. Exhaustion—emotional and physical—sent me to dreamland almost immediately.

Baghdad burned. The thick, black smoke roiled over the skyline like an apocalyptic snake. Car and store alarms blared. Chunks of buildings crashed to the street, cracking the concrete like stones rippling in an empty pool. The continuous sound of gunfire jarred my brain. When I did get a brief respite from the noise, I panicked, because then I could hear screams of terror. The stench of burning garbage. Of rubber. The sickly sweet odor of fried skin.

My partner had left hours earlier. I'd stayed behind—voluntarily—to tie up the last loose end, a diplomat named Rajeem who'd gone into hiding in the Fadhil district. In addition to leaking classified information, which had gotten five American soldiers killed, he'd raped and murdered a few orphans.

My mind kept returning to the pictures I'd seen, the horrified expressions on those dead boys' faces. The blood. The damage a full-grown man can inflict on supple young bodies.

If I had my way, Rajeem would've seen my wet work up close and personal. I didn't get to use a knife often; consequently, I'd spent way too much time planning how to cut off Rajeem's dick and balls with one slice. How I'd keep him from bleeding to death before I pried his jaw open and rammed his genitals down his own throat as I watched him choke to death on them.

But circumstances changed, as they did so often in war, and there was no safe way for me to get close to Rajeem. I had to satisfy the parameters of my op with a simple kill shot to the head. I felt cheated, but I finished the job.

I shuffled through the melee on the streets, hunched over, dirty burka dragging through the rubble, my head covered, but my eyes hyper-alert. I was another injured Iraqi woman, running from destruction and certain death at the hands of the Allies. No one bothered me. No one knew I'd strapped my stripped-down rifle to my right leg under my burka. Scary, how women are part of the background. Scary, how realistic the dreams were becoming. I even smelled smoke.

Smoke. I coughed and opened my eyes. Saw the French blue curtains in the guest room billowing against the red sky.

I sat up. I wasn't in Baghdad or lost in a dream. I was at home. On the ranch. In South Dakota. The sky never looked red like that unless . . .

Something was on fire.

I raced to the window. The chicken coop was engulfed. Orange flames licked the black sky like angry demonic tongues.

Hope.

I dropped to all fours and crept down the quiet hallway toward Hope's room. No flames crackled, no stifling heat, nothing but a bluish-gray haze filled the space. At her door, cool wood met my palm. The metal handle wasn't hot, so I pushed inside.

The windows were closed; smoke hadn't breached the room. My gaze zeroed in on the small white foot dangling off the edge of the bed. "Hope. Wake up."

No response.

She was still sprawled on her stomach with the towel askew. "There's a fire. Wake up."

She didn't move.

I shook her shoulder. My fingers connected with sticky wetness. I felt a bump on the back of her neck that hadn't been there earlier.

Cold fear seized me. I pivoted into a fighting stance as my eyes scanned the room. No one jumped out at me. I picked up the receiver from the nightstand and punched in 911. The line was dead. Damn damn damn. And I'd left my cell phone on the coffee table in the living room.

On instinct I flung back the quilt and cradled Hope to my chest. Her weight didn't register as I hustled from the room. Despite the muscles in my chest being strung rubber-band tight, I inhaled deeply, dashed down the steps and out the front door. Once my bare feet hit concrete, I headed for the gazebo.

Hope didn't stir as I set her on the ground. I raced back inside the house, grabbed my cell phone, and dialed 911 as I sprinted back outside to keep vigil over my sister.

After dispatch rattled off their initial spiel, I said, "This is Mercy Gunderson. 43007 Gunderson Way. There's an injured woman here who requires immediate medical attention. At least one structure on the property is on fire . . . No, ma'am . . . I'm outside . . . Yes, ma'am . . . Thank you."

My cell rang not three seconds later. Jake. I flipped it open. "Mercy! You outta the house?"

"Yes."

"Where are you?"

"By the gazebo. Where are you?"

"On my way."

Two minutes later Jake came hauling ass around the corner. "You okay?"

"I'm fine. But . . . someone broke in and hurt Hope before they set the fire."

"What? Hope is here?" He looked at the cell phone clutched in my hand. "Did you call it in?"

"Yeah."

"Good. Stay with her. I have to see if TJ put Queenie and Comet in the stables in the old barn. The north side of the small barn and the grass beside it are on fire, too."

Shit. Three fires? "Anything else burning?"

"I don't know. I'll check and be back."

Jake seemed startled when I grabbed his forearm. "The horses aren't worth risking your life."

"I know, but I ain't about to let an animal burn to death if I can get 'em out."

I phoned Sophie and asked her to come help. Hope would need coddling, and I'd be too busy putting out fires to tend her. I circled the outside of the house checking to see if anything had been damaged.

An ugly black stain darkened the white siding beneath the kitchen window, as if someone tried to torch the place but couldn't get it to ignite, so they moved on to destroy the next thing. Or had they moved inside?

Why hadn't I heard anything? What had happened to my finely honed powers of observation?

Right. I'd dulled them in the bottom of a whiskey bottle.

Frustration built. I couldn't help my sister. I couldn't stop the buildings from burning down. I couldn't do anything but stand there helplessly as my life careened out of control.

Do something.

Like what? Get my apron wet in the well and help beat the flames back like the pioneer women had done?

An ambulance ripped up the driveway, ending my mental breakdown. Two pumper trucks; two sheriff's cars, sirens wailing; six pickups and assorted SUVs followed. Not gawkers, volunteer firemen. Vehicles were abandoned, shouts exchanged as the fireproof suits went on.

I flagged down the ambulance crew. "She's over here."

The male EMT was Geneva's brother, Rome. "Is it Sophie?"

"No. It's Hope. I don't know when, or how, but someone hit her in the neck and I know I shouldn't have moved her in case it's a head injury, but I couldn't tell if the house was on fire, too, and I couldn't just leave her—"

"You did fine, Mercy. We'll take it from here."

I put my lips to his ear. "She's pregnant."

"Good to know." When I didn't budge, Rome peered in my eyes. "Take a deep breath. Do I need to treat you for shock?"

Was it that obvious? "No."

"Good. See if the firefighters need anything. I'll find you as soon as I'm done with Hope. See? She's already stirring."

I squeezed her hand. She squeezed back.

As I skirted the concrete birdbath, I heard boards collapsing and a *whoosh* of air. I saw a shower of red and orange sparks soaring into the dark sky. Guess I wouldn't have to worry about painting the chicken coop.

A few firefighters were in the pasture attempting to keep the grass fire from spreading. One guy stood sentinel by the propane tank. Others were hosing down the flames licking up the side of the barn.

Damn. There was a gas tank on the far side of the other smaller barn. Jake and the ranch hands used it to fill ATVs, chainsaws, and yard equipment. Jake had been dealing with the horses; he probably hadn't talked to the firemen.

I glanced at the wooden structure. Yellow flames shot into the air, then sparks fell to the ground like gigantic lemon drops. One tiny flare and the blast radius might be enough to ignite the dry grass on this side of the barn. Then the haystacks, the cars, the farm and fire equipment, and the house were in danger of catching fire.

Run.

Instead of running away, I sprinted across the yard, yelling for the chief. Pebbles tore my feet. A chunk of logging chain embedded in the dirt by the old hand water pump tripped me, and I took the brunt of the fall on my knees, rather than twist my ankle again.

I looked up.

Fire danced across the shake shingles. An ember broke free and landed directly on top of the rusted metal gas container. Followed by two more. And two more after that.

Too late.

My heart stopped. I didn't stick around to watch it explode. I scrambled to my feet and ran like hell, screaming my fool head off.

The hair on the back of my neck stood straight up. I heard *whump whump whump BOOM*. Bright light flashed behind me; a blast of heat followed. Something solid hit me, slamming my body into the earth.

I couldn't see, I couldn't breathe, I couldn't move.

Shouts, footsteps, the whine of mechanical equipment drifted around me. Couldn't anyone see I was dying?

An eternity passed before I realized the unnamed entity shielding me was warm and panting like a dog. The object shifted. Rough hands frantically pushed at my tangled hair. Warm, moist lips grazed my ear.

"Come on, Mercy. Talk to me. Yell at me. Do something."

I opened my eyes and stared into Dawson's soot-covered face, inches from mine.

"You okay?"

I sort of nodded.

"Ah hell, I knocked the wind out of you, didn't I?"

I nodded again.

"I shouldn't have hit you that hard. But I heard you yelling and saw how close you were to the tank and I just—"

"Overreacted," I choked out.

He didn't crack a smile. "Better safe than sorry."

"I guess." I wiggled. His jeans scratched the front of my bare legs, gravel dug into the back of my thighs. "You're crushing me."

"Sorry." Dawson scrambled off and held a hand out to help me up.

"Thanks."

"No problem." He frowned and tipped my chin up, his eyes searched my face. "Have the EMTs check you out."

"Why?" I didn't give a damn how bad I looked.

"To make sure you didn't scorch your lungs. Or I didn't break your ribs."

"Oh."

The tip of his shaking finger gently traced my cheek. "There's a bloody scratch here, too. If it gets infected, it'll scar." He plucked debris from my unbound hair, letting it fall between us like confetti. His other wrist rested on my collarbone and his palm circled my neck as his thumb caressed my jawline.

"Mercy?" Rome's voice broke the moment. "Can I see you for a second?"

"Umm. Ah. Sure. I'll be right there."

Dawson gave me an unreadable look before he stepped back and rejoined the firefighters.

Something had just happened. But I'll be damned if I knew what.

SIXTEEN

Hope had sustained a concussion. The blow hadn't broken the skin, which puzzled me. When I questioned Rome, he told me the sticky stuff I'd felt on the back of her neck was some kind of hair product.

Sophie volunteered to spend the night while I handled the details in the aftermath of the fire. At Rome's request, Doc Canaday swung by. After examining Hope, he'd assured me she and the baby were fine and prescribed a few days' bed rest.

I returned outside to watch the commotion wind down. The remaining firefighters loaded up the hoses on the last pumper truck. A couple of hours had passed since the gas tank had blown, yet the acrid, sour smell of smoke still hung in the air.

We'd lost the chicken coop. Both barns were charred on the outside but otherwise unscathed. No stray embers ignited the haystacks, just the pasture directly behind the barn. Luckily, wind hadn't been a factor, but the firefighters cut a square fire line a hundred yards back just to be safe.

From a purely investigative angle, nothing made sense. The two most important structures were left standing. It bugged me that so many people were on the scene so quickly. Why? We weren't exactly on the main drag. And yet the sheriff, the fire department, and most of our neighbors all showed up in record time. Almost as if they'd been waiting for something like this to happen.

Or planning it.

I shivered.

Sheriff Dawson stuck by the firemen as they made one last

sweep of the smoldering pile for additional flare-ups. In the still-ness, the low baritone murmurs were comforting somehow.

Thin tendrils of smoke rose from the rubble. I wandered to the porch. At three in the morning the thermometer read 77 degrees. I couldn't make myself go inside to clean up, despite the fact I stank like smoke and sweat and fear. First time all night I realized I'd been putting out fires in what I'd worn to bed. Good thing I slept in ratty old shorts and a tank top and not naked.

I grabbed the hose and cranked the spigot. Holding my lips to the stream of water, I greedily welcomed the cool wetness in my throat, wishing it'd quench the burning in my lungs.

Washing my arms and legs proved difficult with one hand. I held the hose above my head and doused myself, closing my eyes as the icy cold water flowed over my body. Mainly I wanted the smell gone. It brought back memories of war. Of death. Of the first time I'd run for my life through smoke-clogged streets while everything and everyone around me burned.

I'd felt as sick and helpless and confused then as I did now. Filling my cupped hand with water, I inhaled the liquid through my nostrils. I coughed until my lungs were clear.

Once I could breathe again, I noticed Jake standing at the end of the sidewalk. "Is everything okay?"

"For now, the horses are in the west pasture. *Unci* kicked me out, so I'll head home, unless you want me to stay."

"I'll keep an eye on things. Doubt I'll be able to sleep anyway."

"Then I'll see you in the morning." He vanished.

A sliver of moonlight gave the quart of Wild Turkey on the wicker table a halolike glow. I palmed the bottle and sat on the porch steps, fighting the urge to take a big swig.

After the last pumper truck pulled away, Sheriff Dawson crossed the yard in that loose-hipped, confident stride exclusive to cowboys, bull riders, and law enforcement officers. Since the poor man could lay claim to all three, he came by that swagger honestly.

I couldn't help but watch him.

Dawson was an imposing man out of uniform. I still didn't trust him, but my body didn't seem to give a rat's ass. My mind kept flashing to what an impressive sight Mad Dog must've been in a pair of leather-fringed batwing chaps. After a long hard ride with a 1,500-pound bull between his legs.

When a spark flared inside me, I realized I hadn't hosed myself down nearly enough to deal with him.

Dawson plopped next to me. Without comment, he plucked the bottle from my hands, placed it against his chapped lips, and drank steadily.

"That's what I needed." He gulped another mouthful and handed it back.

I let the bottle dangle in my right hand between my dirty knees.

He frowned. "How did you get all wet?"

It should've bothered me, the way he stared at the clothes clinging to my body, especially since he didn't bother to pretend he wasn't looking closely. Very closely.

"An accident with the hose."

He grunted.

"What'd Klapperich say?"

"Arson."

"No. Really? How long did it take him to come up with that brilliant theory?"

Dawson's muscled forearm abraded the inside of my thigh as he snatched the bottle. "Is that a character flaw, thinking everyone around here is incompetent?"

"If the cowboy boot fits—hey! Quit drinking all my whiskey, Dawson. Aren't you supposed to be on duty?"

"Do I look like I'm on duty?"

I gave him a once-over. Scuffed boots. New blue Wranglers. Championship belt buckle. Gray T-shirt smeared with black soot. Hooded eyes. "No, you look like you were on a date."

"I wasn't on a damn date."

"You got here pretty fast after the call went out."

His gaze returned to my face. "What were *you* doing when you noticed the chicken coop was on fire?"

"You asking me if I torched my own buildings?"

"Hell no."

"Is this an official interview, Sheriff?"

"Smart-ass," he muttered. "Would it kill you to cooperate with me just once?"

"Fine. I was sleeping. Hope didn't want to go home, so she crashed in my bedroom while I was tossing and turning on the floor in the guest bedroom."

"Hope was staying with you?"

"Just for tonight."

"Does it happen often?"

"No. It was kind of a last-minute thing."

"Who knew she was here?"

"No one. Why?"

His eyes narrowed. "She was attacked in *your* bedroom. I don't need to spell out what it means, especially to a smart cookie like you."

Instead of stinging him with a rude comment, I closed my eyes. I heard the steady swell of crickets. No other animal noises caught my attention. Damn. Something was wrong besides the absence of wind. I couldn't place my finger on it. It was like someone was watching me.

Tingles raced up my spine.

Dawson's big hand closed over mine. His ragged thumb swept a continual arc over my knuckles, and his breath tickled my ear. "Talk to me."

I shook off the lure of his touch. "Ssh. I'm listening. Do you hear that?"

"I don't hear anything."

"Exactly."

He went still and listened.

Then I heard it: pebbles shifting on the path between the house and the barn. Someone *was* out there. No time to run inside for a gun. My adrenaline kicked in, and I was on my feet and slithering through the darkness before Dawson knew I'd left.

Everything fell away and I became one with the night. I dropped to my haunches in the shadow of the ash tree. Listened for the sound of clothing rustling. Or heavy breathing. Or more footsteps.

Nothing.

A twig snapped. By the machine shed? I couldn't tell. I crept closer.

My bare feet barely registered the bite of gravel as I tiptoed to the corner of the barn. The odor of charred wood lingered. Should I cut through? Surely the not-so-sneaky bastard wouldn't be stupid enough to hide in the barn.

Part of me wished for my rifle and scope, but I knew I'd be tempted to follow my training and shoot first.

Screech. Bang. The clank of the gate opening.

A diversion? Or was the idiot really taking off through the field with a quartet of nasty bulls ready to give chase?

My senses narrowed to auditory. Fury charged my system, but I kept my breathing normal. Then I heard light footfalls creeping alongside the barn. I braced myself to attack.

One leg appeared, then two. I kicked my foot between the gait midstride and the person toppled to the ground.

Before I had a chance to immobilize my prey, the man rolled me and I landed on my ass.

I jumped up. So did he. He rushed and knocked me into the side of the barn, pinning me against the warped wood.

"Jesus Christ, Mercy. What the hell are you doing?" he hissed in my ear.

Dawson? How had he gotten over here so fast? "Me? What were you doing?"

"My goddamn job."

I snorted.

"Don't start."

"Well? Did you see anything?"

"Besides a coyote hightailing it out of here?"

"A coyote? Where?"

"Over by the propane tank. It must've smelled the burning feathers or something to bring it this close in."

So much for my sharpshooter's instincts. "You didn't see any-one?"

"No."

Even if my vision wasn't perfect in one eye, I had a hard time believing I'd miss an animal that size. I got the feeling the sheriff hadn't seen a coyote. "Quit screwing with me, Dawson."

"What do you mean?"

"Since when has a coyote grown smart enough to open a gate?"

"You heard the gate open?"

"Didn't you?"

Pause. "No."

I attempted to shove him. "I'm sick of your lies. Who are you really working for? Kit McIntyre? What do you get for trying to burn my place down, Dawson?"

"Why would I do that?"

"That's what I'm asking, dumb-ass."

His hand swept from my forehead down to the base of my skull.

My muscles went rigid as a 2x4.

"Either you're in shock or you've got a head injury. Because no way in hell did I do this, and you should know that."

I hated this. I thrashed against him.

Then Dawson had pressed my left cheek against the wood, layering his sweaty face to mine. "Mercy, say something."

"Let me go."

"Why won't you let me help you . . . dammit. Stop squirming." He released a pent-up breath. Slowly he angled back, muttering something.

I looked up at him.

Big mistake.

Those steely gray eyes locked on mine.

And I became acutely aware of how close we were. Of the solid feel of him against me and the fast beat of his heart against my chest. Of his ragged breath beading the perspiration on my skin. Of the adrenaline pumping between us like a dare.

Even our reactions to the situation were strangely synchronized.

My gaze dropped to his mouth. "Dawson—"

Then that mouth was on mine. His lips glided back and forth insistently until my lips parted for his. His hands came up from manacling my wrists to cradle my head. He fed me sweet kisses, hot kisses, hungry kisses, wet kisses. Kisses that plainly told me he'd imagined kissing me like this and wasn't about to let the opportunity pass him by.

I wasn't an idiot; I didn't even pretend I wanted to push him away.

Neither of us had expected this complication. Hadn't seemed to stop us from wanting it. Acting on it.

My last coherent thought for a while was *holy shit.*

Not a breath of wind stirred as our breathing leveled. I braced myself for that awkward moment when you realize you've done something incredibly stupid. When you want to kick your own ass and the ass of anyone else dumb enough to be within kicking distance of you.

Then his warm mouth searched for mine again. Damn if my lips didn't open. Damn if I didn't sink into the kiss like I hadn't been kissed in years and had to stock up for those cold, lonely nights I found myself alone. Embarrassed by my emotional greed and physical need, I pushed his shoulders and ripped my mouth from his. "Let go."

"Not until you look at me."

I didn't want to look at him. In my mind's eye I saw his male smugness. A cocky, I-gave-it-to-you-good smirk, and I created several smart-ass comments that would diffuse the situation and give me the advantage.

I opened one eye at a time. No such expression distorted his face. "What?"

"Don't pretend this thing is one-sided, or let loose a scathing remark that'll cut me down to size. I couldn't take it after . . ."

I bit my tongue and studied the spots scattered on the T-shirt stretched across his chest. Crap. Had I *drooled* on him?

He stepped back and raked a hand through his hair, making the strands stick up like baby chicken feathers. "Look. I can stay tonight—"

"No. I appreciate the offer, but we'll be fine."

"You won't give an inch, will you?"

"If whoever did this sees your official vehicle parked out here all night, they'll think I'm scared and then they win."

"It's not about winning, Mercy. It's about your safety."

"I've got eight guns, eight thousand rounds, and a really bad attitude. That's all the protection we need."

"Not what I meant and you damn well know it."

I smoothed my shorts, trying once again to hide the ugly wounds on my upper thigh from his prying eyes. "So we lost our heads. It happens."

He brooded, studying me suspiciously.

"Dangerous situations trigger reactions and a heightened sense of awareness. Kind of like combat stress."

"*That's* your explanation for what just happened?"

"Yeah. Why?"

"Because it's a bullshit excuse."

"You have a better one?"

Dawson laughed. "Not an excuse, but a theory I might tell you sometime when you aren't being such a pain in the ass."

"Why is that funny?"

"Because after all that's happened, you still don't trust me, do you?"

My cool detachment took over. I looked him dead in the eye and answered, "Nope."

It didn't faze him. He stared back with equal aloofness.

Which pissed me off. "So I'd appreciate it if you didn't blab what just happened to everyone in the county."

"No problem. No one would believe it anyway." He spun on his boot heel and swaggered off.

Well, hell. That hadn't gone the way I'd planned.

Early the next morning the phone rang and I answered it quickly to keep it from disturbing Hope. "Hello?"

"Mercy? Good, you're there."

A second passed before I placed the gravelly voice. "Rollie?"

"Yeah. I was afraid that uppity Sophie Red Leaf wouldn't let me talk to ya if she answered."

"So you disguised your voice?"

"Yep. You free for a bit this morning?"

"Sure."

"I'll swing by to getcha in about fifteen minutes."

I grabbed my Sig and a water bottle. The day was sticky. Even the tease of moisture was a blessed change from the oppressive dry heat.

I meandered down the driveway, debating on whether a truckload of gravel would fill the gouges from the fire trucks and fire crews. Not that we pampered a green swath of manicured lawn anywhere on our place. Watering ornamental grass was a waste when we didn't have enough water for our cattle. Or when our grazing land resembled a dust bowl. Or when one of our wells could go dry at any time.

Along the road, lavender starflowers waved in the wind, the cheery yellow centers nature's smiley face. During my childhood, I decapitated those flowers and used the pretty blossoms as the crowning glory on my mud pies. My mud pies still looked better than my real pies, much to Sophie's dismay.

I rested my forearm on top of the mailbox. A vehicle barreled toward me from the north, reminding me of the night I'd almost become a hood ornament. So many bad things had happened in the interim I'd forgotten about it. I wondered if Dawson had forgotten, too.

Rollie grinned from inside a rattletrap Chevy pickup. The jagged end of his braid swept the seat as he leaned across to open the passenger door. *"Hoka hey."*

"Hey." The makeshift vice-grip door handle clanked as I slammed the door shut. "Nice hat."

His fingers swept the black felt brim. "My official PI hat. Makes me look mysterious and smart, eh?"

"Definitely. So, are we on official PI business, boss?"

"Yep."

"Where we going?"

"Just for a drive so I can talk to you about them Warrior Society kids." He shot me a sidelong glance as he shifted to third. "You still interested, right?"

"Yeah. But I didn't think you were."

"Guess mebbe I was curious so I asked around some."

"You could've told me over the phone."

He grunted. "Huh-uh. Face-to-face meetings only in this line of work. Do you know how much private and dangerous stuff people overhear because of phone conversations and the like? I prefer a controlled environment." Rollie slapped the seat between us and a cloud of dust arose. "Like this one."

Lucky me. "So how'd you get the information? Or is that a PI secret?"

Seemed Rollie might hedge. Finally, he sighed. "Verline. She was friends with Sue Anne. And with that Lanae girl who just up and took off. Verline went to talk to Bucky One Feather

yesterday about what was going on with the Warrior Society. He
told her."

"Just because she asked?"

"No." Rollie shuddered. "I don't think she asked nice. Them
pregnancy hormones are nasty."

True. I thought of Hope the night she'd come to my rescue at
the rez rec center. Not typical behavior for her. "What'd Bucky say?"

"Just he's scared he'll wind up dead. He wouldn't tell Verline
who was in charge. But he did mention you and your sister took
a whack at them. That true?"

I nodded.

"Didja learn anything new?"

"Not a damn thing. It's frustrating." I directed my gaze out
the window to the undulating prairie, rock-strewn hills, and
the plateaus rising from nowhere—the unique topography that
comprised our land. The austere beauty of the Badlands on my
right; on my left, the pine-covered grandeur of the Black Hills
and the jagged point of Harney Peak in the distance. I'd been on
this road so many times I could've driven it in my sleep. I never
tired of the dramatic view. What did that mean?

That this is where you belong.

Gooseflesh broke out on my arms.

I faced Rollie. "Did you say something?"

"No. Why? You look like you seen a ghost."

No ghost. Just phantom ancestral voices talking inside my
head. I'd rather it had been a damn ghost.

"Mercy? What's wrong?"

"Ah. Nothing. Is that the only reason you called?"

"No." He lit a cigarette and relaxed back, driving with his left
hand. "Heard about the fire, hey."

"Everybody heard."

"I was on my way over to help when dispatch came on the
scanner and said it was under control. Lucky thing it didn't
spread."

Not surprising Rollie listened to the police scanner. "Yeah. It
was hard to believe that so many people showed up to help out."
An enormous blackbird took flight from a broken fence post; the
wings beat an iridescent blue in the blinding sunlight.

"Folks wanting to help out surprises you?"

"No. That used to be my biggest complaint about living here. Everybody knew everybody else's business. Now that doesn't seem like the worst thing."

Rollie coughed and spit a loogie out the open window. "It ain't. It's what kept your dad sane after Sunny died, that sense of community and continuity. Sometimes it's a pain in the ass, but it's better than the alternative."

"Like starting over someplace new?"

"Uh-huh. You lose the history and the connection. Once it's gone, you ain't ever getting it back and you become an outsider. Your family ain't never been outsiders. Even after you've been gone two damn decades, the community considers you one of their own, Mercy. Being here is your destiny."

I ignored the *destiny* comment.

"Case in point: them freaks that bought the Jackson place? They're outsiders. Always will be. And I'll bet a hundred bucks not one of 'em bothered to lend a hand when your place was on fire last night, did they?"

"Not that I know of."

"You been by since they put up the electric fences?"

"Been meaning to . . . I've had other things on my mind."

"I'll take you past it before I run you back home. I ain't gonna slow down, 'cause them white supremacists would probably love to shoot an old savage Injun guy like me, eh?"

"I'd protect you."

"You carrying?"

"Always."

After Rollie's comments, I studied the scenery with a sharper eye. Cracked soil, ranging in color from chalk white to bleached orange, signaled cattle had overgrazed this section. Huge clumps of sage plants overtook the landscape, but it was still butt-ugly. Barbed-wire fence stretched as far as the eye could see. I recognized the scraggly copse of poplar trees marking the turnoff to the Jacksons' driveway. Some things never changed.

Whoa. And some things changed more than I could imagine.

Electric fences surrounding the house and yard distorted the landscape into a military image reminiscent of the cold war.

Warning signs were plastered everywhere. The skeletal forms of buildings being constructed loomed like metal monsters.

Three ATVs were positioned as guards inside the fence. And Sheriff Dawson was hunkered against the front bumper of his patrol car, red and blue lights swirling around him as he talked to another guy inside the fence.

I muttered, "Crap," and plastered my back against the seat, out of Dawson's line of vision. I blamed the bullfrogs jumping in my stomach on cruising downhill, not on my seeing Dawson. Or thinking he might've seen me.

"Changes them folks made are spooky, ain't it? Couple of other people were seriously interested in buying it. They would've been a better match."

Who would've been a better match? The Florida Swamp Rats? Kit McIntyre? I wanted to know; yet I didn't.

"Gotta be doing something hinky there," Rollie continued, "with all that security, doncha think?"

"That's what Iris Newsome thinks. She's been bugging me about signing some kind of petition banning additional building or some damn thing."

"Might not be a bad idea. Rumor around Viewfield is they're from some religious sect where they have multiple wives."

Lost in my own thoughts, I shrugged. I wondered what Dawson was doing out there. Routine traffic arrest? On a secondary gravel road? Didn't he have a more productive way to spend his time? Like looking for my nephew's murderer?

Rollie sighed. It wasn't a happy sigh. It was a weary sigh I used to hear from my dad.

"What?"

"How long you had a thing for Sheriff Dawson, hey?"

My fingers rubbed my mouth. Was it obvious my lips were still a little puffy from last night's encounter with Dawson? No. Rollie was perceptive, which made him good at his job. But I was good at mine, too, so I didn't answer.

"Mercy. You know I ain't gonna let this go."

"Who says he doesn't have a thing for *me*?"

Rollie squinted at me through the smoke curling by his eye. "Same difference."

Big difference, but I doubted he'd see one.

He said, "I should've known."

"Known what?"

"That you'd go for a fella like him."

"What makes you think you know anything about the type of guy I go for now?"

He followed up with a mean laugh laced with coughing spurts. "Because Dawson is just like your dad."

That observation jarred me to the core. My mouth opened to argue, but he beat me to the punch.

"Don't deny it. Dawson is big guy. Stubborn. Good-looking. Kinda mean. A little on the shady side. Another cowboy in a uniform."

"My dad wasn't shady."

He grunted. "I won't argue that point, outta respect for the dead."

I bit my tongue.

"Besides, I thought you had some trust issues with the sheriff."

"I do." Denial or explanation of the change would sound like an excuse, or worse, a confession. I didn't need to give Rollie Rondeaux any personal ammo on me because he'd use it.

"I understand the attraction to someone who ain't good for you. Been with a woman like that a time or two myself. Worth a tumble but I'd never turn my back on her."

My teeth left another chomp mark on my tongue. His situation with Verline wasn't my business. However, I had a perverse need to keep my personal business with Dawson out of the public domain. "Do I have to ask you not to blab this, Rollie?"

"Nope. I don't diss on my employees."

"Got more than just me working for you?"

"Officially? Nope." He grinned. "Unofficially? More than you can shake a stick at, Mercy girl."

I smiled. Couldn't help it. I'd always liked Rollie.

He dumped me off at the top of the driveway. "Keep in touch. You hear anything, you need anything, call me."

"For another face-to-face meeting to keep Big Brother from overhearing us?"

"Yep. Or mebbe, keep me in the loop because I'm worried about you."

• • •

Back at the ranch, Theo convinced Hope he could take care of her, so she'd left with him. Sophie shushed me during her soaps. Yay. At loose ends again. Damn. I needed a job.

You could run for sheriff.

Right. That didn't help my immediate boredom.

Then I remembered I'd told Jake I'd check out the large flat-bottomed grazing section he'd tentatively earmarked for buffalo. Tooling around in my dad's truck would clear my head. Nothing more relaxing than spending a summer afternoon on the high prairie. The dips and valleys of the terrain showcased subtle changes, changes the uninitiated wouldn't notice.

Much as I tried to pretend otherwise, I wasn't the uninitiated. For the first twelve years of my life I'd soaked up Dad's words and wisdom like a sponge. So I recognized the yucca seedpods changing colors from creamy white to brittle tan. The spines were faded from green to gray due to dust and drought. The clumps of yellow tumblemustard popped up sporadically, sweet and lovely as the thorny bushes of wild pink roses.

I spied an entrance to the west pasture. I unhooked the barbed-wire loop between the posts; yeah, we employed some high-level security measures on the Gunderson Ranch. Why Kit felt the need to sneak around boggled my mind. With seventy-five thousand acres, some of it bordering public land, there was no way we could police it all.

I dragged the rustic gate open. The tires *tharump*ed across the corroded cattleguard. I hopped back out to close it. Far as I knew we weren't keeping cattle in this section, but I'd been schooled early on in the importance of keeping all gates shut. Old habits die hard.

I inched my way in. Fire was a constant worry. Dad's concern during drought years reached the point he wouldn't allow any vehicle that wasn't diesel in any of the pastures after the middle of July because of increased fire danger from the catalytic converters. And when the ranch hands or Jake traveled from one section to the next, they followed a distinct path. No reason to cut up every square inch of earth just because we could.

Contrary to what the tree huggers thought, most ranchers were heavily invested in conservation efforts. Hard not to be when one depended on the land to live.

I putted along, listening to the meadowlarks and hoping to hear the distinctive trill of an oriole. Looking for any sign of the much-reviled prairie dogs. Despite PETA's claim, prairie dogs were not fuzzy, cute little animals being persecuted by trigger-happy landowners in the Wild West.

Prairie dog towns—a series of interconnected tunnels culminating in hundreds of holes—would pop up and ruin miles of grazing land. The oversized rats were good for nothing except lunch for larger predators. Or for target practice.

The truck chugged up a small rise. Once I reached the top of the plateau, I noticed the stock dam below. Bone dry. Traces of gypsum lined the reddish-black banks. I remembered the dam being a prime spot for duck hunting.

How long had it sat completely empty?

I drove, lost in the solitude. Recognizing buttes and ravines I'd forgotten existed. Watching antelope streak across until their white tails were a memory. I'd spent so many years hating the financial uncertainty of ranch life, the never-ending work, the sacrifices this chunk of earth demanded from my family, that I'd lost the pure joy of having a concrete place to call home. In this day and age of globalization, having a home wasn't a given.

Half the soldiers I knew had nothing but an APO box to call their own. They were too young to have established themselves outside their parents' domain. Married soldiers lived in base housing. Singles lived in barracks or apartments close to the base. Few actually owned houses. Even fewer owned property. Like most soldiers engaged in war, it's hard to plan for a future when you're not sure whether you've got one. When you don't know if you'll ever see that proverbial white picket fence.

So I had the one thing wars were fought over: a bit of earth to call my own. And I'd be damned if anyone was going to chase me from it.

SEVENTEEN

My cell phone chirred, waking me from my unexpected siesta in the truck. "Hello?"

"Mercy? It's Geneva."

"Hey. What's up?"

"Look, do you think you could come over?"

The reception out here sucked. Or Geneva sounded frantic. "No problem." I squinted at the tiny numbers on the receiver. Whoa. I'd been dozing for an hour. "What time?"

"Umm. Now? I need to talk to you about Molly. And what happened with Sue Anne. Molly is really freaked out. The priest has even been by, and he can't get through to her. No one can."

Had Geneva expected Molly to buy into the church's automatic Sue-Anne-is-in-a-better-place line of bull? How could she expect me to reassure her daughter when I hadn't been able to find solace regarding Levi's murder? Or with the fact Sue Anne had been killed on my doorstep?

"Yeah. I'll swing by."

"See you in a bit." And she hung up.

I made the turnoff to Geneva's place and cruised down the driveway. No kids came running out to greet me, which I hate to admit was a disappointment. No kids in the sandbox, on the bikes, or on the trampoline. This time of day had always been the "golden hour" for ranch kids. Chores done, supper on the way. Perfect if you wanted to sneak five minutes to yourself. These days that probably meant fighting over PS2 or a GameCube.

Geneva came out of the house with measured steps, wiping her palms on the towel hanging from the front of her belt loops.

"Hey, Gen, what's up?"

"Same old, same old."

"Where is everyone? Inside?"

"No. Brent took them to Wal-Mart in Rapid City." I followed her to a picnic table in front of a cluster of chokecherry bushes heavily laden with the bitter red fruit.

"I wanted to have uninterrupted time together to talk."

That weird spidey sense that I'd recently developed kicked in. "I thought I was here to talk to Molly?"

"No. I want to talk to you."

It wasn't like Geneva to mask her motives. "Talk about what?"

"Everything that's been going on around here."

"Everything meaning . . ."

Geneva scowled at me. "Gee, I don't know—Albert, Levi, and Sue Anne all turning up dead on your property. And I believe the only one you didn't discover personally was Albert."

Okay. "I know—"

"You'll get your turn to talk, but can you just listen to me to first?"

I nodded warily.

She picked at a cracked piece of barn-red paint on the picnic table. "Dawson getting appointed sheriff seven months ago shocked a lot of people. None of us knew how sick your dad was. Guess we all figured if the invincible Sheriff Gunderson really was that bad off, then the prodigal daughter would return home."

Prodigal? That was bitchy. I waited for her to regale me with snippets of gossip on who in the community had decided I'd been reincarnated as the Wicked Witch of the West for not holding bedside vigil or Dad's hand as he'd died. But her snappy tidbits didn't come. Consequently, my back snapped straight.

"You haven't been around for years, Mercy. Yet, the more things change, the more they stay the same." Geneva looked me over like I was a soil experiment. "Strange thing is, you've probably changed less than the rest of us."

"Meaning what?"

"You're still waltzing around, no real responsibilities. Coming home when you feel like it. Traveling to exciting places all over the globe."

Whoo-yeah. Mideast hot spots were all the rage. The discos were hopping and jam-packed with celebrities. The exclusive spas were first class. The shopping was to die for.

WTF?

I expected her to grin and say, "Just kidding," but I was doomed to disappointment when she remained mum.

Was she serious? No responsibilities? My days consisted of carrying out executions. How did her days compare? Rounding up cattle, checking the outlying fences for dry rot, hanging clothes on the line, whipping up a batch of chokecherry jam. The potential for deadly mistakes was considerably less in her world.

"Aren't you going to argue with me?" she demanded. "Remind me that you have serious responsibilities, too?"

It was like she was baiting me. "Why should I defend myself? You've already made up your mind as to what type of irresponsible person I've become. Or have always been."

A small sneer curled her upper lip. "You know, at times in the last twenty years, when you'd come back on leave, I felt sorry for you. Other times I've been incredibly jealous. I've never allowed either feeling to affect our friendship."

Until now, apparently.

"I should be happy you're here and happy there's a possibility you'll stick around permanently." A wistful look was there and gone. "Sometimes I still feel like that crazy high school girl with nothing to worry about besides dances and rodeos and whether Dad would let me drive the car Saturday night. And other days it seems I've been a wife and mother my whole life.

"But you've done everything you set out to do. Left the family homestead and let someone else handle the responsibilities and drudgery. Traveled extensively." She twisted her wedding ring around. "While I stayed here."

"Geneva, you never wanted to leave South Dakota. You wanted to marry Brent and live on the family ranch. There's nothing wrong with that. It just didn't fit with how I wanted to live."

"So why do I feel you're rubbing your life and your accomplishments in my face?"

"What?"

Geneva leaned forward; her eyes were cold and cruel. "What's it like to play at running a ranch? To have financial security? Not be forced to sell off chunks of your property just to pay your taxes? To employ a tribe of peons to do the chores? To appoint an accountant to keep track of the ranch finances? To hire a maid to cook and clean and wash your clothes?

"Do you have any idea how much that pisses the rest of us off? You showing up like nothing's changed? Acting like you own this county? Driving around in your dad's pickup or your fancy-ass sports car as if you don't have a care in the world? We are all struggling, Mercy. Us. Your friends. The people you grew up with. And it's like you're . . . mocking us."

I heard my molars crack I'd clenched my teeth so hard.

Geneva continued spewing poison. "If you decide to sell to one of those out-of-state hunting outfits—rumor has it they've offered you millions of dollars—the value of *our* ag land will increase. And unlike you, we won't *have* a choice. We'll be forced to sell. And it'll be all your fault."

If anyone else had spouted those nasty accusations, I would've walked away, without refuting their stupidity and without looking back. Instead, I remained in place, letting the hatred brimming in my best friend's eyes burn me from the outside in, like I'd been dunked in lava.

I took a minute to let my temper cool. "You finished?"

Geneva nodded. Cautiously.

"Again, I'm not going to defend myself. But I will remind you why I haven't been here for the last twenty years 'playing' at being a rancher.

"While you've been home, surrounded by the people you love, even when doing the drudgery and chores you supposedly despise—canning and cooking and cleaning and washing diapers—with unfettered access to clean water, fresh food, a real bathroom, and a real bed, complaining in your air-conditioned house about the high price of gas and electricity, and about the ridiculousness of war as you sit in front of the big-screen TV, I've been in Afghanistan and Iraq. Living in the desert. Eating sand. Getting shot at every damn hour of every damn day. Watching old, crippled civilians and young, hopeful soldiers die right in front of me. Wishing I could have one normal day of joyriding around in a vehicle where I'm not afraid a car bomb will go off and blow me and a hundred others into bloody chunks. While you're complaining how life hasn't treated you fairly, I haven't been on vacation, Geneva. I've been in hell."

The corner of her eye lifted, a cross between a wince and a twitch, but besides that, her face remained a porcelain mask. And I wanted to see it crack.

"We all make choices. You made yours, I made mine, but you have no right blaming me for a damn thing. And just because I don't constantly whine about my responsibilities doesn't mean I don't have any."

"I can blame you for one thing."

My dark gaze hooked hers.

"From the moment *you* came home things in this area have been a nightmare." Geneva ticked off the points on her finger-tips. "Albert Yellow Boy was found dead on *your* land. Levi was murdered on *your* land. Molly's friend Sue Anne was killed on *your* porch. And last night someone lit *your* buildings on fire. Maybe the gossip about your family being cursed is true."

"You blaming all that on me, Gen?" I never imagined Geneva and I would grow apart. As the reality of the situation glared me in the face, a deep sense of loss started to sink in.

"Also, I am warning you to stop contacting my daughter. Sue Anne was murdered the very day she talked to you. The day before that you'd talked to Molly. She feels you bullied her into betraying her friend. She's scared."

"She should be. Three of her friends are dead. This isn't a video game where if you screw up you hit Reset and start over."

"I know that," Geneva snapped. "Just because I'm not living in a foreign country dodging bullets doesn't mean I'm naïve. That's why I'm telling you to stay away from Molly. Don't call her. Don't stop by. I couldn't take it if anything happened to her. Or to one of my other kids. I'm not like you, Mercy."

I flinched. I couldn't help it. "How aren't you like me?"

"You don't understand how much my family means to me."

Trying to gain control of my temper and my tongue didn't work. For once I didn't give a crap if she thought I was the coldest, meanest bitch on the planet, because at times I was.

Like now.

"You think *I* don't understand? Why? Because I haven't given birth I'm incapable of understanding love? Or the loss that comes with it? I've lost a helluva lot more in the last two *months* than you have in the last twenty years, so fuck that, Geneva."

She notched her chin higher and continued the self-righteous glare.

"I might not be able to break the Gunderson curse, but I can break the curse of having a friend like you."

After I stormed to my truck, I cranked the music as loud as it would go and burned rubber in my race to escape.

My mood was black. I practically ripped off the doors at Clementine's so I could belly up to the bar. Inside, no one gave a shit about my attitude. The assorted customers were busy adjusting their own moods with various grain-based remedies.

Some shifty, stringy haired biker squatted on my bar stool. I tapped him on the shoulder.

He turned. "Yeah?"

"Get off my chair."

He laughed. "Yeah, right."

"Now."

Before he opened his maw again, I fisted his leather vest in both hands and threw him on the concrete floor.

He hit. Hard.

The buzz in the bar stopped briefly.

I straddled the stool and didn't bother to look behind me. If one greasy finger touched me, I'd kill him.

He must've sensed my murderous intentions because he disappeared.

Muskrat lifted a brow.

I threw my keys at him. "Don't let me drive."

"You got it. Whatcha drinking?"

"Two shots of Cuervo. In single glasses."

"Lime?"

"No."

Muskrat lined them up. I worked my way from left to right until they were empty. Took two minutes, tops.

"More?"

"Just one. And a pitcher of Bud Light."

The golden liquid went down the hatch before Muskrat finished pulling the pitcher.

He slid an empty pilsner glass in front of me and I said, "Good man."

"Anything else?"

"Does the jukebox take fifties?"

"Twenties."

I dug a wad of money from my purse. Peeled off a hundred and handed it over. "Then I need change."

"You wanna start a tab?"

"Yeah." I peeled off another hundred. "Tell me when I've used this up."

Muskrat frowned at the cash.

"What? If you tell me my money's not good here, I'll get shit-faced someplace else, Muskrat."

"Your money is good, Mercy."

"Then what?"

"Nothing." He punched buttons on the cash register and passed me five twenties in change. "Pick something good."

"Dwight, George, and Gretchen coming right up."

He sort of smiled.

I played every song I loved, liked, and the stuff making the rounds on country radio. A Benjamin buys a lot of tunes. I parked my ass back on the stool, glaring at the bowl of soggy pretzels Muskrat not so subtly placed by the pitcher. "What the hell is this?"

"A buffer before your next round."

"Thanks, Mom."

Muskrat gave me a flinty-eyed stare.

A measure of guilt made me amend, "Works for me."

I crunched pretzels, sang along to "Little Sister," and drank.

And drank some more. I leaned across the bar. "You sure you didn't water down that tequila? 'Cause I don't feel anything."

"You will."

I drained the last of my beer. Looked around.

Interesting crowd. No one I knew. Maybe it was time to make new friends since I was a pariah to the few I had.

Even Geneva had turned on me. I could understand her wanting to protect Molly, but she didn't have to go off on me with such a vicious, personal attack. Fuck that. Fuck her. Fuck everyone on the whole fucking planet.

The tequila hit me like a donkey kick to the head.

Thank God. Rarely did I purposely pursue a falling-down drunk, but when I did I wanted instant gratification.

I sucked down a glass of beer to ensure I wouldn't sober up in the next ten minutes.

More folks crowded in.

My gaze landed on a young, buff cowboy at the end of the bar. Mmm. Mmm. Mmm.

He lifted his head.

Ooh. Check out those baby blues.

He smiled.

I went one better and crooked my finger at him.

He sauntered over. Hooked his thumbs in the belt loops of his skintight Wranglers so I could see his Badlands Circuit Rodeo Champion belt buckle.

"Hey there, darlin'," I said, full of tequila charm.

"Hey there, yourself."

"Nice buckle."

"Thanks."

"How long it take you to win it?"

He grinned. "Four years."

"Still rodeoing?"

"Now and again." His smile dimmed. "So, didja call me over to hear my roping and riding stats? Or for something else, sugar?"

"Actually I need a dip. Whatcha got?"

"Skoal."

"Flavored?"

"Hell no."

"Bandits?"

"Bandits and Long Cut."

"Bandits it is."

He reached in his back pocket and pulled out a can. Popped the lid open, held it out, and the smoky scent of tobacco wafted up.

I picked a pouch and slid it back by my left molars. I couldn't stand to have chew under my lip. The tang of mint and tobacco burst in my mouth. I fell into that category of "social" tobacco users; I could take it or leave it. "Thank you . . . what'd you say your name was?"

"I didn't. But it's Riley."

"Thanks, Riley."

"My pleasure."

He didn't ask my name and I didn't offer. "Whatcha drinking?"

"Jack and Coke."

I motioned to Muskrat. "My friend Riley here needs a Jack and Coke." I poured myself another beer from the pitcher.

Gretchen Wilson belted out "One Bud Wiser."

"Do you believe in karma, Riley?" His pretty, smooth brow wrinkled with confusion. Probably didn't know what karma meant. No matter. I gifted him with my party-girl grin. "Never mind. Let's dance, cowboy."

We stopped in front of the jukebox. I led until he got over whatever made him uneasy. Then we did a jitterbug/two-step combo. Whoo-ee. The kid could move. Must've looked like we were having fun because two other couples joined us.

Yeah, I'm a real trailblazer.

While Martina McBride warbled a sappy tune, we knocked back our drinks. Riley kept sneaking strange looks at me. I suspected ol' blue eyes wanted to scamper off, but was scared I'd toss him on his ass if he tried to escape my evil clutches. Smart man. Still, it wasn't my thing to force him to stay in my company, so I cut him some slack. "Could I get another Bandit? For the road?"

Riley offered his can again. "You leaving?"

"No. I don't want to monopolize your time." I dropped the extra pouch in my shirt pocket. "Thanks for the dip."

"Thanks for the drink."

He had a nice ass. Lewd, but I openly ogled that fine bit of Wrangler-clad flesh as he strutted out the door. I sucked down my draft, feeling my thirty-eight years. Truth was, he was too young for me. Too green. I needed a man with at least a couple years of a steady sexual relationship under his big belt buckle. A man who knew his way around a woman's body. A man with stamina.

Someone like Dawson.

"Fuck that," I said out loud to shut up the smarmy voice inside my head.

"You'd like to fuck that. Too bad your luck ain't holding."

I didn't respond. Just drank. Steadily.

Laronda slithered into the space next to me. The gold bracelets on her arms clattered like a rattlesnake's tail as she waved down Muskrat.

Her overprocessed hair brushed my cheek like a piece of cheap carpet. Too bad I didn't smoke. One flick of the Bic and her starched mane would flame up like underbrush in August.

"Maybe it's not bad luck. Maybe it's your attitude."

"Fuck off, Laronda." I reached for an empty ashtray.

"Then again, maybe it *is* your age."

"You want to go a round or two with me tonight?"

"No. I was taught to respect my elders."

Shake it off, some helpful voice inside my head suggested. I didn't listen. I spit a stream of tobacco juice. It missed the ashtray and splashed on her manicured hand.

"Watch it!" Her gaze narrowed until her ratlike eyes nearly disappeared. Her laugh rang as phony as every other thing decorating her person. "You are a class act. No wonder you're sitting here alone glaring at your beer."

After she paid for her vodka sour, she sashayed away to dick with someone else.

The alcohol soaked in. On my return from the bathroom, I paused to observe a game of darts in the back room. Barely thirty seconds passed before I smelled her. Coating her slimy skin with cheap perfume wouldn't mask the venom in her blood. I waited for her to open her big trap and her forked tongue to emerge.

It didn't take long.

"I suspected you'd be back here trolling."

"You would know all about that."

"Ooh. Meow. You are an old sourpuss, aren't you?"

Jesus. I needed another drink, and I was already three sheets to the wind. I started to walk away.

"Hey, I'm talking to you."

Laronda made the mistake of sinking her claws into my shoulder.

Instinct kicked in. I grabbed her hand and twisted her arm behind her back. "Don't ever touch me."

"That hurts!"

"Good."

"Let go."

I did.

When she whirled around to attack me, I smashed her back into the concrete block wall until her head cracked. I braced my forearm across her windpipe, hindering her hands with my free arm and blocking her legs with mine. Boring. I could take her even when I was shitfaced.

"Don't touch me. Don't talk to me. Don't look at me. If I even think you're breathing in my direction, I will fuck you up. Understand?"

Laronda glared, but didn't answer.

So I pressed harder on her throat.

Her eyes began to water. Her face turned as red as the cherry in her sissy-ass drink.

"Are you clear on that?"

She tried to nod. When she couldn't, she panicked.

I let her.

She thrashed.

I let her.

I whispered, "Stay away from me."

She thrashed some more.

I didn't care. I had a burning desire to get her to that elusive point right before she passed out where she couldn't breathe. Where she thought she might die. And my apathetic eyes would be the last things she'd see.

"Mercy," he said my name sharply. "Let her go."

I removed my forearm. Laronda coughed and gasped, dropping to her knees, which I figured was a natural position for her.

It'd be smug and voyeuristic to watch her wheeze, so I faced John-John. "What?"

"What were you doing to her?"

"Um . . . punching her dance card?"

"Not funny." He leaned in to sniff my breath. "I oughta have Muskrat throw you out for that stunt."

"Do it. I don't give a damn." I sidestepped him. The crowd granted me a wide berth as I headed back to my lonely bar stool.

At the bar I upended the remaining beer.

John-John edged up beside Muskrat. "Are you drunk?"

"Close." I hated the sympathetic look in his eyes. "You tossing me out?"

He shook his head.

"Good. Then bring me another round."

"I don't think—"

"Leave her be, John-John." Muskrat swapped the empty glass for a full one. "She's entitled."

For that, Muskrat deserved a big tip. I toasted him and blew him a kiss.

"So whatcha gonna do for fun next?" John-John asked. "Kick a few senior citizens?"

"Dance. Think any of these guys will give me a spin?"

Muskrat snorted.

"You could always use force. That seems to work for you."

"Fuck off, John-John." I smiled meanly. "Then again, some guys prefer to be dominated, don't they?"

"I see you overdosed on vitamin bitch today," John-John shot back.

"Knock it off, both of you," Muskrat said.

"I'm just getting started." I twirled on my bar stool. Grabbed the first guy who walked past: a fifty-year-old biker with faded prison tats, and a gray soul patch around his hard mouth. "Wanna dance?"

His four teeth made his grin interesting, if not downright charming. "What the hell. My old lady ain't here."

We danced. I drank. I found another willing victim to two-step to "Right or Wrong" by George Strait. Another fearless young Indian brave slow danced with me to Keith Urban's "Raining on Sunday." The partners and songs began to blur.

Dancing didn't alleviate the too-tight feeling of my skin. The booze didn't diminish the ache in my soul.

When I returned to my seat for another shot, John-John placed his hand on my drinking arm. "Is this helping, doll? Because you don't look like you're having fun."

"I don't know what fun looks like anymore." I closed my eyes and knocked back a shot. It made me very, very dizzy. I was very, very loaded. I'd passed the *I love you, man* stage and reached the *my life sucks* stage.

"Where were you before you decided to drink yourself into oblivion?"

"At Geneva's fortress of self-righteousness."

"Did you two have a fight?"

My soft laugh held a bitter edge. "Takes two to fight. She treated me to a diatribe." I shivered. The excessive alcohol had thinned my blood. Or, if I believed Geneva, I was already cold-blooded. "I don't want to talk about it."

"Let me know when you do." He slid a Coke in front of me. "Can you take a break from straight shots?"

"I'd probably better."

I drank the soda. Ordered another. Took a break to rid myself of some of the booze, but I didn't run into Laronda in the bathroom. Maybe she'd slunk back underneath the rock she'd crawled out from.

The door blew open. Several soggy bikers stumbled in. Thunder rattled the rafters. Clementine's didn't have windows, so I couldn't tell if lightning accompanied the rain.

I dug out the Skoal Bandits and nestled it in my cheek. The weather fit my mood; I was sinking in my own little cesspool. I didn't notice the subdued noise level in the bar until he bulled his way in behind me.

"I need to talk to you."

Why did his deep voice cause a quiver in my belly? "Go away, Dawson."

"Talk to me here or I'll drag you to the office. Your choice."

"Your girlfriend called you, did she?"

"She's not my girlfriend."

The silence in the bar was short-lived.

"Did she whine to you about me being mean to her? Boo fucking hoo."

"Did you physically threaten her?"

"Yep." I still hadn't turned to look at him.

"Why?"

"Because I felt like it, that's why."

"This isn't helping."

"So? I don't give a rat's ass. Slap the cuffs on or get away from me."

John-John was watching and listening from behind the cash register.

Dawson wrapped his hand around my upper arm. "Mercy—"

I whirled around. "Just because you kissed me does not grant you the right to touch me whenever you want, Dawson. Get your hand off me or I will break it."

John-John fumbled a lowball glass.

Dawson increased his grip. "Just because you kissed me doesn't grant you the right to blow me off when I want to talk to you in an official capacity, Gunderson. Laronda threatened to press charges, and there's a whole bar full of witnesses to back her up that you attacked her unprovoked. So if you don't want to end up in jail, listen to me."

"Unprovoked? Bull."

Dawson put his hot mouth against my ear. "Play along."

I snorted. "Like that'll happen."

"I'll haul you outside. We'll decide what to do from there, but you can't stay in here."

"Do I have to apologize to that phony bitch?"

"No."

"How do you know she won't follow us to make sure you're arresting me?"

"It's pouring outside. She's not gonna get her hairdo wet or else she'll look like a drowned cat. And if she presses the issue, I'll dissuade her."

It was bizarre, holding an intense conversation without making eye contact with him. "How? With your cowboy charm?"

"If I have to. Or I'll have *you* press charges against her for attempted vehicular assault."

That comment took a second to sink in. "You *knew?*"

"No, I didn't know, I figured it out. And I don't appreciate your acting so damn surprised that I was doing my job."

"So why the hell didn't you tell me that bitch tried to kill me—"

"Because you would've killed her." He paused. His rapid breathing stirred my hair; shivers cascaded from my scalp to my toes. "And she's not worth doing time for."

My head swam. From too much booze, too much anger, too many unanswered questions, and too many secrets. Dawson's deep voice whispering in my ear wasn't helping clear my mind. "You looking to throw me in jail for attempted assault?"

He made a noise, half growl/half laugh. "You? In a bed? Fifty feet from my office? With a door that locks? That's punishing me, not you."

Sexual heat flashed through me, igniting a more dangerous edge than anger. My head said, "Not now," but I angled my face until his lips grazed my temple. "Dawson—"

"Dammit, Mercy. Don't do this. Don't say another word until we're out of here."

Before I could respond, he yanked me off my bar stool.

"Come on. Outside." He didn't bother to lower his voice.

"Let go of me."

Dawson dragged me through the gathering crowd.

I tried to twist out of his hold. "Keep your hands off. I didn't do anything."

"That's what they all say."

He herded me past the jukebox. I caught a glimpse of Laronda's puffy red hair and her Cheshire grin. "Where are you taking me?"

"One guess."

I stopped. "I am not going to jail."

Dawson loomed over me and glared. "Move it. Outside."

I spun on my heel and marched to the door without looking back. My body pulsed with irritation. Burned my ass to back down from Laronda. It went against everything I did. Everything I was. My job was to take down bullies, not to turn tail and run.

Outside, rain slapped my face. No wind, but it was pitch-black except for glints of lightning. The absence of light, the continual deluge, my inebriated state, and my bad eye were a bad combination. I stumbled through potholes that'd become mud puddles. I patted my pockets.

No keys.

A jagged line of lightning illuminated Dawson standing right in front of me. My heart jackhammered when he grabbed my shoulders. "Don't touch me."

"Tough shit. What is wrong with you?"

"Why don't you tell me? I'm sure you've compiled a mile-long list like everyone else in this godforsaken county."

His palms slid over my collarbones in a long caress up my neck to hold my face in his hands. Rain streamed down his cheeks, tiny droplets clung to the tips of his hair. "Talk to me."

"I can't."

He shook me a little. "No matter what I do or don't do, you still don't trust me. Why were you drinking yourself into the gutter and picking fights tonight?"

"I don't know."

"Yes, you do. Tell me."

Booze, nerves, fear, and frustration made me rant. "You wanna start with the dead bodies showing up at my place? Or that my nephew was murdered? Or that some bastard tried to burn down my house and barn? Or that someone broke into my home and assaulted my sister? Or shall we skip to the part where I remind you that you're not doing your job, the job my father did with pride for years. The job my father handpicked you to do because he . . . couldn't do it anymore, and goddammit, I can't believe he's dead and I didn't get to say good-bye. I'm dealing with this shit by myself. Again. Why am I always the one left holding the goddamned bag?" My breath hitched.

"Mercy—"

I waved off his show of pity. "But because I'm Wyatt Gunderson's daughter, people trust me, and expect I can solve their problems. I don't want that trust. *You* should want it. This"— I gestured to the scant space separating us—"is just making it worse."

"Worse? How could it be worse? No one trusts me, least of all you. And I'm sick of you thinking I'm inept and I don't give a shit about three dead kids. I am not an insult to the office that your father held for so many years."

"Really?"

"Yeah, but me defending myself isn't what this is about, is it?"

No. "Just leave me alone. Why do you even care what the hell I think?"

Dawson locked his soulful eyes to mine. "I care because I saw the strongest woman I know lose it tonight. You're on the edge, Mercy, and I'm part of the reason you're there."

I looked away. Damn him. The flashes of lighting bounced strobelike around us and made me woozy. I swayed to the ground.

But Dawson followed me. We were on our knees, in the mud, rain pelting us, thunder crashing around us.

"Hey." He attempted to move my tangled hair from my eyes.

I knocked his hand away. "Take a hint, Dawson. Go."

"No. Why won't you trust me?"

"Give me one reason why I should."

"Because your dad did. And on some gut level you do, too."

He'd said the one thing that guaranteed my emotional reaction. Grief punched me hard and knocked the fight right out of me.

Dawson softened his hold. Evidently he'd made his point.

Tempting, to curl in a ball and weep for everything I'd lost in the last two months, including my dignity. Naturally, I wouldn't give into such a female reaction, especially not in public. I clenched my teeth against the gathering tears, but my protective shields were worthless.

He hauled me to my feet. "You're in no shape to drive."

"No kidding."

"Where are your keys?"

"I gave them to Muskrat."

"Good. Let me take you home."

I didn't argue. He clasped my hand in his and directed me to his truck.

Silence filled the humid cab. Windshield wipers slapped inef-fectually against the pouring rain. Even with the heater cranked full blast I couldn't keep the bone-rattling chills at bay. Resting my forehead on my knees, I concentrated on breathing.

The truck stopped. My body seized up. Dawson didn't ask; he just picked me up and carried me inside my house.

Two times in less than a week I'd let him treat me like a baby. It'd make my humiliation complete if I started bawling like one.

The house was dark. I shook so hard Dawson almost dropped me going up the stairs. In the bathroom, he sat me on the toilet, shut the door, and flipped on the shower. Steam filled the small space.

Dawson fell to his knees in front of me, leaving gloppy mud splotches on the fluffy pink bathroom rug. When my fingers wouldn't cooperate, he said, "I'll help you get undressed." He unhooked the buttons on my blouse. "Then I'll put you in the shower to warm you up."

The cadence of his voice soothed me, even when my body twitched like he'd zapped me with an electric cattle prod whenever his callused fingers connected with my bare skin.

My soaked boots came off next. Then sodden socks. He made me stand and reached around to undo my bra, slowly dragging the satin straps down my shaking arms. Dawson's eyes never left my face. He popped the buttons on my 501s, shimmying the tight, wet jeans and my underwear to the floor. One-handed, he pulled aside the shower curtain and helped me over the steep tub ledge.

The hot water hit my chilled skin and I sighed. "You can go now."

"Huh-uh. I'm not leaving until I know you aren't gonna pass out and smack your head into the soap dish."

"Suit yourself," I muttered under the spray. When the shakes were under control, I shampooed. As I rinsed, vertigo seized me, I stumbled into the wall.

Dawson wrenched back the shower curtain. "I knew it. You shouldn't be—"

His gaze didn't make it to my face for the longest time.

I noticed he'd taken off his wet shirt and boots. Everything inside me went haywire, seeing him half naked. Without thinking, I trailed my soapy fingers across his smooth, muscled chest. He was so warm. So solid. So . . . here.

He sucked in a harsh breath. "Don't. Unless that was an invitation."

"And if it was?"

Dawson studied me. The muscle in his jaw snapped like chewing gum. "You gonna blame this invite on booze?"

"No."

"You gonna blame this invite on anger, self-pity, or combat stress?"

"No."

"Do you suddenly trust me?"

I thought about it for a minute. "Not really."

He stared. Then that damnably appealing cowboy grin appeared, slow, sexy, and hot as sin. "Two out of three works for me." Dawson stripped off his jeans and climbed in.

His mouth and hands were on me before he'd jerked the shower curtain closed.

"Wait," I said, breaking my lips free from his. I hooked my index finger next to my gums to remove the tobacco pouch from my mouth, tossing it toward the sink.

Dawson frowned at it. "Were you chewing?"

"Yeah."

"I quit last year."

"Good for you." My arms circled his neck, and I plastered myself against his slick body.

"God, I miss that sweet minty taste." He traced my lips with the tip of his tongue. "Give me a taste of what I've been missing, Mercy," he said, and crushed his mouth to mine.

He kissed me until I felt I was drowning. In him. In the shower spray. In my own confusion. But for once I didn't fight the deluge; I just let it carry me away.

EIGHTEEN

I woke the next morning with a freight train roaring in my ear and pinned beneath a railcar. I squirmed. The snoring stopped. A rough hand dragged up and down my naked back in a sweetly intimate wake-up call.

"How's your head?" he murmured.

I mumbled and hoped he'd take the hint and let me sleep.

Dawson rolled me on my back, gently pushing away my snarled hair. He stared at me until I worried that warts had popped up on my face overnight. Or was he in shock by how bad I looked in the morning? I hadn't been a fresh-faced, dewy-eyed ingénue for years. "What?"

"You let me stay."

"I wasn't exactly in any position to throw you out."

His left eyebrow winged up. "Complaining about the positions we tried last night?"

My body burned hot as a branding iron remembering the sexual heat and the intensity and the synchronicity between us. "No. Good thing I practice yoga, huh?"

"Very good thing." A shy smile tilted the corners of his mouth, then spread across his rugged face. Not necessarily a movie-star-handsome mug, but well worn. Interesting. A little tough, a little tender.

I smiled back.

"Although I *am* an old man and I'll probably be feeling it all day."

"Doesn't seem like you'll need to raid Mr. Pawlowski's stash of Viagra anytime soon."

"Hey, that was almost a compliment, Gunderson."

"It *was* a compliment, Dawson." I traced the boxy shape of his jawline with my fingertips.

He turned his cheek into my hand and kissed my palm. "Are you gonna throw me out now?"

"I should. But how about if I make breakfast first."

When Dawson headed to the bathroom, I escaped to the kitchen.

Cooking is not my forte. Food might help settle my stomach, although I couldn't blame the way my insides jumped solely on too much liquid fun from the previous night.

While the coffee brewed, I tossed a half stick of butter and frozen hash browns in the cast iron frying pan, microwaved a package of bacon, and scrambled a half-dozen eggs.

I'd never mastered morning-after chitchat. Sex has never been a big thing for me, maybe because I'd gotten used to the feast or famine cycle of it. Been a dry spell lately.

The stairs creaked; my heart rate spiked. Christ. I'd had Sunnis shooting at me and I hadn't reacted this skittishly.

Dawson poured himself a cup of coffee. "Want a reheat?"

"Sure." I slid my mug across the counter and flipped the hash browns.

"If I were a gentleman I'd say you didn't have to go to all this trouble, but damn, it smells too good to lie."

The grandfather clock chimed seven times. "You proved you aren't a gentleman a couple of times last night."

"Mercy—"

"Butter the toast, Dawson. Everything else is almost done."

He mumbled and grabbed the butter dish.

Once we sat down, I couldn't help but watch him devour every morsel. Been a long time since I'd seen a man enjoy a meal with such . . . gusto. I shivered discreetly, recalling being on the receiving end of such single-minded concentration in another room of the house.

When we finished the meal, I poured more coffee.

He said, "Wanna talk about it?"

"About what? Last night?"

"Yes, but not the slamming, jamming sex. About before. Why

you were getting drunk and picking fights at the bar." Dawson held up a hand. "This is not an official interview. I'm asking as your friend."

"Oh. So we're friends now?"

He grinned. "Friends with naked benefits. Who pissed you off last night?"

"Geneva."

His smile morphed into a frown. "Haven't you been pals with her since you were both little cowgirls?"

"Yeah. Makes me wonder how long she's been holding off on telling me how she really felt about me."

"What'd she say?"

"That I'm a spoiled jet-setting 'hobby rancher.' It was time for me to grow up and become a responsible member of society. But if I sell my ranch, I'll ruin her life . . . oh, and the lives of every single person in Eagle River County. A little contradictory, doncha think?" I sighed. "And Kit was sniffing around the other day basically saying the same thing."

"He wants you to sell to him, naturally."

"Naturally."

Dawson's gaze sharpened. "He threaten you?"

"No more than he did the last time."

"I'm serious."

"I am, too, *friend*. The truth is, I sort of went off on him when I found out Trey's been his employee for the last year."

"You didn't know?"

"Not a clue." I brooded into my coffee cup. "Does it make you wonder who else is in his employ?"

"Yeah. Kit hasn't been telling anyone, even the people who work for him, who his investors are."

"So Trey doesn't know?"

"Nope. Neither does Laronda."

"You asked her?"

"In a manner of speaking."

Part of me wondered how far Dawson had gone to pump Laronda for information.

"Evidently Kit thinks I'm the only thing standing between him and owning the ranch."

"All the more reason to watch out for him. He's up to something."

I stood and refilled my cup. "I can handle Kit no problem."

His chair scraped on the linoleum. From behind me he said, "I recognize the dismissal, so I'll drop it for now. But if you need to talk, you know where to find me, okay?"

"Okay." That was surprisingly easy.

"I have to go home and change before going into the office. Can Jake or Sophie give you a ride to your truck?"

"Yeah, don't worry about it."

"Can I get one for the road?"

I set down my cup and rummaged in the cupboard. "I don't know if we have any Styrofoam cups with lids, Dawson."

He turned me around. "I wasn't talking about coffee." Then his mouth came down on mine hard and he kissed the living daylights out of me.

I could scarcely breathe when he finally pulled back.

"Mercy Gunderson, you make me lose my ever-lovin' mind."

Dawson left without another word, which was good because I was pretty speechless anyway.

An hour later, I looked up from the *Tri-State Livestock News* when Jake said, "I'm borrowing the truck for a little while today. I need to haul the ATVs over to Bernie's place. They're running like a pack of crippled old dogs."

"How about if I do it and save you the trip? I wanted to talk to him anyway about Axel, and this'll give me a reason to show up."

"Sure." Jake didn't demand to hear my plans, wasn't his way, but I sensed his curiosity. "Another thing. Queenie's back in the old barn. We need to talk about options with her. She's old and that sore on her leg ain't healing. The vet's done everything he can."

No one wanted to put down a horse, least of all Jake. "Whatever you think. You know I trust your judgment with the livestock." I paused. "Where are the other horses?"

"TJ and Luke are keeping them at their place. With the ATVs out of commission they'll need them for a couple of days."

being stonewalled at every turn? Because of my gender? Because I wasn't all Indian? Because of my father's connection to law enforcement? Or was it something else? God. I knew how Dawson felt—inept and like an outsider. I slammed the door hard and smacked the steering wheel with the heels of my hands. "Goddammit!"

"My dad gets that reaction a lot," came from the passenger's side of the truck.

Startled, I whirled toward the kid crouched on the floorboard, clutching an enormous backpack. My eyes narrowed. "Axel?"

"Yeah. You're Mercy. Levi Arpel's aunt, right?"

"What are you doing stowed away in my truck?"

"I need a ride to town."

"Why don't you ask your dad?"

"He's busy welding or some such shit."

I laughed. "Nice try. If you're gone, your dad will blame me."

"No, he won't. He'll think I called my ma and she picked me up on the road. She does it all the time so she don't gotta talk to him. Besides, it ain't like I'm a prisoner. I can come and go when I want."

"Yeah?" I gave him my best no-bullshit stare. "That's why you're hiding on the floor instead of sitting on the seat?"

"Okay, I *am* sneaking off. Dad wants me to stick around and help him. I got stuff to do today." Axel licked his lips. "I heard you asking him questions."

"So?"

"So if you give me a ride to town, I'll give you some answers."

I cranked the key so fast it almost snapped in the ignition.

When we cleared the tree line, Axel popped up like a gopher out of a hidey-hole. "Thanks."

I shot him a sideways glance. Scrawny kid. Probably took a rash of crap for being small. With his smooth skin and slight frame he seemed younger than Levi and the others. "I don't see any reason to beat around the bush, Axel. Tell me about the Warrior Society."

Axel recited what I already knew, almost by rote. But slowly, as if he expected to drag it out until we reached town and he'd make his escape without really giving me any new information.

Screw that. I jammed on the brakes and the back end skidded. "Enough bullshit. I've heard this. I want to know how you managed to leave the group when no one else could."

He slumped in his seat. "Because of Albert. He started running away. His ma called my ma and blabbed some of what Albert had told her about the group. Even though my folks are divorced, Ma talked to Dad and they both forbid me from participating."

"And you quit just because they demanded it?"

"I didn't have a choice. I'm the youngest in the group, and I don't got a car or a cell phone. I didn't want to seem like a pussy or a little kid to them, so I told everyone I thought it was a stupid group, against tradition, and that's why I wanted to quit."

"But you didn't believe it was?"

"At first, it was really cool to be a part of it. Part of them. But then . . ." Axel studied his fingernails. "Then it changed when they came around. When school got out, my ma sent me to Rapid City to live with my cousins for the summer, so I really didn't have a choice."

"So why are you back here now? This isn't a safe place to be."

No answer.

I kept pushing. "I can't believe if your parents sent you away before any of your friends were killed that they'd let you come back now." *Ping.* Lightbulb moment. "They don't know you're here, do they?"

Axel shook his head. "I heard what happened to Sue Anne. Freaked me out. I needed to get back here. My cousin's buddy was coming to the rez, and he gave me a ride. Dropped me off on the road and I hid out in Dad's shop. I was gonna call one of my friends to pick me up, but I heard you were headed into town and I thought I'd hitch a ride."

Kid probably heard the desperation in my voice as I'd tried to talk to his father. Truth was: I *was* desperate and wasn't about to blow this opportunity. "Fine. I won't turn around and take you straight back to your dad if you tell me something."

"What?"

"Who are the leaders of the group?"

Silence. He wouldn't even look at me.

"I'm not kidding, Axel. Tell me."

Axel spun in his seat. "Or you'll what? Dump me out here and make me walk to town? *Shee*. Wouldn't be the first time I had to walk. Nothing you threaten me with is as scary as what they'll do to me if they find out I talked to you."

"Yeah? Maybe being seen with me in town is all it'd take to tip them off that you and I were chatting, so why don't we skip the secret bullshit pact and you tell me what I want to know." .

He blanched. "You were the one."

"One what?"

"The one who got Sue Anne to talk. You're the reason she's dead."

That statement ratcheted my guilt up another notch and I lashed out. "Wrong, I wasn't the one who slit her throat. They did. And they'll do it again. Maybe to you."

"You don't feel a bit guilty for getting her killed, do you?"

My patience shattered. I grabbed him by the shirtfront and shook him. "You have no idea what I feel. No idea what it's like to see that girl carved up and covered in blood and discarded like garbage. They bound and gagged her and left her to bleed to death on my porch. *My* porch, Axel. I couldn't help her. I couldn't save her. Just like I couldn't save my nephew. And I'll be goddamned if I'll sit around and watch these sadistic fucking . . . *murderers* kill anyone else. . . ." My voice cracked and trailed off when I noticed his eyes were wide with fear.

I released him abruptly, sucker-punched by shame. Bullying a young kid wasn't the answer to any questions. Ever. I slammed the truck back in gear, hating that I'd probably brought this dead end upon myself by violence and intimidation.

Axel broke the silence in the cab when we were on the outskirts of town. "Stop here."

I pulled off to the side of the road, expecting him to jump out and run like hell.

He didn't. He fiddled with the straps on his backpack. "It was shitty, what I said to you. I know you're not any more responsible for Sue Anne getting killed than I am for bringing her into the group in the first place."

Seemed I wasn't the only one suffering from guilt.

"So I just wanted to say thanks for the ride. And I'm sorry about Levi. He was . . . cool."

I nodded.

Axel opened the door. He paused.

I held my breath. *Please. Please help me.*

His knuckles were white where he gripped the dash. "Know what? You're right. I'm sick of this shit. Out County Road Nineteen, about eight miles past that old ranch where them religious freaks took over, there's a National Grasslands sign. Go about another half mile closer to the rez, where the land turns hilly and there's a deep ditch on the left side. Straight down that steep hill, along the bottom of a dried up creekbed, are some trees and stuff. Where the bushes end is a flat spot with a fire pit ringed with stones. That's where we're meeting tonight with the leaders. Just after dusk." He bailed out of the truck and took off across the field.

I spun a cookie in the road and headed home. I wasn't exactly sure of the area Axel had been talking about, but I knew someone who would be. "Hey, boss. I need your Indian tracking skills. Can you pick me up at my house in an hour?"

Rollie and I didn't talk much after I filled him in on what I'd learned from Axel. We both knew it wasn't my expert PI skills that'd gotten me to this point, but sheer dumb luck.

We bumped along, seemed we were counting the miles by inches. The road curved sharply and the terrain went from level to hilly. Rollie slowed and parked in a pull-off in front of a set of grooved tracks, which disappeared over the edge of the hill. "I'm pretty sure it's down there."

"You coming?"

"Nope. I'm too damn old to go traipsing around in the muck. I'll wait here and play lookout. If I honk the horn, stay put."

I hiked down the hillside to find a spot close enough to the action so I could hear and see what was going on tonight, but far enough away that I'd be part of the scenery.

At the bottom, in a flat area scraped clear of foliage, sat a fire pit ringed with the large flat stones Axel mentioned. Smaller white ones lined the inside. Were those the rocks Chet told me he'd seen the guys hauling? Is this where they performed all the rituals?

My gaze scanned the terrain. A couple of boulders had tumbled down and were imbedded in the rocky slope, but weren't big enough to hide behind. I homed in on the sparse scrub oak bushes scattered along the back of the draw.

I could enter about two hundred yards down from the ridge. Seemed to be my best option. To test the theory, I crawled from the backside through the underbrush, pushing aside decaying leaves and breaking off low-lying branches so I'd have an unobstructed view. I mentally marked my spot and hiked up to my access point, leaving a clear set of footprints to Rollie's truck, in case the Warrior Society members were practicing Indian tracking skills.

"Well?" he demanded.

"I'll be shaving it close to keep them from seeing me, but I'm sure I can make it work. If not, and they do see the whites of my eyes . . . I doubt any of them can outrun me." None of them could outshoot me, but it probably wasn't smart to bring that up.

"Good." Rollie aimed the truck at the ditch and spun a U-turn. "Now, when you come out here tonight, make sure you don't drive past and miss it."

"You have a string or something I could use as a marker? Since I'll be coming from the other direction?"

"Check under the seat."

I unearthed a piece of white nylon rope. I jumped out intending to comb the ditch for a stick.

The driver door slammed. "Hang on, I've got a stake." Rollie rooted around in the truck bed, holding out a short chunk of metal as thick as a piece of rebar.

"This'll work." The parched earth had little give, but I screwed it in deep enough so the wind wouldn't blow it over. I tied the cord around the top. No one would see my flag unless they were specifically looking for it.

After we'd returned to the truck, Rollie said, "You gonna sneak in, using some of them stealth tactics Uncle Sam taught you, eh?"

"That's the plan."

He opened his mouth. Shut it. Fumbled for another cigarette. Still, he didn't speak his mind. He puffed away as we tooled down the gravel road in silence. It freaked me out a little because Rollie rarely curbed his tongue.

"Spit it out, Rollie."

"What are you gonna do? Especially if you hear something about them killing Levi? Pull out your Desert Eagle and mow 'em all down? Show 'em 'No Mercy' hell-bent on vengeance?"

Feeling belligerent that he'd found a flaw in my plan, I retorted, "If I do, it's no less than what they deserve."

He shook his head, staring at me, his eyes bleak, his weathered red face wrinkled with concern.

"Jesus. What now?"

"If you are capable of mass execution, then you ain't no different than the terrorists you been fighting the last few years. Think about it before you do something you can't undo."

Rollie flipped on the radio. Conway Twitty's "Tight Fitting Jeans" effectively ended all conversation.

We didn't exchange another word until we said good-bye as he dropped me off at the top of the driveway.

Dog-tired, I trudged upstairs. I had a long night behind me and I might have a long night ahead of me. I crawled between the sheets, still tangled from my romp with Dawson, and conked out.

Around dusk I donned gray-and-black camouflage. Tied my hair in a ponytail and swirled greasepaint on my face. I loaded the pockets of my flack jacket: binoculars, Bowie knife, my Browning High Power, my Sig, and an extra clip for each just in case. Rollie's warning flashed in my mind. What *would* I do if I heard a confession?

Worry about it if and when it happened.

It weirded me out, dressing for recon in my frilly, floral bedroom. Seemed I'd performed this ritual in another lifetime. Last time I'd been in Iraq. Last time I'd been 100 percent.

The disjointed sensation lingered as I climbed into the truck. I didn't play the radio. My mind blanked, my sole concentration on breathing slow and deep so it would look like I wasn't breathing at all.

I cruised the edge of the road. The second my headlights caught the flash of white, I parked in the ditch and turned off the engine. Cut the interior light, slipped out the passenger door and eased down the steep incline.

The ground was mucky from the rain. My boots felt like cement blocks from the caked-on mud. When I reached the spot where I'd cleaned out the underbrush, I belly-crawled into position on my elbows.

Seven figures were crouched around the bonfire. I didn't recognize anyone with my naked eye so I pulled out my binoculars.

The attendees had coated their faces with red and white war paint, making it hard to tell who was who. Moser stood sturdy as a tree. The sunken chest belonged to Randall. Short one, Little Bear. Bulky guy . . . Bucky. Axel was tasked with dragging material for the fire from the outskirts of the group. A broad-shouldered man sat with his back to me. His face was aimed at the rocks, so I couldn't see it.

A strange feeling unfurled in my gut.

The guy standing, doing all the talking, seemed familiar, but I couldn't place him either. I listened.

"—making such a big deal about it."

"We're making a big deal because our friends are dead. And you can't give us no good reason why. This wasn't 'sposed to be part of it. Albert's accident—"

"Yeah," Moser interrupted. "We shoulda told the cops the truth about what happened. Now people are talking. Chasing us down and asking questions. Thinking we're killing people. Ain't gonna be long before—"

"Did your ancestors surrender when faced with adversity? Remember what happened to Lakota warriors when they practiced their religious rituals? They were slaughtered. If anyone knew, especially law enforcement, that a bunch of young Indian males were renewing some of those sacred rites, it wouldn't matter whether or not Albert's death was accidental. They'd arrest you." He pointed to each person. "All of you. You'd spend the rest of your lives in the penitentiary."

No one answered him.

I'd heard that voice before. Where?

Axel tossed the pile of tumbleweeds on the fire. A flash of eager yellow flames engulfed the desiccated plant, instantly burning it into red coals. As he poked the embers, he said, "We ain't talking about Albert. We're talking about the others. Did you kill them? Levi and Sue Anne?"

Everyone jabbered at once.

The big man stood, lifted his arm to the sky. Metal glinted in the fire's orange glow. He fired in the air. Twice.

Immediate silence.

My heart pounded like a tom-tom. Not many men that size in this county. Three I knew of off the top of my head. One was dead. One worked for the man who'd threatened me. One had woken in my bed this morning. The man started to turn— I wanted to squeeze my eyes shut—but I kept the binoculars trained on him. Even as my hands shook and the pitiful mantra of *please don't let it be him* began a loop in my head.

The brightness of the fire illuminated the man's wrinkled red face. Not Dawson, thank God.

Hiram Blacktower.

But my relief was short-lived when I realized the man Hiram was talking to, the man in charge, was Hope's boyfriend, Theo Murphy.

NINETEEN

As soon as I swallowed the sourness rising up the back of my throat, I was damn glad I hadn't brought my sniper rifle. I imagined Theo's face in the crosshairs of my scope. One trigger click and his head would explode like a watermelon.

Breathe.

I refocused. Chaos ruled. Moser shouted accusations at Theo. Bucky and Little Bear were pointing and yelling at Hiram. Randall sat on a rock, rocking, his arms wrapped around his up-drawn knees. Axel watched the scene unfold with strangely wise eyes, stirring the coals out of reflex, not need.

Hiram raised his gun and fired again.

Silence fell.

Theo said, "Thank you, honored leader."

Axel snickered.

Theo whirled on him. "Have something to say, Axel?"

"To you? Yeah. This is bullshit. I don't know why you're in the Warrior Society anyway. You ain't Sioux." He spoke in Lakota to Hi.

Hiram shook his head.

Theo snapped, "In English."

Guess I wasn't the only one who didn't understand the language.

Axel didn't look at Theo. Nor did he miss a beat when he switched to English and addressed Moser. "Didja invite them 'cause they offered to buy us booze? Is that really what the Warrior Society is about? Getting drunk and letting anyone in as long as they bring us a suitcase of Coors? *Shee*. How's that make us different from the rez gangs, eh? Just 'cause we ain't selling meth don't mean what we been doing is right."

Moser twitched. Little Bear angled his head from the fire, leaving his face in shadow.

My rage festered in the surreal stillness.

"We were doing just fine on our own. For a while, I was even proud of the group we started. A place where we talked about our Lakota heritage, learned our traditions. Ever since Moser brought in this white motherfucker"—he pointed at Theo—"and this half-baked half-breed"—he aimed his slender finger at Hiram —"*they've* taken over. Now they're dressing in buckskin and war paint? Telling *us* how to be Indian? How screwed up is that?

"Some of our *kolas* are dead and these guys are saying *so what*? Ain't that what we were trying to get away from on the rez and everywhere else? Adult white folks dismissing us as worthless thugs? Or savages?"

Bucky said, "Axel's right. That horse coulda thrown any of us. Why'd we hide the truth?"

"It's too late to make it right now. Who woulda been in trouble anyway? We'd be headed to juvie, not the pen. But didja ever wonder how he"—Randall gestured to Hiram again—"knew *exactly* where to dump Albert's body? It was like he already had a place all picked out."

All faces turned toward Hiram.

"We let Blacktower take advantage because we was all too drunk to realize both of them had other motives. *White man* motives. Makes me sick. Especially when I heard what you guys did to Lanae. There ain't nothing in our history, or any Lakota ritual, about raping a virgin as a sacrifice to the Great Spirit. These assholes just wanted a young piece of dark pussy, and they used us to get it."

Warning chills raced up my arms. Axel was playing fast and loose against a guy with a gun. Not smart.

"That's enough, Axel," Theo warned.

Axel paid no heed. "I ain't gonna listen to this bullshit. I sure as hell ain't gonna take part in something that's gonna hurt any-one."

"I'll remind you that this sudden burst of conscience will not absolve you of your past actions in any of these situations, either in our eyes, or in the eyes of the law," Theo said.

Axel laughed. "You can do whatever you want, 'Great White Chieftain' or whatever dumb-ass name you wanna be called. And you better let me do the same."

"Or what? What makes you think you're safe?"

Nothing thinly veiled about that threat.

"If anything happens to me, like what happened to Levi or Sue Anne, I got someone who'll spill everything that's been going on with this stupid group to the sheriff. And then he'll come after you."

"You wish," Theo sneered. "Sheriff Dawson won't do a damn thing based on the scared ramblings of a fifteen-year-old kid when he hasn't done squat about two clear cases of murder." An arrogant expression crossed Theo's face. "He doesn't care about dead Indians. Only thing he cares about is getting elected sheriff. And since high school kids can't vote, and neither can the people on the rez, I don't think he'll be too concerned."

Part of me wanted to defend Dawson; a bigger part feared Theo had made the right assessment.

"Wrong. If I tell him that you—"

"I'll tell him that you failed my class, which isn't a lie, and you'll make up all sorts of lies to cause problems for me."

Axel said, "You asshole."

"And if any of the rest of you really want to push it, I'll inform the sheriff I suspect you guys"—he gestured to Little Bear and Moser—"killed Levi because he'd cozied up to your old girl-friend, Sue Anne. How long you think it'll take before he connects the dots to Sue Anne's murder?" He faced Randall. "You're not out of it either. Albert ran away from home and hid out in your basement. Not to mention Bucky, here, stole the horse, that killed Albert out of his uncle's pasture. Don't forget you all participated in the mating ritual, some of you several times. Not one of you here is without guilt."

Dead silence.

"Don't screw with me, boys; I've got you by your little teeny balls."

Axel spit on the rock by Theo's feet. Then he said to Bucky, "We're outta here. For good."

Bucky shot Hiram an anxious look before he chased after Axel. I gave the kid credit; he didn't turn his back to the man with the gun until they were out of sight.

Theo glared at Moser, Little Bear, and Randall as they backed up, also intent on escape. Without a word they fled. An engine sputtered, roared to life, and broke the quiet.

Hiram plopped on a rock. "This ain't going the way it was planned."

"No, really? Brilliant deduction." Theo stood. "Stay here and put out the fire."

"Where you going?"

"To follow those little shits and see if I'll need to do any more damage control."

"*More* damage control? What'd you do?"

"What needed done. What you and that asswipe Kit were too civilized to do."

Hiram shook his head. "That ain't your job. You're supposed to be convincing her to sell. Period."

"She will. Soon." Theo disappeared up the hillside.

I listened until I heard his vehicle drive away. Then I pushed back through the bushes and unsheathed my knife. Ten seconds later I had that knife at Hiram's throat.

"Drop the gun." My voice was an unrecognizable growl.

He didn't argue.

"Kick it next to the fire."

Hiram stretched his leg. With the toe of his boot he sent the gun skittering over the barren ground like a silver spider.

I dug the blade in, drawing blood so he knew I wasn't bluffing. My knife skills were rusty. I looked forward to a hands-on refresher course.

"Did you kill Levi?"

"No!"

I didn't believe him. "Did you kill Sue Anne? Leave her to bleed to death on my porch?"

"No. But—"

"But what?"

Another pause and he blurted, "I think Theo did."

"Did he kill Albert Yellow Boy, too?"

"That was an accident, I swear."

"Convince me."

"Moser, Little Bear, Bucky, Randall, Theo, and me were out here doing fast mounts and dismounts. As Albert climbed on, a rattler spooked the horse and it reared. Albert tried to get loose, but his shoe caught in the stirrup. The horse threw him sideways and broke his neck. Killed him right away."

"Why'd you move him to my land?"

"We thought a dead boy, especially a friend of Levi's who'd been in trouble, would convince you and Hope to sell the ranch faster."

"Was that scare tactic Theo's idea?"

"Yeah."

"Why should I believe you didn't kill Levi as an additional incentive for us to sell?"

"That wasn't in the plan. We figured Wyatt would leave the estate stuff to Hope. With him dying . . . she'd need someone else to depend on."

"It never occurred to you she could depend on me?"

"Ah. No. Kit introduced Theo and Hope, thinking Theo could feed us information on everything that was going on, while convincing her to sell to us."

"You purposely set up my sister with that piece of shit?"

"Nobody twisted her arm to crawl in his bed, Mercy."

I hissed and dug the blade edge into his Adam's apple. "Wrong answer, Hi."

"Okay, okay! Yes, Kit set them up."

"When?"

"About five months ago."

Jesus Christ. They'd planned to get their grimy hands on the Gunderson Ranch before my dad was even in the ground. "How did Kit know Theo?"

"After Theo moved here, he came into the real estate office asking about local land for sale. He was scouting for that group in North Dakota he used to work for; them guys wanted a place to run a huge herd of buffalo.

"Kit promised Theo if he could talk Hope into agreeing to sell to Kit's investment group, he'd set a side a large section for them buffalo guys to buy. Problem was, we didn't know Theo was such a wild card. He wormed his way into them kids' group by talking about his 'Indian blood' and his understanding of Lakota rituals. When Theo bragged that he could get them kids to do anything he wanted, including hurting themselves and each other, it freaked Kit out. Everything was s'posed to be handled on the QT. He sent me to keep an eye on him."

"Theo, the almighty Indian leader, didn't care you were babysitting him?"

"No. Since I'm Lakota, he acted like I was Tonto to his Lone Ranger. Them kids didn't care who hung around either as long as there was enough booze flowing."

"Were you there when they raped Lanae?"

He swallowed hard and I smelled his guilt.

"Did you participate?"

Eerie silence.

"Answer the question."

His voice was barely a whisper. "Yeah, but I was drunk."

My hand awaited instructions from my brain.

One quick slice, the barbarian in me urged.

Get more information first, the dutiful soldier retorted.

I breathed. Weighed my options.

Another voice broke through my rage. Not my dad's. Rollie's. *Don't do something you can't undo.*

It took effort, but I forced the blade from his throat. I had enough information. I could've walked away. Instead, I exchanged the knife for the Sig and placed the barrel at the base of his skull. Although we were ten feet from a fire, Hiram shook uncontrollably. I didn't care. "Was Dawson involved in any of this?"

"No."

"None of it?"

"None of what?"

"Hiding the truth, Hi."

"I don't know what you mean."

The man was so stupid it shocked the hell out of me this

Warrior Society stuff stayed under the radar on his watch. "Yes, you do. Kit. And you. And Trey. And Laronda. Who had a hand in setting fire to my buildings? Whose idea was it to assault me? Or was it an attempt to kill me? And do you know how pissed off I am that Hope bore the brunt of that attack?"

No answer.

I grabbed his hair and yanked. "Don't so much as twitch again or I'll put a bullet in your addled fucking brain."

Hiram whimpered like a kicked dog. "Don't hurt me."

"Like Trey tried to hurt me by whacking me at Clementine's?" That crack in my vulnerability still burned my ass.

"Trey done that on his own. He was just supposed to—"

"Supposed to what?"

"He's a good-looking kid, and we thought because it'd worked with Hope—"

"That I'd fall on my back and spread my legs for him? Jesus. You guys are stupid."

"So we were wrong, but we didn't have nothing to do with none of the rest of that stuff."

I let my voice explode in his ear as I pushed the gun deeper into his skin. "Convince me."

"C-come on Mercy, you've known me for years. You think I'm c-capable of that kinda stuff?"

"I didn't think you were c-capable of rape, you sick bastard, but you managed to do that. And now I see why Josiah wants nothing to do with you. You don't have a shred of honor, Hiram Blacktower." I leaned over his shoulder and whispered, "Give Kit a message. He won't know where, he won't know when, but I am coming for him."

I smacked Hiram in the back of the head with the gun grip hard enough that he tumbled off the rock. He fell face-first in the mud, and groaned once. I didn't know if I'd knocked him out or if he was faking it.

I didn't care. And I sure as hell didn't stick around.

I drove home on automatic. Once I had cell service I called Hope's home phone. No answer. I tried her cell. No answer. Feeling unnerved and pissed off, I swung by her trailer. No sign of her car. No sign of Shoonga. The house exhibited an unoccupied aura, but I beat on the flimsy aluminum door anyway. No answer.

It scared the living hell out of me to consider that she was probably staying with Theo.

My options were limited. I could hightail it to the rez and try to find Theo's house. I remembered something about four miles out of Eagle River. Right. Driving around in the dark, on the maze of unmarked gravel roads, in four directions, in the middle of the night, would not be discreet. If I did show up, I'd tip him off I was on to him, and I wanted to retain the element of surprise.

I had no choice but to wait until morning. It'd give me time to come up with a plan to get Hope away from Theo without rousing his suspicions. It'd also give me time to hit upon a way to execute Theo that would look like an accident. Dawson would be suspicious of a single .45 shot to the head.

I left a series of messages on Hope's cell phone for her to call me. No matter what time.

Thunder rattled the windowpanes. Rain? Two nights in a row? In a drought? A portend of doom for sure. I hugged the porch support beam and studied the changes in the sky. Dark clouds scuttled across the stars. A heavy, damp wind blew from the north, leaving a film on my skin sticky as pinesap. As a precaution against it being damaged by hail, I parked my Viper in the machine shed.

About two a.m. I returned inside and prowled from room to room, too restless to sleep. I opened my bedroom window to allow the fragrant scent of summer rain to waft in. Eventually the soft patter on the tin roof lulled me into a dreamless light sleep.

The morning dawned grim. Humid wind whipped across my face; sticky air clogged my lungs. My clothes clung to my skin like Mylar.

Something beside the electrostatic charge in the atmosphere was making my skin buzz. I didn't need caffeine. I was already hyper-alert and too wired to do yoga, but meditation might help.

I crossed my legs lotus style, let my eyes drift shut, and envisioned the influx of oxygen into my lungs as slow as sipping water through a straw. Releasing the air first from my belly in a single long stream, then a silent hiss reversing course through my lungs, up my throat, and out my nose.

I'd performed the ritual a dozen times when my cell phone rang and I lost every bit of relaxation.

Caller ID read: *Hope*. Finally. "Hello?"

"Mercy?"

"Hey, sis. Where are you? I've been trying to call you since last night."

Silence.

"Hope?"

A soft sob.

My heart rate shot through the leaky roof. "What's wrong?"

"Theo. Oh God, Mercy, he already hit me after I dropped the phone. We've been out since before sunrise, and I'm so cold and scared and I can't help shaking—"

The unmistakable sound of flesh hitting flesh ricocheted in my ear, followed by Hope's sharp cry. The plastic phone case cracked beneath my increased grip. "Hope? What the hell is going on?"

Dead air. Rustling as the phone was passed. Theo said, "Mercy, the ever-vigilant daughter, who returned to save the family ranch from the greedy hands of evil land developers. Sounds like a bad movie of the week." A mangled bray of laughter. "The truth is, I can't trust Hope not to snivel, so listen closely.

"Hiram told me what happened last night after I left. You sneaking around, spying on us like you're some army secret agent? Pathetic. You're a truck driver. Anyway, Hiram is scared shitless; Kit is pissed off and says he's not paying me for doing my job of getting into your sister's pants."

I heard Hope screech, "What? You bastard—"

Another sharp crack sounded, and I knew he'd smacked her again.

Oh yeah, jail was too good for this son of a bitch.

"You understand my dilemma. I can't go back, so I need money to relocate. With a little . . . ah, persuasion, Hope told me how much cash is stashed in your daddy's safe. Around thirty thou, right?"

"Roughly."

"Get the money and bring it to me. Come alone. You fetch the sheriff or bring Jake or that faggot John-John, or one of those brain-dead ranch hands or even that dog, and I'll kill her. Immediately. Messily. I'll make sure it's as painful as possible before she dies.

"Come unarmed. If I see you carting along anything resembling a gun, knife, bow and arrow, or even a big rock, I'll kill her. Don't wear a coat either; I'd better see nothing but your bare arms.

"Last thing. Come on horseback. I catch sight of an ATV or a pickup or a dirt bike, I'll kill her. Right in front of you."

"Wait—"

"Hope means nothing to me. But I know she's all you've got in the whole wide world. I'll take great joy in blowing her brains all over the precious Gunderson Ranch just to see you suffer, bitch. So think about what'll happen if you're planning on doing one goddamn thing to double-cross me. We clear on that?"

"Yes. What am I supposed to carry the money in?"

"A plastic garbage bag."

"Where do you want me to bring it?"

"Call Hope's cell phone once you've got the money and are mounted up." He laughed again, and it was like a rusty corkscrew in my ear. "Ought to be interesting, riding a horse after all these years. You pissing your pants in fear, little soldier? Can you do it? Even to save your sister?"

I ignored his taunt. One thing at a time. "We don't have cell phone reception everywhere on the ranch. I want to make sure once you hang up you're not taking her someplace where I can't get in touch with you, because you want an excuse to slice her up."

"Don't worry about that. Worry about getting me the money in time. Worry about me not getting antsy and shooting her just because she's annoying and I can. You have thirty minutes."

I heard Hope whimper, "No. Let go."

"Just in case you think I'm bluffing." A loud snap echoed

through the receiver and Hope screamed. "I broke her wrist. Next it'll be her nose, and I'll work my way down from there."

The connection went dead.

Thirty minutes.

Clutching the cell phone like a lifeline, I ran into my dad's office. Although the safe combination hadn't changed in years, my shaking fingers fumbled the dial. Four tries later, the last number clicked and the heavy door swung open. I stuffed a plastic garbage bag with stacks of bills. Didn't bother to count it. Didn't matter if it was every penny we had.

I took the stairs two at a time. In my bedroom, I jerked my gun cases from under the bed. Like hell I was going in unarmed.

My gun of choice was my compact Taurus Millennium Pro .45—the Walther P22 wouldn't do enough body damage for my liking; the 9 mm Glock didn't have a safety. I changed from sweats into baggy jeans. The metal was cold against my bare skin as I shoved the compact Taurus in the small of my back. The safety didn't catch on the waistband, so no chance I'd accidentally shoot myself in the butt. One gun and an extra clip wasn't nearly enough firepower, but it'd have to do.

I tucked my jeans into my worn Lariat boots. I considered taking the Chinese throwing stars from my bag of tricks. But under duress my aim with them wasn't great, the exact opposite of my firearm skills, and I couldn't risk hitting Hope with one of the flying razors.

On went my white ARMY OF ONE T-shirt. I glanced at the clock. Seven minutes had ticked by.

I spied an old backpack on the top shelf in the closet. Pulling it down, I dumped the contents on the floor, then transferred the cell phone, the money, the gun, and the clip into the backpack. Scanned the room. Good to go.

The easy part was done.

I sprinted outside. The air was heavy, a thick mass of swirling cold fog. Rain pelted me. Thunder rumbled. I slogged to the barn and froze once I realized what I'd have to do.

The irony wasn't lost on me; Queenie was housed in the stall where my mother died.

How was I supposed to overcome thirty years of terror and

climb on the back of a horse in thirty seconds? I didn't even know if I remembered how to saddle one.

My mother's voice drifted into my mind: *Saddle up the same way every time, Mercy; that way you'll never forget a step.*

Blood pulsed in my ears as I headed for the tack room. I grabbed a halter and a lead rope, and draped them around my neck. Then I peeled a wool blanket off the stack and unhooked a saddle from the wall, equipment that had been used recently. I threw the blanket and the saddle over the rail separating the stalls.

My hands shook. The bridle jingled like Christmas bells. I needed to calm down. I didn't have the luxury of spending time with Queenie to alleviate her fears or mine.

The creak of the hinges on the wooden gate sent goose bumps all over my body as I trudged inside the stall to face my demons.

The second I scooted sideways into the stall, Queenie reared. I leaped back, covered my head with my arms, and cowered by the exterior wall.

She whinnied. Almost sounded like a mean laugh.

God, I couldn't do this. Whether the horse was scared from the storm blustering off and on for the last day, or by me, or a combination of both, there was no way I could get close enough to slip the halter on. Say nothing of leading her out of the stall, saddling her, and gaining her trust so she'd take the bit.

And that was all *before* I'd have to climb on her back and ride her hell-bent for leather into a raging rainstorm.

The saddling process emerged from my blocked memory banks, but I wasn't in any shape to actually go through with it. My body shook; my clothes were soaked, not from rain but from nervous sweat.

While I fought with myself, Queenie snuffled and backed into me, butt first. Swished her tail. Crowding me. Putting me in the direct line of those powerful hind legs and deadly hooves. I suffered visions of my mother stuck in this same situation before vicious kicks knocked her to the stall floor.

The fine hairs on my nape tingled from the electricity in the air. Thunder crashed, rattling my nerves and the wooden walls.

I chanced a look at Queenie. Bad weather spooked the most even-tempered mare. Her sides heaved; her ears were pinned flat against her head. She sidled to the left, limiting my opportunity to get around her.

Damn horse knew I intended to put on the halter. Knew I was afraid to approach her. She kept trying to get me behind her, pushing me farther into the corner, keeping me from her left side.

I reached for my calm center, and my senses were assaulted by the stench of horseshit, the bitter smell of wet hay, old urine, and mud. The musky aroma of horseflesh, my own nervous sweat, and a phantom whiff of my mother's Emeraude perfume tainted with blood—all nightmare scents reminding me of the worst, most terror-filled afternoon of my life.

Go away go away go away. Breathe. In. Out.

I wasn't that helpless eight-year-old girl. I couldn't shrink in mortal fear in a smelly barn while a madman tortured my sister.

My personal pep talk didn't help. The past had hold of me, and I couldn't make myself move. I couldn't ever remember being petrified on this level. Not even when I'd been separated from my team in Kabul for two days and nights, hiding from patrols amid dead Afghan women and children.

You can do this, Mercy girl.

Dad?

No answer.

The loss of my father hit me like a Scud missile, yet I realized death wasn't strong enough to break the hold he had on me, especially here, on this piece of land he loved.

I could do this.

I *had* to do this.

Holding the halter by my side, I took a step toward Queenie, my blood pulsing in my ears, my heart lodged in my throat.

She did a quick little hop, tossing her head. We bobbed and swayed, a weird shuffling combination that might've looked like a mating dance if I hadn't been too scared to see the humor in it.

"I know we'd both rather be doing something else, but for now, I need you to work with me, because it's been a long time since I've done this."

Her ears swiveled my direction.

Maybe she'd cooperate now that I'd confessed my failings. When I inched forward, she lifted her front left leg, tossed her head and cleared her nostrils, blowing snot everywhere.

Nice. But I'd dealt with much worse bodily emissions from dead soldiers. I shook off Queenie's gross-out tactic.

Another footstep closer. "Come on and stand still, girl. I won't hurt you. See?" I reached out and placed my palm on her warm neck. Held up the halter so she could see it. Stroked her velvety brown coat. She flinched and tried to sidestep me again, but I stood my ground and kept touching her. Trying to reassure us both that this was okay.

"Good girl, Queenie." I patted her and murmured nonsensical words. Hoped like hell she couldn't hear how fast my heart beat with primal fear. Next I touched her nose, pushed down gently, a signal to get her to lower her head. "Let me slip this on."

Talking soothed her. I kept up a running dialogue in the same quiet cadence. She stayed still while I lifted the nylon halter and slipped it over her nose, buckling the strap below her left ear.

She blew out a frustrated breath.

"Doing great, girl. Almost done. Let's get you saddled up. Then you can run off all this aggravation."

Hurry hurry hurry kept racing through my head.

I grabbed the lead rope and threaded it through the ring on the bottom of the halter, under her jaw. After I opened the stall door with my elbow, I led her into the main aisle of the barn. Having her in a less confining space didn't alleviate my fears.

Water pooled on the dirt-packed floor. I figured Queenie would bolt if I gave her the chance. Instead of letting the lead rope drop and ground-tying her, I looped it through the D-hooks imbedded in the log support beam outside the stall with a quick release knot.

The roof vibrated from another clap of thunder.

I lifted the saddle blanket from the railing. Humidity made the wool damp. I settled the blanket on her back, a little high on the withers. I hoisted the saddle, careful not to toss it on her too hard.

Luckily Queenie didn't hump her back. Although when I

skirted her to reach her right side to check the cinch and drop the stirrups from the saddle horn, she did a little crow hop. The saddle slid so it ended up cockeyed. I managed to keep my panic at bay, even as I remembered how the cumbersome saddle sliding under the horse's belly had set off the temperamental Thoroughbred that'd killed my mother. I straightened the saddle, pulled the cinch under her belly, and tightened it through the cinch ring.

I untied the lead rope. Walked her a few steps forward and back, then rechecked the cinch. Sure enough, she'd puffed up her belly with air before I'd fastened the cinch and it was already loose. I tightened it a little more and grabbed the bridle.

The dim gray light affected my vision. I leaned closer and squinted, noticing Queenie's gums sagged around her mouth, a sign of age. I remembered Jake mentioning we might need to put her down soon. If she was sick, was riding her a danger to me?

Hurry hurry hurry.

I unhooked the halter, letting it dangle below her jaw. My right hand trembled as I held the top of the bridle and pulled it up over her head and ears at the same time as my left hand gently tried to push the bit into her mouth. Stubborn old nag wouldn't open up. I slid my finger into the toothless place in the back and pushed until she opened. I quickly slipped in the bit. "See? That wasn't so bad."

I swear Queenie gave me that *you-kidding-me?* look, and a tiny bit of hysteria crept into my laugh. I removed the halter and draped it over the railing.

Clutching the reins, I directed her to the barn door. I opened it and noticed the rain had let up. The sky was an odd shade of silver, misty clouds hung low, thick like fog, but cast no shadows on the patches of ground the color of wet cement.

I snatched the backpack off the peg and threaded my arm through one strap. Flipped open my cell phone and dialed.

The bastard didn't answer until the seventh ring. "Yeah?"

"I have the money. The horse is saddled and ready to go. Tell me where you are."

"I was beginning to think you wouldn't call."

"Where are you?"

"On the ridge above the ravine on the west end of the creek. Know where that is?"

Wouldn't be wise to snap at him that I knew this land better than he ever would. I visualized the grazing section. No trees or rocks or any shelter of any kind. So much for a stealth entry. Even a gilly suit wouldn't offer camouflage in such a wide-open area. "Yeah, I know where it is. You at the top of the creek? Or the bottom?"

"Middle. And you've only got five minutes left. Did you do that on purpose? You planning something?"

Fear snaked up my throat, choking me.

Before I could croak *no*, he said, "Maybe you need another incentive to get moving?"

I heard Hope whimper, "No, don't!" followed by her high-pitched scream and then nothing.

Rage burned away any remaining fear. I jammed the phone in my left rear pocket and prepared for the last step.

Riding.

The mount up should've scared me, but I was unexpectedly calm as I scooted Queenie close enough to get a leg up. On my first attempt she swung her butt sideways and I lost my balance, crashing into the support beam behind me.

"Come on, girl, I don't have time for this."

I tightened my grip on the reins and tried again, shoving my left foot in the stirrup. Even as the saddle shifted and Queenie decided to reverse, I threw my right leg over. My butt hit the contoured leather of the saddle.

I was on a horse for the first time in thirty years.

No time to give myself kudos. I slid the backpack around. With the reins in my left hand, I rooted until I found my weapon. I shoved the gun in the small of my back and settled the garbage bag full of cash on my lap.

I pressed my heels into Queenie's sides. She walked until we cleared the barn and the yard. Trotted as we passed the stock tanks. Once we hit open pasture, I gave her her head and we hit a full gallop.

And it still wasn't fast enough.

TWENTY

Queenie's strides ate up the prairie. Rain warred with the swirling fog, though I scarcely noticed the conditions. Remembering how to ride a horse wasn't like remembering how to ride a bike. I jounced in the saddle, out of kilter with the animal's natural grace. The anger and fear pounding in my blood was synchronized to Queenie's erratic hoofbeats. I needed patience. Prudence. A faster horse.

I spurred her harder when she lagged. The ridge Theo had picked stretched above a small spring-fed stream and wasn't as verdant as in years past. I tugged the rein in my right hand; Queenie didn't hesitate at the switch in direction. As we galloped along, I peered over the edge. Nothing below us but chunks of shadowed shale and clumps of stony soil, colorless as the sky.

Queenie slowed down considerably. I nudged her with my heels again. She grunted annoyance but picked up the pace slightly. Poor girl was struggling. Her sides billowed with each heaving breath. I'd make sure Jake pampered her when this was over, but right now I longed for a riding crop to urge her on.

The crest banked and Queenie lost her footing. She bobbled, righted herself, and slowed to a snail's pace. We'd made it three-quarters the length of the ridge when three things happened simultaneously: a loud crack reverberated through the canyon, an engine gunned somewhere ahead of me, and my horse came to a dead stop.

When Queenie fell, I fell. The flank strap loosened, and the saddle and I pitched sideways. I smacked the ground on my left side hard enough to make my teeth clack together like castanets. Searing pain shot across my collarbone, up my neck, and down my arm. I didn't hear that distinctive pop, but I immediately knew I'd dislocated my shoulder.

The reins snapped from my hand. The gun slammed into my lower spine before it jiggled loose from my pants, and hit the mud. My foot popped out of the stirrup, saving my leg from getting pulverized beneath fifteen hundred pounds of dead weight.

My ankle was wedged beneath Queenie's withers. Grunting against the pain, I wiggled my foot until it was free. The plastic bag caught air and whapped me in the chest. Ignoring the intense agony, I shifted to reach for my gun. I patted the soggy ground.

Nothing.

White-hot spears of fire zipped through my left side as my shaking fingertips connected with the Taurus's short barrel. Almost . . . Nope. Still too far.

Gritting my teeth, I slid my hand higher, inching my fingers down the smooth slide, what seemed a millimeter at a time, until I could curl the tips around the barrel. The breath I'd been holding exploded in a rush as I nestled the gun in my palm.

The sound of a revving engine edged closer.

I was out of breath and out of time. Through the adrenaline rush of surviving my worst nightmare, I realized that for me to retain the element of surprise, it had to look like Queenie's body had incapacitated me. I needed a diversion.

Resting the gun temporarily on the ground, I rustled in the garbage bag, snapped the rubber band on a stack of money, and released a crumpled handful of bills. The wind whipped the loose cash in a swirl of green, a tornado of color against the slate sky.

Despite the pain screaming in my shoulder, I pressed my body to the mud. My heart pumped like an oil derrick. Hot sweat poured from every pore, mixing with the cold rain, making my skin greasy with fear. I thumbed the safety, and cradled the gun to my chest beneath the bag. From beneath lowered lashes I watched and waited.

Theo appeared. Alone. Cautiously alert. A measly .22 clutched in his hand. He spared me a quick glance, then focused on the money blowing across the grazing field toward Nebraska.

My brain was stuck on one thing: Where was Hope? Why wasn't he holding her hostage to ensure my cooperation?

Because she's dead.

No. I refused to think along those lines or I'd go crazy and do something stupid. *Be smart. Be patient. Breathe. Listen.*

Theo took two steps toward me.

I had one chance to make this work; I hoped like hell Theo's reflexes were slow. His greedy gaze focused on the bag of money. When he reached for the bait, I lifted the gun and put two bullets in his knee.

Theo's screams echoed as he fell to the ground, clutching the flapping chunks of bloody skin where his kneecap used to be.

I rolled to the right and sailed to my feet, kicking his .22 aside and out of his reach. My useless left arm hung like a slab of meat. Through the brilliant haze of pain, I aimed the Taurus inches from Theo's face. "Where is Hope?"

He was blubbering. It didn't appear he'd heard my question.

To get his attention, I jammed the muzzle between his eyes and yelled, "You've got three seconds to tell me where my sister is."

"Up on the ridge."

"Alive?"

Blubber. Blubber. Blubber.

I whacked him on the forehead. "Alive?"

"Yes."

"Then why isn't she here?"

"She passed out after I . . . shit, it hurts."

"After you what, Theo?"

"You'll hurt me if I tell you."

"I'll hurt you worse if you don't tell me right goddamn now what you did to her."

Through his mumbles I heard, "I broke her nose."

Red rage consumed me. I flicked on the safety, gripped the barrel in my hand, and clocked him in the side of the head with the grip.

Theo screamed again.

"You are a sick fuck, beating up a defenseless woman. Did you kill Levi, too?"

"No!"

Again, I hit him with the butt of the gun. Same spot. Only harder. His girlish shrieks didn't soften my purpose.

"I'll ask you again. Did you kill Levi?"

"No." He was sobbing, rocking like a lopsided egg. "I swear. I didn't kill him. I swear."

"But you killed Sue Anne."

He nodded.

"Why?"

No response.

"Don't think I won't beat you to get answers. We both know you aren't man enough to withstand the kind of punishment I can dish out, so start talking."

"Sue Anne was going to tell the tribal police, the principal, and the community center director I raped Lanae."

"When did Sue Anne tell you this?" When he seemed reluctant to answer, I smacked him again. He screamed again. "Answer the question."

"After you talked to her that day on the rez. I followed her home from work that night." He whimpered and rocked. "It hurts."

"Tough. Why did you leave Sue Anne to die on my front porch?"

"To make it look like the same person who'd killed Levi killed her."

Then why hadn't he used a gun on Sue Anne? Why had he used a knife to slit her throat? "You admit that, yet you expect me to believe you didn't kill Levi?"

"No. I swear—"

"Did you set fire to the buildings?"

"I tried."

"Why?"

"If you died, Hope would be in charge." He rocked back. "Hope wanted to sell from the start. Don't blame me—"

"Save it. Take me to her. Stand up."

"I can't."

"Do it."

"But it hurts."

"Too bad. Get *up*." Injured or not, I kept my eyes on him every single second. Slowly, Theo rolled to his good knee. His thin shoulders heaved. Looked like he was throwing up. He moaned loudly. He took his own sweet time wobbling upright to stand on one leg like a drunken crane.

The second he was vertical, his stance changed. When he lurched sideways and threw the rock at me, I reacted instinctively. I fired two shots at his heart, one shot in the center of his face.

The blasts knocked him back, knocked him flat, and he was dead before he hit the dirt. I didn't need to double-check. I hadn't missed. No one survived three direct hits from a large-caliber gun from ten feet. No one.

Wiping the sticky blood spatters on my face with the inside of my wet forearm, I assessed the situation. One dead guy. One dead horse. One ATV. Me, basically a one-armed bandit. My gaze landed on Theo. Tempting, to put my boot on his hip and send his body careening down the hillside. Let the buzzards and the coyotes take care of his worthless carcass, just like in the old days of the Wild West.

But that'd make it difficult for the rescue workers to bring his body back up. No point hiding the fact I'd killed him. It'd be a true test of my acting skills to work up an ounce of remorse.

Crouching down, I threw my gun in the garbage bag on top of the money and dragged it behind me. I limped between Queenie's twitching body and Theo's sprawled form toward the ATV. At least I wouldn't have to rifle through a corpse's pockets for the keys; they hung from the ignition like a silver charm.

I tossed the bag in the back of the four-wheeler. Didn't help. Jesus. My shoulder socket burned as I climbed on and started up the machine.

Rain beat on my face. Thunder crashed and lightning spiked close by; my skin tingled, and the hair on the back of my neck prickled. When the back end of the ATV skidded out, I forced myself to slow down on the rain-slickened embankment. I couldn't save Hope from the bottom of a ravine.

Just ahead a big cottonwood loomed above a misshapen lump.

Hope. Motionless.

Just like Levi.

No. Hot fear lanced me and I refused to look to the sky for the circle of crows. Once I reached her I cut the engine and bailed off, momentarily forgetting about my shoulder, but the instantaneous pain was a raw reminder.

I slipped in the muck, falling to my knees. Hope was curled up in a ball; her broken wrist flopped between her breasts like a dead trout. I leaned as close as I could without losing my balance. Blood crusted the middle of her face like a strawberry birthmark. I placed my finger on her carotid artery.

A faint pulse, but a pulse nonetheless. Thank God. I smoothed my shaking hand over her face, her arm, her throat; everything was icy cold.

Since I couldn't pick her up I gently rolled her flat.

Burgundy spots of blood polka-dotted her white shirt. I didn't see additional injuries. Hope might be in shock, but I wouldn't have to field dress wounds before calling for medical attention.

It took four frustrating attempts to remove the cell phone from my left rear pocket with my right hand. Between the moisture and my trembling limb, the silver box squirted from my grasp like a slippery bar of soap. I plucked it up, crud and all, and hoped it hadn't broken in my fall. I dialed 911.

Explaining the severity of the situation to dispatch didn't go smoothly. Then again, babbling in a thunderstorm about an injured pregnant woman, a man I'd shot to death, and a dead horse could've sounded like a crank call.

After hanging up, I immediately called Jake. He knew exactly where I was on the ranch, but I had to talk fast to convince him to go to the house and stay there so he could lead the ambulance to us.

Now all I had to do was wait. As good as I was at the waiting game, it'd be a miracle if I didn't go insane. I didn't dare sit down or I'd pass out from pain. So I paced.

How many times had I been in situations like this? All over the world? Injured, waiting for help to arrive? Praying that everything would turn out all right once it did?

Dozens. Upon dozens. And as I paced in that sodden field, I realized I wouldn't miss that part of my life a bit.

• • •

From my vantage point, I saw Jake gallop in on his horse Ace, the ambulance close on his horse's hooves. The lights flashed *red blue red blue* in a blur, but the siren was silent. Two patrol cars finished up the motorcade. Jake's mount shied and jerked hard to the left, instinctively fleeing from the dead horse and the scent of blood. He spurred in my direction.

The ambulance followed Jake. I pointed to my sister, lying on the ground. Rome and a guy I didn't know jumped out. Hope didn't stir as they checked her.

Jake dismounted and tied Ace to the cottonwood tree. He loped over and his gaze flicked me top to bottom. "You ain't looking good. What's wrong with your arm?"

"Dislocated my shoulder when I fell off the horse."

His eyes went wide. "You *rode* out here?"

"Yeah. Long story." I paused, returning my focus to the medical crew. "Sorry about Queenie. It happened so quick."

"Might've been a heart attack. Not your fault."

Our eyes met again. No recrimination in his, just concern.

"I'm not hurt as bad as Hope."

"But bad enough." Jake yelled, "Got another injury here that needs attention, Rome."

"No. I'll be fine. Just get Hope stabilized."

"She is," Rome said as he pushed to his feet. "Let me see you."

"How is she?"

"Unconscious. The sooner we get her to Regional Hospital, the better. She isn't in immediate danger so they aren't sending the helicopter, especially in this weather."

"What'll happen once she gets there?"

"They'll probably determine whether the break on her wrist requires surgery and reset her nose. We'll have to wait and see on the prognosis for the baby."

I'd forgotten about that. "So can we go right now?"

"Whoa. *You* aren't going anywhere." When he placed his hand on my biceps, my arm stung like he'd smacked me with a crowbar and it was difficult not to shriek with pain. "I'll have to call for another ambulance for you."

"What? Why can't I ride with her?"

"Can't have two injuries in the same cab. Against county policy."

Another reminder of why I hated bureaucracy. "I am not going to sit here and wait for a fucking joyride while Hope is in surgery, Rome."

"Calm down."

"I am calm."

"If there was any way around this—"

"There is. Fix me first."

His startled gaze met mine. "Are you serious?"

A large figure was slogging across the field. Dawson. Through gritted teeth I said, "Yes. You've done this before, right?"

"Yes."

"Then do it."

"Dammit, Mercy, it doesn't work like that. We need an ortho to reset it—"

"No. You do it. Now." I shuffled closer. "I *am* going to the hospital with Hope in that ambulance. I don't care if I have to ride into Rapid City on the damn roof one-handed."

"You're in shock."

"Quit being a chickenshit. You aren't going to make it worse."

"Mercy, I don't think—"

"Don't fucking think," I hissed. "Just do it."

Resigned, Rome sighed and pointed to Jake's hand. "Give her your glove so she's got something to bite down on."

Jake whisked off a thick glove and rolled it up lengthwise. "Open," he said, and I unclenched my jaw. He worked it in my mouth across my tongue, stretching it until my teeth were covered in leather. "You sure about this, Mercy?"

I nodded.

"What do you need me to do?" Jake asked Rome.

"Brace yourself and hold on to her. No matter how tough she thinks she is, this is gonna hurt like a son of a bitch."

No lie. I bore down, focusing on the rough texture of the glove against my tongue. The tangy taste of the sweat-stained leather and dirt burst in my mouth.

"Easy." Rome placed his hand on my collarbone and I almost launched into orbit from the agony of that simple contact.

Jake became an immovable wall on my right side; my shoulder was jammed into the center of his chest. His left hand gripped my left hip. He wrapped my fingers around his right wrist and whispered, "Squeeze."

I should've fallen back on my yoga training and deep *uji* breathing. Instead, I held my breath and my body rigid. Despite my claims, Rome couldn't just pop it into place; he'd have to maneuver the bones back into proper position.

When Rome jiggled my arm back and forth, I squinched my eyes shut and swallowed the nausea. My breath stuttered in a muffled scream. Shit. That hurt.

"Easy. Almost got it."

Liquid streamed down my face, couldn't tell if it was tears or rain. I increased my grip on Jake's wrist.

After a harsh jerk, something popped. It grated, bone grinding on bone, making my knees buckle from sheer blinding pain. The glove in my mouth couldn't stifle my agonized howl. Saliva dribbled out the corners of my lips. Jake hauled me upright and held me steady while Rome finished the torture.

Rome twisted until everything snapped into place. I grunted, and the soggy glove dropped from my mouth. The burning sensation morphed into a constant throb. Rome gently lowered my arm as I buried my face into Jake's neck, sagging against him.

I couldn't catch my breath. I shook like a wet dog. I should've been mortified that I looked weak, but I hurt too bad to care.

Dawson said, "She okay? What happened?"

Rome said, "Dislocated her shoulder."

"Shit." Then, "Why isn't she getting treatment down by the ambulance?"

"Because I just reset it for her."

"Christ! Are you kidding me?"

Jake was stroking my hair and murmuring softly in Lakota.

"You aren't supposed to—"

"I know," Rome snapped. "She insisted."

"What in the hell were you thinking, Mercy?" Dawson said.

I stepped back and gazed at Jake, mouthing *thank you*. "I'm thinking it's time to get Hope to the hospital." I didn't look at Dawson until he blocked me in.

"Not so fast. You have to answer some questions first."

"Later."

"Now."

I blinked the moisture from my eyes. "Then you'll have to cuff me, Sheriff, nothing besides metal bracelets will keep me here. Nothing." I lowered my voice. "But we both know I can take you in a ground fight, so don't even try to stop me."

"Don't push me, Gunderson."

"Don't think I won't shoot through you, just like I shot through Theo, to get to my sister, Dawson."

Hard cop stare. "You admitting you shot him?"

My hard stare right back didn't waver. "Yep."

Rome and Jake crowded in around me. "Mercy isn't going anywhere besides the hospital," Rome said.

"Back off," Dawson warned. "That's a county ambulance you're driving. Last I knew, you worked for me."

"Last I knew, it was an elected position," Rome retorted. "And if you want to keep the job as sheriff come election time, you'll let her go right now."

"You threatening me?"

"Just stating the facts. After what she's been through in the last month, not to mention what she went through today, she doesn't need this right now."

Dawson's gaze moved between the three of us. I gave him credit; his eyes didn't linger on me. No one would suspect he'd rolled out of my bed yesterday morning.

"Fine. Answer this, Miz Gunderson: am I gonna run across any other bodies up here?"

"No."

He pressed his nose to mine. "The second you're cleared from the hospital, the *second*, I expect you in my office."

"Rome," the short guy shouted from beside Hope's stretcher. "She's ready. Let's go."

Jake wrapped his jacket around me and said, "I'll stick around, see if Dawson needs anything else. Once this is done, I'll call Sophie and we'll head to the hospital."

I nodded.

Jake and Rome kept me sequestered from Dawson as I

climbed into the back of the ambulance and endured the hellish back-roads ride into Rapid City.

Rome must've done a good job setting my shoulder. The emergency room doc injected a muscle relaxant, slid my arm into a sling, and told me to have the VA follow up.

Hope's wrist didn't require surgery. The on-call ortho gave her a local anesthetic, reset it and her finger. The ear, nose, and throat doc was called in, and she reset Hope's nose. Near as anyone could tell the pregnancy hadn't been compromised.

Hope hadn't regained consciousness. The staff assured me she was fine, just under a self-imposed hypnotic sleep. I remembered the catatonic state Hope had lingered in for days after she'd shot Jenny Newsome, and I wasn't surprised that's how her body and mind dealt with trauma.

How did I deal with trauma? I paced.

Jake and Sophie showed up. Sophie clucked around me like a grandmother peahen. I let her. She volunteered to stay with Hope while Jake drove me to the sheriff's office. The sooner I got it over with, the sooner I could get back to the hospital. And tell my sister I'd killed her lover. Yeah. I could hardly wait for that conversation.

On the ride back home I didn't want to talk. Jake didn't seem to care. "Did Theo tell you he killed Levi?"

I directed my attention out the window. Not that I could see anything beyond the wall of grayish-blue clouds and ribbons of silver drizzle trickling down the glass.

"Mercy?"

"He said he didn't kill him."

"And you believe him?"

"I don't know. He admitted that he killed Sue Anne and that he'd set the fires, so I think he would've bragged if he'd killed Levi." Theo's words: *I wanted to make it look like the same person killed Sue Anne and Levi* taunted me. Theo hadn't known how Levi had died. Hope had kept her promise.

"If he didn't do it, then who did?"

"I don't know. It doesn't make sense." I told him everything Hiram and Theo had told me.

Jake's jaw was so tight I expected it'd crack. "Do you think Kit might've done it?"

"Again, I don't know."

"What a piece of shit," he said.

I didn't know if he was talking about Theo or Kit since the description fit both of them. "Did you know about Hope and Theo?"

"No." He sighed, rubbing the side of his mouth with the back of his hand. "Well, that ain't true. I knew she was seeing somebody, but I wasn't sure who."

"Dad didn't know?"

Jake shook his head. "As far as Wyatt knew . . ."

"What?"

"It ain't my place to say."

"Then whose is it?" I faced him. "Spit it out, Jake."

He switched lanes to pass a rusted-out VW love wagon with Oregon plates. "First, I wanna know if you've hidden a gun in that sling."

"The sheriff has my gun, remember?"

Jake shot me a sardonic look. "We both know you have more than one gun."

"I'm unarmed for a change. Come on. Tell me."

"A few weeks before Theo came into the picture, Hope and I had . . . gotten together again."

I braced myself for my burst of anger. None came. Huh. Maybe the pain meds had mellowed me. Then his real meaning hit me. "The baby is yours?"

"Maybe. Hope had been feeling awful poorly, just like before with Levi. But I chalked it up to her being heartsick because of Wyatt dying. Then when *unci* told me Hope was pregnant . . ."

I hated that he never seemed to finish a sentence. "And?"

"And before I could talk to her about whether it was mine, Levi was killed. She had plenty of other things on her mind." He paused to gather his thoughts. "Wyatt knew I stuck around all these years because of Levi. He never understood why Hope wanted to keep it a secret, 'specially after Mario Arpel died, but he accepted her decision. Now I feel like it's happening all over again."

Jake had hovered on the outskirts like an obedient dog, abiding by Hope's wishes, waiting for scraps, when he should've stood up to her and demanded his paternal rights. But that wasn't Jake's way. Which is why Jake and I were never a good match.

I thought back to the dance. Hope and Theo had been discreet. Theo hadn't sat in the front pew with her at Levi's funeral. He hadn't horned his way into anything, besides his interest in the ranch. "You think anyone in the community knows Hope was with Theo?"

"Not many." He frowned. "Why?"

"Then there's no reason for you and Hope not to go public with the fact she's carrying your child."

Jake turned toward me so fast he jerked the wheel and the back end of the truck skidded out. "What are you talking about?"

"Hope needs someone to take care of her; we both know that. Since the odds are good that lump in her belly could be your child, she should turn to you." I was spinning this so hard I made myself dizzy. "Secret lovers bonding over tragedy. People love that romantic claptrap."

Jake's wide-eyed gaze remained on me instead of on the road. "You're plum crazy."

"You get a second chance to raise a child with her, and you get to look like a hero not only in her eyes, but in the eyes of the community."

His face might've held skepticism, but his body language read interest. "Got it all figured out, doncha?"

"You have a better idea?"

"Nope. But I'd sure like to know what kinda drugs they pumped into you at the hospital." He cocked his head and nervously slid his hands up and down on the steering wheel. "Weren't more'n a coupla days ago you threatened to pierce my forehead with lead because of my past with your sister. And you were convinced I'd do anything to get my hands on the ranch. Now it's like you're holding an invisible shotgun to my head and telling me I gotta fall in line with your plans. What gives?"

How did I explain? Could I? Without sounding like a sappy Hallmark greeting card?

"Since all this has happened . . ." Raindrops beaded on the window, zigzagging a random pewter path before the wind wicked it away. "I'm tired of fighting, Jake. War. The ranch. With everyone around me. With myself. At my age, it's hard to swallow my pride and admit that even when I thought I hated this place, I've never really fit anywhere else."

Jake didn't comment, which wasn't a big surprise. The rest of the drive was silent.

When we turned up the rutted driveway I'd traveled a million times, Jake looked over at me and said softly, "Welcome home, Mercy Gunderson."

For once I was grateful for his stoicism as I blinked back my tears.

Amid the clouds of misty fog I could tell the ranch was deserted. I don't know if I expected Dawson to be lying in wait for me. I wasn't disappointed, but I couldn't shake the feeling I hadn't seen the worst of this day.

Jake parked the truck behind the big barn while I trudged up the porch steps into the house. I needed a hot shower to wash away the grime and blood. Right after I downed a shot of whiskey or two to blur the grimy, bloody images in my mind.

I debated on how I'd unhook the sling to get my clothes off without help, when I heard a car pull into the yard. Great. Maybe Dawson had come looking for me. I knocked back a mouthful of fortification before I shuffled back outside.

Iris Newsome lingered at the bottom of the steps, her wrinkled face pinched with concern.

After the day I'd had, the last thing I needed was to hear her boring-ass pitch about my responsibilities as a landowner as she waved a petition in my face.

"Good Lord, Mercy. I just heard what happened."

I frowned. "Bad news travels fast."

"Is Hope all right?" Iris peered over my shoulder before those sharp birdlike eyes pierced mine. "Is she here?"

"No. She's at the hospital."

"Oh. That's good. Unless . . ." Her hand fluttered by her sagging chin. "Did she lose the baby?"

How had Iris known about the pregnancy? I knew for a fact Hope wasn't babbling near and far. "They're keeping her overnight for observation."

"And you're here? Instead of being at the hospital with your poor sister?"

Stung by her chiding tone, I found myself nodding. "Temporarily. I have to turn myself in to the sheriff for questioning."

"Why?"

"Standard procedure."

"Isn't it a clear case of self-defense?"

Did I look as confused as I felt? I eased down the steps, giving my brain time to clear a path through the pain meds and the whiskey. I doubted Dawson had released the fact I'd shot and killed Theo to the general public, especially since I hadn't been officially interviewed. So how did Iris know what'd gone down only a few hours ago?

Logic said she'd been listening to a police scanner. Still, my spidey sense tingled. I had to play this cool. "Well, Dawson is cautious."

"Cautious? The man is a buffoon. You'd think he'd be more concerned with figuring out who put two bullets in Levi, rather than putting you and Hope through more hell."

My stomach pitched, my vision went blurry. Dawson had insisted on keeping Levi's manner of death under wraps. Only a handful of people knew how Levi had been executed.

Including the murderer.

My thoughts rewound to Levi telling me he had someone to talk to. Someone who understood what he was going through. Someone who knew that section of land, Levi's brooding spot. Someone who lived close by with easy access.

Snippets of conversations popped up. When Levi had said "she," I'd assumed he'd meant Sue Anne. But "she" was Iris Newsome. A trusted family friend. A woman who was no stranger to tragedy. A mother who'd been grieving for her child for years.

A psycho who'd bided her time to take retribution on the person who had killed that child, by killing *her* child.

If I'd felt murderous rage before, it was nothing compared to how I felt now. But I was at a serious disadvantage to act on my violent impulse, unarmed, injured, and drugged up.

Before I could take action, Iris knocked me off balance, whipped me around, jerking my head back by my hair. A knife appeared in my peripheral vision.

"I'll sign your stupid petition, okay? You don't have to strong-arm me."

"Don't get cute with me, Mercy."

"I'm not. What is going on? Why are you—"

"It's too late to play dumb. Put your right hand in your front pocket."

I got it halfway in. "That's the farthest—"

"All the way." She dug the knife deeper into my windpipe until my hand was completely buried in the pocket.

The knife tip gouged my throat with each jarring footstep. Blood ran and mixed with the rain as she frog-marched me through mud puddles to the fence.

"No one will believe I slit my own throat."

"I'm not going to use the knife. You're about to take a swim in the stock tank." Iris clucked her tongue. "Such a pity. You lost your balance, bumped your head, and fell in. Not so unbeliev-able that you'd drown with an injured arm."

"How long did you plan this?" I demanded.

"Drowning you? Spur of the moment." Iris pulled my hair with enough force she ripped chunks out. "But I'll enjoy watch-ing Hope grieve over you, too. Move it."

At this point I had nothing to lose by goading her. "God won't condone you killing Levi because of Jenny's death. That eye-for-an-eye stuff is bullshit. Aren't you supposed to turn the other cheek?"

"I'd followed the Christian way and forgiven Hope . . . until *she* got knocked up. The little whore didn't deserve a baby after I'd lost mine. Hope needed to suffer humility, just like I did, so she'd know what it's like to be childless and alone."

Iris's comment from the day of Levi's funeral floated back to me. *I see her, and it's just not fair.* Iris hadn't been talking about Hope grieving over Levi; she'd been talking about Hope being alive instead of Jenny.

She thrust me against the stock tank until the steel rim bit into my upper thighs.

It'd be impossible to fight her off without the use of my hands. Yet I wouldn't let her drown me like a rat. If I kicked sideways and knocked her over, it'd give me a chance to run.

Iris yanked my head back. "Don't fight it. I hear drowning is peaceful."

"You vindictive bitch."

She twisted the tip of the knife deeper into my flesh. "You have no idea. I *liked* that Levi always trusted me. I *liked* the look on Levi's face as I shot him in the heart. I *liked* watching those big brown eyes widen with fear as I put the barrel to his head and pulled the trigger. "

She'd described his last moment so vividly Levi's terror beat in my blood. Gunpowder filled my nostrils. My heart stopped beating. My head pounded. I was suffocating. I was dying.

Mercy. Focus.

I shook off the shock and the muzzy feeling, bringing up my foot to deliver a snapping side kick to her knee.

A loud ringing clank echoed next to my ear. Then the knife dropped from my throat, the death grip in my hair loosened.

With both hands immobilized, I lost my balance and crashed sideways, but I managed to twist and land on my back, not my shoulder. The air left my lungs in a rush.

Through the blood rushing in my ears and another helping of excruciating pain, I heard *thwack thwack thwack.*

Once I could breathe again, I focused on the rhythmic noises. I wiggled my hand out of my front pocket and rolled to my knees. Slowly, still fighting dizziness, I raised my head and saw Jake standing over Iris's prone body wielding a flathead shovel.

Jake swung over and over. Smacking her in the head, taking chunks out wherever the steel edge hit: her arms, her legs, her back. Blood glistened on the steel. Red spatters smeared the wooden handle and covered Jake's forearms.

I forced my gaze to Jake's face and saw agony, rage, madness, and bloodlust. With every downstroke, a hitching wail broke forth from his mouth.

Bracing a hand on the lip of the stock tank, I stood on shaking legs. Jake didn't miss a beat. *Thwack. Thwack. Thwack.* I cleared my heart from my throat. I shouted, "Jake. Enough."

He froze and looked over at me, the shovel stopping in midair.

I recognized that shell-shocked look. I'd seen it on soldiers. On civilians. In the mirror.

"Mercy? What? How . . ." He glanced at the body at his feet.

"Take a deep breath and put down the shovel."

He swung the shovel again. The corner connected with the muddy ground next to Iris' face. I admit, I cringed for a second, fearing he'd splice her head like a ripe cantaloupe.

"I-I heard her talking. When she said she liked killing him and how scared he was at the end . . . I-I lost it."

"It's okay, Jake."

"No, it's not!" He stared at Iris's body, seeming to really see it, to really see what he'd done to her, for the first time. His face lost all color. "Oh God. I did that?"

The shovel slid from his blood-covered hands and clanked against the rim of the stock tank. He dropped to all fours and began to dry-heave.

We didn't have time for him to have a crisis, even when it was justified. I hobbled over to him. "It's over. You avenged Levi. You saved my life. No shame in that."

"But look at what I did to her. Jesus. No. Don't look. I can't look. . . ." More retching sounds, more keening sobs.

Iris's body was seriously fucked up. Deep gashes cut through her clothing. She looked like . . . someone had beat her to death with a shovel. "Jake. Listen—"

"You don't understand. I'm Indian. She's white. When Dawson sees her like this, he ain't buying it was self-defense."

"He won't find out."

Jake lifted his face. "What did you say?"

"Pull yourself together because we have to get rid of this body right now. We're planting Iris someplace else."

He sputtered, "B-but that's wrong."

"What's wrong is she murdered your son. She was a malicious, bitter woman, and if you hadn't killed her, I would have. And trust me, the way I planned to do it? No one would've mistaken it as self-defense."

There was that look of fear I'd gloried in when I'd made my late-night visit. He'd fall in line. He had no choice.

"Why are you doing this?"

"Doing what? Getting rid of her body?"

"No. Protecting me."

"Besides that you're indispensable to the ranch?" I locked my eyes to his. "Because whether I like it or not, you're family, Jake. We take care of our own."

A beat passed. Jake nodded once. "What now?"

"Get an old blanket and a tarp and bring the truck over here. Hurry."

As Jake drove the rig around, I made sure Iris's keys were in the ignition of her Honda. Jake and I rolled her up in the moth-eaten burlap tarp. Neither of us was particularly gentle with her remains; she didn't deserve dignity.

With my bum arm I wasn't any help loading her into the truck bed. I already knew a dead body is tough to maneuver. Jake was learning firsthand.

"Now what?" he panted.

"Take her to that ravine about two miles north, where the Newsome Ranch borders ours. It's a ways out, which makes it perfect. Get on the rutted road that snakes down and dump her in the gully, but make sure she isn't on our land, and make damn sure you leave nothing that can be traced back here. You'll have to be really careful because I've heard those crazy religious freaks keep a close eye on things."

"I know. What'll you be doing?"

I grabbed the blanket and pointed to Iris's car. "Halfway between here and their place I noticed the fence was down, so I'll drive in as far as I can go. Then I'll double-back across the field on foot."

"You really think once someone finds the abandoned car they'll believe she walked that far? By herself?"

"I don't care because it won't be our problem."

Jake gave me a once-over. "You wearing that to the sheriff's office?"

Mud covered my shirt. Every piece of my wet clothing clung to me. My boots squished. The last thing I wanted was Dawson grilling me on why I'd stopped home and cleaned up. Showing up gross and dirty at the sheriff's department was a great alibi.

"Yeah." My gaze moved over him head to toe. "You have an extra set of clothes?"

"In the tack room."

"Stop and change afterward. Wrap up those clothes in the tarp and stuff them in the grease barrel in the machine shed. We'll burn them later. I'll need gloves. Or rather, a glove."

Jake rummaged around inside the cab. He waved a yellow cotton glove liner and held it out for me. "This ain't the first time you've done something like this."

A statement. Not a question that required an answer.

TWENTY-ONE

Jake dropped me off at the sheriff's office and I went in alone. I didn't need to worry that in a rush of guilt he might blurt out what'd he'd done to Iris Newsome. I already had enough problems.

Dawson was making me wait. I didn't blame him.

In the small reception area, I sat on a chair and studied the framed map of South Dakota. During my childhood I'd been fascinated by the thick red marker lines outlining our small county. In the hundreds of times I'd been in this office, sitting in this same hard plastic orange chair, I'd never been in this position: waiting to explain to law enforcement why I'd killed a man.

After Jake and I parted ways, everything went according to plan. He dumped the body; I dumped the car. I closed my eyes as a bout of nausea washed over me. The endless walk through the foggy pastures had been a nightmare. My body nearly shut down from the pain. My mind had suffered enough trauma. My main focus had been trudging to the road before I passed out from shock.

The office door opened. I heard Dawson's boots thumping on the tile floor. When the noise stopped, I opened my eyes and looked up. His face read pure business. A frisson of fear danced up my spine. I'd be damned if I'd show it. "Sheriff."

"Miz Gunderson. Come back to my office." Expecting I'd follow, he ducked into the room that'd belonged to my father.

The overwhelming urge to run beat at me with a child's guilt. Like somehow Dad would know I'd done a bad thing. Like the walls would pulse his disappointment until it reverberated through me and made me confess. I swayed as I rose to my feet, swallowing the cry of pain racking my body.

"You okay?" Kiki said behind me.

"Just tired." I gritted my teeth and shuffled to the office, sliding into the ladder-back wooden chair directly across from Dawson's neat-as-a-pin desk. Kiki sat between us at the corner of the desk and pulled out a notebook.

"I've asked Deputy Moore to record your statement," Dawson said. "Start whenever you're ready."

For a moment I was at a loss on where to begin. I exhaled with deliberate slowness and talked about what I'd overheard at the Warrior Society meeting regarding Albert Yellow Boy's accidental death. How I realized the adult leader of this group was Theo Murphy, the man my sister was sort of seeing, and Levi's teacher. I relayed my conversation with Hiram Blacktower and his claim that Theo worked for Kit McIntyre. I shared my frustration about not being able to track down Hope after the meeting. Then Theo's early-morning phone call demanding I bring him money so he could leave town. Being forced to listen as he assaulted Hope.

My retelling of the events sounded clinical. Precise. Probably made me sound cold, but I was used to detailing everything to my CO with as little emotion as possible.

Both Dawson and Kiki were quiet after I finished.

Finally Dawson asked, "Let me get this straight: Theo Murphy confessed to killing Sue Anne White Plume?"

"Yessir. That is correct."

"After you shot him in the knee?"

"Yessir."

Dawson angled across the desk. "Theo Murphy also confessed to killing your nephew, Levi Arpel?"

I looked him right in the eye and lied. "Yessir."

Another round of silence.

"Tell me again about how you came to shoot Theo Murphy twice in the chest, once in the head."

"He was on the ground after I'd immobilized him by shooting him in the kneecap. After he'd told me what I wanted to know, I instructed him to get up and take me to my sister. He took a long time getting up, which I attributed to the injury. When he turned, he threw a rock at me and I fired at him."

"Instinctively?"

"Yessir. My training as a soldier is to shoot to kill, not to wound." Maybe I should've phrased that differently.

"But at no time during your confrontation with Theo Murphy did he fire at you?"

"He threw a rock at my head, sir."

Dawson scowled. "Let me rephrase that. Did Theo Murphy fire his *gun* at you?"

As I answered, "No sir," I realized I was completely screwed.

"Thank you. Hang tight. We'll be right back." Dawson motioned to Kiki, and they exited the room.

But I heard them arguing in the hallway.

"I'll remind you that Wyatt Gunderson would do exactly the same thing." Pause. "No. Wyatt hired me because we both believe in following the letter of the law. No exceptions. Not even for the former sheriff's daughter."

More voices joined in. The argument escalated until Dawson bellowed, "Enough."

The door creaked. Dawson's heavy footsteps stopped behind me. "Mercy Gunderson, I'm placing you under arrest for the shooting death of Theo Murphy." He read me my rights.

I thought I didn't have a drop of adrenaline left in my body. I was wrong.

"Please stand."

I rose slowly but became light-headed. Dawson's hand on my right shoulder righted me.

"Easy. Just take it nice and slow. No hurry."

I asked, "Where am I going?" even when I already knew.

"Downstairs to booking."

Despite the dread churning in my belly, my back snapped straight. I marched out of the room to the set of locked doors at the end of the hallway. I'd been downstairs dozens of times. Always by choice. Not so this go around.

Dawson punched in a code, and the guard buzzed the door to let us in.

Kiki joined us. I studied my mud- and blood-spattered boots.

No one spoke during the walk downstairs. I was booked and fingerprinted. Kiki helped me undress. I wore the faded blue baggy pants and shirt of the jail uniform. My personal effects were tagged, but I was allowed to keep the sling. Magnanimous of them.

Kiki didn't say a word as she led me to the empty cell. I settled myself on the cot, trying to act brave, when I felt anything but. Her face was bright red with embarrassment as she hit the button and the doors clanked shut, locking me in. She whispered, "Sorry," and I was alone.

Not really alone. I stared at the surveillance camera before I closed my eyes and pretended to sleep.

I sat astride a Palomino, galloping along the lip of a craggy canyon. No saddle. No fear. My horse and I were fluid, gliding in perfect synch. Graceful. Beautiful. Focused.

The buckskin fringe on my dress flapped in the wind. The bone beads at the end of my braids clacked with each thundering hoofbeat. Cool breezes stemmed the sting of the sun's blistering rays; I tipped my face to the cloudless turquoise sky. I twined my fingers in the horse's silky mane, angling across the stallion's bare back to urge him to run faster.

We crested the last steep slope, me and my trusty steed. I dug my knees into the horse's withers. In a burst of speed we reached the peak. The horse was covered in sweat, and I could barely hang on.

The mountainous area spread out before me, like the Alps in the opening scene of *The Sound of Music*. I rubbed my eyes. This wasn't where I was supposed to be. This wasn't the ranch. This wasn't home. I heard a noise, a cross between a war whoop and the higher pitch of an Indian woman's tremolo. Then I saw them. My mother. My father. Levi. Running across the fertile plain, replete with wildflowers. Laughing. Mom and Dad swinging Levi high into the air like he was a small child.

I waved, shouting for their attention. No one noticed me. I kicked the horse into a full gallop. Muddy clods splattered my face. As I swiped the sludge from my eyes, I lost control of the horse. It was headed straight for them. Blindly, I tugged on the reins. The thick leather strap in my right hand morphed into a rattlesnake the size of a python. It slithered from my grasp, sinking enormous fangs into the horse's left flank. The horse screamed and reared, bucking me off into the muck.

Then the Palomino twisted and plowed my mother to the ground like she was a bowling pin and those gigantic hooves pummeled her head like a boxer's speed bag.

Levi pulled a gun out of his grass-stained shoe. He fired. The horse shrieked; flames shot out of its muzzle. An owl screeched above us. The horse shrank to the size of a mouse. The bird of prey plucked up the rodent and disappeared.

I crawled to my mother, only to watch her bloody, mangled body disintegrate into a pile of snow-white ash.

Panicked, Levi turned to my father.

A snub-nosed revolver appeared in Dad's hand. He braced his feet in an official cop's firing stance and took two shots. One bullet lodged in Levi's brain, one in his heart. Levi crumpled to the ground. He, too, fragmented into nothing.

The bright day blurred to gray.

Dad pivoted my direction. He wore his sheriff's uniform. The gun morphed into a shovel and he swung it at me like a mace. "It's your fault. She'd be alive if not for you. They'd all be alive if not for you."

Words I'd always feared—but he'd never uttered—sliced through me.

His face aged. He shriveled into a stoop-shouldered old man. The scenery distorted. We were in the desert outside of Baghdad. Sand stung my face, obscuring my vision. The roar of tanks. Low-flying aircraft buzzed. Bombs boomed. Placid wisps of clouds changed into plumes of angry black smoke as the city behind us burned.

As Dad stalked closer I shouted, "Stop!" He kept coming until a land mine detonated and blew his leg off. The blast didn't knock him down. He stood, one-legged, in the middle of a minefield, bleeding. Dying. Waiting. For what? For me to run to him and save him?

The *buzz buzz* of warning alarms grew more insistent. I scanned the heavens. Not a compelling turquoise, but black.

Rockets shrieked past, white vapor trails clung in the sky. Everything was black-and-white. Seemed I was stuck in a *MAD Magazine* comic book, *Spy vs. Spy*. Was I a bad guy? Or a good guy? I
glanced down and saw black flak gear, head to toe. When had I
become a bad guy?

The warning *buzz buzz* reverberated around us. I yelled, "Dad.
I'll be back."

An enormous white cowboy hat concealed his face. "You always say you'll come back, but you never do."

"I will. This time I swear I'll come back for good."

Buzz buzz.

Dad hopped forward on his good leg. The blinding explosion
knocked me flat. When I couldn't see him anymore, I screamed.

"Mercy?"

I awoke with a jolt. A cement ceiling and gray walls swam
into view. I wasn't in Iraq. I blinked, remembering I was in jail. I
didn't know which was worse.

My name was repeated again, louder, amid another buzz.

"Mercy. Answer me."

I swung my legs to the floor and faced Dawson.

He hung on the other side of the bars, concern lining his face.
"You were screaming."

"The price of being a soldier."

"Does that happen often? Combat nightmares?"

"Often enough." I kept my expression bland. "You here checking to see if there's any rest for the wicked, Dawson?"

"Not even close."

Our gazes clashed. The questions in his eyes went unspoken.

"Then what are you doing down here?"

"Came by to check on you and to give you these." He held out
a plastic bottle containing my pain meds from the hospital. "Kiki
found them in your jacket pocket."

"Isn't that against the rules? Giving a prisoner drugs?"

"Probably. But I've dislocated my shoulder and I know it
hurts. No reason for you to suffer."

As I wobbled toward him, I noticed he wasn't wearing his
gun, and he wasn't keeping a discreet distance between himself
and the iron bars like he was supposed to.

"If I was a tough girl, I'd insist I didn't need the painkillers."

"Not to worry. You're plenty tough." He cleared his throat. "I brought you a bottle of water."

I curled my hand around the bar and studied him. "Why are you doing this?"

Dawson's dark gaze never wavered from mine. "You know why."

I frowned.

"Here. Hold out your hand." He dumped the pills into my palm.

I popped the pills in my mouth and snagged the water bottle he'd wedged through the biggest slat. I drained the whole thing and passed the empty back to him. "Thanks."

"You're welcome. You want some food brought down? Kiki said you didn't eat earlier."

"I'm not hungry."

We stared at each other in the utter silence.

"I thought you might like to know I talked to Hope."

"She's awake? How is she?"

"Bandaged up, but okay. She's worried about you."

"Did you tell her . . . ?" I hadn't thought how I'd break the news to her that I'd killed Theo. A big part of me worried she'd think I belonged in jail.

"Yes. She knows about Theo. She isn't upset with you, Mercy."

How had he learned to read me so quickly? "She knows he killed Levi?"

"That, too."

"Is she by herself?"

"No. Jake and Sophie are staying with her."

At least she wasn't alone. Not like me. I squeezed my eyes shut as I rested my forehead against the cold metal. I wouldn't cry. I wouldn't feel desolate. I wouldn't feel go goddamn isolated. God. I should be used to it by now.

Rough, but warm and gentle fingers tentatively caressed my cheek through the bars. I couldn't make myself pull away. I needed simple human contact, if only for a minute or ten.

"Dawson," I said hoarsely. "The camera. Someone might see."

"I don't care."

His breath drifted across the top of my head in a soothing, steady stream. He continued the tender strokes up and down my jawline until I finally retreated, even when I didn't want to.

He stepped back. "You'd better crawl onto the cot before the meds kick in and you crash on the floor."

Only after I'd stretched out did he make any move to leave.

"Get some rest. I'll see you in the morning." The buzz of the doors unlocking sounded, and he was gone. I had the strangest feeling he hadn't gone far.

I laid there staring at the ceiling until the painkillers made me sleepy. Dawson hadn't apologized for arresting me. It was weird to think I would've thought less of him if he had.

The next morning I was first on the docket at the courthouse, so there wasn't time to completely cleanse myself of the filth still clinging to my hair and skin. As a soldier it bothered me not to have the time to spit and polish myself for the brass.

Mike O'Brien, the state's attorney, summarized the situation for Judge Brunson. I listened to him read Hope's statement. Dawson read my statement and added his own observations. He carefully explained his reason for arresting me. I didn't fault him, but I seemed to be the only one. My friends in the courtroom were rife with animosity.

In the end, I wasn't charged. Theo Murphy's death was ruled justifiable homicide by self-defense.

I went home.

EPILOGUE

Two weeks later . . .

My duffel bag was nestled in the dirt and weeds next to my feet. I slouched on the bottom porch step, taking it all in. I heard Sophie and Hope chatting through the screen door. Across the yard, Jake and TJ took advantage of the cool morning and readied the old wooden machine shed for a coat of paint.

Things were better between Jake and me. Being forever tied to a dark secret has an upside, apparently. He'd taken my advice, reached out to Hope, and she'd latched onto him like a lifeline. Consequently, he and Hope shared the news with the Viewfield community and Eagle River County about their impending bundles of joy. Hope's ultrasound during her stay at the hospital in Rapid City revealed twins. No one said a word about paternity, including me.

They were helping each other through the grief of Levi's murder. They'd moved into the main house. I'd even given up my bedroom. Once Vivi cleaned Dad's rooms, I hauled my few belongings downstairs and didn't feel like a squatter who'd get kicked out when the real owner returned. Dad wasn't coming back, but his presence was everywhere and always would be.

As I listened to the crescendo of the cicadas, and the wind chimes pinging in the sweet morning breeze, an Eagle River County patrol car crawled up the drive and parked.

Shoonga started to bark. I wrapped my hand around his collar and shushed him.

This was the first I'd seen of Dawson since my court appearance. Wasn't the first I'd thought of him. He'd been busy wrapping up cases—starting with Albert Yellow Boy's.

Estelle had stopped by. Learning Albert's death had been accidental like Dawson suspected hadn't eased her mind; in fact, it seemed to anger her. She'd made an offhand comment about how things were different (read better) for Hope, because Levi's murder was resolved, unlike Albert's death being chalked up to just another Indian kid's dumb mistake. Sophie shooed her off before I'd had a chance.

Geneva called daily to apologize and I let her calls go straight to voice mail. I'd talk to her eventually, just not while I was emotionally and physically raw. We'd been friends long enough that she had the right to earn my forgiveness.

Even Molly had swung by to plead her mother's case and she'd come bearing kittens. An entire bucket of the little purring furballs. I'd like to claim I wasn't moved by her sweet and over-the-top gesture, but truthfully, I was. I kept the biggest kitty as a barn cat. The male tabby didn't follow me everywhere like Shoonga did. It amazed me how quickly I'd gotten used to that dog demanding my attention and affection, and how easily I gave it. I even let him sleep in my room, just because it drove Sophie crazy.

Four days after I was released from jail, someone reported Iris Newsome missing. When her abandoned car was discovered a day or so later, Dawson organized a search party. It took them two days to find her remains, which were nearly unrecognizable after wild critters snacked on her bitter old skin and bones. Still, the coroner ruled her death suspicious. Dawson hedged when locals questioned him on his investigative findings, and it was the first time I hoped he'd slack off investigating a homicide. Rumor had it members of the LifeLite Church were on the top of his suspect list, due to the petition Iris had been circulating, which gained posthumous momentum.

Iris Newsome was buried between her beloved daughter, Jenny, and her husband, Merle. Jake and I attended the ceremony, although neither of us wanted to. Oddly enough, without heirs, the Newsome estate was in limbo. I had every intention of using the money from Dad's life insurance policy to buy that small acreage the instant it went on the market, if for no other reason than to screw with Kit McIntyre. He and I weren't done. Not by a long shot.

Dawson ambled toward me, wearing his uniform, sans ugly hat, sans dark sunglasses. "Mercy."

"Sheriff. You just cruising by, or are you here on official business?"

He ignored my smart question and hunkered down to my eye level. He smoothed his fingers over Shoonga's coat in a manner that let me know he was a dog person. His shrewd eyes swept over me, lingering on my sling. "How's the shoulder?"

"Annoying."

"I'll bet."

Jake whistled and Shoonga took off.

Traitor.

Dawson jerked his chin toward my duffel bag. "I heard you were leaving."

"Yeah."

He shifted his stance, looking everywhere but at me. Finally, he said, "You coming back?"

Silence.

"Yeah."

"Good." He ran his hand through his hair. "Look, I wanted to—"

I couldn't deal with whatever he needed to get off his chest. "I wanted to drive my Viper to Denver and fly out from there like I usually do. It's just another damn thing I can't do with a broken wing."

"Better than a broken neck," he muttered.

"True."

"Need a ride to the airport?"

"No. Rollie is picking me up in a little bit."

He lifted both brows. "Rollie?"

"Seems strange, huh?"

"Very."

Rollie had inserted himself into my life on a regular basis. I was still sorting out my feelings about that, too, not sure I needed him to act like a surrogate father.

"How long will you be gone?"

"Three weeks." I lifted my sling. "I'm hoping this will get me the sympathy vote and speed up the process."

"Good luck. If that administrative bunch at Fort Bragg is anything like the marines, they'll take however long they want with the outprocess paperwork."

"The army is more organized than a bunch of jarheads, who just bull their way through everything." That caught his attention.

Dawson's eyes tapered to fine points.

"I'm kidding, Sheriff."

His gaze narrowed farther. "I thought we'd moved beyond you calling me Sheriff, Mercy."

"That was before you arrested me."

He didn't defend himself, but I sensed his patience stretching as he fought to stay polite. "So what are your plans when you get back?"

"Riding, roping, and arithmetic. I'd better learn everything about how to run a ranch. Jake already has his hands full."

"Maybe you should tell that to Rollie. Since you two are so chummy, he's been hinting to anyone that'll listen you'll be working for him as a PI."

Rollie. What a troublemaker. I still owed him a favor. I wondered how long before he'd collect. "Or maybe . . ." I floated a dramatic pause. "I'll run for sheriff."

That steely blue gaze collided with mine again. "Are you serious?"

"Why? Does the thought of me running against you make you nervous, Dawson?"

He snorted and snapped the stem on a fat yellow dandelion growing out of a crack in the cement.

I could let him off the hook, or I could make him squirm.

Guess which one I chose?

"Besides, a little friendly competition would be good for you. No one else has announced their candidacy, have they?"

Another snort.

"I wouldn't want you to think you've already sewn up the election this many months out."

"Sewn up. Right."

"Plus, it might be fun. Fighting with you has been . . . interesting so far."

Lightning fast, Dawson inserted himself between my thighs and curled his warm palms over my knees. His face was inches away; his body not nearly close enough. "Here's something to remember if you decide to run against me; I don't fight fair. So if you think the fact that you are a g—"

"Girl?" I supplied with a hint of venom.

"No." He lightly butted his forehead to mine. "I was going to say a *grunt*. Actually, I was going to say a lowly *army* grunt, but you outrank me."

"Yep." I cocked my head. "Clever, having your old CO try to crack my service files."

No surprise or remorse crossed his face. "That didn't take long to get back to you."

"Uncle Sam likes to keep a close eye on his investment." I smiled. "Maybe you should start saluting me, Marine."

"Like that'll ever happen." Keeping our eyes locked, Dawson brushed his lips over mine. Softly. Teasingly. Repeatedly. Never fully connecting our mouths.

A quiet, disgruntled sigh escaped from me.

He angled back. That sexy cowboy grin appeared. "Heal up, Sergeant Major. Then I'll take you on, anytime, anyplace. Officially or unofficially."

My heart thumped.

Dawson gently tucked the wilted dandelion behind my ear. He leisurely traced the outline of my jaw from my temple up one side of my face and down the other with his knuckles. "I'm glad you're sticking around, Mercy. Eagle River County is more . . . interesting with you in it."

For all the cowboy swagger Dawson packed into his exit, he should've been wearing chaps and a white hat, and riding a horse.

I looked around at the historic place that for better or for worse, had always been my home. I listened to the bawling calves. I smelled manure and warm earth and marigolds and Sophie's lemon sponge cake.

This was my life now. I wasn't the only Gunderson who'd cursed the land, the sky, and the futility of pretending we had control over either. Or questioned the sacrifices we'd made to live out here, in the middle of nowhere. Or the middle of paradise, depending on the day and my mood.

Wasn't everything in life about sacrifice?

Yet even in the middle of nowhere, I wasn't alone; I had the ghosts of the past, the blood, the sweat, the tears, the joy, and the sorrow of those ancestors who'd gone before me to keep me company.

Instead of feeling trapped by that knowledge, I was freed.

ACKNOWLEDGMENTS

First off, I can't say enough about how wonderful it was to work with my terrific editor, Trish Lande Grader. I'm honored to have had her expertise and vision for this book as well as the insight from Pocket editor Abby Zidle, and to get me (and Mercy) on the right course. A sincere thank-you seems inadequate.

Thanks to my agent, Scott Miller.

I need to thank several people in my life who read through this book in its various stages: Mary LaHood has been a steady, honest, and valued critique partner for years; my buddy, author Toni McGee Causey, for letting me bounce ideas off her up until the very end; and also to my author friend Mary Stella, who has offered support in many forms; and my blonde trouble twin, Cat Cody.

My First Offenders blog pals, Jeff Shelby, Karen Olson, and Alison Gaylin, who are so much more than "just" blog partners; and Jeff, the hilarious video announcing the "deal" was above and beyond, my friend.

A twenty-one-gun salute to the folks at H-S Precision in Rapid City for letting me shoot the prototype sniper rifle and for not balking at my bajillion questions.

And a huge debt of gratitude to the soldier/sharpshooter who gave me the lowdown on army life in wartime.

Thanks to our friends Mark and Lisa Sanders, who graciously opened their beautiful ranch to us, patiently answered every question I asked about life as a rancher in western South Dakota, drove us all over the gorgeous chunk of earth they call home—anytime I asked. Truly, your friendship and generosity knows no bounds. I'm humbled . . . and jealous, 'cause damn do I love your spread.

To J. Carson Black for all her expert equine help, many, many thanks . . . and yes, I do throw good fillies.

To my family, daughters Lauren, Haley, and Tessa, thanks for not minding when I'm in my own little fictional world. And lastly, a big wet kiss to my husband Erin, for his unwavering belief in me and this unpredictable career of mine, and for being the real gun expert behind the scenes.

I owe a big thank-you to all the readers, librarians, bookstore personnel, and fans who've contacted me and have been supportive from the very first book. It means more than I can possibly express.